MAGGIE HAMAND

THE ROCKET MAN

First published in Great Britain 1995 by
Images Publishing (Malvern) Ltd.
Upton upon Severn, Worcestershire

British Library Cataloguing in Publication Data

A catalogue record for this book is available
from the British Library

ISBN 1 897817 46 0

Text typeset in 10 pt Garamond

Designed and Produced:
Images Publishing (Malvern) Ltd., Worcestershire.

Printed and Bound:
Butler & Tanner Ltd., Somerset.

ACKNOWLEDGEMENTS

I would like to thank all those people in London, Vienna and Paraguay who helped me in my researches, and those whose continued belief in this book sustained me through the long struggle for publication. I must also thank my family and above all my husband Jeremy, who alone knows how many tears I have shed over this book.

PART ONE

VIENNA

I

When Hans Müller committed suicide one cold Sunday in January nobody could understand why he had done it, least of all his wife, Lieselotte. Katie Haynes had spent hours holding the distraught woman in her arms, listening to her howling over and over, 'Why did he do this? Why? Why?' To this neither Katie, the police, nor Müller's UN colleagues could provide an answer.

The funeral was held the following week in the Vienna Central Cemetery. Lieselotte stood at the graveside, clothed in black and veiled, her hands clasped, standing as still as if frozen by the icy wind. At Lieselotte's side, her sister held the Müllers' six-month-old baby. A sombre crowd stood behind them, and all around stretched the endless long avenues of gravestones, the bare trees, and the wide paths sprinkled with dirty snow.

Katie looked at her nervously from across the empty grave, holding her own daughter's hand, watching the men prepare to lower the coffin, afraid that her friend might break down completely, or make some desperate gesture. Katie wondered for a moment how she would feel if it were her own husband Bob who was being buried, but she could feel nothing; either her imagination was wanting, or the idea failed to move her. She pushed this thought to the back of her mind, not wanting to admit that Lieselotte grieved her husband's death with a depth that she could not match.

Men lifted the coffin with ropes and manoeuvred it towards the grave. Katie instinctively drew backwards, pulling Anna with her, though the little girl didn't seem at all upset, just wide-eyed, curious. Icy raindrops suddenly began to fall from the heavy sky. To Katie's left, a man tapped her arm to attract her attention and held an umbrella over her head. Katie, surprised, glanced up at him; he looked at her quite solemnly and didn't smile.

He was wearing a shapeless dark overcoat, a man in his mid-forties, she would guess, with an unusual face, a face you would not easily forget with its strong and mismatched features; a craggy nose, a mouth that was too large, cool blue-grey eyes, and dark hair, just starting to recede in front, exposing the high forehead. He held a Russian fur hat, and it was this, together with the sheer size of him, that made her think he was almost certainly a Russian.

It was very cold; the wind blew in gusts against them, and the trees suddenly tipped down showers of water. Anna tugged at Katie's sleeve and said that she wanted to go home; Katie gathered her under her coat. The priest, seeming anxious to finish, hurried through the service, but the men were struggling with the coffin, the ropes and the earth slippery with the rain. Water ran off the side of the umbrella and soaked Katie's shoulder, so she leaned closer to the stranger beside her, and he offered her his arm to lean on. Despite his size he did not seem solid, but tense and taut, full of suppressed energy. Without being aware that she was doing it, she gradually leaned closer to him, till the whole of her side touched his through their thick coats.

When the earth was thrown onto the coffin she shuddered, and to her horror found that tears were running down her face. She hoped the man wouldn't notice; but he had. He pulled off his thick glove, reached into a pocket, and pulled out a clean white handkerchief which he offered her; she was surprised at the pale hand which emerged from the bulky sleeve, so fine and sensitive looking. She took the handkerchief, smiled at him politely through her tears, and let go of his arm.

When the burial was over, just as they were all turning away, Lieselotte stepped forward and gently tossed a single red rose into the grave.

Everyone was anxious to get away quickly because of the rain, which continued to fall in an icy, drenching stream. Katie went over to her friend, took her hand and squeezed it, but Lieselotte seemed in another world, and turned away, distracted, leaning on her sister. Katie stood for a moment with Anna, lost and disoriented. She looked around to see if there was anyone she knew and saw the Russian – if that's what he was – standing on his own under his umbrella, lighting a cigarette. She glanced at him once or twice and noticed that he hardly took his eyes off her.

Lieselotte went on ahead; Katie followed more slowly, with Anna. They walked down the long avenue between the trees, past some mounds of earth from freshly dug graves, covered over with large sprays of evergreen foliage and topped with fading flowers. Anna stared at everything, fascinated. To one side a woman in an Austrian hat with a bitter, much-lined face swept the path with her broom.

As they walked along the path, she realised that the man with the umbrella was walking beside her. Smoke from his cigarette drifted across her face.

'Do you know Müller's wife?' he asked her. He spoke English in a smooth, deep voice, and with a definite Russian accent.

'Yes, she's a good friend of mine.'

'How is she taking this?'

'It's terrible for her, she can't understand. Nobody can understand. Why did he do it? When they just had the baby . . . Why?'

He did not reply at once; in fact, she thought he wouldn't reply at all. Then he said, very softly, 'I think perhaps you are asking the wrong question.'

She looked at him, startled, but he looked away. A moment later he excused himself and walked back along the path. She was left feeling puzzled, perturbed; she didn't have the slightest idea what he meant.

After the funeral Katie drove straight to the airport to meet Bob. Like Hans, he worked for the International Atomic Energy Agency in Vienna, and despite a recent promotion he still travelled extensively. Katie had been longing for him to come back, having had to deal with Lieselotte's grief unsupported. She hated his long absences and had more than once urged him to pack it in. His contract was coming up for renewal again at the end of the year, and she had told him she couldn't face another three years in Vienna, isolated from her family and friends, and unable to find any satisfying work. But where to go was a problem; Bob was American, and she was English, and neither of them were keen to settle in one another's countries.

They waited at the arrivals barrier, Anna jumping up and down with excitement. Bob had missed her fifth birthday, and she was expecting a present. Katie scanned the crowd but it was Anna who saw him first; she ducked under the barrier and ran towards him, shouting, 'Daddy! Daddy!', jumping up at him so eagerly that he put his suitcase down and swept her up in his arms. Her face was bright and flushed as she hugged him, and he kissed her, saying, 'Well, how's my little princess? Are you five now, huh? Let me look at you.' Katie had to wait till he had given Anna her birthday present before she was able to kiss his cheek.

Despite travelling all night he looked quite unruffled, his clothes uncrumpled, his face close-shaven, and his hair neatly combed back from his forehead. Although she had looked forward so much to his return, her first emotion was of irritation at his composure. They walked off towards the car.

'Everything okay? Give me a real kiss.'

She kissed him again, on the mouth this time.

As they crossed the arrivals hall, she said, in a quiet voice, 'Bob, did you hear about Hans?'

Bob went on walking. He said, 'Yes, I did hear. It's tragic, shocking.' Anna skipped on ahead, oblivious; Katie had to call her back. Bob started to talk but an airport announcement drowned out what he was saying.

'Bob, slow down.' She grabbed his free hand, he squeezed it and began walking more slowly. Katie showed him where she had parked their car and he loaded the suitcase into the boot. She said, 'You look tired. Do you want me to drive?'

'No, I'm fine.' But he seemed tense and preoccupied, and, when Anna was strapped in, he let her climb into the driving seat. On the autobahn, while Anna ecstatically played with the doll he had bought her, he asked, 'What happened with Hans exactly?'

'She'd gone out for a lunch with friends and then for a walk in the Vienna Woods. It was a week ago last Sunday. Hans said she should have a day off, she hadn't left Jochum since he was born, so she left him with Hans. When she got back he was dead and Jochum was crying in the cot.'

'Did he leave a note?'

'Yes, but it didn't say why. Just that he couldn't live with himself any longer and that he knew they would be happier without him. He said his affairs were in order and his will was with his lawyer.' Katie hesitated. 'He said that he loved them but that was the only thing that was at all personal.'

'And the police are happy with this?'

'I think so. I don't think there's any doubt that it was suicide.' Katie's voice trembled for a moment. 'But Lieselotte doesn't understand why. They seemed perfectly happy at home, with the baby, and everything. He wasn't that depressed, he hadn't threatened it or anything.'

'People who really mean to kill themselves rarely do.'

'She thought it might be something to do with work. It couldn't be, could it, Bob?'

'No, I don't think so. But I suppose we'll have to go through all that. Maybe I'd better go straight into the office.'

'Oh Bob, please don't do that. Surely it can wait till tomorrow. Anna would be terribly disappointed.'

He turned round to Anna and smiled. He said, softly, 'Okay.' Anna was the key to his heart; he would do almost anything for her. Katie looked ahead, concentrating on her driving. She said, 'It's all been rather difficult. I was lonely, without you.'

Bob patted her thigh. 'Well, I'm back now.'

When they got home Bob had a shower and Katie made some lunch. Bob came up behind her in the kitchen, towelling his hair.

'Was there anything in the papers?'

'About Hans? No, I'm sure there wasn't.'

'I'd better call Lascalles.' He went back into the bedroom. Through the open door she could see him on the phone, fiddling with the telephone cord. Katie felt irritated. His work always came first; she shouldn't have expected anything different. She let him talk for ten minutes and then went to the door to mime that lunch was ready. Bob smiled at her and held up his hand to ask her not to interrupt.

She could hear snatches of the conversation. 'I really don't think I have anything that will shed any light on it. No, I don't. I can't understand it. No, everything was just fine. Yes, it was unfortunate about Gavrilov but then I did warn you about that when it was first suggested . . . No. No other problems that I know of. Hans seemed quite happy about it. Have you written to Cruz? I see. No – tomorrow at eleven will be fine. Yes, of course. See you then. Okay.'

He hung up but remained seated on the bed. He looked suddenly overwhelmingly weary. Katie went up to him and put her arm on his shoulder and he looked up at her. Only then did he ask the question which she might have expected from him first: 'And how is Lieselotte?'

The next morning, when Bob had left for work, Katie went into the city centre to meet her friend Nihal Senanayake for their regular Tuesday coffee. The weather had turned milder and it was still raining, and as Katie walked down the hushed, pedestrianised streets near the Stephansdom a lone street musician played a mournful, haunting tune on a flute. Katie felt herself overwhelmed for an instant with that particular melancholy of the expatriate, a feeling of being always isolated and detached, living in a culture she didn't belong to despite her fluency in the language; an outsider, an observer, mixing mainly with a population of transient foreigners. As the daughter of a diplomat, she knew this rootless existence only too well, and by now it had lost its appeal.

She wandered down the Graben, looking into the shop windows, passing the time till they were due to meet at eleven. She settled herself in a corner at Hawelka's and they brought her coffee with a glass of water on a silver tray. Nihal, as usual, was late. She saw him at last through the window; he was unmistakable, his short, dark figure advancing out of the rain. He fumbled with the door and hung his coat and umbrella on the hat-stand. Slightly out of breath, he sat down opposite her, putting his newspaper and a sheaf of documents on the table.

He ran his hand through his damp hair, realigning the broad white streak which he considered very distinguished, and smiled broadly. Katie silently accepted that he knew her too well to feel he had to apologise for his customary lateness. Then he pulled a face.

'What is it?'

'My shoes leak, and my socks are wet.'

'Why don't you buy a new pair?'

Nihal looked sheepish. Katie knew that he was always short of money; as a freelance journalist his income was erratic, Vienna was an expensive place to live, and she knew he sent a lot of money home to his ex-wife and children in England. Nihal was, like her, a Cambridge graduate, one of those highly educated Sri Lankans who are more English than the English; Katie always felt at home with him. Their friendship went back a long way, to the days they both worked at the BBC World Service in London. Katie had relied on him heavily when she first came to Vienna; he knew everyone and everything. She met him once a week to exchange gossip; today, as she had anticipated, he wanted to know about the suicide.

'How was the funeral?'

'Miserable.' Katie didn't want to go into too many details; Nihal, of course, was always looking for a possible story, and she knew that he would view anything she said principally for its news potential; she didn't hold this against him, after all, journalists are like that. The waiter came and they both ordered coffee. Katie sipped hers slowly, skimming the milk off the top with her spoon.

'Nihal, at the graveside I was standing next to this Russian. At least I'm pretty sure he was a Russian.'

'What did he look like?'

'Tall. Brownish hair, thinning a bit. In his forties.'

'Going grey?'

'No. His English is very good, a deep voice.'

'Tall? Over six foot?'

'Oh yes, at least.'

'It's probably Dmitry Gavrilov. He was with Müller on that last inspection in Brazil.' Nihal lit up a cigarette. 'I'm doing a piece on this new safeguards deal there, looking into all the background. No-one at the IAEA thinks his death has anything to do with that, do they?'

Katie knew he asked her this in case Bob had said anything to her about it. She was instantly defensive.

'Bob never talks to me about work, you know that. Anyhow, he's been away.'

Nihal asked, 'And what does Lieselotte make of it all?' As Katie didn't answer, he tried again, 'You're a good friend – she must have said something to you – what does she think?'

Katie drank the remains of her coffee. 'Oh, I think she's too shocked to think anything.'

There was a silence. Nihal extinguished his cigarette, staring at Katie and obviously wondering if it was prudent to push things any further. Abruptly he changed the subject. 'Actually, since you mentioned him, I had a briefing with Gavrilov last week. He's one of the new breed, you know; here because he's good at his job and not just for political reasons . . . I found him very impressive.'

Katie was staring out of the window. She was thinking of the coffin going into the ground, of how she had stood by the grave in the rain, of his intent face as he had looked at her, and the way he had offered her his arm to lean on.

Nihal sat at his desk in the hallway of his small flat in the Tulpengasse. He inhaled deeply on his cigarette and watched the smoke drift up towards the ceiling, lit by an ancient Anglepoise lamp. He had not yet written the first sentence. That was always the most difficult; where to begin. Once he had got beyond that things usually started to flow.

He tapped in the first sentence of his article.

> In September 1990 President Collor de Mello of Brazil publicly threw the first spadeful of lime into a 320-metre deep concrete lined shaft in Amazonia which the military had built to test a nuclear weapon, thus heralding the official end to Brazil's nuclear weapons programme.

He paused, put down his cigarette, went on typing, gathering speed.

> A few weeks ago, on 28 November, at Foz do Iguaçu, Brazil and Argentina signed a far-reaching treaty in which they agreed to end their nuclear arms race and open up all their nuclear installations to international safeguards. President Collor has also made public the demise of a secret military plan, code-named Project Solimões, which was rumoured to show that Brazil had been within a year or so of having the bomb.

Nihal was typing without a break now; his cigarette, neglected, burned out in the ashtray.

> Brazil's secret nuclear weapons programme goes back a long way. In 1975 West Germany signed a controversial deal to supply Brazil with a complete nuclear fuel cycle. This included four nuclear power stations, a uranium enrichment plant, and a reprocessing plant. All this would come under IAEA safeguards. But it has been known for years that Brazil has meanwhile been running a so-called parallel programme, under the control of the military, and that some of the West-German know-how was transferred from the safeguarded installations to the military ones.

Nihal paused for thought. If only he could get something out of Bob Haynes or Gavrilov about the inspection . . . Haynes was hopeless. He was a real organisation man, would never reveal anything that might reflect badly on the IAEA. On the other hand . . . On impulse, Nihal picked up the little pale blue IAEA phone directory and flicked through the pages. The Director of Information had arranged for him to have a briefing on uranium enrichment technologies from Dmitry Gavrilov last week; Nihal had found him refreshingly open, honest, and ironic. Perhaps if he could get to see him again he could steer the conversation round to Brazil.

He rang the extension number. Gavrilov answered at once.

'This is Nihal Senanayake . . . you remember . . . yes. I'm looking at my notes from that briefing you gave me last month. There are a few things I'm not clear about. I'll be in the building later this afternoon, I just wondered . . .'

'Yes, of course. I'll be in my office at five-thirty, come to see me then.'

Nihal hung up. He thought, he is not going to tell me anything about Brazil. It's a waste of time. Still . . . He looked at his watch. If he was going to see Gavrilov at five-thirty, he didn't have much time. He typed out a couple more paragraphs, saved what he had done so far, found his coat, put his notebook in his pocket, and set out in the freezing cold for the UN building, wondering again what had made him decide to live in this beastly climate.

The Vienna International Centre stands on the banks of the Danube, three large towers surrounding a central rotunda. The towers are curved, wider at the ends than in the middle, and inside the curved corridors soon prove disorientating. Nihal had been in the building countless times and still had trouble finding his way around it. It was said that even people who had worked there for years had been known to go downstairs to the coffee machine and fail to find their way back to their offices again.

For once, he arrived on time. Gavrilov's secretary, a pretty Austrian girl called Hilde, showed him in. Gavrilov got up from his desk and indicated that Nihal should sit down on one of the comfortable chairs at the other side of the room.

Nihal sank into the chair with pleasure. He opened his notebook. They went over various abstruse points about the workings of gas centrifuges. Then Nihal said, 'I wanted to ask you about Brazil.' He explained about his feature. What puzzled him, he said, was why Brazil had so unaccountably changed its mind on accepting safeguards; after all, it was only a short while ago that the Brazilian Government had voted against accepting international inspections.

Gavrilov sighed. He seemed to realise at once that the first part of the conversation had been a ruse but showed no irritation. 'Well, of course we have had all the accounts from Brazil and now the results of the inspection. You know I cannot reveal anything about this. I can give you some general information, the kind of thing you could already get from published reports. Probably you know it all already. There were some recent leaks in the Brazilian press – you read Portuguese? No? Let me see, I have some copies somewhere.'

Gavrilov went over to a bookcase and found what he was looking for. He returned to his desk and began reading aloud. 'The Valadares Centre claims to be operating 990 centrifuges. But over the past two years, the Centre has added three buildings, M-1, M-2, and M-3, covering a total of 24,000 square metres. This could hold about 6,000 centrifuges.'

'But these are not operating?'

'Not yet. Of course you are aware that the Brazilians have had a lot of problems with their centrifuges. Probably they have been rather unlucky, they are very tricky things to run. So, if we are to believe what they say, they are not very efficient.'

Nihal sat silent, waiting for more; Gavrilov suddenly became more expansive. 'Of course once the Valadares plant reaches a certain capacity the desirability of safeguards becomes overwhelming. That is why the IAEA was so anxious that there should be a full-scope agreement. Do you want some figures? What is so worrying is that if they had 3,000 centrifuges up and running, which is certainly possible in the not-too-distant future, and if they had stockpiled 150 kilogrammes of 20 per cent enriched uranium, which I'm not saying for a moment is the case, it would not be possible on present performance, but *if* – then Valadares could produce the 20 kilogrammes of highly enriched uranium needed for a bomb within a week.'

A chill went through Nihal. Then he repeated, 'But why did the Brazilians change their minds, do you think? Have you any ideas?'

'You are asking the wrong person. I am only a technical man, you should ask someone who was in on the negotiations. But you have your own theories, I expect? What is the drift of your article, anyway? What else are you mentioning?'

'Well, quotes from the Brazilian representative on the IAEA board last September saying Brazil would never accept international safeguards. And Project Solimões . . .'

'Ah, yes, of course,' said Gavrilov, and an amused smile crossed his lips. 'Project Solimões.' He stood up and walked to his desk. He delved into his jacket pocket and pulled out a packet of cigarettes; then he glanced at his watch. He said, 'It's six-thirty, they turn the air-conditioning off. Can you believe it? If you work late you suffocate. I'd like to smoke, shall we go down to the bar?'

So they went down to the bar and bought two double whiskies and Gavrilov lit his cigarette. He asked, and Nihal wasn't sure whether there was irony in his voice or not, 'You don't have any inside information on Project Solimões, I suppose?'

Nihal shook his head.

Gavrilov leaned forward in his chair, glanced sideways, as if to check the coast was clear, began to talk in a deep, rich voice. His English was really excellent; he spoke fluently, with only an occasional hesitation as he sought for the right word or phrase. 'Look, I am going to tell you something that I shouldn't. No doubt you have heard other similar stories. I think I can trust you not to use this, not directly. I've read a lot of what you write, and you are not going to compromise your convenient relationship with the IAEA, am I right?'

Nihal raised an eyebrow and smiled.

'You wanted to know about the visit to Valadares. It was suggested that I go as an observer. As you may know, our names all have to be put forward thirty days before the inspection. No objection was made by the people at the Brazilian Nuclear Energy Commission, the CNEN. But when we got to the Valadares Centre, there was a great deal of arguing. We all stood in the entrance hall for two hours – this is the maximum time that inspectors can be kept waiting according to the agreements that have been drawn up for such inspections.

'It seemed to be me they objected to. They said, "Why have they sent a bloody Russian?" Of course this is not an unknown humiliation, Russian inspectors are always being turned down all over the world. I explained that I was only an observer, it was not so important that I go, but it was vital that the inspectors went ahead, set up the seals and the cameras, took their readings – so it was agreed that I should stay outside. I stood outside the main centrifuge hall, with two soldiers on either side, then the director came down to see me.

'He said he was very sorry, took me up to his office. He was a little man, with a moustache and an obviously military bearing – Rear Admiral

Gonçalo Oliveira Mourao, if you want his full name. He said there had been a confusion, a breakdown in communication between them and CNEN. They were very sensitive about their technology, there had been much opposition and resentment to the idea of international inspectors, they had not been told there was to be an observer too. He himself thought this was quite wrong, there was no reason at all why I should not view the cascades. They were not hiding anything. And here he smiled a charming smile; the kind of smile incidentally you must never trust.'

Dmitry inhaled deeply on the end of his cigarette, stubbed it out, and looked Nihal directly in the eye. Nihal was not taking notes; he didn't want to do anything that might stop Gavrilov in mid-flow; he was in fact astonished that he was telling him all this, not least because he was a Russian, and in his experience Russians always gave away as little as possible.

'So I went back down to the cascade hall with the director and a soldier. We put on the white coats and the radiation badges and went in. Of course there isn't much to see, the centrifuges are all encased in the outside containers. I was not allowed to go up the steps and look down on the pipework.'

Gavrilov took another cigarette, offered one to Nihal, who accepted, and lit up again. 'They took me round and Oliveira explained that they had a lot of problems with their centrifuges. There were imbalances in the Maraging steel and he told me they had lost quite a few. One of the centrifuges actually crashed while I was there.'

'Really? What did it sound like?'

'Like a gun going off. It gave me quite a shock, I can tell you. Actually it's not a problem, they just leave it there till the plant is finally decommissioned. I remember that Oliveira laughed and said to me, "You see? We have not been so lucky, but we have done nearly as well as you Russians, I think." "And much better than the Americans," I replied. One must never miss an opportunity to get at the Americans, you understand. You know about the American attempts to design gas centrifuges, don't you? They tried to build them too big – the Americans always have to do things big. It never worked, of course, and they abandoned this project.' Nihal had the impression that Gavrilov was really enjoying himself; he was intrigued; he had no idea what was coming next. Gavrilov took another gulp of his whisky and carried on.

'So we went from one end of the hall to the other. We were standing right at the end of the line – it was hard to hear him because of the thump of the hex solidifying against the walls of the containers. I could see Cruz and Müller packing the samples, I was going to go over to them but Oliveira shook his finger at me. "Let us not interrupt them," he said. "They are very busy. Come up to my office." Of course you do not argue or disagree somehow if there is an armed man standing by your side. So we went back to the office, and after a short chat he left me there in the company of some straight-faced soldier.'

'Didn't you think this was all a bit suspicious?' asked Nihal.

'Suspicious? Well, of course, in a way it is suspicious – but this kind of thing goes on all the time, you know that. It's a bit humiliating, I suppose, to be treated as some kind of industrial spy, but then, we Russians are used to such things. Well, it's a humiliating thing to be a Russian nowadays.'

He paused for a moment, turning the glass round in his hands. 'Anyway, the real point of this long story is this; while I was waiting in the office Oliveira told me something I thought you might like to know. If you use it, please don't attribute it to me. You see, there is no question that these military types would love to build a bomb. He said to me: "Of course, the decision not to make a bomb is purely political. We have the capability. The first nuclear bomb was exploded nearly fifty years ago. It would be inconceivable for Brazil not to master a technology that is fifty years old."'

II

The inquest into the death of Hans Müller took place two weeks later in a building near the Rathaus. Bob went with his other colleagues from the IAEA and Katie went with Lieselotte. She sat next to her on the wooden bench, holding her hand, hoping to give support, but Lieselotte sat expressionlessly through the whole proceedings.

The evidence was fairly straightforward. The cause of death was unquestionably the pills and barbiturates which he had taken on a empty stomach, washed down with whisky; death had occurred within the hour. Müller's doctor testified that the pills used were not the non-addictive ones he had prescribed recently when Müller had complained of inability to sleep. There was no explanation for where the drugs had come from; the small brown bottle bore no label, so it had not been possible to trace them through the local pharmacies; perhaps he had obtained them on one of his frequent trips abroad. Doctors abroad might prescribe less cautiously, and in some countries it was often possible to obtain such drugs over-the-counter.

Then there was the question of the suicide note. It had been written on his own notepaper, with his own pen. It was unquestionably his writing. The fact that the writing had deteriorated at the end of the note could have been due either to emotion or to the fact that he was confused or already slipping into unconsciousness after taking the drug. The coroner made the point that his wife had said that she thought the note was odd; it seemed stilted, not how he would have normally expressed himself. There was also the fact that the lawyer's name was misspelt, though again, this could have been caused by stress or confusion. At this point Lieselotte turned to Katie and she could see that she was hoping something might be made of this; but the coroner did not seem to think this was evidence of any foul play.

The police had found nothing to indicate that it had not been a straightforward suicide. There had been no marks on the body, scratches or bruises, which might have indicated a struggle, and no signs of forced entry or disturbance to the flat. There had been no other fingerprints on the bottle. None of the neighbours had seen or heard anything untoward. Müller's colleagues said that he had seemed to have been depressed and anxious recently at work, though none of them could give any reason for this, except the stresses of travel and long periods spent away from home. Reference was made to the arcane nature of his work, but the Deputy Director General of Safeguards, Georges Lascalles, said that there was nothing Müller had been involved with that could have brought him to this brink; the matter had been looked into internally very thoroughly and nothing suspicious had been uncovered.

The coroner summed up; it appeared to be an open-and-shut case. He said he had sympathy for the wife; often in these cases the bereaved relatives could not see any reason for a suicide. Above all she should not blame herself. A verdict of death by suicide was recorded.

They stood up to go. Lieselotte's face was blank. It was all over so quickly; Katie felt cheated, that her friend had deserved more than this. Katie put her arms round her and hugged her; then she asked Lieselotte home for a coffee or a drink but Lieselotte said she had to go back to baby Jochum. She told Katie she would be leaving Vienna soon – she was going back with her sister to Cologne as soon as everything was arranged in order to be near her family. Hans's death meant the loss of her diplomatic status and privileges and there was nothing left but painful memories in Vienna.

On the stairs outside, where one or two journalists, including Nihal, were waiting to catch anyone who might be able to give them a quote, Katie saw Dmitry Gavrilov. He was standing against a pillar, his hands thrust deep into his coat pockets, and he did not look at all happy; in fact, he looked agitated and disturbed. A man she did not recognise, presumably also from the IAEA, came up to him and said something in his ear; he shrugged and shook his head. Then he looked up and saw Katie, he must have seen her, he looked straight into her face, but he did not acknowledge her at all; instead he turned and walked hurriedly down the steps and out of the building. Katie felt shocked, as if she had been cruelly let down; the whole brief scene had left an unpleasant impression.

Left unexpectedly on her own, Katie made for the Café Central. She loved this place; it was one of her favourite haunts, one of the few consolations for her of Viennese life. The high ceiling was arched like a church, ribbed with gold and supported on gleaming marble columns; the tables were also topped with marble, but despite this, perhaps because it was usually full, it didn't echo too loudly nor seem cold. Katie found a table in the corner; she ordered coffee and took out her book.

She was unable to concentrate. She knew that she was going to miss Lieselotte terribly. Although she'd known her for some time, Katie had really become close to Lieselotte when she'd had her baby, remembering her own isolation when Anna was tiny, cut off from her family and friends and coping with Bob's frequent absences. Now she saw her almost every day and at the thought of not doing so felt suddenly empty and depressed. She put her book away, stared blankly into space, looked around her. With a faint shock she saw Gavrilov, over by the window, reading a newspaper. He turned the page and refolded it, glanced up and his eyes met hers. She looked away. A little later she glanced at him again and for the second time their eyes met; this time she smiled to show that she recognised him.

She looked down at her coffee. He got up and came over to her table; she had known that he would. He was a little nervous, made a gesture towards the empty chair beside her. 'Do you mind?'

'No, please do.'

The waitress came and he ordered more coffee. He turned to her: 'Some cake?'

'No, I shouldn't.'

'Yes, why not? I hope you are not dieting, like all these other Western women? You are thin enough already.'

She smiled, he ordered and the waitress went away. He said, 'I'm sorry, we weren't introduced.'

'I'm Katie Haynes.'

He started slightly. 'Oh, I see, you're Bob Haynes's wife.' He took out a cigarette, tapped it on the packet. 'I'm sorry, do you mind if I smoke? I should give up, I know, but you see I have so few other pleasures. I'm Dmitry Gavrilov – you can call me Mitya.'

'Mitya.' She pronounced the name slowly, as if tasting it, exploring it with her tongue. 'So you work with Bob? In Safeguards?'

He nodded.

'What do you do there?'

He looked at her, hesitating, as if uncertain what to say. Then he said, quite slowly and deliberately, 'Actually I am an expert in uranium enrichment.'

'And have you been at the Agency long?'

'Six months.'

The coffee and cake came. Katie cut a sliver off the corner of her gateau, savouring each mouthful; Gavrilov consumed his quickly, without seeming to notice particularly what he ate. Katie, thinking that he might prove after all to be boring and moved by some impulse of mischief, said, 'I was always against nuclear energy myself.'

'Were you? Good for you.'

'Why do you say that?'

'Well, somebody has to be against it, ask all the right questions, try to make sure it's as safe as possible. If we had had that kind of pressure at home we might not have had Chernobyl.'

He looked straight at her, and she had to drop her eyes, unable to meet the intensity of his stare. She said, 'What do you think, then? Do you believe in nuclear power?'

He looked away and then shrugged. 'Is there an alternative? We can't all be idealists. Some of us have to deal with the realities. You're an idealist, I take it.'

Katie said, 'I don't know.'

'Well, what do you believe in?'

She laughed. She thought, what a question. 'Well, I don't know. God, I suppose.'

'Do you? I thought so, at the funeral. At one point you started to cross yourself.'

'I was brought up a Catholic. What about you?'

'Oh, I don't believe in religion. It's all right for people who want to believe in fairy tales.'

'There's a lot of psychological truth in fairy tales.'

They looked at one another and both laughed. Immediately the mood changed and lightened. Katie liked the way he smiled; he didn't do it very often, but when he did it changed his whole face. She particularly liked the way the corners of his mouth turned slightly down and his eyes wrinkled. Katie asked, 'Where do you live? You don't live in the Russian compound now?'

'No, we live just the same as everyone else. Needless to say many people are unhappy about it, they complain that they are not so well off as they were before. Well, that is what we Russians are good at, complaining. I have a flat in the 19th district. Is that far away?'

'No, we're in the Weinberggasse.'

'Well, then, I'm just round the corner.'

'And your family?'

'I'm on my own. Divorced. No children.'

She thought she detected a note of bitterness in his voice. She would have liked to ask him more, but she didn't feel able to. Instead, she found herself asking the inevitable question about the political situation back in Russia.

He sighed, as if he had been asked this question a thousand times. 'What can I say? Things are terrible. Let me quote you one of your English poets: "Things fall apart, the centre cannot hold . .."'

'" . . . Mere anarchy is loosed upon the world,"' echoed Katie. 'I know it well; The Second Coming. Yeats is one of my favourite poets.'

'Is he?' asked Gavrilov, studying her face. 'What else do we have in common, I wonder?'

He lit another cigarette, and then, very casually, he put his free hand next to hers where it rested on the table. She was not sure if this was deliberate. She let his fingers rest next to her own, instead of taking her hand away; it was like the first act of infidelity. Unthinkingly she looked around, to see if there was anyone she knew; and then she saw them. Two figures, a man and a woman, stepping out of the brightness of the street and standing by the entrance. She watched them take off their expensive camel-hair coats, hanging them on the coat-stand just inside the door.

Katie looked away at once. She knew who they were; she didn't want them to see her. She turned to Dmitry and saw him watching her, curious. 'Somebody you know?'

She pulled a face and saw the woman, striking in a bright red dress, sit at a table not far away, half hidden by a marble column; her husband sat with his back to them. Katie was relieved; they hadn't seen her. She glanced at them once more, just to make sure, and saw the woman do the same; their eyes met; they couldn't now avoid one another. Katie gave a tentative wave, hoping they might leave it at that, but the woman got up, and came across to them, exuding wealth and confidence.

She was one of those Latin American women of indeterminate race, with thick, black hair wound elegantly into a pleat, honey-coloured skin, and the face of a model, her features fine and taut as a racehorse. When she smiled she was quite bewitching. She held out her hand to Katie; it was covered in ostentatious gold rings and bangles. 'How amazing to find you here. But of course, you live in Vienna, don't you.' Her voice was soft and smooth, with an American accent. She turned around. 'Wolfie, shall we join them? You don't mind if we join you, do you?'

Katie moved round to make room for them. She introduced everyone; 'Liliana and Wolf Richter; Dmitry Gavrilov.' Richter sat down heavily. He was in his late forties, perhaps fifty, a little overweight. He had a pampered look about him, as if he was used to a life of luxury; except that his face was rather hard. He greeted them politely, but he didn't look pleased. Katie was dismayed; there were few people she felt more uncomfortable with than Wolf Richter and Liliana.

She shot a glance at Dmitry to try to indicate her feelings, to apologise for inflicting this on him, hoping he would realise that they were not her friends, but failed to catch his attention. Richter himself seemed bored. He drummed his fingers impatiently on the table, looked at his watch. They ordered coffee; Richter's mobile phone warbled. He answered it and started arguing, loudly and in German, about a delivery that was late; it was clearly an important deal, he mentioned large sums of money. Dmitry suppressed a little smile.

Liliana was looking at Richter with admiration. 'Poor Wolf, he can never get away from the phone,' she said. When Richter finished the conversation Liliana reached over and took Katie's hand. 'Oh, I do love your ring – did Bob buy it for you? We're only here for a few days, but you must join us for dinner – is Bob here? Look, I bought this dress, let me just show you . . .' She chattered on, unaware that Katie's faint smile was really a plea for her to stop. In spite of Liliana's babble she could hear that Richter had finally started talking to Dmitry, the conversation had become technical, and Richter's heavy face seemed almost animated. He was describing arcs in the air with his hand, making gestures as if to show how things fitted together, and he drew diagrams on the serviettes. Dmitry's expression was unreadable as he smoked his cigarette and listened. Despairing suddenly of the impossibility of the situation, Katie got to her feet.

'I'm sorry,' she said, 'It's lovely to see you like this, but I have to go. I have to fetch Anna from kindergarten.' In fact this wasn't true; she had asked a friend to collect her today, in case she was delayed at the inquest. But it worked; Liliana kissed both her cheeks and released her. Richter gave her a bored, dismissive wave.

Gavrilov had also got to his feet. He briefly said 'Goodbye' and followed Katie out into the cold, bright sunlight. She stood there for a moment, agitated and uncertain.

He asked, 'Are you going home by tram? We are going the same way, I think.'

A large red Mercedes coupé was parked across the road. There was a driver and another man in dark glasses staring down the street. Katie was sure that it was Richter's and not for the first time she wondered whether his activities were legitimate. She began to walk hurriedly up the street without answering Dmitry's question.

'Who is this man?' he asked rather abruptly, watching her face intently.

'His name is Wolf Richter. I don't really know him. Liliana is an old friend of Bob's.'

'What do you know about him?'

'Very little. I know he's very rich, but I never quite found out why, I think he had money in his own right, not just from Liliana. He's a bit of a playboy – the pair of them spend money like water. He's an engineer of some kind, I think. Bob told me he had his own technical research institute or something.'

He was walking close beside her. 'Research into what?'

'I don't know, I really don't. Why?'

'Have you seen them often?'

'No, just in Paris, a couple of times. As I told you, they're not my kind of people.'

'When were you in Paris?'

She was suddenly on her guard; there was something about his questions, casual though he made them, that alerted her. She thought he was too interested; these were not the questions of someone enquiring into the background of someone they have casually met. She wanted not to answer, but this seemed too difficult. 'In the spring – May, or June, I can't remember.'

'And he has his institute there?'

'No, that's in Germany. In Paris he has a luxury apartment in the Place des Vosges.'

'And you went to his apartment?'

'Yes.'

They were standing at the tram stop. A cold wind blew, and she shivered. He moved behind her, putting himself between her and the wind. Katie noticed this gesture, and the thoughtfulness of it, but didn't dare say anything to him. They waited for the tram in silence. She felt horribly confused.

'How did you meet him?'

She wondered if he was just trying to make conversation, but she didn't want to say any more; she was spared, because at that moment the tram lurched into view. They stepped up into it, punched their tickets and went to sit near the back. Katie looked out of the window at the elegant buildings as they sped along, trying to ignore the disturbing sensation of sitting so close to him. How had she met the Richters? It had been in Paris, eighteen months ago. She and Bob had gone there for a long weekend by themselves, the first time they had been away without Anna. Bob had said that he wanted to look up an old friend from New York who had married a German living in Paris. They had a flat in the Place des Vosges. Katie hadn't wanted to go, preferring to spend time on her own with Bob, but he had insisted. The flat was very expensive, all white and gold with carefully chosen objets d'art. Richter had opened some champagne. Liliana, appearing in a model dress, had said that it was her birthday. 'Come down with me,' she said to Katie, 'Come and see my birthday present.'

They had run downstairs and across the square, still clutching their glasses of champagne. It had been raining; Liliana tripped across the puddles in which the baroque streetlamps were reflected. She took her to a nearby garage and proudly pointed to a large Rolls-Royce. The chauffeur was patiently waiting. The Rolls-Royce was pale blue and had Liliana's initials painted on the doors. Liliana had said, 'Go on; come inside.' The chauffeur had opened the doors for them and Liliana had instructed him to take them for a drive. Liliana opened a compartment and pulled out a bottle of champagne. There was a little gold box which she opened; it contained fresh cherries dipped in chocolate. Liliana laughed with delight, like a small child. 'Look how he spoils me,' she said. 'When I met Wolf, I decided, this was it. I was always going to marry money, you know. I don't care what anybody says, it is the only thing that matters.'

Katie had thought, what am I doing here? She felt awkward and badly dressed, and didn't want to get drunk. She sipped some more champagne and looked out of the window. 'Did you marry for love?' asked Liliana. Katie had looked at her, startled, because she didn't know the answer. No-one had ever asked her this before and it struck her now that to have said 'Yes' would have sounded false. Katie was not romantic; she thought people married for much more pragmatic reasons. She remembered saying, 'I think I married because I wanted a child.'

Was this an admission that she hadn't loved Bob? In many ways, this visit to Paris had been a turning point for Katie, a crystallisation of her feelings of dissatisfaction with her life and the loss of her ideals and values. Meanwhile, Liliana had rattled on, telling her that her father, Luiz Carneiro de Amaral, had been a wealthy man in Brazil, a coffee baron, living in a huge colonial style house in the very centre of São Paulo. But her father had divorced her mother and they had lived quite modestly. Later, she had regained her father's favour, but before this happened she had resolved to become wealthy in her own right. She had gone to New York; she had been a Penthouse model. This was when she had met Bob. Katie had been somewhat shocked by this, wondering what other hidden aspects of his life there were that she had no knowledge of.

Liliana had taken her back to the flat. Then they had all gone to dinner in an expensive restaurant and later to a nightclub. Katie had danced with Bob and then with Wolf himself. They had not returned to their hotel till nearly six in the morning, Katie feeling ill and dizzy with exhaustion, and had then slept till midday, both of them waking with terrible headaches. She remembered asking Bob why he had never told her about Liliana before and where Richter's money came from, but didn't get any real answers. She had been miserable; Bob had accused her of never knowing how to enjoy herself. That evening had been the cause of one of their rare and memorable rows.

Recalling this, Katie felt more than ever that her life had taken a wrong turning since she'd left the BBC in London and come here to take what had turned out to be a dead end job with Radio Blue Danube. She had given up work to be a mother, partly because Bob had wanted this, and now found herself without prospects. This was not the life she had envisaged for herself. She had a sudden feeling of desperation, made worse by an intuition that this man next to her was as acutely aware of her physical presence as she was of his.

The tram took them to the bottom of the Obkirchergasse and they walked up the street together.

Gavrilov suddenly asked, 'Was Lieselotte happy with the verdict?'

'No, not really, I don't think. She's still not convinced it was suicide, but it's so hard for her to accept.'

Gavrilov stopped abruptly. 'This is where I live. Do you want to come in for a coffee?'

She stopped too, and stared at him. She knew she ought to say no, but instead she nodded. The flat was in a small modern building, and he took her up to the second floor. She walked into a sparsely furnished room, with just a table and chairs, a bookshelf, and a black leather sofa. On the table were the remains of his breakfast, a pile of papers, and a photograph in a frame. He hurried about, clearing the plates from the table, taking her coat, going into the kitchen and putting on the kettle. Katie didn't know what to say to him.

She walked over to the table. She looked at the photograph, of a woman with two children. He came up behind her. 'My sister, Olga, and my two nephews, Kolya and Volodya,' he said. Katie picked it up and studied it more closely. His sister had the same eyes and mouth as he did; she was a striking-looking woman. The boys looked rather solemn. Katie said, pointing to the youngest, 'This one looks like you,' and Dmitry immediately looked pleased. 'Do you think so?' he said. 'Everybody says so. Fortunately neither of them really take after their father.'

She put the photograph back. He was standing right behind her; he was far too close. He had taken off his jacket and wore a thin white cotton shirt, and she had the sense that she could hear his heart beating beneath it, feel the warmth of his skin separated from her by this fragile layer. What was she doing here? She half turned, intending to step away from him, but the movement only brought her closer to him, touching him; he put his arms around her and began to kiss her hair, her neck, her ear, and then, as she turned her head up to him, her mouth.

She stepped back from him, leaning against the table. He was looking at her, and there was something in his gaze, in the whole expression of his face, which moved her irresistibly. She had never felt such desire, it hit her like a pain deep inside, and she found that she was trembling. She turned her back to him, and quick as a cat he put his arm round her waist, pulling her back with him onto the sofa. His hands found their way under her clothes, pulling them aside, touching the naked skin. She let him touch her, caress her, everywhere; before long, she encouraged him. He aroused her quickly; the soles of her feet burned, a flush spread over her and then she was crying out with pleasure.

Now he started to fumble with his own clothes. She was instantly frightened. She said, 'If we're going to . . . these days . . . shouldn't we use . . . ?'

He seemed not to know what she meant at first. Then he said, 'I have one in the bedroom. Let's go into the bedroom.'

His bed was unmade; they fell upon it. There was a large plate glass window opening onto a balcony, screened from the flats behind by a wall of conifers; the pale winter sunshine penetrated into the room, dappling the sheets with faintly moving shadows. She lay naked on her back while he stripped off his clothes, fumbled in the drawer by the bed, and then he turned to her. Although he was a big man he wasn't fat, but his skin was curiously pale, as if he had always been starved of sunlight. He leaned forward, touching her, she opened her legs, and he entered her easily, as if they had been doing this for years.

He stroked her firmly, gently, almost with reverence; he seemed far more interested in her pleasure than in his own. She closed her eyes, as she usually did, but he wouldn't let her; he said, 'Look at me, I want you to look at me; tell me what you like; do you like it like this?' and she had to respond to him. She found she loved everything about him; his size, his smell, his touch, the way he was gentle but also so quick in his responses. He seemed not to tire of her and she, who had seldom come easily with Bob, lost count of the number of times she reached orgasm.

Finally, they lay still. She pulled the sheet over her and lay with her back to him, pressed against the warmth of his body, half dozing, exhausted. With one hand he gently stroked her long, thick hair.

They lay like this for some time. Then, abruptly, the phone rang. He picked it up and spoke a few words, in Russian, then hung up. He turned back to her but it had broken the spell. She asked, 'What is the time? I must get back. Anna will be wondering where I am.'

He sat up, his arms resting on his knees. He said, 'If you like you can have a shower.' She thought she had better. She had the instinct at once to conceal from Bob what she had done. She went into the tiny bathroom and showered hastily. She looked curiously at the clutter of shaving gear, a bottle of Russian after-shave and some mysterious pills in a packet with Cyrillic script, and to her relief, saw nothing to suggest that there had been another woman there recently.

By the time she had dressed he had made some coffee and the pot stood steaming on the table. He sat on the sofa in a shabby dressing gown and suddenly looked much older.

He indicated that she should sit down, said, 'I did ask you in for a coffee.'

'Thank you. But I have to rush, I'll be late to collect Anna.'

'It's okay.'

She didn't feel embarrassed in his presence, as she might have done, but she felt anything she said would be superfluous. He was silent as well, so she said nothing, not even asking whether she would see him again. She gulped down the coffee and went to the door, aware all the time that he was watching her. She turned and shut it firmly behind her, ran down the dark staircase. In a few moments she was outside in the sunlight, walking up the hill. Everything seemed normal in the street; a car swept up the hill, a lady was walking her dog, the sun was still shining palely. It was half past two; she was not even much later than she had said she'd be, she wouldn't even have to give an explanation. It was that simple. She had thought that she would never do this, as so many of her friends had done; there had been no agonising, no soul searching, nothing. She had simply gone to see a man she hardly knew for coffee and emerged a little later an adulteress.

III

It was part of Nihal's routine when he was at home to meditate every evening; not that he was religious, but he found the mental discipline rewarding. He was just coming out of his meditation, sitting cross-legged on the floor, when the telephone rang. The answer-phone was on, but he leaned over and picked up the receiver before it cut in.

'Hello?'

'It's Mitya Gavrilov. You remember, we met . . .'

'Of course.'

'I was wondering . . . I have something which might interest you. Actually, nothing to do with the IAEA, but perhaps we could meet?'

Nihal was so surprised by this invitation that he took a while to answer. 'I'll be up at the Agency tomorrow.'

'Yes. Well, I'm afraid we've just had a circular round from the DG, reminding us that no-one is to speak to the press without getting clearance through the press officer. You're quite well known up there. I suggest we meet in town.'

Nihal suggested a bar near the Rathausplatz, not far from his flat. They arranged to meet that evening at nine.

Nihal hung up, went into the gloomy kitchen and lit a cigarette. He sat in the dark and stared out of the window.

Gavrilov frankly puzzled him. A few years ago it would have been inconceivable that someone in his position should be acting as he was.

Nihal had checked his background, and found that he had worked as a nuclear scientist in some of the Soviet Union's most secret research establishments. He'd been abroad for conferences, but that would have been always under the watchful eye of the KGB. Nihal knew the system; they had to sign before they went that they would co-operate with intelligence; they had to report every foreign contact. To speak to the foreign press at all would have been utterly forbidden.

Of course, in recent years that had been changing. Nihal remembered how, almost overnight, the Russians at the UN had suddenly begun wearing Western-made suits, mingling freely with people of other nationalities and openly criticising their own regime. The Russians were now employed at the UN on the same basis as everyone else; gone were the days when the slightest misdemeanour would have them on the next plane back to Moscow. They could live where they liked, make friends with whom they liked, could say, more or less, what they liked. On the other hand, here was a senior scientist who must possess a vast amount of secret knowledge. How free was he, really?

The bar was crowded when Nihal arrived. There was no sign of Gavrilov so he ordered a beer and sat in the corner, reading a paper. Gavrilov joined him shortly.

They sat opposite one another and both lit up. Nihal found that he was pleased to see him; he thought that perhaps they felt an affinity for one another because they both lived on their own and neither of them quite belonged anywhere.

Gavrilov, unexpectedly, jumped straight in. 'I think it might prove worthwhile for you to investigate the activities of a man called Wolfgang Richter. He's a German, aged late forties, early fifties. He's from Stuttgart. He has his own technical research company – I believe something to do with rockets.'

'Rockets?'

'Exactly.'

'Any other clues?'

'No, not really, though I imagine some of his work will have been published. You could look in the *International Aerospace Abstracts*, that kind of thing.'

'Okay.' Nihal stubbed out his cigarette. 'That's it?'

'That's it.'

They were both silent for a few moments. Nihal felt a sense of great disappointment; he'd been hoping for a lead about Brazil. He took the opportunity to get back to what was preoccupying him at the moment.

'I saw you at the inquest into Hans Müller's death. Was everyone happy with the verdict?'

Gavrilov's face changed at once; he was suddenly much more cautious. 'I think so.'

'So no-one thinks there's more to it?'

'Well, you're not the only person this has occurred to, obviously. But we've had endless meetings, and there is no evidence.'

'Look,' said Nihal, 'It smells to me. What evidence are we talking about? I've been thinking about it. You have had all the statistics from the Brazilian nuclear authority, CNEN, isn't it? going right back to the inauguration of the Valadares Centre. Presumably I can assume that all adds up.' Dmitry made a gesture which implied that he could indeed assume that. 'But supposing the information was not correct – supposing they had under-declared it. The military could presumably give the wrong information to CNEN. You don't think the military could conceal anything from them?'

Gavrilov sighed. 'Well it's possible, but I wouldn't have thought so. Not unless there were people at CNEN who agreed with it. For that kind of thing there would have to be bribery, corruption, the fixing of data on a grand scale, probably right up to the top. The new director at CNEN, Pereira da Silva, he's undoubtedly – how do you say? – on the side of the angels. He is a long-standing enemy of the military programme.'

'But how near are they to getting the other centrifuge halls in operation? Did the inspectors get to see that?'

'They inspected everything that was declared to them.'

'So the IAEA is just taking their word for it, that they only have the one cascade hall functioning.'

Gavrilov regarded Nihal seriously. 'Nihal, we always just take their word for it. If a country says they have x number of reactors, x reprocessing facilities, x enrichment plants, then that is the number we go and inspect. Of course inspectors couldn't be allowed to look all over somewhere like Valadares. It is a military research establishment. They do research into nuclear submarines and nobody is going to be allowed to poke around wherever they like. Nor are they going to be allowed to go in and see where they are assembling their centrifuges. I know exactly what you are thinking. Of course I have thought it myself. So has everybody else. We are not blind to the possibilities. I have discussed all this with the DDG myself.'

Gavrilov lowered his voice and leant a little closer to Nihal across the table. 'All right, supposing they were operating another cascade, one they did not allow any of us to see. Perhaps Hans Müller had his suspicions. Is this the kind of scenario you are suggesting? It is not very likely, it is extremely unlikely, but I suppose it is just about possible. Unless we had any evidence, what could we do about it? We could hardly go back to the Brazilians and say, on the basis of supposition, that they are not playing ball. There has been so much opposition to the idea of IAEA safeguards in Brazil that it would be disastrous politically. They might pull out of the whole thing.'

Nihal offered Gavrilov another cigarette and they both lit up. Nihal said, 'So a suspicion isn't enough.'

'No. You know how it is – the IAEA might, because a light bulb failed somewhere and the surveillance cameras did not record anything, be unable to establish absolutely that there has not been a diversion of nuclear material. But everything else is in order. How can one report a country to the UN Security Council for breach of its NPT obligations over a failed light bulb?'

'I think they killed him.'

Lieselotte sat hunched up on the chair, her hands wrapped round her head. For a few days she had been calm, waiting for the verdict of the inquest, but now that this was over, it was all coming out: the grief, the fear and the anger.

'Who?' Katie's German was fluent, and Lieselotte's English was hesitant, so they always spoke German together.

'I don't know who. You know as well as I do – he could have discovered something wrong in Brazil.'

Katie put her arm around her. 'Liese, that doesn't make sense. Bob told me they have been into everything. He organised that inspection, he said everything was in order.'

'Yes, but they might not know. Why should they know? Anyway, they won't let me talk to anyone. I asked if I could talk to the people who were there on the inspection and they said no. There was an Argentine, he's left the IAEA, Cruz, I think. And a Russian, Dmitry Gavrilov. Why won't they let me see them?'

This unexpected mention of Gavrilov's name affected Katie so profoundly that she actually started. She had been trying not to think about him, determined that things should go no further. Lieselotte was immersed in her own thoughts and noticed nothing. Katie said, trying to concentrate on the moment at hand, 'Perhaps if you wrote again they would let you. If it made you feel better . . .'

'I don't want to see them to feel better. I shall never feel better. I want to find out the truth.'

'Liese,' Katie took her hand; this was hard to say. 'Liese, if there were something wrong, they wouldn't have to go round killing people to keep things quiet. Half these countries are running rings around the IAEA all the time, you know that.'

'I don't know it.'

'Well, you have to be more cynical.'

'You're telling me Hans's job was worthless.' Lieselotte was angry with her now; she stared at her fiercely.

'No, I'm not saying that, Liese. I'm sure he believed in what he was doing, just as Bob does. I'm saying that there are flaws in the system, that's all – and they don't have to kill people to cover it up.'

Lieselotte stood up and walked to the window. In the next room the baby started crying. She turned and ran in to him, and Katie could hear her talking to the baby, in the same sweet, crooning voice that any other mother would. Lieselotte came back, the baby held against her shoulder, nuzzling his warm head. She stood in the doorway and for a moment her face was tranquil, almost happy. Then the pain flooded back, and she began to cry again. 'Thank God I have my baby,' she sobbed, holding him tightly. 'If I didn't have him, I think I would die.'

Katie was sure Bob hadn't noticed that anything was wrong with her. Well, why should he? Although inwardly she felt as if something fundamental had changed, that she was not the same person as before, there was nothing obviously different about her or her behaviour which would have led him to think that she had been unfaithful. What she had done was completely out of character, and this made her wonder if she really knew herself, and worse, whether Bob knew her at all. The fact that he'd noticed nothing irritated her, as if she felt he ought to have been able to look inside her and see that she was in inner chaos.

The worst thing was that she couldn't stop thinking about it. She kept seeing Dmitry's room, the pale sunlight dappling the bed and falling on his white skin, remembering the way he had touched her. And yet, he hadn't rung her. Why? Suppose he didn't feel anything special for her, had just been desperate to go to bed with someone? The very idea made her feel humiliated. But no, surely that couldn't be. No-one could behave like that unless they felt something; and besides, he knew that she was married. Perhaps he thought it was best for her to make the next move.

As a result of this one brief hour, an hour which might not in the end have any significance, everything in her life seemed to be suffering. She had some translating work to do, and she was now behind with it. In the morning when Anna went to kindergarten she had intended to sit down and get on with it, but she was too agitated to concentrate. She hadn't slept well, and she found herself being short and bad-tempered with Anna. That was the worst thing of all; how could she have behaved like this, risking her marriage, when she had a child?

But now, as she cleared the table after a late supper, she couldn't help noticing that Bob's eyes were on her. He followed her into the kitchen as she was making coffee and put his arms around her.

'Honey,' he said, 'I've been wondering, you never say, about having another baby . . . Are you depressed about it?'

His words broke unexpectedly into Katie's thoughts. Nothing had been further from her mind. Bob was very keen that she should have another baby; he didn't want Anna to be an only child. Two years ago, Katie had got pregnant for the second time, but had miscarried at twelve weeks, and since then had not conceived; well, it was difficult, with Bob away so much, and she usually didn't hesitate to point this out to him. Bob was much keener than she was to have another child. Katie remembered only too well the depression she'd suffered after Anna's birth, the loneliness of looking after the baby on her own, and she didn't know that she wanted to repeat the experience. Despite this, the loss of the second baby had been deeply upsetting.

'I don't know, Bob. I'm really not sure I want another baby.'

Bob took the tin of coffee out of her hand and put it down on the worktop. 'Katie, forget the coffee. Come to bed.'

'I don't want to go to bed. Bob, I want to talk to you about Lieselotte. She's a bit unstable, I think that's understandable, but now she has this weird idea – she thinks that somebody might have killed Hans.'

Bob sighed and let go of her. He picked up the coffee tin and began measuring spoonfuls into the filter.

'But we've been into that. The DG actually had a whole session with her explaining what had been done and how carefully we had looked into this.'

'She said she wanted to talk to the other people who'd been on that trip and that she wasn't given permission.'

'No, well, that wouldn't be right.'

'Why?'

'Because it would put them in a very awkward position, they are not allowed to give out any information to anyone, that's a condition of their being given permission to carry out inspections. Besides, it wouldn't tell her anything. No, Kaisler is completely right there.' Bob turned to Katie. 'Look, is Liese getting any help? Is she seeing a therapist or something?'

'Her doctor's put her in touch with someone.'

'Good.' Once again, he put his arms around her, began kissing her; this time she couldn't resist. They went to bed and made love quickly and without ceremony and then Bob went instantly to sleep. Going to bed with him this time felt strange; instinctively she shrank from it. When she had gone to bed with Dmitry she had felt she was betraying Bob; but in going to bed with Bob she felt even more strongly that she was betraying Dmitry.

The phone rang. Startled, Katie looked up from the German-English dictionary and picked up the receiver.

'I want to see you.'

It was Dmitry. The deep voice and the liquid Russian vowels were unmistakable.

Katie hesitated for a moment. 'I don't think that's a good idea.'

'We could meet in town, maybe, at the Café Central. I just want to talk to you.'

She said, without thinking, the first thing that came into her head: 'Lieselotte wants to see you. Can I bring her along too?'

He was silent for a few moments, as if trying to think through all the implications. Then he said, 'Yes. Yes, of course.'

'On Wednesday morning?'

'Yes, that's fine. What time?'

'Eleven o'clock – I'll see you then.' She hung up. So he had rung her, finally; Katie felt both relief and agitation. She looked across the room to where Anna was playing with her doll on the carpet, talking to herself, and she realised that her heart was thumping in her chest so loudly she was surprised Anna didn't notice. What was she doing, seeing this man? What good could come of it? Anna looked up at her and smiled, and Katie smiled back, a false, deceitful smile, because she was not thinking of Anna or her best interests, she was thinking of herself.

Lieselotte had made herself up for the occasion. The bright lipstick and darkened eyes emphasised the paleness of her fragile face, making her look like a china doll. Her hand trembled slightly as she lifted the cup of coffee to her lips. Katie realised at once that she was necessary in this meeting as an interpreter. Neither Gavrilov's German nor Lieselotte's English were up to a difficult conversation.

Lieselotte had seemed grateful to Katie for arranging the meeting and hadn't thought to ask how this had come about. Katie had made a point of telling her that Bob would disapprove and that it would be better if she didn't tell him. Now, sitting here, she felt she was deceiving him on two fronts.

Lieselotte came straight to the point. 'I know you went to Brazil with Hans on this last trip. You stayed with him, didn't you, in the same hotels? Surely you men talk about these things. There wasn't anything that went wrong, was there? He didn't make a mistake? There wasn't another woman or anything was there? Nothing that could have made him do something like this?'

Katie translated into English. Dmitry considered for a moment before replying: 'He didn't tell me if there was. I'm sure there wasn't another woman, I don't think you need worry about that. He talked a lot about you and the baby. I know he felt badly about leaving you alone so much.'

'And was there something else worrying him?'

'Well, only a few things to do with work, I think, internal office politics, nothing else.' Dmitry looked uncomfortable; he said, 'This must be very distressing for you. I –'

Lieselotte seemed to understand without Katie's intervention. She cut in quickly, still in German. 'No, no, what's distressing for me is not to talk about it. I think about it all the time, it goes round and round in my head, it's a relief sometimes to be able to talk about it. But it's no use, is it? I don't suppose we shall ever know. The police are not interested in taking it any further. I thought of hiring a private detective, but what would be the point? He would not have access to the IAEA.'

Dmitry waited while Katie translated.

'If he did it wouldn't help him. I can assure you that they have been through everything, all the papers, reports, they've checked very thoroughly. I have been to the meetings and it's all been taken very seriously.'

'This is what Kaisler told me. But it is not enough. I tried to explain to the police, but they didn't listen. There is something wrong with the letter. It's not something I can explain, but it isn't right.'

'Do you have the letter?'

Lieselotte reached over with uncertain fingers and rummaged through her bag. She took out the letter, still folded in a plastic bag as a piece of police evidence. She pushed it over to him. 'Can you understand it?'

Katie smoothed it out on the marble table top and read it out to Dmitry. He studied it as she read, their heads close together. Once again she felt the thrill of his touch.

Dmitry asked, 'What isn't right about it?'

'I said to the police, this is not the way he would have written. Could somebody have dictated it? I don't know. And why did he spell the lawyer's name wrong? He knew this lawyer well, I can't see him making a mistake. And I asked myself, could it be some clue? I couldn't see it, the police couldn't see it. But what haunts me is, how can you force somebody to write a suicide note? If you know you are going to be killed anyway, why should you make it easier for them? Why write the note, why swallow the pills? What do they threaten you with? I wouldn't write such a note. What would I have to gain if they were going to kill me anyway?'

'You would have something to lose,' said Dmitry, 'If they threatened to harm the baby. Wasn't he in the house?'

Nobody said anything. Then Lieselotte, obviously shocked at the simplicity of this threat, said quietly, 'Yes of course, why didn't I think of that?' Katie looked at Dmitry, equally shocked. She felt uneasy with the way the conversation was going, feeling that Dmitry, far from reassuring Liese as she had hoped, was only fuelling her misguided suspicions. She thought this last remark was a dreadful, unforgivable thing for him to have said. It only occurred to her later that he came from a society where people might naturally think of such things.

But Lieselotte did not seem to mind this in the least; perhaps she was pleased that somebody was taking an interest, that she could talk openly about her anxieties rather than listen only to the social niceties. Dmitry looked at the letter for such a long time that Katie began to feel embarrassed. They were both silent, watching him. He stared at the paper, he frowned, he turned it over, he even lifted it and held it up to the light. Katie and Lieselotte looked at one another.

Lieselotte said, 'It is our notepaper – the watermark shows that, if that's what you were looking at.'

Katie translated and Dmitry abruptly folded up the note and handed it back to Lieselotte; she took it and put it back in her bag.

'I shall never believe it; I shall always have doubts,' she said. 'The most terrible thing is that I shall never know. If he was under pressure of some kind, if he was murdered, it would be terrible, but perhaps it would be better, at least I wouldn't have to blame myself.'

'But why do you blame yourself?' asked Katie, putting her hand on Lieselotte's arm, 'Whatever the reason, it is nothing to do with anything you did.'

'How do you know what I might have done? You weren't there. I knew something was wrong, I should have done something to help him. I didn't help him, I was angry with him. He was never there, he was working, he was preoccupied and depressed. I had to cope with the baby all by myself, I resented it and I let him know that.' Her voice became angry; she turned away from Katie.

Dmitry watched this exchange, uncomprehending, looked to Katie to help him, but she said nothing. Lieselotte glanced at her watch. She said, leaning forward, to Dmitry, in broken English, 'It is so kind of you to see me like this. It has helped me, a little. I know you must not say anything. Thank you.' She stood up. 'I must go, Katie. No, don't come with me, my sister is waiting. I'll be fine. I'll ring you tomorrow.'

Katie kissed both her cheeks, and watched her cross the café floor, weaving in and out between the tables. To her surprise, Gavrilov also made ready to leave. 'Katie, I'm sorry, but I also have to go – I have a meeting. But please, can we meet again?'

'I don't know.' She was startled. She had expected to have to fend him off, to explain that she couldn't see him and endanger her marriage, and that what had happened between them was not to be repeated, but now she felt bereft at his sudden departure.

'Tomorrow?' He was insistent.

'It's Saturday. I have to look after Anna.' Then she said, 'Well, perhaps I can leave her for an hour or two with Bob. Can I ring you later?'

He wrote his number on the back of his card and handed it to her as he left. The card had his name printed in both English and Cyrillic under the IAEA symbol of the atom in a laurel wreath.

Before she left Katie memorised the number, tore up thc card into tiny pieces and left them in the ash-tray.

Dmitry took the lift straight up to the twentieth floor and strode into his office. His secretary appeared instantly in the doorway, a sheaf of messages in her hand. Hilde was an ideal assistant, knowledgeable and efficient; she was unflappable, and seemed to intuitively understand his moods, never taking things personally. An Austrian with a Russian mother, she spoke both English and Russian fluently. They switched back and forth easily between the two languages.

He told her to hold all but urgent international calls and to leave him undisturbed for half an hour. She opened her mouth to protest but then thought better of it, putting the heap of messages to one side to give him later.

Gavrilov shut the connecting door between his office and hers, swivelled his chair round to face his computer screen and hesitated for a moment before logging in. He summoned up a menu and began putting in the series of passwords.

As he waited for the file to be retrieved, he stood up and went to the window. He could see the giant Ferris wheel at the Prater amusement park and the cold winter sunlight sparkling on the icy waters of the Danube. He lit himself a cigarette; he felt so agitated he could hardly stand still.

Why was it that Hans Müller had inserted into the misspelt name of his lawyer one of the passwords to the file on that last mission to Brazil? It had taken only the addition of two letters. Was it simply a way of explaining that his death was somehow linked to that trip, or was it more specific than that? Was he pointing to some information contained in that file? He had been taking a chance in any event – the probability of someone who knew this ever seeing the letter must have been very slight. Only a handful of people within the IAEA who were authorised to see that file would have recognised it.

Dmitry sat at his desk and frowned. He had been disturbed all along by the memory – and it was not altogether clear, because it had been late and he, like Hans Müller and Eduardo Cruz, the second inspector on that trip, had been drinking in the bar – of Müller coming to him on the last night and saying, while Cruz was buying more drinks, 'There's something I want to talk to you about. Can I come to your room later?' Dmitry had sensed from his attitude that it was something important; he had the feeling that Müller wanted to make some kind of confession. But in the event Müller had never come. At the airport, when he had reminded him, Müller had shaken his hand dismissively and said nothing.

Dmitry turned to the screen and looked through the report on the inspection at Valadares. First the inspectors had checked the ledgers recording in detail the receipt of uranium hexafluoride at the plant, the throughput, and the ratio of product to the unwanted residue or 'tails', and these were compared with the reports sent to the IAEA. All this appeared to be in order. Seals had been affixed to some of the storage cylinders so that these did not need re-checking, and to various valves and flanges to make sure that material could not be drawn off. The seals contain certain unique markings which are photographed and compared with original photographs; any tampering with the seal would show up as a distortion.

The report showed that they had checked the setting up of the cameras which took still shots of the inside of the plant every couple of minutes, making it impossible for any tampering to go unnoticed. Seals were also attached to the camera housings.

Then readings had been taken at various points to measure the uranium hexafluoride samples from the product, feed and tails lines and check that only uranium with a low level of enrichment was passing through the tubes. Radiation levels were checked, which again would indicate the presence of highly enriched uranium. Then the inspectors had looked at the pipework on top of the cascades. If the centrifuges were connected in parallel more uranium hexafluoride could circulate to a lower degree of enrichment; if in series, enrichment could increase up to the 90 per cent or more needed for weapons grade uranium.

Dmitry read through the whole file twice. There was nothing

wrong with it; there was no problem or anomaly that he could see. He knew the kind of figures you could expect from a plant this size; there was nothing to ring any alarm bells. He checked the date it had last been updated; 4 January, the Friday before Müller died. It would be possible to check who had made the last changes. He exited from the file and crossed the room, sinking down into the chair and resting his feet on the low table.

He sat still for a while, deep in thought. Eduardo Cruz had been at the end of his contract with the IAEA. He was now back in Buenos Aires, working for the Argentine Atomic Energy Commission. Dmitry looked at his watch. It was ten o'clock in Buenos Aires; he went to his desk, shuffled through some papers to find the number he had written down, and tapped it out on the phone.

The call took some time to connect. At length a voice answered. The woman took details of who he was and put him through without delay.

'Ah; my Russian friend,' said Eduardo. 'What can I do for you? I think of you every time I read about the situation in your dear country. They are rationing vodka, now, I hear. What a mercy for you that you are in Vienna!'

'They have been rationing vodka for some time,' said Dmitry patiently. 'But I wanted to ask you something: have you heard anything recently from the IAEA?'

'No.'

'Has the DDG not written to you?'

'Not that I know of, I have been away on leave. Perhaps there is something in this huge pile of mail. What is it about?'

Dmitry said, 'Did you know that Hans Müller committed suicide?'

There was a long silence on the phone, through which Dmitry could hear the echo of a distant, disembodied voice carrying out some conversation in an indistinguishable tongue beyond the faint hiss and crackle. Then Cruz said, 'I knew that man wasn't right in the head.'

'How?' asked Dmitry swiftly. 'How did you know that?'

'Oh, just a feeling that one has,' said Cruz. 'Nothing positive at all. Look, I am shocked by what you tell me. This is terrible. Does anyone know why?'

'I don't think so. That's why I'm calling. I was wondering whether he said anything to you which could pour light on it. Or if there was anything about the inspection, anything at all, which didn't seem quite usual.'

'No; no, of course not. If there had been, I would have mentioned it at the time. We spoke about this ourselves, then when I came back, I had a long talk with Haynes. Wait a minute, I have the letter in front of me now. It asks me to write in confidence to the DDG.' There was an uneasiness, a faint hostility even, in his voice.

'Yes, of course,' said Dmitry. 'It's just that since I was there . . . I have been asked all these questions myself, of course.'

'Of course,' said Cruz. There was another pause. Then they both started speaking together; Dmitry gave way. Cruz went on: 'I'm afraid I don't know what's in your mind. Are you actually querying the inspection report? If you're thinking that Müller made some mistake or had taken false readings, anything like that, well that's just not possible. We checked everything together on the site you know. That's how it's done.'

'Yes,' said Dmitry quietly, 'I know how it's done.'

'Well,' said Cruz, 'If I think of anything, I will put it in my letter. Maybe then you will get to hear of it later on.'

Dmitry mumbled 'Yes of course. Thank you,' and hung up. He sat in silence, twirling his pen. He knew in the instant that he put the receiver down that he had made a bad mistake; as soon as he implied any suspicion about Müller, it implied suspicion about Cruz too. Of course the man had sounded hostile. And supposing something really was going on, he had simply tipped Cruz off. No, he supposed the letter from the DDG would have tipped him off. But then, the DDG would have worded things rather differently. He would have been far more subtle. He would have known how to put it so as not to cause any imaginable offence.

He didn't notice Hilde come in; she stood attentively in front of him, a file in her hand, waiting for him to look up. He did so eventually; his eyes gradually focused on her. She said, in Russian, 'Your half hour is up.'

He met her amused smile with one of his own.

The Belvedere Palace was like a hall of mirrors. It was all white and gold and Katie's shoes rang out loudly on the wooden floor as if asking everyone to turn and stare at her. Wherever she looked she saw images of herself and her Russian lover. Katie, having arranged to meet somewhere public, and to give Bob an excuse – 'Just going to look at the Klimts, darling' – and to protect herself from what might happen – was now afraid that someone she knew would see them together. And anyway, it was no use. As soon as she saw him she was trembling with desire for him; she wanted only to be alone with him.

She moved away and looked out of the window, at the view of stone roofs and the formal gardens laid out in squares with paths running between the box hedges. Everything was covered with a fine layer of frost and snow.

Dmitry came up to stand behind her. He said, 'I don't want to see any more paintings. Let's go back to my apartment.'

She said, 'I'll have to call Bob.'

She rang Bob from a call-box and said she had bumped into a friend and would be late. Was that all right? She was going somewhere for coffee with her; it was Marianne. Dmitry stood next to her and watched her tell this string of lies without any trace of expression on his face. Then they caught the tram and went back to his apartment. All the way there she was pierced with desire for him, almost in pain, not knowing how she could bear waiting, and yet almost enjoying the pain of anticipation. They almost ran up the road together and the moment the door closed behind them they were stripping off their clothes.

As she lay down on the rug on the floor to receive him, he hesitated; despite his urgency, he reached back to his discarded coat and withdrew a condom from the pocket. Then he rolled her over, put his arm round her waist and pulled her towards him, entering her from behind. In this position he seemed to go in deep, so deep; the sensation was so exquisite that she begged him to go on, but he, too, must have been very aroused, and came quickly, crying out loudly, as if in pain. He curled over her, stroking her, covering her back with kisses. Then they went to the bedroom and made love again, this time more slowly and tenderly. She did things with him that she would never have considered doing with Bob; she confessed to him every secret desire.

When they were finally lying quietly with their arms around each other, Katie asked, 'Has it been like this for you with anyone else?' and he said, 'No, of course not, how could it have been? You are not like anyone else.'

This tenderness disturbed her, because she so much wanted and needed it; Bob never said such things. But what she was doing was frightening; she wasn't sure she could cope with it. She turned away from him suddenly. 'I shouldn't be here. I can't carry on like this, seeing you, deceiving Bob. I feel so ashamed.'

'No,' said Dmitry, touching her face, 'That is the lovely thing about you; you are shameless.'

'But only with you,' said Katie, 'I'm only like this with you.'

IV

Nihal knew within a few hours of beginning his researches that he was onto something potentially very big.

The index to *International Aerospace Abstracts* contained various references to Wolfgang L Richter dating back to the mid-1970s. There was a paper given at an Aeronautics conference in California in which Richter said he had developed 'A bi-propellant rocket engine with low thrust and high performance . . . it has been made possible to achieve unlimited burning without ageing, short pulsing time, high reliability and low cost.' This paper gave the name of a company after Richter's name; *Raketenforschung GmbH.* Nihal had looked up some other papers; they were all in the same vein. The later papers referred to his company as RASAG, *Raketen und Aufklärungs-Satelliten AG.* It was all technical stuff, way over his head. He looked through one or two general scientific and aerospace magazines. In one there was a small piece about the German company seeking investors for developing a low-cost satellite launching system.

In the Space Directory Nihal had found a listing for the company, RASAG. It was based in Stuttgart and was a small enterprise, developing low-cost rocket technology. Richter was the president; the chairman was a man called Karl Weiland. That rang a bell; Weiland, he recalled, was one of the Nazi rocket scientists from Peenemünde who had at one time been a consultant to NASA.

This was interesting. He rang RASAG's offices in Stuttgart and spoke to the PR man, Becker, who promised him a brochure in the next post. Becker, who spoke excellent English, emphasised that the company was carrying out space research and that it was entirely independent of the German Government. They planned to offer rocket launches which would be far cheaper than the existing choices, making satellite technology available to a wider range of companies and nations than at present.

But when asked where they were going to launch the rockets, Becker suddenly refused to say, telling him that a deal with an unnamed country was under negotiation.

Richter's history was not hard to unravel. A brilliant young engineer, he had won his first research contract while still at university. He had then gone into industry and joined two of the wartime German scientists, Sänger and Pilz. At first, his company had received huge contracts from the West German Government, and was given the use of government research facilities. But in the mid-1970s the Government cut all ties with Richter, who appeared to have then hit a lean time, trying to raise money for his research.

In the mid-1980s he married Liliana Carneiro, then one of the top models for fashion magazines; her lean, honey-coloured face decorated their covers, while, on the inside pages, her slender bronze body was draped with the most expensive clothes. This marriage bought Richter into a new world of wealth, power and prestige. He began to be more successful in raising money, mainly from private investors, and before long had recruited Weiland, one of the last surviving Nazi rocket scientists, and formed RASAG.

Nihal then telephoned the Nazi-hunting agency, the Jewish Documentation Centre, conveniently situated here in Vienna, to find out about Weiland. Some years ago, Nihal had interviewed one of the few British scientists attached to the US Air Force team which had liberated the concentration camp at Nordhausen, where rocket parts were fabricated by Polish slave labour. This man had spoken movingly of the mounds of corpses, the starving and beaten prisoners, and the small children, conceived by raped camp workers, running round hungry and ill-clothed. Nihal believed that at least twenty thousand workers had died making the rockets. He recalled that this scientist had also been present at the interrogation of some of the scientists, including Wernher von Braun; he had a list somewhere of their names, and wondered if Weiland had been among them. At this time Nihal had also visited the massive bunker at Eperleques in the Pas de Calais, a huge German wartime factory for the assembly and launch of the V2 rocket. As he had trudged in the cold March rain round this grim, abandoned place, in which thousands of half-Jewish Germans, together with Polish, Belgian and Russian prisoners of war, had slaved and perished, his spirit had quailed. He had indeed felt it to be, as the monument at the entrance proclaimed, 'One of the sacred places of human suffering.'

Weiland would now be in his eighties. Like von Braun, he had been a card carrying member of the Nazi party. For years, again like von Braun, he had worked with NASA and achieved acclaim. His presidency gave a certain prestige to RASAG, even if he played no active part, but it also linked it to this unsavoury past.

But Nihal was puzzled. Under the UN Space Treaty, no private organisation could put a rocket into space. There was also the Missile Technology Control regime, by which Germany was bound. In fact, the whole thing was distinctly odd. The very idea of a private company selling cheap rocket technology to whoever wanted it was horrifying. If no-one knew about it yet, he thought, they certainly ought to.

Katie lay in bed with Bob. She tossed and turned, and couldn't sleep. Her conscience tormented her, she had lied and wanted to confess to him, but she couldn't. Anyway, what would be the point? It would simply hurt him, and there was no reason why he should know anything. She had resolved to end her relationship with Dmitry at once.

But how could she give this up? Why was sex so good with him, so much better than it had ever been with Bob? She didn't understand it. She rolled over again, pulling the covers off Bob, and he grabbed them, impatiently.

'What the hell is the matter with you? Can't you let me sleep?'

She said, 'No. I want sex.'

She had never said anything like this to him so simply and directly. He half sat up on one elbow, astonished.

'Are you feeling okay?'

'Don't you want to?'

'Well, of course, I always want to.' He put his hand on her thigh, stroking her. She rolled onto her back, put his hands where she wanted them. He, obviously excited by this initiative, was already erect, getting ready to penetrate her. She pushed him back.

'No, not yet . . . carry on like that.'

'Like this?'

'No, not exactly . . . here.'

It was impossible. He didn't seem to understand what she wanted and it humiliated her to have to ask. She realised that she often pretended more pleasure than she felt in order not to hurt his feelings and that in the long run this hadn't been good for them. Yet it hadn't always been like this; she had sometimes wondered whether Bob was simply bored with her. She imagined, for a moment, being with Dmitry. Even thinking about him excited her.

Bob was inside her now, and she slipped her own hand down between them and made herself come. Once was not enough for her now; she went on, and he went on, and then in the end she came once again, with him; he lay still, on top of her, his arm vaguely stroking her arm, obviously puzzled.

After a while he rolled off her. He lay on his back, his eyes open.

Katie, feeling desperate, sat up, took his face in both her hands and forced him to look at her. 'Bob, I'm so bored. I want to leave Vienna. Can't you get another job?'

'Why this, suddenly?'

'Well, Lieselotte's going, there's nothing for me here and . . . oh I don't know.'

'As it happens I was thinking about trying something else. Give me time, I'll see what I can do.' He was silent for a few moments. 'Is that the only reason?'

Katie lay back in the semi-darkness. 'What other reason could there be?' The question hung between them, the silence filled with tension. Katie felt her heart beating, afraid that he suspected something. She realised that she had never been truly intimate with Bob, had never really shared her inmost thoughts; she had always been aware of having to play a certain part, had never been able to let go and be herself, in case Bob disapproved of her. Now she was afraid to confront him, afraid of his reaction. This realisation was a shock; she had known Bob for years, had lived with him, had a child with him. How could she feel more intimate with a man she hardly knew, whose language and culture were entirely different?

She turned back to Bob, half intending to say something, but to her relief she found he was already asleep.

When Bob came home from work the next day he told Katie that it seemed Hans Müller had had a mistress. An anonymous woman with a Viennese accent had rung up the IAEA claiming that Müller had got her pregnant and demanding some form of compensation if they didn't want her to publicise the fact. Apparently she had asked to speak to the DG, and when told this had not been possible she rang, separately, half a dozen people in the organisation, including the Director of Information and several people in Safeguards. She had sounded angry and distressed and had said vicious things about Müller. Everyone who had spoken to her had been shocked by her abusiveness; it had left a nasty taste in the mouth.

Katie too was dreadfully shocked. She turned the oven down so as not to ruin the supper and followed Bob into the living room. 'Oh God,' she said, 'I hope Lieselotte doesn't hear about it. Do you think it's true?'

Bob shrugged. 'Well, you never know what any of these people are up to on the side, do you?'

Katie turned away from him, unable to meet his gaze.

The phone rang. It was Lieselotte, in great distress. She had just been phoned by the woman claiming to be Hans's mistress. She had put Jochum to bed and finished packing her things; she was due to leave for Cologne in a couple of days. The woman, whoever she was, had said obscene things to her about what she and Müller had done together. Lieselotte could not bear to repeat them. She had wanted to hang up but had not felt able to; she had listened almost against her will because she had been so tormented by her imaginings that she thought anything would be bearable if only it were the truth.

The woman had said that if Lieselotte didn't send her money she would give the story to the papers. Lieselotte had said that she would do no such thing and had hung up. Then the woman had phoned again. This time she had been in tears. She said that Müller had told her terrible lies. He had said he was going to leave his wife and hadn't done so. He had promised her money to keep quiet. She had told him she wasn't going to keep quiet. She had threatened Hans that she would tell his wife and he had told her if she did she would regret it.

Lieselotte had pleaded with her to stop, had said that it was destroying her, that she did not believe her, and that she could not be talking about her husband. She had said she was going to ring the police and if she called again she would have them trace the call. She had hung up; the woman hadn't called back again.

'The trouble is, I really can't believe her,' said Lieselotte. 'Perhaps I am naïve, but I just can't believe it. Not Hans, not with a woman who sounds like that.'

Katie didn't know what to say. Would Bob react the same way, if he found out what she had been doing? She struggled to think of something sensible, something which would calm her friend, but she couldn't. 'Have you told the police?'

Lieselotte said, 'Yes, I called them. They said they would send someone round.' Her voice suddenly went flat.

'Do you want me to come over?' asked Katie.

'No,' said Lieselotte, 'No, it's all right. My sister is here. We're going on Wednesday. I'll write to you. I knew you would hear about it from the office, I just wanted you to hear it first from me.'

Katie said her goodbyes, hung up and went back into the kitchen. Bob was standing there, staring out of the window.

Katie asked, 'Bob, do you think it's true?'

'I don't know.'

'But you worked with Hans.'

'Well, I didn't know him that well. It's possible, of course, when people are away so much, of course it is.'

'Have you been unfaithful?' The words escaped her before she could stop herself; she was horrified, afraid he would turn the question back on her. But instead he laughed. He turned to her and embraced her. 'Is that what's worrying you? No, of course not, honey. Why should I be, when I have you?'

When Dmitry heard the story from Hilde he felt somehow disgusted with everything. He didn't know what to think. Of course, if people were prepared to cover up something, if they were prepared, in an extreme case, to murder someone to silence them, they were not likely to shrink at paying some woman to lie and make an unpleasant scene like this to make it seem as if there was a personal reason for the suicide. All the same, to destroy someone's image of their dead husband seemed the ultimate in cruelty. But then – perhaps he was completely wrong. It could be true. Didn't he himself know what emotional messes people could get into, people who on the surface were conventional, reliable. Why shouldn't this be true of Müller? He sat at his desk and stared at the wall in front of him. He wished again that he hadn't rung Eduardo Cruz.

He tried to think clearly. He couldn't be sure what was imagined and what was real. Everything was an impression; the expression on the face of Oliveira at the Valadares centre when he had said they had nothing to hide; the look in Müller's eyes when he had asked Dmitry if he could talk to him later at the hotel in São Paulo; the tone in Cruz's voice over the telephone. Did you know these things, or were they just imagined? He thought probably you knew. He had known that Katie wanted him from the first minute he had seen her, probably before she had realised it herself. He was usually right about people. Perhaps he should simply trust his instincts.

On the other hand, what could he do? He was never going to be able to prove anything. His first impulse had been to go and see the DDG again and tell him about this latest detail, but he knew that he would be in trouble for having spoken to Lieselotte, and he was already aware that he had made himself unpopular by repeatedly voicing his doubts about what had happened. Besides, it had revealed nothing. As far as Lascalles was concerned the business was closed.

Dmitry sighed. Of course, if there were a problem in Brazil, it could be sorted out behind the scenes without the IAEA ever getting wind of it. It was unlikely that the Brazilian military could get away with anything they might be doing for long. If something was going on, it was likely that the Brazilian authorities would discover it before the IAEA. They would simply sort things out internally. They would say there had been problems with their accounting, that sort of thing. The IAEA turned a blind eye to minor safeguards transgressions all the time. Or perhaps somebody could, behind the scenes, ask the head of the Brazilian Nuclear Energy Commission to look into it. Perhaps he would mention this to the DDG.

Dmitry walked across the room and stared out of the window at the city lying under a thin layer of snow. The whole history of Brazil's parallel programme had been a maze of deception. In 1986 the military had gained greater control of the parallel programme when CNEN had been put under the direct authority of the National Security Council, which was made up of the President and heads of the armed forces, instead of the Ministry of Mines and Energy. When austerity measures had curbed spending on Brazil's nuclear programme, secret bank accounts had been set up abroad to make sure the military programme did not suffer. Various top nuclear energy officials in Brazil had acknowledged that they had been involved in clandestine trade to build the Valadares plant. This included declaring false end uses for German lathes for machining cylinders for gas centrifuges. The former chairman of CNEN had even publicly revealed that Brazil had obtained a wide variety of nuclear equipment by mis-labelling them as 'tractor parts' in the shipping documents.

Dmitry sat down at his desk again and rested his face in his hands. Everybody was aware of this. People had known about it for years. There had been criticisms of the whole West German nuclear deal; the US in particular had warned them against it, saying there was no guarantee that Brazil would not use the imported expertise for military uses. But since Brazil had not then acceded to the Nuclear Non-Proliferation Treaty there had been nothing much that could have been done about it by the IAEA. In a way, it was almost funny. It was farcical. You could shrug your shoulders about it and get on with the job and hope that nothing would come of it; indeed, hope, as seemed to be the case in Brazil, that governments would see sense and decide against the bomb for their own financial and political reasons. It was all right somehow as long as individuals did not come into it. But if things had got to the point where people were prepared to kill to cover up such goings-on, if a safeguards agreement was being deliberately and cynically breached, everything suddenly appeared quite different.

And why shouldn't they be prepared to kill? Enormous sums of money were at stake in nuclear trade. The military were already up to their necks in clandestine deals. There had been a long history of corruption. Perhaps one or two people had been bumped off already, in Brazil; little people who didn't matter. Perhaps a technician who had been prepared to talk had had an accident, been run over by a car or that sort of thing. Nobody would know or care about it. He knew it only mattered so much to him because he knew Hans Müller personally, had met and liked his distraught young wife.

The phone rang. Dmitry almost jumped, startled. He picked it up. It was Nihal, reporting on what he had found. Dmitry listened for a long time in silence. When Nihal had finished, he stayed silent for so long that Nihal had to ask him if he was still there.

Dmitry reached across his desk for his cigarettes. He thought for a moment, wondering whether it was necessary to say this, and then deciding, on balance, that it was best if he did. 'By the way, Nihal, this is important – you won't tell anyone I suggested you look into this, will you?'

Katie, again, heard nothing from Dmitry. After a few days she could bear it no longer. She dropped Anna off early at kindergarten and rushed back to his flat, hoping to catch him before he left for work.

There was a long pause before he answered the door. He was unshaven, wearing his dressing gown. He started, surprised to see her, and stood for a moment staring at her. Then he said, abruptly, 'Come in.'

She walked into the room. There was some music playing quietly: some Beethoven string quartet, she recognised it from a long time ago. It was cold in the flat, as if the heating hadn't yet come on. He didn't say anything to her at once; for a moment she felt terribly uncomfortable, afraid that she might have disturbed him at a time when he wouldn't welcome it, or even, the thought crossed her mind for an instant, was with another woman.

She said, 'I thought I owed you an explanation.'

'What for?'

She looked at him. Within seconds they were kissing one another; within minutes they were in bed. It was too cold for either of them to want to get up afterwards. It had started to snow outside; the curtains were drawn back but it was still quite dark inside the room. He switched the bedside light on. They lay together in the small circle of light it cast, which emphasised the darkness all around them; he put his arm around her shoulder.

With his free arm, slightly awkwardly, he reached over to get a cigarette.

'Do you have to smoke so much? Doesn't it worry you, that it'll kill you?'

Dmitry turned and looked at her. 'Well, for you, I will try to smoke less. But this one, I must have.' He lit up and inhaled deeply. Leaning against him, Katie felt suddenly relaxed, intimate.

After a while she said, 'You must tell me about yourself. I don't know anything about you.'

'So you want my life story, do you?' He looked at the clock. 'Well, I don't have to be in till ten. Maybe there's time to at least begin.'

He began to talk, slowly, slightly hesitantly, as if finding it hard to find the words to say in English things he had never before expressed in that language, perhaps even in his own. He told her about his father's death when he was eight; how things had been hard for them; how he had been determined to excel at school. He had worked hard at science because he was good at it, but also at languages, because it had been his dream to travel abroad. He achieved a gold medal at school and went to Moscow State University where he was a serious student, preoccupied with work. There he had his first serious girlfriend; she was from Cuba. She used to teach him Spanish. He had long ago lost touch with her. He had also met his wife, Masha, there though he hadn't actually gone out with her or married her until much later.

Katie asked, tentatively, 'What went wrong with your marriage?' but he answered vaguely. They were wrong for one another. Katie must know what goes wrong with marriages – what had gone wrong with her own? It was not anybody's fault. Masha had not liked his work. Of course he had worked in secret research establishments; the Russians were absolutely obsessed with secrecy, and for her this was not easy. Well, what else was there to say? His life had been very boring. His career had followed a logical progression. He had worked hard, but had never particularly excelled at anything. If he had, he wouldn't have come to Vienna. The Russians didn't like to let their top scientists go abroad.

At that point she asked him, 'Didn't you ever want to rebel?' and he looked at her, surprised. 'Look,' he said, stubbing out his cigarette and turning towards her, 'You had better not have any illusions about me. I was – how do you put it? – a clean-cut Russian boy, a Komsomol type, a Party member. Of course uranium enrichment is a sensitive area; it has as many implications for atomic weapons as for nuclear power. So I have had to be careful. Rebellion – whatever you mean by that – is not possible. Of course, inside, it is a different matter. You get sick of everything. You know the system is absolutely rotten, but on the other hand, you don't think much of the West either. So you just carry on, but inside . . . inside there are these little devils lurking.'

Katie smiled; she could believe this.

'Of course all the hypocrisy can't help eating away at you. But I will say this for us, at least when we repeated all this stupid stuff we knew it was all shit. That's why the Americans are so dangerous, because they believe their own propaganda.'

Katie turned to look at him. Forgetting what he had said earlier, he reached out for another cigarette. Playfully, she took it away from him. Then she asked, 'But you didn't ever work with nuclear weapons?'

'No, not directly, of course – well, that's not quite true. I did my military service in the Strategic Rocket Forces. I spent four months one summer in Novaya Zemlya – do you know where that is? It's the huge island north and east of Archangel where they test the rockets, and nuclear weapons too, actually. We worked in huge concrete silos deep underground. The control post had to be manned around the clock of course, so we used to work eight-hour shifts, day and night.'

Katie moved closer to him, pressing herself against him; he rolled over, embracing her; she felt her skin melting into his. There was a momentary playfulness in his eyes, as if he enjoyed shocking her by what he was saying. 'We worked with the huge Scarp missiles which began to be deployed in 1965,' he said softly. 'They stood 34 metres high; the warheads were 25 megaton thermonuclear devices, equivalent to 1,250 Hiroshimas – they used to make obscene jokes about it as they lowered the warheads onto the rockets.'

Katie could barely imagine such a thing. She wondered what it felt like, to actually stand and look at such a bomb. Were you afraid? Awed? Disgusted? Could the imagination even take it in? She pulled back from him a little, asked, 'But how could you stand it?'

'Well of course I was not very happy about being there at first, but in fact it was not really such a terrible experience. A lot of people coped by not thinking about it, just drinking, playing cards, sleeping, going into the nearest small township in search of some distraction. But let me try to explain to you how it was. Imagine: you come out of the missile silo at three in the morning –and of course it's a polar day, there's no night – you are in broad daylight, with this wind blowing in your face. You are completely disoriented from working different shifts and the lack of day or night. I cannot describe to you the beauty of this austere landscape. The sea is green, and so clear you can look right into it; there are icebergs floating; the rocks are black and covered with lichen and dark moss; and of course the immense sky. I used to walk for hours by myself, I went without sleep, at times I thought I was hallucinating. It was an almost mystical experience.'

Dmitry reached out for the bedside table and lit another cigarette; he lay back and exhaled with a long sigh. 'Let me admit it: there was something seductive about being in the presence of so much power. I used to think about it when I walked by the sea for hour after hour. Like someone looking over the edge of an enormous cliff and feeling the urge to jump, I used to wonder if we might actually fire them, just to see what would happen, or indulge in some perverse urge towards destruction. Now I suppose the main danger is we will use them on ourselves.'

Katie didn't know what to say. She felt she should have been shocked by what he was saying, but instead she found it thrilling; she was awestruck by the vision of him associated with something so dark and powerful. She could almost feel her mind doing an about-turn, rethinking all her attitudes. 'So that means that when I was in the sixth-form at school and signing up with CND and going on disarmament marches, you were there in the missile silo, you were one of those people that I so despised, who could have pressed the button.'

Dmitry laughed. He said, 'So you think people like me should have protested, do you, have refused to dirty our hands. Well, it was easy for people like you to turn your back on it, to say this was nothing to do with you, you disapproved of it, but what were you risking? What kind of a choice do you think we had? It wouldn't even have occurred to us to try to avoid our military service or refuse to do what we were told. Anyway, it was our patriotic duty. You have to realise that at the time I was doing my military service we had less than 600 missiles while the US had over 1,700; it wasn't till 1971 that we overtook them in actual numbers. So we were definitely able to think of them in terms of defence –'

Katie said, 'Stop. I understand. You don't have to try to justify yourself to me.'

'I am not justifying myself.' He put out his hand and touched her tenderly. 'So, you went on peace marches, did you? I wouldn't have thought it.'

'It was the thing to do,' said Katie. 'I suppose when it comes down to it that's why we do most things.'

'And that's why you're here with me.' He was not looking at her as he said this; as always Katie didn't know if he was being ironical or not. She felt uncertain; he seemed at that moment so distant, foreign. To overcome this feeling she put her arms around him, and said, 'Make love to me.'

'What, again?' He looked astonished. Katie rolled on top of him, and the look in his face, so intense, so pleased, stirred her; she could feel, too, that he was aroused again. Then she said, suddenly, she didn't quite know why, 'Do you think Hans *did* have a mistress?'

He said, emphatically, stubbing out his cigarette, 'No, I don't. Do you believe all that business? I don't think he was like that.'

Katie said, 'You sound so disapproving. What about me? Aren't I doing the same thing?'

Dmitry said, 'No, you misunderstand. I didn't mean that. I meant that the whole thing sounds wrong. I talked to his secretary the other day and she said it was the first time she had heard of it. I think that's a bit strange. Usually when someone is having an affair, his secretary is the first to know.'

Katie said, mischievously, regretting that she had raised this question and trying to turn his attention back to her, 'Does your secretary know about us?'

'Hilde? No, it's too early. But if you ring me at the office, she'll soon know, of course, won't she?'

V

Nihal had arranged to meet Katie at the Café Central; they hadn't seen one another for two weeks. For once she was later than he was, so he sat in the corner and made notes in his black pocket-book.

He had spent the morning ringing round his contacts on the newspapers but had received a disappointing response. One said that the story sounded too improbable and asked him to check it out more fully. A second said that Nazi rocket scientists were too old hat, they didn't think it was sufficiently interesting. Only finally, when he spoke to his old editor Martin Dudley, now with a magazine called *North-South,* purporting to be the Third World's answer to *The Economist*, did he get some genuine interest and a commission. However, it was only for a short piece, about 600 words, for the technology section.

When Katie arrived he was surprised at her appearance. She looked miserable, had dark shadows under her eyes and seemed listless as she sat down opposite him, pulling off her shawl and draping it over the edge of the chair; nor did she seem as pleased as usual to see him. Yet despite this, she looked, as she always did, lovely, with her clear skin, thick hair and that indefinable aura of sensuality which emanated from her.

He felt sorry for her and wanted to cheer her up. He put his hand on her arm and squeezed it. She looked up at him and smiled; not for the first time, he wondered what it would be like to make love to her.

He asked, 'Katie – what's the matter? It's not this business with Lieselotte?'

'No . . . well, I suppose it is, in part. Liese left yesterday. It was difficult saying goodbye, I'll miss her, and I don't know how she'll cope. I'll go and visit her sometime, but, you know, it's difficult.' She put her chin on her upturned palm and sighed. 'Of course, all that was terrible, but it isn't that. Actually, Nihal, the truth is I'm having an affair.'

Nihal was shocked. He had always thought that Katie wouldn't do such a thing, or that if she did, it might have been with him. He asked at once, 'Who with?'

She waited until the waitress had finished putting their coffees on the table. Then she said softly, with a nervous glance around her, and with a lowered voice, 'Nihal, can I trust you? If you tell anyone else, they'll tell somebody, and then in the end Bob will hear.'

'Of course not. My lips are sealed.'

'It's Mitya Gavrilov.'

Nihal was silent for a long time, startled. What was going on? Could this be coincidence? It was as if Gavrilov was working his way into every corner of his life – but why? However had this come about? Then he remembered Katie saying they had met at the funeral.

He asked, 'And Bob hasn't noticed anything?'

'No, no, I don't think so, I don't think he's guessed anything.' Katie leaned over and helped herself to one of Nihal's cigarettes. It was a long time since he had seen her smoke; it rather suited her. 'Actually, I've become rather good at lying, Nihal – in fact I hate myself. I never thought I would do anything like this.'

Nihal was now recovering himself. 'Well, I must say I have been wondering how long you would stick it out with Bob.'

Katie exhaled sharply. 'Why do you say that? What's wrong with Bob?'

'Oh, nothing, really. But I've never thought he was your type.'

'Well, who is my "type"? I wouldn't say Mitya was my "type". Nihal, please be serious. I'm in torment. I know you've talked to him, but I've no idea what he feels about me.'

Nihal laughed. 'Well, I certainly don't know, he hasn't said anything. He's rather a dark horse, our Mitya, don't you think?'

Katie stared into her empty coffee cup, aware of Nihal watching her, almost mocking her. She was suddenly angry with him. There was no-one else she could confide in, and now he was making fun of her. She felt her cheeks turn red. Nihal said, 'You're too serious about these things. I don't suppose it'll last; why don't you just enjoy it while it's happening?'

Katie thought, because I am not like that. Far from it; she was in a state of constant agitation. She had managed to meet Dmitry two or three times last week, by one subterfuge or another. She had taken Anna to nursery early and gone to his apartment straight away for 'breakfast'. They had gone to bed and then Dmitry had left for work, late, leaving her to spend an hour or two in his flat before going to collect Anna. At first it interested her to be there, looking at his books, helping herself to what food he kept in the fridge, feeling she was somehow prolonging her contact with him, but soon she began simply to feel empty. Then she had told Bob she was going out in the evening to a film with a friend and gone to see him instead. She didn't recognise herself any more; she would not have believed before that she could have had such an appetite for sex. She never discussed with Dmitry what was going to happen to them and he never asked her any questions about her marriage with Bob. Perhaps it suited him as it was. She supposed it would be up to her to raise this issue.

The trouble was, she wasn't sure what she wanted herself. She had asked Dmitry once whether he wanted to go back to Russia at the end of his three-year term and he had said simply, 'Of course. No Russian ever wants to leave his homeland.' She could not imagine herself and Anna going off with him to live in some ghastly place like Irkutsk or Novosibirsk; besides, it would be too cruel to separate Anna and Bob. These UN affairs were usually doomed; people came to the end of their contracts; part of the attraction was in the foreignness, the clash of cultures, but when it came to it, people ended up cleaving to their own lives and their own countries. She knew that Nihal, too, knew that only too well.

Nihal snapped his fingers in front of her face. She looked at him, and, despite herself, laughed.

'Oh Nihal, you must think I'm ridiculous.'

'Katie, let me ask you – if you see Mitya – he's never talked to you about his work, has he? He hasn't said anything?'

Katie gave him a long stare. Once again she had the uncomfortable feeling of there being more under the surface than she was aware of. Then she looked away. 'No, of course not. We don't talk much anyway. When we do manage to get together we've got better things to do.'

She regretted the remark as soon as she had made it; she realised that in doing so she had offended Nihal. She stubbed out her cigarette into the coffee cup and put out her hand to him, but he was already getting up to go.

Nihal's short article about cheap rockets for the Third World appeared in the technology section of *North-South*. Nobody paid much attention to it. He was surprised when, three days later, he had a phone call from Martin Dudley in London. Dudley sounded unusually animated.

'There's a letter that's arrived here today relating to your article,' he said. 'It was sent anonymously. It is absolutely extraordinary – none of us know what to make of it. It appears to be a photocopy of a contract – well, more than a contract, it's more like a kind of treaty – between your Richter's rocket company and the Government of Paraguay. It's two years old, and appears to have been signed by President Stroessner himself.'

Nihal shot forward in his chair. 'What?'

'I have to tell you, it's the most bizarre document. We can't imagine whether or not it is a fake. It's several pages, all typewritten. Do you want me to read it to you?'

Nihal could hear pieces of paper rustling in the background at the other end of the phone. He sat down at his desk with a pen in his hand. Snowflakes whirled outside the window; Nihal's feet were cold. He was trying to economise on the heating; his landlady was finally cutting up rough about his rent arrears, and his wife in London was demanding more money.

Dudley said, 'I won't read it all, but I'll give you the gist. It concerns a large area of land north of Mariscal Estigarribia. Article one: Full rights which include the right to enjoy the territory without restriction. Only representatives of RASAG will be allowed to fly over the territory. Article two: All representatives of RASAG will enjoy immunity from any prosecution by the state. RASAG will exercise sole disciplinary control. Article three: Only persons authorised by RASAG will be allowed to stay in the territory. The State will be compelled if requested by RASAG to evacuate all other persons and keep them away . . . And so it goes on. It's the most crazy thing I've ever heard. Neo-colonialism is not the word. We rang the Paraguayan Embassy, both here and in Bonn, but they wouldn't comment on it, wouldn't confirm if it existed or not. We have no idea who sent it to us. You don't have any other leads, do you?'

'I was going to try to interview Weiland or Richter.'

'Well, we'll pay you to go to Stuttgart. See if you can find out if testing has begun in Paraguay. I want to see if we can run something before anyone else gets onto it. There are some things you ought to check out. For instance, isn't Germany a signatory to the Missile Technology Control Regime?'

'Yes, but I don't know how much impact that has. The regime as I understand it is not a treaty or even a formal agreement, simply a statement of intent and a list of items the adherents pledge not to export. But there are ways of getting round this as you know, you just get sensitive parts made elsewhere. Besides, the destination is important, exporting to Paraguay is not the same as to the Middle East.'

Dudley said he would fax the document to him and hung up. Nihal had use of an office in the foreign press association building. There was a fax machine there; any journalist hanging around might see and read it. He put on his coat and hurried round to the Bankgasse. Who could have leaked the document, if it were genuine? Some disaffected person from the Paraguayan Embassy or from RASAG? If the deal had been made by Stroessner, perhaps it was all off anyway; Stroessner had been ousted nearly two years ago. Nihal knew almost nothing about Paraguay, but he was sure it was Stroessner's son-in-law, Rodriguez, the head of the armed forces, who had taken over. He seemed to recall that Rodriguez had promised to democratise, but no-one seemed to be taking his reforms very seriously. As one journalist had put it, same dog, different collar.

Nihal collected the fax from the machine, then went up to his office and checked the mail. It was cosy in his office; much warmer than his apartment. He supposed that if his landlady ever kicked him out he could always camp in here. He made himself comfortable and read through the faxed papers. The document had a genuine look about it, and anyway, why would someone fake such a thing? It was so improbable that it had to be real. If it was forged someone had gone to a lot of trouble; there were stamps, signatures. It was very odd.

He rang RASAG and got through to the public relations man, Becker. Becker denied all knowledge of it. He sounded angry and demanded, 'Where did you get this information?' Nihal said that he wanted to come and interview Richter. Becker said that was impossible; Richter was a very busy man. Anyway he was not in Stuttgart at the moment. Nihal said that obviously they must be planning to test their rockets somewhere. Was he denying that it was in Paraguay? Becker said he was not in a position to comment further.

Nihal rarely felt a sense of urgency, but this time he did. He realised at once that this was a real scoop, and that everyone would be onto it. He must get in first. It was a major story; the kind that reputations could be made on. What's more, all he had in his favour was a slight head start; he wouldn't have much chance against the resources of a national newspaper team.

He picked up his copy of the *International Who's Who* and found Weiland listed there. They had the address in Palm Springs, Florida; all he needed was the phone number.

He picked up the phone, and began dialling.

Dmitry was going back up to his office, stepping into the lift on the ground floor when he saw Katie, Bob and Anna hurrying to catch it. He saw Katie's face change and whiten momentarily when she saw him, then she turned away, busying herself with her child. Bob waved and Dmitry held the door open for them; Bob put his arm around Katie and walked with her into the lift.

The doors glided shut and Katie lifted Anna up so that she could press the button to the twentieth floor. Anna giggled and Katie kissed the top of her head as she put her down again.

There was a moment's awkward silence. Then Bob said, 'Katie, let me introduce you – this is Dmitry Nikolayevich Gavrilov. Dmitry, this is my wife, Katie, and my little girl, Anna.'

Dmitry bowed, slightly awkwardly, and smiled at the child. She stared back at him with curious eyes, grey-green, the same colour as her mother's. They were the picture of a happy family; probably they'd been for lunch in the restaurant, and now Anna wanted to see her father's office, play with the computer keyboard and things like that.

Katie said, 'We've met.'

'You have?' Bob looked startled.

'At Hans's funeral, very briefly, but we weren't introduced.' She looked at Dmitry and gave him a frail smile before looking back at Bob.

She was so cool. How could she be so cool? She stood in front of him, no more than two feet away, staring ahead at the lift doors, her hair swept elegantly back from her face and pinned up, exposing the long white neck. He had to resist a powerful desire to bend down and kiss it; he couldn't help imagining her as she had been, only a few days before, lying across his bed, naked, abandoned.

The lift juddered to a halt and they stepped out. Bob said, 'Katie, why don't you take Anna into my office? I just want a brief word with Gavrilov.'

Katie took Anna's hand and stepped out of the lift without meeting Dmitry's eyes. He watched them walk hand in hand along the corridor, Katie's head bent down as she listened to what Anna was saying. He realised with a jolt that Bob was talking to him.

'I gather you're still not entirely happy with the inquiry into Müller's death. You don't have any reasons for this, do you? Anything that we don't know?'

Gavrilov stared at him, a little wildly. How was it possible to have any kind of normal conversation with this man?

'No. No, I don't.'

'You don't think that it's a little irresponsible to be spreading rumours if you don't have any particular reason?'

'Rumours?' Dmitry stiffened; he wanted to get away. He felt in his pocket. 'I just remembered – I forgot to go to the bank.' He pressed the button for the lift. Bob was still standing there, looking at him. He sensed the man's hostility.

'You could damage the Agency's reputation. That isn't what you had in mind, is it?'

The lift arrived and Gavrilov stepped into it; the door glided shut before there was time for him to answer. At random, he pressed the button for the eleventh floor; he had no idea what was on the eleventh floor, but perhaps he would now find out. What was Bob talking about? Had somebody seen him talking to Nihal? Or was this sudden onslaught actually nothing to do with this at all, but because Katie had given away some clue that she was seeing him?

Katie lay curled up on the sofa reading Anna her bedtime story. Anna's warm, sleepy head lay on her shoulder; her eyes were already drooping. Katie came to the end, put the book down, gently kissed Anna's cheek and smoothed her hair. Anna yawned, and she found herself doing the same. Anna snuggled up against her and closed her eyes; Katie felt unusually calm and peaceful. Bob was laying the table for supper.

Anna gave up the struggle against sleep and closed her eyes. After a few minutes Bob came over and lifted her up in his arms. Anna stirred and put her arms round his neck, let him carry her off to bed. Katie watched him carry her so proudly and tenderly, and was stricken by her folly in risking her marriage. Seeing Dmitry in the lift that afternoon had been a shock; she realised she was a fool to think she could keep it quiet for ever. Sooner or later something would happen and she would give herself away. Besides, seeing her lover and her daughter together had brought home to her how it was not only Bob she was deceiving. If she and Bob split up, what would happen to Anna? It was unthinkable.

Bob came back and they sat down at the table, starting their meal in silence. Katie realised, with a stab of panic, that she had less and less in common with Bob, that there was nothing to talk to him about. But of course, how could it be otherwise when she couldn't share with him the problem that was most on her mind?

Bob said, 'I'm going to Paris, Katie. For a job interview.'

'Who with?'

'The division for the advancement of science in UNESCO. I don't think it's what I want, but I thought I'd go and see.'

She knew that he was doing this because of her, because she wanted to leave Vienna, and she was touched. She still had the chance to save her marriage. Once the affair was safely in the past, once there was no chance of its flaring up again, perhaps when they had left Vienna, she would tell Bob everything, and ask his forgiveness. It was totally destructive, having this secret between them, she could see that.

He helped himself to some salad. 'Katie, you see Nihal a lot. Do you know what story he's working on?'

'No. I didn't know he was working on anything special, he hasn't said anything to me. Why?'

'I just saw him talking to Gavrilov the other day. You know we are not supposed to talk to the press without permission, and I know he hasn't got it. Besides, I don't trust that guy. I saw him talking, the other day, to someone in resources who I know is KGB. I wouldn't want Nihal to get the wrong end of things.'

Katie stared at him, aghast. She wondered if Nihal and Mitya had been talking about her. And what was all this? It was almost as if Bob knew something and was warning her. Or did he suspect there was something between them? Why had he mentioned this? He never usually spoke to her about anything to do with work.

She tried to think of something to say to him. 'Well, don't you ever talk to the people from the CIA? That man we met at that party in the summer –Williams I think he was called – you said he was CIA.'

'Yes, but that's different, honey. That's just socialising.'

Katie felt irritated. 'How do you know who's KGB?'

'Oh, you just know these things. Hey, what's the matter? You're not eating.'

'I've had enough.' Katie put her fork down on the plate. 'I don't suppose there's anything in it. Nihal talks to everyone, you know that.'

'Oh, you and Nihal, with your wishy-washy liberal backgrounds. You know these bloody Russians have been the problem with the UN from the beginning. That's why we've never been able to do half the things we want to. They say it's all changed, but it hasn't, in fact if anything it's worse, because now it's even more difficult to know what games they're playing.'

Katie had an instinctive urge to rise to Dmitry's defence, but quickly controlled herself. She started to busy herself, clearing away the plates in the kitchen. Bob followed her and watched her in silence for a while. Then he said, his voice suddenly soft and concerned, 'Katie, what is it? What's wrong with you these days?'

Katie straightened abruptly and in doing so knocked a vase of flowers over. The water gushed down onto the floor and she grabbed at the vase, the flowers slipping through her fingers. Bob was stunned for an instant, then he bent down and began picking up the flowers from the floor.

Katie sat down on the kitchen stool and suddenly burst into tears. She could sense that Bob was alarmed with her behaviour and that made it worse. He straightened up and put the flowers back in the vase, making a hopeless attempt to arrange them properly. 'If you don't tell me what's the matter how can you expect me to help?'

'You wouldn't understand. It's nothing. Oh, I don't know, I just feel depressed. You don't understand what it's like, being stuck here at home with Anna all the time; and she gets bored as well. It's not easy to make friends here – and I'm sick to death with my translating. Endless, boring, technical documents, and never seeing anybody. Besides, I can't concentrate on it properly, I only get two hours in the morning and then it's time to pick up Anna. What am I doing with my life?'

Bob said, more softly, 'Well, that's why I'm thinking of changing things. I don't want you to be unhappy. But you seem, lately, I don't know . . . almost hostile to me. Okay, I know I'm not always good at showing my feelings, but you know how much I love you.'

'Oh, Bob.' She dried her eyes and kissed him, then, awkwardly, turned and carried on with tidying up the kitchen. Bob just stood there and looked at her. She felt transparent, ashamed, and that it must be obvious to him that she wasn't telling him the whole truth.

On the way to bed Katie went into Anna's room. Bob was already there, smoothing out the covers and tucking Anna's kangaroo under the duvet. He kissed her forehead and straightened; Katie's eyes met his. She saw that he was cautious, guarded with her, and she suddenly couldn't bear it. With a sudden impulse to make things right between them she reached out and put her arms around him, holding him tightly for a long time.

Nihal arrived at Dmitry's flat as he had arranged at nine. He shook the snow from his coat and hung it up on the hook behind the door. Nihal accepted the drink he was offered and handed Dmitry the by now much folded copy of the RASAG contract.

Dmitry read through it quickly and frowned. He said, 'Well, it could be genuine, but actually this looks to me like a classic piece of Soviet *disinformatsia*. I didn't know they were still doing this these days.'

'Is there anything specific that makes you think this?'

'Well, it all sounds wrong. Possibly the whole document is a fake. On the other hand, it could have been acquired and leaked by the intelligence services – quite possibly the KGB. Once they saw your piece they might have decided they'd better act quickly. They have this section of the first chief directorate, you know . . . it's called "active measures".'

Nihal laughed and said that he was only a journalist.

Dmitry shrugged and handed back the copy. 'Of course this is all quite out of date these days. I would imagine that if what you say about Richter is true, the Americans would be equally unhappy about his activities. But don't they practically run Paraguay? It's hard to imagine they could do this without US support. The whole thing is a bit odd, don't you think?'

'Where is this place, Mariscal Estigarribia, I wonder?'

Dmitry got out his atlas and they opened it on the table. He shone the lamp on it and they sat and looked in silence.

Maps are curious things, thought Nihal. Places seem more distant, more exotic, in maps than in reality. Though he'd travelled a great deal, he'd concentrated on Asia and Africa, where he could get by with English, and he had never been to South America; it was a part of the world he did not know at all. In the interior of Paraguay was an area known as the Chaco. It appeared to be dry forest and grassland. It was sparsely inhabited. There was a town called Mariscal Estigarribia on the Trans-Chaco highway which crossed the country from Asunción to the border with Bolivia. He knew that if he were actually standing there, it would seem quite normal; only after he had come back and looked at the map again would it seem to him that he had been somewhere distant and remote; would in fact have difficulty believing he had ever been there.

Dmitry turned the page. He looked at the map of Brazil, and Nihal asked, 'Where's Cachimbo – where they drilled those test bores?'

Dmitry pointed to one of the most remote spots in the centre of Amazonia, a place to which there were no roads. Then he sat back and lit a cigarette. He said, 'Are you thinking what I'm thinking? There's something about it, isn't there? The world is so small, there is nothing secret in it any more, and yet here we are . . . with strange, perhaps evil things going on in the dark heart of a continent.'

VI

Nihal sat in the lobby of the Anschloss Garten Hotel, Stuttgart, checking his tape recorder for the third time. He had spare batteries in his bag; he had a stack of tapes, enough to record several hours of conversation; he had copies of his article; he had the photocopy of the contract. Getting an interview with Weiland had been surprisingly easy. He had said he was researching a book on the history of the rocket and Weiland had assented at once. He had said he would be in Stuttgart that week and would meet him at his hotel.

At five minutes to eight he was walking along the silent corridor, looking for room 589. He knocked sharply at the door; Weiland opened it himself. He was a thin, slightly stooping man; very frail; his skin was mottled, but the thin silvery hair was elegantly combed back from the high forehead and his eyes were clear, unclouded and piercingly blue.

'Come in, come in,' said Weiland. 'Would you like a drink?'

Nihal asked for some orange juice. He looked around the room; it was a large suite, probably the hotel's best, comfortable and expensive but with that soulless familiarity of the large hotel chain. To his surprise Weiland was alone. The door at the far end was ajar and there was a light on behind it; Nihal wondered if there was someone else there, listening to what was going on.

They sat opposite one another on green silk chairs. Nihal started with general questions about the early days of rocket research at Peenemünde. Weiland wandered a little as he spoke, jumping from

Peenemünde to his time working for NASA; he added little to what Nihal knew already.

He asked Weiland about his presidency of RASAG but the German didn't seem to want to go into that at first; he spoke at length about his work with Wernher von Braun and his particular genius. He argued that because von Braun had had the gift of being able to convince non-technical people about the potential for space research, he had been largely responsible for persuading Kennedy to put money into the moon landing programme. It was a pity, said Weiland, that he had latterly under-estimated his enemies. He hoped that Richter would not make the same mistake.

Nihal, seeing his cue, pounced upon this point. Would the German Government really allow Richter to build the rockets on German soil? Wasn't it likely to become a political hot potato?

Weiland considered for a moment. He said that he thought that it might. So far, Richter had only tested prototypes. Whether there would be a different reaction when he went into mass production he couldn't say. People had become stricter in recent years about rocket research. There was the Missile Technology Control Regime. Of course, peaceful space research was permitted, but sometimes people failed to make the necessary distinction between the two. But the genius of Richter's design was that most of the basic parts for the rocket were simple components that could be bought off-the-shelf.

'But do you think these rockets will actually work? There must surely be a great many technical problems to overcome?'

Weiland leaned forward in his chair, his hands trembling slightly, but a glimpse of an old fire coming into his eyes. 'Ah, but it's based on a principle we were developing in the last desperate days of the war, when we were trying to find cheap ways of building rockets. This was developed for an anti-tank rocket, something we called the *Wasserfall*, the waterfall. Like the RASAG rocket, this used compressed air instead of costly pumps to – how shall we say – to press the fuel out from the tanks to the combustion chamber. I am sure it will work, because we tested this many times and certainly we had considerable success with it . . .'

'But this is fascinating. I would be very interested to see the factory here. I would also, if it were possible, very much like to see the testing site in Paraguay. Obviously this rocket technology will be of great interest to many Third World countries.'

Weiland did not react at all to the mention of Paraguay. He became rather vague. He said, 'Oh, I don't think that is very likely. I don't think Herr Richter will like to give permission to journalists. Of course, I can ask him, but . . .'

'Where exactly is the rocket site?'

'Do you know Paraguay? No? Well, in the interior of the country is an area called the Chaco – actually some writer referred to it as the green hell, and that I think is very apt: this area is almost totally uninhabited and is under military control. We have rented a large area of land there. It is pretty inaccessible. In case you were to have any ideas about venturing there yourself, I don't think I could recommend you go and have a look without written permission, indeed, without being accompanied by some of our staff.'

'This contract that you made with the Government – its terms seem rather extraordinary. Don't you think there will be criticism?'

'What do you know about the terms of the contract?' Weiland's voice was suddenly as sharp as broken ice.

'I have it here.' Nihal produced the photocopied document. He handed it to Weiland whose hand wavered a little as he took it; he gave it a glance; his expression hardened. 'But this document is a forgery. An utter forgery. Where did you get it?'

'It was sent to me.'

'Who by?'

'An anonymous source.'

Weiland was silent, deep in thought. He seemed to have been taken by surprise and didn't quite know how to deal with this; Nihal saw anger in his face as he stared at the document. Weiland looked up and said with finality, 'I am sorry, I have never seen this document before. Is that machine still running?'

'Yes.'

'Switch it off.'

Nihal did so, instantly. He had finished his orange juice; he couldn't eke it out any longer. It was clear that the interview was over;

he folded up his notebook, then decided on one last try. 'I'm very keen to interview Herr Richter, I am intrigued by his ideas. You don't think you could suggest this to him?'

Weiland made an impatient gesture with his fingers. 'Herr Richter is a very busy man. I could ask him, but I doubt he could spare the time. Besides, he is not here. I believe he is in Paris.' Weiland stood up, supporting himself with his arm on the side of the chair. An idea occurred to Nihal; it was rather a long shot, in fact it sounded to him quite wild, even as he said it: 'I've heard rumours that the Mennonite communities at Filadelfia are very anxious about this rocket project. There has even been talk of plans to sabotage a launch.'

'Sabotage?' Weiland took a step towards him, and his voice rose in pitch, almost to a falsetto. 'Please, tell me where you heard this.'

'I'm afraid I can't reveal to you my source.'

Weiland turned and went to the door, an amused smile suddenly crossing his face; 'No; no, of course you can't. I quite understand. Let us hope it is no more reliable than your other sources. But thank you very much for telling me; we will look into it.' He stepped forward and Nihal, rather reluctantly, shook his outstretched hand. As he left the room Nihal had a distinct impression of Weiland's hand reaching out towards the phone.

Katie thought that Bob's absence in Paris was an ideal opportunity to talk things over with Dmitry and to end their affair. She had asked the girl downstairs to babysit for the evening and, after reading Anna a story and tucking her into bed, she hurried down the hill, wrapped in her coat, holding her arm out to balance herself because of the ice underfoot. It was bitterly cold. Fine snow was falling, swirling above the white pavements. She tried to think through what she was going to say to Dmitry, and her heart felt heavy, because she was not sure that she would actually have the strength to say what she wanted. At the same time, she was excited at the thought of seeing him tonight; she had never had a whole evening on her own with him before.

She crossed the road and squeezed between two cars parked outside the house. As she did so she noticed there were two men sitting in one of them; she saw them, but didn't give it any further thought. When she got to Dmitry's door she hesitated for a long time before ringing the bell. He opened the door at once, as if he had been waiting right behind it.

Katie walked past him into the room. The table was laid for dinner. There was a bottle of wine already open and two glasses. Katie didn't kiss him, and she didn't sit down. She hovered awkwardly in the centre of the room.

Her expression must have given her away. Dmitry asked, 'Is something the matter?' He made a move towards her and she retreated suddenly, moving behind the sofa, afraid that if he touched her she might break down or lose her resolve.

The words she had tried to rehearse came out only with the greatest of difficulty, and failed entirely to convey what she was feeling.

'I decided tonight that we should talk about all this. I mean, about what is happening.'

'Happening?' Dmitry looked puzzled.

Katie blundered on. 'I mean, I can't just carry on like this . . . if we do, sooner or later I will have to tell Bob . . . I thought it might just be easier . . .' she took a deep breath; 'I thought that perhaps we should just end this.'

She hadn't meant to put it so bluntly. Dmitry almost jumped, startled, looking at her as if he had suddenly been woken from sleep; there was such an unmistakable expression of dismay in his face that she suddenly knew that he must feel for her what she felt for him. She could not bear the fact that she had hurt him, he looked so confused, bewildered, so she reached out at once to comfort him; they held one another for a long time, Katie crying, Dmitry murmuring soothing words to her. As soon as she started to cry she felt better; the tears seemed to drag out with them all the other feelings she had been fighting back over the last few weeks, and she felt at once a sense of release. Unlike Bob when she cried, Dmitry did not seem embarrassed or uncomfortable; he didn't ask her to stop or try to dry her eyes. He seemed to accept her tears as he accepted everything else about her. 'That's right, cry,' he said softly, 'Then you will feel better.'

When at last she stopped and sat down on the sofa he lifted up her chin and wiped the tears away with a handkerchief. 'There,' he said finally, 'Is that better?'

She nodded.

'Has anything happened today?' he asked her, 'Your husband doesn't think . . . ?'

'No,' she said, 'It's not that, only that I don't know how to cope with this. I don't want to lie to Bob, and I'm afraid of telling him. I know that this has to come to an end sooner or later, so I thought, perhaps it's best to end it now.'

'Why does it have to end?'

Katie stared at him, confused. They sat in silence for a while, but it was a gentle, soothing silence, and Katie began to feel an intense relief, as if all of this had been unnecessary and there was no reason for her to feel such pain. Dmitry stood up. 'Look, don't torment yourself now, you don't have to make any decisions tonight. Let me get you something to eat.'

Katie realised that her feeble attempt to break things off had been a dismal failure. The only thing she wanted was to be here and with him, and she knew that he felt the same, and there was no point in creating an artificial deadline. Why end it before it had to end? Even if it just postponed the suffering, wouldn't that be better, wouldn't anything be better than having to face it now? Anyway, perhaps her feelings would change, perhaps they would burn themselves out, she might wake up one day and look at Dmitry and wonder what had caused this terrible madness.

She lay down on the sofa and looked up at the ceiling. Dmitry took a cassette off the shelf and slipped it into the player. He said, 'I'm afraid this is something rather cheap and sentimental . . . but, well, sometimes I feel nostalgic.'

It was a Russian man singing a series of haunting melodies; in the background someone played an instrument she assumed was a balalaika. She lay and listened, half dozing, while he busied himself in the kitchen. Finally he came and leaned over her to say that supper was ready; she was too tired and sleepy to get up. He ran his hand over her face, along her body, finally resting it over her breast, in a gesture of such affection and intimacy that she felt she did not care what happened, as long as she could remember that moment. Gently, unhurriedly, they made love; then they got up and Dmitry reheated the pancakes, which they washed down with wine and then vodka. Then Katie said, 'I'm sorry – I've been a fool. Will you please forget what I said when I arrived?'

'No,' he said, 'I won't forget it, but I will ignore it, if you like.' And he gave her one of his rare exuberant smiles.

At one in the morning she said she must go. She put on her coat, and then went and looked out of the window to see if it was still snowing. She couldn't help noticing again the white car parked within sight of the apartment; unlike the others, its windscreen was clear of snow. The outline cast across the ground by the street-lamp contained the shadow of the two figures within. 'Are they going to sit in the car all night?' she asked, half to herself, 'They'll freeze to death.'

Dmitry got up suddenly and came over to the window. 'What are you talking about?'

'There are two men in that white car over there,' said Katie. 'They were there when I came here.' A realisation, prompted by his alarmed response, came to her, and she felt her hair prickle with fear. 'They're watching somebody, aren't they?'

He looked momentarily out of the window, taking care that the curtain fell behind them so that they wouldn't be visible, and then drew her away from the window. 'When did you notice this?' he demanded.

'I saw them when I came. I didn't think. They're not anything to do with you, are they?'

'I have no idea.'

They looked at one another in the silence, neither of them quite sure what to say.

'Are they your people, or what?' asked Katie, after a while.

'My people? What do you mean, my people? Do you mean the KGB? No, of course not. Why should they be?'

He seemed seriously worried and it alarmed her terribly. Then she said, 'You don't think Bob might have hired a private detective?'

'Well, why not? it's possible.' Relief seemed to pass over his features for a moment. Then he frowned. He started to walk up and down the room. Katie felt her heart fluttering in her chest like a trapped moth. She didn't understand what was happening.

Dmitry had poured himself another vodka. He continued to walk up and down, the glass in his hand. 'Katie, does Bob ever talk to you about his work?'

He said it almost casually; he was not looking at her. Katie was suddenly on her guard. Since Bob had put that tiny seed of doubt about him into her mind, she had wondered what she would do if he asked her that question, and how, if he did, she would reply. She looked at him; she could see that he was as tense as she was; it was as if something physical had entered the room and come between them.

'Yes,' she said, trying to sound natural, 'Of course, sometimes, why not?'

'What kind of things?'

'Just office gossip, nothing important.' She felt as if she was feeling her way along a narrow ledge in the dark, wanting to put a hand out for support, afraid of touching nothing but emptiness. She said, 'Mitya, I really am frightened. They won't do anything, will they? Should we go to the police?'

'No, I don't suppose it would do the slightest good to go to the police. All the same, I'd better do so. It's what the UN security people advise. Look.' Dmitry went to his jacket and took two folded sheets of A4 paper from the inside pocket. It was headed 'Points relative to personal security' and consisted of fourteen paragraphs in poor English. It gave instructions for people to change their routine, check the car for signs of tampering, watch for people approaching the car when halted at traffic lights, never opening the door to strangers and reporting any suspicion of being followed to the police. Katie read it with mounting alarm. It meant that people took this kind of thing seriously. It implied that somebody might want to kill you.

'Where did you get this?' she asked.

'From the UN security people.' Dmitry took the sheets of paper out of her hand. 'Actually, I like this document. Did you notice point three: "Be as unpredictable as possible in all your actions?" I'm not sure the IAEA would approve.'

Katie laughed, and for a moment the tension eased.

Dmitry drained another glass of vodka and said, 'Tell me about Bob.'

'Why are you so concerned with Bob suddenly? asked Katie, feeling more than a little suspicious. He had never asked about him before, in fact had scrupulously avoided it. 'You've never asked me anything before, you haven't asked me if I still love him, you haven't even asked me if I still go to bed with him . . .'

'Do you?'

'Yes.'

She said it to hurt him, and she succeeded. He turned away from her suddenly, as if she had slapped him. She said, 'Well, what do you want me to do? Do you want me to leave him?'

He spoke coldly, off-handedly. 'You must decide yourself, if you want to leave him. I've told you, what happens with your marriage is up to you. I can't decide for you. All that is nothing to do with me.'

'I think it's very much concerned with you.' She had begun to shake with anger. 'I think I was right when I came, I think I should just walk out of here right now and not come back.'

He winced and closed his eyes. 'You must do what you want.'

She crossed the room and snatched her shawl up from the back of the chair. 'Oh, what I want, what I want,' she said, 'That's so easy for you, isn't it, to put everything onto me. What about you? What do you want?'

He looked suddenly very tired. He sat down on the edge of the sofa and examined his fingernails. 'Please go now, Katie. This isn't going to get anywhere.'

'No, of course not, if you won't answer me. Yes, I'd better go. I'll call you.' She slammed the door on her way out.

As she left the building and walked up towards her own flat she saw a car parking. A few minutes later, the white car started up, pulled out into the road and drove away past her up the hill.

Nihal took a bus to the railway station. He thought he might as well go back to Vienna and asked at the ticket office for information about trains. Then he thought he might go to Paris; after all, Richter was in

Paris. Dmitry had even given him his address in the Place des Vosges. He wondered, not for the first time, where Dmitry had got the information. He rang the airport. There was a flight in just under an hour. If he took a taxi he would make it.

From the airport he booked a room at a cheap hotel near the Place de la République and arrived there just before ten, exhausted. He sat down on the bed and took off his shoes. He stared at the pink flowery wallpaper and wondered whether this had been the right decision. After all, he could hardly just turn up on Richter's doorstep and demand an interview . . . or perhaps that was exactly what he should do.

He lay back on the bed and noticed that the wallpaper also covered the ceiling, giving him the sensation of being gift-wrapped in a box.

Almost immediately the phone rang.

Imagining that the woman at the desk must have some query, he picked up the receiver. At the other end of it was a woman's husky voice. She asked, 'Is that Nihal Senanayake?'

'Yes.'

'I have to talk to you about RASAG.'

There was a few seconds' delay before the full implications of this hit Nihal. A cold sensation swept through him. He thought, I didn't even know I was coming here myself, how on earth could they know? Who was this woman?

'About what, exactly?'

'I gather you have some information that could be very important to us.' She spoke almost breathlessly; he found it hard to place her accent. French, perhaps, but also something else.

'Who am I speaking to?'

'That doesn't matter. But I would like to see you. Can you meet me tonight? I will be at the bar in the Hôtel Crillon. Do you know where that is? It's in the Rue de Rivoli. Can you be there in an hour?'

Nihal looked at his watch. 'How will I recognise you?'

'Oh, don't worry about that – I will recognise you. You must come alone; I'll see you there.' Then the phone abruptly went dead.

Nihal remained sitting on the edge of the bed. He thought,

someone has followed me all the way here. I didn't mention this to anyone. What was going on? He would go; he had to.

On the way to the hotel, on the metro, Nihal kept looking around him to see if there was anyone still following him. He tried to do this without it seeming obvious; but it was impossible to tell. He tried to memorise the people in his carriage and watch who got off with him at Concorde. It was much more difficult to spot someone than he would have imagined. He began to wonder if it had been a good idea to come alone. Perhaps this was a set-up, and they intended to get rid of him – but this was absurd; nonetheless, he began to regret his remark to Weiland about the Mennonites.

As soon as Nihal spotted the woman in the Crillon Bar he knew it had to be her. She was sitting at the bar facing the door and had long, blonde hair, long legs, the most exquisite fine features, and wore dark glasses. As he walked in she gave him a little wave. She looked like something out of a 1960s spy movie. Everything about her was expensive; she wore model clothes and clutched a crocodile-skin bag. Nihal went over and sat on one of the barstools next to her. She swivelled round to face him, sweeping the hair back behind her ear with a haughty movement of her hand. Then she said, dropping her voice to a soft, seductive tone, 'You must help us. You must give us this information.'

'What information?' Nihal supposed he would have to buy her a drink; he dreaded to think what it would cost. 'What would you like to drink?'

'Oh, it doesn't matter. I have a drink here.' It was bright pink with a twist of lemon in it and the glass was frosted; she held it by the narrow stem. She merely touched the glass to her lips as if to cool them, then put it down gently on the bar. 'Come, you must tell us, about this sabotage plan.' She moved closer to him; the crocodile-skin bag pressed against his leg. He tried not to reveal his distaste for it. The scent of expensive perfume, not too strong, but subtle, emanated from her as if it was in her very breath. 'Lives could depend on it,' she said.

A bowl of peanuts stood on the bar; Nihal dipped into them; he never missed the opportunity of some free food. 'But I don't know your name,' he said. 'Or where you're from.'

She hesitated and looked away, took another sip of her drink. She said, 'Sylvia Mellors.'

Nihal thought at once there was something wrong with the name; whatever else she was, she was not English. Her voice, at the very least, was foreign, perhaps French, a hint of Spanish. She laid her hand delicately on his arm. 'Please, tell me what you know. It could be dangerous for you. There are certain people who want to know very badly. If they want to get this information from you I don't suppose you would be able to keep it to yourself – do you understand me?'

Nihal did understand her. He felt completely out of his depth; in fact, he felt frightened. He had no idea who this woman was; whether she was working for some intelligence service or for RASAG. Nihal thought he'd have to play this very carefully. He was alone, and no-one even knew he was here; he should not have allowed himself to be so vulnerable. 'It's only a matter of rumour. I could tell you who my source was; but anyway, why should I reveal anything if there's nothing in it for me?'

'Perhaps there could be something in it for you,' she said, turning away slightly, tossing back her hair, and picking up her drink. 'You want to meet Wolf Richter, don't you?' She spoke the name almost with awe.

'Yes, I do. In fact, it might be better if I could talk to him directly.'

'I see,' she said. She removed her glasses and looked at him; he wondered for a moment whether she had not been, or was now, a call-girl, because there was something professional in the way she seemed by her look to make him feel attractive, important, while her eyes gave nothing of herself away. 'And you can tell me nothing now?' she asked him, softly.

'No.'

She looked away. She seemed suddenly to have lost interest in the conversation; she ran her finger lazily round the rim of her glass. Then she touched the slice of lemon with the tip of her finger and put it to her tongue. She said, 'Herr Richter will ring you tomorrow, then, at your hotel.' She did not look at him as she spoke.

'That's fine.' He got down from the stool; there was no way he could do so with dignity. 'Good-night then, Miss Mellors.' He tried to put a note of irony into his voice; she glanced up at him with a little smile as if she had recognised it. Then he turned round and, feeling somewhat foolish, left the hotel.

Nihal waited all morning in the hotel for the call from Richter, but it didn't come. In the late afternoon he went to the Place des Vosges and stood across the square. The lights were on in the upstairs windows but it was impossible to see anything through the pale blinds. He crossed the road to go and ring the bell and passed a grey Peugeot in the square in which two men were sitting; one of them was talking into a car phone. It seemed to have an unusually long aerial. Of course it was very likely that someone would be keeping a watch on Richter's apartment. This reminded him that he, too, might easily still be being followed.

He went into the entrance and rang the bell, but no-one replied. He thought of standing there and waiting in case Richter came back, but decided that if he was being followed they might be alarmed at this behaviour, so he gave up and went back down to the metro, returning to his hotel to collect his bags.

The receptionist produced his key and a note written on a used envelope. She said someone had phoned on behalf of a Monsieur Richter. If he rang the office in Stuttgart they would make him an appointment.

Nihal beamed at her and gave her an unusually generous tip.

Weak afternoon sunshine filtered into the DDG's office. Dmitry sat, his back to the window, frowning, staring at the papers in front of him. He had made a contribution earlier on; long ago the meeting had lost his attention. He was wondering why Müller had made changes to the report on that Friday, the last day before he died. There was actually no reason why he should not have done; the report had not been finalised yet. It could take months before the reports were completed and passed back to the governments concerned; results had to come back from the laboratories, everything had to be checked. He wondered if anyone who did not have access to the file could make changes to it. Passwords could be stolen; there were other ways to get round computer security systems.

This opened up a new train of thought. There had been a great deal of concern recently about whether hackers could get into the IAEA's data base and extract or tamper with information. Safeguards data were held on both of the IAEA's mainframe computers, on which other data – including library and public information data – were stored. The Safeguards Division had been asking for some time to have one computer solely for their use to try to make it more secure. So far at least this request had not been granted.

But if there were no hard copies of earlier drafts of the report, how could he check whether Müller – or indeed anyone else – had altered something? There must be some back-up tapes. He had no idea how long these were kept for; but every night the data would be copied from the discs to large reels of magnetic tape in case there was a power cut or other disaster which might otherwise wipe out the database. He thought he would check with Panini, the computer systems manager. Maybe it would be possible to check that nothing had been changed by seeing what was on the back-up tapes.

He became aware that it was very quiet in the room. He looked up suddenly; everyone was staring at him. Somebody must have asked him a question. He had no idea what it was about. He had not the slightest idea where on the agenda they were. He could feel himself flushing with embarrassment and didn't know what to say.

He stood up. 'I'm sorry, can you excuse me for a moment. I've just remembered something very urgent.' He picked up his papers and then, in confusion, put them down again. He stepped sideways, nearly knocking his chair over as he did so, and left the room, aware of the astonished glances of his colleagues.

He took the lift down to the computer system's manager's office. Dmitry had met Panini before and knew that he was always harassed. He had a dishevelled look and his face bore the habitual expression of a man who maintained great patience in the presence of idiots. His office was chaotic; the phone was constantly ringing; every problem concerned with the Agency's computer systems landed on his desk. He made the point over and over that it was never the computer or the systems which were at fault, only ever the operators, but of course nobody believed him; it was always easier to blame the machines.

He looked up when Dmitry walked in, waving him into a chair as he conducted a conversation in French on the phone. He was clearly not pleased to see him; he knew at once it meant more work. Finally he hung up. 'What can I do for you?' he asked.

'We were just considering a hypothetical situation,' said Dmitry, plunging right in. 'How far back do the back-up tapes go, if for any reason data was lost and we wanted to reconstruct the database?'

'Up to six months.'

'But you don't keep them daily up to that time, surely?'

'Oh, no. We keep them daily for a week. Then we keep a weekly tape, so within any month you can go back to the previous week. Then after that, we keep a monthly tape, but the maximum is six months.'

'So if some data was changed, for example, and remained on the file for a certain period, perhaps only a few days, it would be a matter of luck if we could find it?'

Panini frowned. 'Yes, well, it would depend on whether the back-up tape we kept happened to fall within that period.'

'So if I'm talking about something that goes back about two months . . .'

'You might be lucky. You might not.'

'I see.' Dmitry paused for a moment. 'Well, I'd like to look at what is on the back-up tapes for a particular file.'

'I thought you said this was hypothetical.' The phone rang; Panini picked up the receiver, listened for a moment, said 'I'll call you back,' replaced it and then, on impulse, took it off the hook. He looked at Dmitry with raised eyebrows.

'Well . . . it may be. I wanted to check something.' Why did this make him feel so uncomfortable? It was a perfectly reasonable request to make; no-one could challenge his right to do this.

'It's just one file, is it? You're authorised to see it, I suppose? I'll have to check.'

'Of course.'

'You realise once I pull it off the back-up tape there won't be any password protection. Do you want it as hard copy or on disc? Have you done this before? There are certain procedures we have to go through. You'll need an authorisation . . . Fill all this out and I'll see to it for you.' He put the receiver back on the hook and instantly the phone rang again. 'You're not in a hurry for this, are you?'

Dmitry shook his head.

RASAG's offices and factory were housed in a large building on an industrial estate outside Stuttgart. Nihal was taken up to a little office on the third floor where the secretary introduced him to Becker, a pale, thin man whose anxious-looking face peered at Nihal from behind thick glasses. Becker shook hands limply and said, 'I'll show you around, then you can have thirty minutes with Richter. Please, come this way.'

They went down a metal staircase and Becker opened a heavy metal door into a vast unused space. Sunlight streamed through the high windows but there was not a mote of dust in the air. Becker cleared his throat. 'This will house the production line.' Nihal walked through the empty halls, his feet treading silently on the polished floors, the walls dazzling white, thinking; but this is crazy. How could anyone let him build these things? All Germany would have to do would be to forbid exports of the rocket parts. Germany has strict arms control legislation; surely they must have suspicions about all this?

Becker took him into a side-room where models of the RASAG rockets stood on display together with an array of components. The prototype consisted of units of shining, lightweight metal tubes. Nihal braced himself to lift one and it shot upwards in his hand, light as if it had been made from paper. Becker laughed.

'These are made from cold spun stainless steel. This has high strength and is easy and relatively cheap to manufacture. We simply bolt these on top of one another and group them in clusters of four to make the rocket. We are about to test a basic four-tank, four-engine cluster. This will develop a thrust of 12 tonnes. It might reach an altitude of 15 or 20 kilometres. The eight-engine cluster would be capable of putting a 500-kilogramme satellite in orbit.'

Nihal scribbled all this down in his notebook.

'The propellant. Two of the tanks are filled with kerosene and two with nitric acid oxidiser, and compressed air is used to maintain the pressure inside the tanks as the rocket rises. The rocket is actually steered by controlling the rate of flow of the fuel from the four tanks to the engines . . . at the moment, we simply use an off-the-shelf inertial guidance system.' Becker showed him the models. 'This is the full-sized version – impressive, no?'

Nihal nodded and Becker, seeing that he had no more questions, took him back upstairs. As he entered the main office, Richter swivelled round in his plush leather chair. He looked a little uncomfortable in his expensive suit; his hair was slightly too long, and he had an impatient, irritable air about him. He shook hands with Nihal and indicated that he should sit down at the large round table.

The secretary brought coffee; another man came in, aged about thirty-five, smartly but casually dressed in a floral shirt. Even indoors he wore sunglasses; they were part of the look. Richter had introduced him as Berthold Heinrichs, his right-hand man. Nihal was not quite sure why he was there; Heinrichs sat through the whole meeting without saying anything and appeared to be exceedingly bored.

Nihal put his tape-recorder on the table and took out his notebook. Richter had a dull, inflectionless voice and his English, though adequate, was not good. He said that he was happy to talk to Nihal because he understood that he wanted to write an accurate and factual account of their unique endeavour. He said that he was first and foremost a scientist, but he did not think scientific achievements were enough, science had to be tested in the marketplace . . . for him commercial success was as important as scientific success. He intended to open up space commercially, just as aeronautics had developed from a scientific discipline to a commercial enterprise. There was no reason why access to space shouldn't be within the reach of all nations, not just a select few.

Nihal listened politely for a while, then asked: 'But what about the military aspect? Aren't these rockets likely to be used for military purposes?'

'For military satellites? Yes, of course. Why not?'

'I didn't just mean that. Is there any reason why these rockets couldn't equally well carry a conventional warhead, or even a nuclear one?'

Richter's voice sounded utterly bored. 'Well of course this is an old question. There are many reasons why this rocket is not suitable as a missile. The fuel, to begin with, cannot be stored in the rocket for long periods, it has to be pumped in prior to launch in a long and slightly hazardous operation, and then there is the question of the guidance system. You don't need me to tell you that these days people expect their missiles to be rather accurate. Anyway, in my experience the vast majority of Third World countries are not aggressive towards their neighbours. They are concerned with protecting their own boundaries, they are concerned with their internal problems, economic problems, social problems . . .'

'And what about your launch site?'

'Well, this is not certain. It would help us to have an equatorial or at least tropical location to favour the launch of satellites because, as you must know, we can make use of the earth's rotation. In view of all the rumours which have been circulating we don't want to give out too much information at this time.'

'Can you confirm that it is in Paraguay?'

Richter glanced at Heinrichs and Nihal thought he caught a tiny, imperceptible movement of the corner of Heinrichs's mouth. Richter said, 'Yes. But all this other information you have received is complete nonsense. I am not prepared to discuss such blatant lies. You must of course be aware that not everyone is happy about our activities, because we challenge the present monopolies. Perhaps you should be a little more cynical about accepting such information at face value.'

Nihal, thinking it wise to change the subject, asked various technical questions, and Richter, who seemed happier discussing these technicalities, took his time over clarifying the details. When the interview was over Richter suddenly became quite friendly. He offered Nihal a drink and then, when he refused it, offered to run him to the station. They stepped outside and Richter led him over to a gleaming red Mercedes coupé parked on the forecourt.

Settling himself in the plush seats, Richter pulled on his heavy leather gloves and Nihal, his head hardly high enough to see over the dashboard from the low-slung seats, timidly watched Richter demonstrate how his car could accelerate from 0-100 kilometres per hour in 6.2 seconds. He drove with an intensity more appropriate to someone on some deadly mission than driving to the station. Perhaps this was instructive in showing what Richter was all about.

As they drove at an alarming speed along the autobahn, Richter asked casually, 'I understand you had heard some story about the Mennonites wanting to stop the rocket launch. How do you know this? You haven't been to Paraguay, have you?'

'A friend of mine was there recently.'

'His name?'

'I never give away people's names.'

'Think something unpleasant might happen to them?'

Richter tossed this remark off lightly, his eyes fixed on the road ahead, but Nihal wondered if he was correct in interpreting this as a threat. 'No, why should it?'

'I've given you a lot of information. Don't you think it only fair to return some?'

'I understood the deal was that I would tell you what you want to know in exchange for permission to view a rocket launch.'

'I don't think that would be possible.' They drew up at the station. Richter, having clearly lost interest, tapped his gloved hands impatiently on the steering wheel.

'I'd like to see what you write.'

'I'll send you a cutting.' Nihal climbed out of the car. Almost before he had shut the door, the car had shot away with a screech of tyres.

Dmitry got the files from Panini on Thursday afternoon. At the end of the day, once Hilde had gone home, he went through them but found nothing wrong. There were only some minor changes and corrections which distinguished this from the report he had seen. The odd thing was that there didn't seem to be any difference between the last version on the back-up tapes and the final one, the one which Müller had updated on his last day. On the other hand, this was the last avenue he could think of. There was nothing to be done and perhaps his suspicions were, after all, unfounded. He decided to forget it.

He pulled on his coat and hat and walked down the corridor towards the lifts. The building was deserted; it was eerily quiet. When he got outside there was an icy wind blowing. He walked to the station and sat down on the bench on the platform, waiting for the train. There were only a few people about. Someone came onto the platform and walked past him, his collar drawn up, and stood at the other far end, stamping his feet. Dmitry took out a cigarette and lit it.

The train came. Dmitry was in no hurry to get home and he wanted to finish his cigarette; he was sheltered from the wind and perfectly warm in his thick coat and hat, he felt heavy and lethargic, so he stayed where he was and missed the train. There was no reason at all why he should have done this; there was no other line he could have been waiting for. Perhaps it was because he had a moment's paranoia. But as the train pulled out, he saw that he had not been paranoid at all. The platform was now empty, except for the man in the dark coat standing in the shadows, struggling to light a cigarette in the cold wind.

Dmitry felt suddenly cold. He had been used to routine surveillance before, both at home and at conferences abroad; but this was different. He got to his feet and tossed his cigarette end onto the rails. Then he got out another cigarette and made a big show of failing to light it. With an exclamation of disgust he tossed the lighter onto the rails and walked up the platform towards the man in the dark coat.

'Excuse me,' he said, in awkward German, 'Could you give me a light?'

He knew as he did this that he was breaking the rules; he knew you were never supposed to acknowledge that you were under surveillance. It gave him pleasure to look this man straight in the face; he thought he saw a flicker of alarm cross his bland features. Silently the man offered Dmitry his lighter. Dmitry wondered if he knew that he knew. The man was not tall, in his thirties, undistinguished looking. Dmitry wanted to hear him talk. He handed back the lighter and said, 'How often do the trains come this time of night? Every ten, fifteen minutes?'

The man definitely showed irritation. 'Yes, something like that.' He spoke with a Viennese accent. Of course they would be likely to hire someone local.

'Thanks for the light.' Dmitry went back to sit down further up the platform. He got on the next train, took it as far as Schwedenplatz and changed. He glanced along the platform, but as far as he could tell, he was on his own. There was no point anyway in checking, he wasn't going anywhere, and he assumed they were watching his flat. But now he knew, without a doubt, that there was something very wrong. As he let himself into his living room and sank heavily onto the sofa he was struck by the irony that he had come here from Russia hoping to leave all this behind him, only to find himself in an even more sinister network of espionage, surveillance, and intrigue.

VII

It was a cold, crisp, sunny day in Linz, the kind that always made Nihal feel clear-headed, energetic. He entered the lobby of a rather dull hotel and hovered there uncertainly. He was supposed to be meeting Johannes Becker. Three days ago Nihal had rung RASAG to check some facts and figures and been told that Becker was no longer working for the company. He had rung every J Becker in the Stuttgart telephone directory till he found him; Becker confirmed that he had resigned and after some persuasion agreed to meet Nihal and tell him why.

In his anxiety not to arrive late Nihal was over half an hour too early. To the right of the reception desk was an area with chairs and tables. He chose a seat with a good view of the front entrance and sat down. He felt uncomfortably conspicuous as he unwound his scarf and took off his hat. He didn't ask at the desk if Becker was checked in there or had left a message for him; he didn't want to do anything that would draw any attention to either of them; after all, there were not very many Sri Lankans in Austria. There were only half a dozen businessmen there, four in a group at one table, and another two sitting on their own; they were all bound to remember him.

The time passed very slowly. He glanced at his watch; it was almost twelve-forty-five. Perhaps Becker had been frightened off. Just as he was coming to that conclusion, Becker appeared as if from nowhere. He sat opposite Nihal and glanced nervously around.

'You're not recording this? I won't talk to you if you record it.'

'No, of course not.'

They ordered drinks and Becker moved his chair round next to Nihal so that he also had a good view of the door. 'I've made enquiries about you; I think you're genuine. Look, I have resigned. Please don't believe what he told you at that interview, it's a long way from the whole truth. Richter's not so brilliant as an engineer, he's okay, but he's using second hand ideas and what really gets him going is the thought of making money. I can assure you that anything that will make him money he will do. If he thinks he can make money out of satellites, then that's fine, he'll do it; he'd like to have some acclaim, he'd like to keep his hands clean. But he knows, and everyone else around this outfit knows if they are honest with themselves, that if that fails there's always going to be money for cheap rockets which can lob little warheads over the border at your neighbours when you're not too happy about what they're doing.'

Nihal, sipped his beer, encouraging Becker with his silence.

'Look, let me give you just some ideas of how this operation works. Richter entertains a lot of people in his flat in Paris. He's seen representatives of the military from Chile, Brazil and a number of Middle Eastern countries which I won't name.'

'I see.' It was not surprising, if this were true, that the French secret service would be keeping an eye on him.

Becker lowered his voice and leaned forward.

'In Stuttgart you asked about why the German Government don't stop the export of parts. Well, the point is that no sensitive parts are actually made on German soil, only parts which, arguably, don't need export licences. Other parts come from France, Italy, Switzerland and Austria where the export regulations aren't as strict. The propellant is manufactured right here in Linz; look, this is the name of the company,' Becker wrote it down on a piece of paper and slipped the note across the table. 'But that isn't all. Richter has no doubt told you that he uses a very basic inertial guidance system and actually this is true, but they are working on a much more sophisticated one now. Different parts are exported from different countries and can be put together to make whatever you need. For instance, you can take that television set over there and use certain parts of it to make a guidance system. That doesn't mean that television set is a guidance system, does it?'

'No. I quite see . . .'

'I can tell you there have been secret deals going on this past year with a country I don't want to name, but a country where nobody would allow anything to be exported that could possibly be connected with missiles. You know already one of the advantages of the RASAG rocket is that most of it can be assembled on the site, so it's so easy to transport, also it doesn't need more than a few skilled people to put it together the other end.'

'Yes; I remember you saying that. But what about the Paraguay deal? Is that contract real?'

'Yes, I can assure you of that. It was negotiated with President Stroessner when he was still in power. I can give you the name of the lawyer who drew it up and maybe he will be able to tell you something. They have already launched a prototype there but there was not any publicity. You can be sure the Americans and the Russians have been monitoring it.'

Becker took back the slip of paper from Nihal and wrote down the name of the lawyer, Jürgen Steinhagen, in Zurich. 'You contact him, although I don't know if he would be loyal to Richter or not. He was actually there in Asunción when the contract was signed. If he's willing to see you, he'll tell you quite a story about it.'

Nihal sat silently while Becker took off his glasses, polished them and glanced nervously around once more. His young, smooth face bore the expression of a child who has unwittingly got into trouble at school and is waiting for the inevitable punishment. 'Look; I don't have to tell you, I suspect you are aware of it already, but these people are really big crooks. What kind of person signs a deal like that with a man like Stroessner? Do you know the stories about Stroessner? He used to send his enemies up in aeroplanes and have them pushed out over the Chaco. Probably they fell over the very site where the rockets are to be launched.'

'But Rodriguez –'

Again, Becker did not allow Nihal to finish his sentence.

'Of course Rodriguez may be a different kettle of fish. He has promised to democratise. So far he has been very supportive of the rocket project but I think he will come under heavy pressure. Richter is so nervous about this that he is making other plans.'

Nihal tried to attract the waiter to order another bottle of beer. Becker, seeing his difficulty, snapped his fingers and got instant service.

'Look, when I joined RASAG they were talking mainly about communications satellites. Then they started talking about spy satellites. I have to tell you I was caught up in the idea of it; it was exciting, it was glamorous. Richter certainly knows how to have a good time; he's a good man to work for, he's generous, he's interested, he is not always breathing down your neck. But I don't think he is going to succeed with this Paraguayan project, I don't think anyone is going to let him. He's a little naïve; I don't think he has any idea what's around the corner for him.'

'And what is around the corner?'

'I think he is going to be stopped. Do you think the Americans, the Russians, most of Europe, are going to sit back and let him build these things? The implications are horrific. He will sell them to anybody.'

'Yes; so I understand.'

'I don't mind telling you that I'm frightened,' said Becker. 'You are not the only person who's been ringing me up since I left. There was some guy from the BND but I've made it a rule never to get mixed up with these intelligence spooks. They are all the same, whatever country they are from; they are so suspicious nothing you can tell them will ever convince them what you say is true. They make your skin crawl. Do you know what he suggested to me? That I go back and work for Richter, patch things up with him, and then report back with exactly what was going on. There'd be a lot of money in it. I said no. I know what always happens to people who do these things. They end up hanging in some cupboard with a faked suicide note.'

Nihal looked at him. He was thinking of Hans Müller.

'What are you going to do now?'

'Oh, I've got myself another job. Something a bit safer, a bit more dull, you know? I don't like the way things are going. For God's sake don't contact me at home again. Probably these guys have got my phone tapped. And please don't quote me. I'm just giving you a few leads to follow up. If I were you I wouldn't follow them up anyway. Have you published anything yet?'

'Not much.'

'Well, publish as quickly as you can. You're safer once it's already in print, it's too late to stop you then. Don't be too naïve, will you? If you think of Richter as a kind of harmless boffin you may find yourself with a nasty shock. The man is dangerous.'

Nihal swallowed the rest of his beer. He thanked Becker, picked up the piece of paper with the propellant manufacturer and the lawyer's name on it and put it in his notebook; then he walked out into the cold winter sunlight without a backward glance.

For a few days Katie felt nothing but relief that she had broken off with Dmitry. Their last encounter had left her frightened and confused. Of course, she had thought that things had changed in Russia, but did she know how much? She had no idea of the pressures he might be under. At the same time, she was concerned about him. She felt that it was wrong to have shared what she had with him and then cut off all communication; surely it was reasonable just to ring him and ask how he was? She wandered around the flat every morning, while Anna was at kindergarten, distracted from her work, wondering if she should call him, and always resisting the temptation.

Finally she gave in and rang Dmitry at the office. He picked up the phone instantly; his voice was cool and official.

'Gavrilov.'

'It's me.'

There was a slight hesitation. Then he said, 'Yes, how can I help you?' as if she were a stranger.

She said, 'Is there somebody there with you?'

Again the hesitation; 'Yes.'

'Shall I ring you later?'

'I'll call you back in ten minutes.'

She paced the apartment for ten, fifteen, twenty minutes. Now she would be late to collect Anna from kindergarten. She stood with her coat on, glancing at her watch, giving him another five minutes. Still the phone didn't ring. Finally she gave up in despair and left the house, slamming the door heavily behind her.

Nihal knocked back another shot of vodka and looked at Dmitry. On the table between them were his notes, a cassette player and the tapes of all the interviews, to which Dmitry had listened intently. His features were absolutely still; he held the cigarette packet in his hand, but made no move to open it. Something about his utter absorption affected Nihal strangely. Nothing moved in the room except the tiny leaves of a plant on the table which trembled in the slight draught from the window.

'Well?'

Dmitry suddenly came back to life. 'It is extraordinary. Is there anything else?'

Nihal told him briefly what had happened in Paris. 'What bothered me most was the way they must have got onto me the moment I left that hotel room.'

'Yes, they had you followed,' said Dmitry, 'There's no other explanation.' He spoke straight, matter-of-factly, as if he knew about such things; he was not inclined to treat it, as Nihal might, as a joke.

Dmitry opened the cigarette packet and offered one to Nihal. 'And where does his money come from? Did you find that out? Is it really private investors?'

'So he claims.'

Dmitry raised his eyebrows, lighting his cigarette.

'Well, apparently he has raised over 500 million DM from something like a thousand small investors. It seems he's very wealthy, moves in playboy circles, and found no difficulty in persuading people to put money in. Thanks to Germany's unusual tax loss laws RASAG managed to negotiate an extraordinary deal whereby investors could deduct 260 per cent of what they invested in RASAG from their tax bill, as it's classed as scientific research. There seems to have been something of a fuss about this. I rang the local tax office and they were very shirty about it and told me that it was perfectly legal. I believe they have been told it was out of line but by now RASAG have got what they wanted.'

'And he's financing his whole operation on this?'

'Well of course he's borrowed enormous sums of money, I think about 80 per cent of what he has is credit.'

Dmitry smiled.

'Mitya, I can't explain to you how odd the whole thing is. They had the rocket, the steel tubes, and everything, on display, but no evidence that they had been manufactured there, maybe they had them made by some other small company somewhere. They are just ordinary spun steel tubes – you could have them made anywhere as pipes I should think and no-one would raise an eyebrow. Most of the rocket parts can be bought off the shelf; valves, pipes, and so on.'

'And the propellant?'

'They use kerosene and white fuming nitric acid as an oxidiser. They buy this from a factory in Linz.'

Dmitry frowned. 'But they experimented with this fuel in Russia and I believe they had problems with unstable burning. This solid fuel is also very heavy and that could be a problem for a large rocket.'

Nihal was startled by this unexpected and valuable piece of information. 'Do you know about rockets? I should have talked to you before I saw Richter. I could have asked some more sophisticated questions.'

Dmitry shrugged his shoulders. 'Oh, I'm no expert, I've just read a bit, here and there.'

Nihal watched him, curious. Not for the first time, he wondered whether there wasn't more to Dmitry than met the eye.

Dmitry finished his cigarette, stood up and went into the kitchen, came back with some black bread and salmon eggs which he put on the table. He sat down and poured another vodka, picked up the glass and drained it, and then fidgeted with it, as if wondering whether to say something. Then he asked suddenly:

'Nihal, you know Katie quite well, don't you?'

Nihal thought he knew what was coming. 'Yes, I've known her for years.'

'What about her husband?'

'Bob? No, I don't see much of him. It's Katie I was friends with, from years back, when we were both at the BBC in London, when I was still living with my wife. I always found Bob . . . well, rather boring.'

'Why?'

Nihal shrugged. 'Oh, he's one of those people who will always put the organisation first. He distrusts me, of course, because I'm always looking at the problems. At first I didn't understand why Katie married him but I think it was for security. Of course he adored her.' He nearly added, don't we all.

'I know his contract is nearly at an end. Is he staying on at the Agency, do you know?'

Nihal was beginning to feel uncomfortable. He said, 'I do know why you're asking this.'

Dmitry instantly looked acutely embarrassed and returned to the previous topic. 'So you've sold your story?'

'*North-South* are running a big feature next week. I could have sold something to one of the London papers, but *North-South* are the ones who have supported me. I've got to go and see this Jürgen Steinhagen. It's just a question of checking that this contract is genuine.'

Jürgen Steinhagen rose from behind his massive desk and held out his hand. His offices, in an old and rather pompous building on the Limmatquai, reflected his wealth and success and the financial standing of his clients. Steinhagen himself was a prosperous German in his forties. He had greying hair and wore rimless glasses. They sat down in comfortable leather chairs on either side of a glass coffee table.

Nihal had told him over the phone that Richter had recommended him.

'I haven't seen Herr Richter for some time, I take it he's well?'

'Oh, I believe, very. I saw him last week.'

'How can I help you?'

Nihal handed him the copy of the contract. Steinhagen studied it.

'This is the contract you drew up with Richter?'

'Yes, that's right. Does he have a problem with it?'

'I don't believe so.'

Steinhagen stared at Nihal. He obviously realised that he might have been tricked; he was probably wondering what exactly Nihal was there for and what he should say.

'Are you working for Richter?'

'No, but it's true he suggested I talk to you. He just gave me a tour of his factory and explained his plans to me. I'm a journalist.'

'Ah; I see.' Steinhagen looked puzzled, as if he didn't see at all. He paused for a moment, deep in thought, before answering:

'I have to say, I have rather fallen out with Wolf Richter. I haven't seen him for over a year. May I ask how you got this copy of the contract? Did Richter give it to you?'

'No; a copy of it was leaked to my magazine.'

'Ah.'

The phone on the desk rang. Steinhagen answered it and said he would be a few minutes. He turned back to Nihal. Perhaps he thought that Nihal already knew enough and that no harm could come of talking to him, because he suddenly became quite open and friendly. 'Well, look, let me tell you. I first met Wolf Richter through a business contact and we did various other legal work for them. They actually made contact with Stroessner through me, because I was then doing a lot of work for German companies in Paraguay. I was flying backwards and forwards to Asunción all the time then and I had met Stroessner on a few occasions. I floated the idea to him and he was very interested. It was the kind of grandiose idea that appealed to Stroessner and he said that one day he would have the Cape Kennedy of Latin America.

'I arranged for Richter to come over. We hired this big house in Asunción and we had a good time, I remember it well. There was a meeting with Stroessner and I drew up the contract, rather hastily, I have to add. We did take some rather amazing liberties to which we half expected Stroessner to object. But you see, he was an old man then, he was preoccupied with the question of his succession and I don't think he really gave it too much thought.'

'So did the negotiations go on for some time? How many other people were present? Lawyers? Any other generals?'

Steinhagen shrugged. 'Oh, not very many. Anyone else was immaterial, anyway, Stroessner was the only one who counted. It was a jolly social occasion, you understand. We were in the President's residence, it was a hot day but inside it was very cool with pot plants, marble floors, lots of drinks, nice food and it was all very relaxed. Then we signed the contract.'

'And there weren't any real negotiations? Nobody queried some of the extraordinary clauses in the contract?'

'No. As far as I remember, it was all over in about twenty minutes.'

Nihal was stunned. This was incredible; that the leader of a country should have signed away all control over a large area of their state without formal discussions in about twenty minutes. He went on, 'But the new President? Did he accept this too?'

'I think the whole of the military were quite supportive of the project. All these soldiers out in the Chaco, they have nothing else to do. And remember, Paraguay is desperate for foreign investment. They have particularly been encouraging the Germans and as Richter also intended to develop the area a little – drill for water, irrigation, crop growing for the workers, that kind of thing – he was made more than welcome. The Paraguayans are trying to open up the Chaco and this fitted in rather well. It was a big, prestige project, that might attract other people. And of course it meant getting one ahead of Argentina and Brazil, both of whom have had problems with their missile programmes. Of course, Richter was a little nervous at the time of the coup, but it soon became clear that the contract would be honoured.'

The phone rang again and Steinhagen answered it. Then he looked at Nihal. 'Listen, I'm sorry . . . I am very busy. Is there anything else you need? Please don't quote me on this, will you? I have a feeling Richter is not a man to get on the wrong side of.'

On the plane back to Vienna, Nihal felt satisfied. He had got more or less everything he needed now for his story. It was growing dark. The vibration of the engines made him sleepy. He clutched his bag with the evidence inside it, unwilling to let go of it even for an instant; he didn't want to fall asleep. Nihal was not exactly afraid, but he was aware that he might be being followed, and that Richter, or others, might not want the full details of the story written. He had begun to feel terribly important; he was carrying this immense, this extraordinary secret. Nihal, influenced by his father, had always tried to practise non-attachment. He didn't get worked up about things. He took life as it came. He had never been too much bothered by material success. But this was something different. It had gripped him. It was an obsession. Although he had enough now to write his piece, he wanted to know everything that it was possible to know about Richter's secret designs; he wanted to get to the very heart of it.

He was almost home, near the bottom of the Bankgasse, starting to cross the road, when a grey car came from nowhere and nearly ran him down. The car brushed against him and he fell backwards, sitting down heavily in the gutter in a slurry of icy water. He scrambled to his feet, shaken, and managed to catch part of the number-plate before the car disappeared from sight. His clothes were soaked, and there was a sharp pain at the base of his spine. He felt himself gingerly, afraid that perhaps some vertebra had been jolted out of place, but he was able to walk without any difficulty. How had he managed to miss seeing the car? Perhaps he had been preoccupied with his thoughts and failed to notice the car approaching; he had certainly had his head tucked down inside his collar and scarf to protect himself against the freezing rain. But he was not convinced that it had been an accident.

Nihal let himself into the flat and closed the door with a feeling of relief. He thought about reporting the incident to the police; then decided not to bother. He remembered that some time ago, when a Turkish journalist he knew had been killed in a hit-and-run, the police had done nothing to investigate it. Instead, he rang Dmitry to say he had some news for him and invited him over for a curry the following evening to discuss it.

In the morning Nihal woke up stiff and bruised. His chief emotion was of anger. He rang every car hire company in Vienna, saying he wanted to hire a grey Opel. If they said they had such a car, he asked for the registration number. None of them tallied. Perhaps he had got it wrong. Of course, the car could have been hired outside Vienna; but this was unlikely, because it had a Viennese number plate.

The other thing they might have done was to use a stolen car. He thought he might as well check with the police; he knew they wouldn't give him the information unless he said it was his own car so he rang and said he wanted to report a car stolen. He gave the incomplete registration number, saying he had borrowed it from a friend, and wasn't sure of the number; his friend might have reported it already. Had they had any record of it being stolen?

He had to hang on for some time. The man came back. He said there was no record, and would Nihal please give further details. Nihal said he would ring back and hung up. He stared into space for a while, trying to forget his anger, and then sat down in front of his computer to start work.

Three saucepans were bubbling on the cooker. Nihal wandered from one to the other, tasting, adding spices, and feeling more relaxed. He'd always enjoyed cooking, grinding spices and inventing new recipes and showing off his culinary skills. He was startled when the doorbell rang rather earlier than expected; he went and opened it, still holding a wooden spoon in his hand.

It wasn't Gavrilov. It was Katie. She had snow in her hair and her face looked white, pinched and cold.

He was so surprised to see her that he stood and stared, curry dripping from the spoon.

'Aren't you going to ask me in?'

'Yes, of course.' He shut the door behind her. She walked into the kitchen and paused in the action of taking off her coat. 'What a delicious smell . . . Is somebody coming? I'm not disturbing you, am I?'

'Not at all.' Nihal resigned himself to the fact that the evening would take a rather different shape to the one he had intended. 'If you like you can join us. Is something the matter?'

'I don't know, I'm so miserable. I had a row with Bob . . . I had to get out.' She sat down on the chair and he asked her how things were going with Dmitry. She said, 'Oh, they're not.'

'What did I tell you? I said it wouldn't last.' He patted her thigh delightedly, glad to be proved right. 'So, that's how it goes. You're not the only one who's miserable, Dmitry is also going around looking like he's seen a ghost.'

Katie gave a little start. 'What do you mean, seen a ghost?'

'Well, I saw him at the bank at the UN this morning and he's certainly not himself. Do you want a drink?'

'No,' said Katie automatically and then, 'Yes; yes, actually, I will.'

The doorbell rang. Nihal said, 'Ah, that will be the man himself.' Katie gazed at him with astonishment. Dmitry came in and they both looked at one another in confusion. Dmitry also looked pale and tense and he had dark rings under his eyes.

'Well,' said Nihal, raising his glass to his lips and smiling with ill-disguised amusement, 'The star-crossed lovers.'

'Oh for God's sake,' said Dmitry with an uncharacteristic burst of irritation.

'Sorry, sorry, I meant no harm.' Nihal had not been prepared for the heaviness of the atmosphere which now filled the apartment. He began to realise that he had gone too far and turned to Dmitry. 'Katie just called in unexpectedly . . . Perhaps I should make myself scarce; perhaps you have things you want to discuss together? Shall I go out and leave you to it?' He opened the cupboard door. 'You know,' he said, 'I have run out of rice. Why don't I just go down to the shop and get some? Keep an eye on these, won't you?' He handed Katie a wooden spoon.

As soon as Nihal had gone Katie sat down at the table. Dmitry sat opposite her and poured himself a glass of wine.

'What's the matter?' she asked. 'You look dreadful.'

'I don't know . . . nothing . . . I've given up smoking.'

'Have you? I'm glad.' She looked at him. 'Please tell me, Mitya, what's wrong. Is it because of me?'

'You? Why should it be? No, of course not. You women always think everything has to do with you.'

Katie was hurt; she stood up and moved away from the table. 'Why did Nihal do this? I am furious with him. He could have told me you were coming.'

'And he could have told me.' Dmitry suddenly smiled. 'Come on, Katie, this is stupid. Since we're here – cheers.' He drank down half the glass. Then he fidgeted nervously with the ashtray on the table. Unconsciously, he took a packet of cigarettes from his pocket and opened it. Katie said, 'Mitya, you just told me you had given up.'

'What? Oh, yes, of course. Here, take them. I wasn't thinking.' She took the cigarettes and lighter and put them in her bag. Dmitry watched them disappear with an expression close to panic.

Katie said, 'I'm sorry. I'm no good at this. I shall go mad if I can't see you.'

'You are seeing me right now.'

She went up to him and sat on his knee, and he put his arm round her shoulder and pulled her close to him. They stayed that way for a long time, in delicious proximity; suddenly everything was all right again. Dmitry fiddled absently with her hair.

Nihal rang the doorbell; Katie got up and let him in.

'That looks good,' Nihal pronounced, after inspecting the saucepans, and poured himself a glass of wine. 'Well, it's ready, I should say, except for the rice.' When it was done they sat down at the table; Nihal as always ate with his fingers; Dmitry, and then Katie, followed suit. For the first time that week, Katie was able to eat with enjoyment; Dmitry too began to relax. He poured himself another glass of wine but Katie shook her head.

'If I get drunk I'll never be able to get home.'

'It's all right,' said Dmitry, 'I can run you home.'

So of course she went back to his apartment and went to bed with him. A quality of desperation had entered their love-making, as if they no longer sought to give to one another but tried to take from each other whatever relief could be obtained. Later they lay together in the darkness; distant sounds from the flats above and below came through the walls, but otherwise there was silence. Katie must have fallen asleep. She woke suddenly, feeling wide awake, and, without knowing why, was sure that there was something wrong. Dmitry was sleeping beside her, breathing slowly and evenly; she could hear the alarm clock ticking, the wind blowing in gusts against the windows and the fridge humming in the kitchen. It was very cold. A streetlamp lit the room very faintly through the blinds.

How late was it? Oh God, what would Bob think? She moved to slip out of the bed, but then she heard a sound, and knew at once that there was somebody else in the apartment. Quickly she rolled over and shook Dmitry. Something in her manner must have alerted him because he opened his eyes and listened without saying a word. Then he rolled over, pulling her half under the bedclothes and putting a finger over his lips.

They lay like that for a long, long time. Eventually Dmitry sat up, put the light on, and reached for his dressing gown.

'He's gone,' he said.

'Who was he?' Katie's heart was still beating fast with fear.

'I don't know. A very professional burglar.' He got out of bed and went to his desk, and started carefully to check things, moving swiftly and deftly through piles of paper and skimming through the floppy disks on the shelf by the computer. Then he went and checked his briefcase.

'Have they taken anything?' asked Katie.

'No. But why come at night? They know the apartment is empty all day.'

Katie sat up, the bedclothes pulled up around her. Now, finally, she was terrified. 'This wasn't an ordinary sort of burglar, was it?' she said.

'No . . . I don't know . . . probably not.'

'You have to tell me now, Dmitry. What is it all about? I'm frightened.'

'If I knew I wouldn't tell you, it's much better that you don't know anything.' He still looked puzzled, uncertain, standing in the middle of the room in a pool of darkness cast by the shadow of the lamp. Then he went over to the telephone and punched out a number.

'Nihal, it's Mitya,' he said. 'Yes, I know it's one o'clock. Listen, I have to come over and see you now. No, no, it isn't that. All right then. About half an hour.' He hung up and turned to Katie. 'I'll drop you home on the way over there. You'd better get dressed.'

Katie pulled on her clothes. She was shivering. She said, 'Is there nothing you can tell me?'

'No. Nothing at all. Are you ready? I hope Nihal isn't too angry with me. He sounded pretty fed up about being woken up.'

'Oh, no, he'll love the drama.'

Dmitry looked at her for a long time with an expression on his face that she could not read at all.

In the car they were silent. The drive took only a couple of minutes; he pulled up just round the corner from her flat and she stepped out. Turning back, she said, 'We need to talk. Shall I come on Friday? Just for an hour?' He nodded and she turned and ran. Her hand shook so much in the lock on their front door that she couldn't get the door open; Bob opened it for her. He was in his dressing gown and had clearly been waiting up for her. He was furious, a cold, hard fury which frightened her.

'Where have you been? I tried to ring Nihal but just kept getting his answerphone.'

'I was there, I'm sorry. He often leaves it on even when he's in.'

'You could have phoned me, at the least. I've been going crazy, wondering where you were. You've never been out this late before – were you at Nihal's all the time?'

'Yes, he cooked an excellent curry. I'm sorry – I said I was sorry.' Katie went into the bathroom, anxious to avoid him. Then amazed at her duplicity, she called out through the half open door, 'He wanted me to hear all his tapes, you know, those ragas he's so mad about. They went on for hours, please, don't be angry.' She stepped into the shower and stood there, letting the hot water run over her face, soothing her and removing the evidence of her tears even as they flowed.

When she came out she had composed herself. She walked into the bedroom, wrapped in her towel. Bob was sitting on the bed.

'Did you go to bed with him?'

'Who?' Katie was so startled she couldn't think.

'Nihal.'

'No.' She almost laughed with relief; she looked him straight in the eye and saw that he believed her. She knew that this was the time to tell him the truth, but she couldn't do it. She was afraid of his anger, and besides, she was afraid of the situation with Dmitry; things were more complicated than she had thought, and she needed time to think. Then, as if a malevolent spirit had come into her mind, she remembered something. 'It was our wedding anniversary on Monday.'

Bob stared at her, stunned. 'Is that what's been eating you today? Why didn't you say?'

'I kept waiting for you to remember and you didn't.'

All the anger went out of Bob in an instant. He said, 'God, honey, I'm sorry.'

'It doesn't matter.'

'Yes, it does; of course it does. For once I was here, and then –' he banged his forehead with his hand. 'We'll go out, on Friday. Ask Marianne to babysit.'

Katie towelled her hair, thinking of what she had said to Dmitry. 'No, not Friday – I have the Montessori parents' committee.'

'Well then, Saturday.'

'All right.'

Getting into bed and turning off the light, Katie let Bob cuddle up to her but did not encourage him to make love. She could not believe that she had lied so easily. But she had got herself into a real muddle; she was involved with a Russian nuclear scientist, rather naïvely thinking that things had changed, and realised now that this might not be the case. No doubt he knew many things that Western intelligence would be only too delighted to know . . . she had no idea what might be going on. She lay in the dark, trying to breath slowly and evenly so that Bob would think she was sleeping, but her eyes remained open, staring into the darkness.

'You can tell me what it's all about in the morning,' said Nihal grumpily as he let Dmitry in. 'You can sleep in here – set the alarm if you want to.' The spare room was stuffy from stale cigarette smoke and Dmitry left the window open slightly before going to sleep. He was woken suddenly by the window blowing open in a gust of wind and banging against the bookshelves. Two or three books came down with a thud; Dmitry called out with fear and flung himself to the floor. Nihal was standing in the doorway in an instant, a sarong tied round his waist, his hair standing comically on end.

'What on earth is going on?'

Dmitry said, 'For God's sake. There's someone on the balcony.'

It was very quiet in the room, so quiet that Dmitry could even hear his watch ticking. Nihal shook his head and went to peer out of the window.

'Is there anybody there?'

'No.'

Dmitry relaxed visibly. He got up from the floor and went to look himself. He stepped out onto the balcony and looked for any signs that someone might have been there and any obvious way of reaching the balcony, but there was none. Nihal said, 'I'll get you some coffee. It's nearly six. It doesn't look as if either of us are destined to have any more sleep tonight. You'd better tell me what has happened.'

Nihal made coffee and they sat and looked at one another. Dmitry told him about the intruder.

'So you also think you're being followed?' asked Nihal. 'This is to do with the rocket man as well, you think?' Dmitry didn't reply to the question and asked Nihal if he had found anything out about Liliana's background. Nihal had asked a contact at the Brazilian Embassy and also knew a journalist in Brazil whom he had telephoned but he hadn't heard anything yet. They discussed the situation from every angle. The break-in at Dmitry's apartment was very odd. There were three possibilities; that they were looking for something they thought he would always carry on him; that it was a warning; even, and this was Dmitry's suggestion, that they had wanted to kill him but hadn't done so because Katie was there with him. Nihal didn't ask him who he meant by 'they'.

Dmitry was very concerned about Nihal; but Nihal shrugged. Somehow he couldn't really believe that he would come to any harm. After all, Richter had seen him quite openly, almost everything he had was from Richter himself or from published sources. Nihal asked him if he had told Katie and he said he hadn't, that he didn't want her to know; he was absolutely firm about that. They agreed it would be better not to meet from now on as they might have put one another in danger. *North-South* wouldn't run Nihal's article for another week. Perhaps he should lie low. But, as he pointed out, it was too late now; *North-South* had the story. In any case he was going to the UN environment preparatory conference in Stockholm which would keep him out of the way for a few days.

Nihal decided to tell him about the incident with the car. He did so in a joking way, but the expression on Dmitry's face rather took the fun out of it. 'The trouble is,' said Nihal, 'I can't very well go to the police – it sounds so crazy. What do I say to them? I have been in touch with this rocket man . . .' he giggled. He realised that they had both half unconsciously adopted this label, as if Richter's name was too dangerous to be spoken out loud.

Dmitry stared at him, unsmiling. 'You should take this thing seriously, Nihal.'

Nihal was silent for a long time. He lit another cigarette, gave one to Dmitry, who took it gratefully. Then Nihal asked, 'What will you do? Will you go to the police?'

Dmitry sighed. 'I don't want to, but I think I'll have to go and talk to someone at my Mission.'

VIII

Dmitry was afraid. On the way into work that morning he had been aware of a car following, always at a discreet distance. He had taken a different route to work, one with unexpected twists and turns, and the car, a blue Audi, had stayed with him. It was now beyond doubt that he had been put under surveillance. But why? If this was to do with a cover-up in Brazil, they must know that anything he might find out, he would find out within the IAEA. Why follow him outside it? They followed you to see who you made contact with. But who would he be meeting with? Then there was also the possibility that this was connected with Richter, and that they knew about his contact with Nihal; but then what would they gain from watching him? Whichever way he looked at it, it didn't make sense.

Then he thought, they are following me to find out my movements. That's what they do; to find out where would be the best place to kill me. He immediately dismissed this, it couldn't be true, it was too frightening to contemplate, but then he realised it must be a possibility.

Dmitry rose from his desk. His first impulse was to go and tell the DDG about his suspicions, but he was reluctant to do so. He had a feeling that Lascalles would not believe him. The IAEA would not have the slightest idea what to do about it. Dmitry was himself not sure of what was going on; the whole Richter story was too incredible, and he had no proof that this was connected with this Brazilian business, only the most tenuous of links. He might make an idiot of himself. On the other hand, he felt he had to talk things over with someone.

He picked up the phone, then suddenly put it back again, grabbed his coat, and went down to get his car. He drove the few blocks to the Russian Mission to the UN, an ugly modern brick building in the 22nd district not far from the International Centre. When he got there he was unable to park; there was obviously some function going on. He left the car in a side-road and almost ran up to the building.

People were arriving in twos and threes as he went inside. It was even possible that he himself was meant to be there; the invitation might be buried somewhere on his desk. He crossed the white marble hall; the sound of animated voices drifted down from above. He bounded up the stairs under the huge chandelier of spiky glass which hung like an upside-down wedding cake. The Russian Ambassador to the UN was standing at the top of the stairs. He shook hands with Dmitry warmly and smiled, then turned to the next guest.

Dmitry went into the reception room. He saw who he wanted straight away. Porfiry Ivanovich Vedyensky was standing to one side, talking to two women and another man from the Russian Embassy. Vedyensky was the KGB *rezident,* under cover of Counsellor. Dmitry had crossed paths with him before; Vedyensky had let him know when he first arrived in Vienna that he expected Dmitry to pass him any information that would be of interest, though of course he didn't have to go along with this these days. Dmitry had made a joke of it. Normally he would have avoided Vedyensky like the plague; he didn't like him, or his plump, unpleasant wife; these people were unhappy about the way things were going; too much of their power was being eroded. They knew, too, better than almost anyone else, how near things were to falling apart. But he had no option; he needed him. Vedyensky would know what he should do.

Dmitry did not go up to him at once; that would have been too obvious. He prowled along the tables, took a glass of wine from a tray and scooped up a handful of canapés. He regretted this at once; he was unable to eat them, the dry biscuits and salty herrings stuck in his throat. Then he went back to stand by Vedyensky. The other man smiled at Dmitry; he seemed urbane, charming, but there was no warmth in his eyes. Dmitry took in snatches of his conversation. 'Of course, we are becoming more and more marginal in world affairs . . . the Americans will have their way with everything, there will be nothing to stand in the way of the whole US military-industrial complex . . .'

Dmitry interrupted. 'Absolutely. In this I am in complete agreement with you – I think it is very worrying. Porfiry Ivanovich, please excuse me, if you have a moment, there is something I would like to discuss with you.'

'Good. Talk. Have some of these, help yourself to another glass.'

'It's a serious matter. I can't talk about it here.' He glanced sideways at Vedyensky's companions.

'Well, then, come and see me tomorrow.'

'Shall I come in the morning, early?'

Vedyensky's companions had taken the hint and were drifting away. 'Yes, yes, whenever you like.' Vedyensky looked at Dmitry closely for the first time; his impassive face altered slightly. 'You are very concerned about something, Dmitry Nikolayevich? Not a personal problem, I hope?'

'No, no, it's something to do with the Agency.'

'Important?'

'I think so.'

'Give me a few minutes. I can come down and have a little talk with you.'

Dmitry went and stood by the window and had another drink; he made no attempt to talk to anyone. Fifteen, twenty minutes went by; Vedyensky was still busy socialising. Finally, just when he was thinking of giving up and leaving, Vedyensky came over, put his hand on Dmitry's arm, and said, 'Come downstairs.' Dmitry winced slightly at his touch.

The Ambassador was no longer at the head of the stairs; the hall was empty. Vedyensky ushered him into an office and closed the door behind him. This wasn't his own office; that would have been in the *rezidentura,* the self-contained part of the Mission which housed the KGB. Even the Ambassador was not allowed there without an invitation.

Vedyensky indicated a chair but Dmitry didn't sit down; he was too agitated to sit still. Until now the suspicions had all been in his head; for a moment he wondered whether it was not all a product of his imagination. It also crossed his mind that it was a mistake to raise it with Vedyensky before he had spoken to the DDG. He was so engrossed with these thoughts that he hardly noticed Vedyensky sitting perched on the side of his desk, waiting, quiet, expectant.

'Well?' Vedyensky finally asked. His voice was soft, restrained and yet somehow threatening.

Dmitry prowled up and down in the space between the desk and the window. He wondered if the conversation would be recorded; he was ill at ease. 'Well – it is rather complicated, Porfiry Ivanovich – perhaps there is nothing to it, it may all be some kind of mistake. I am not sure, I have very little to go on.'

'That's all right. Take your time, Dmitry Nikolayevich. Try to organise your thoughts. Start at the beginning.'

Dmitry explained about the Brazilian situation, about Müller's death, about his suspicions. It did not take very long; somehow the story seemed less sinister when spoken out loud. Vedyensky did not react in any way; once Dmitry had finished, he said very quietly, 'And you have no proof of this?'

'No. I have only my suspicions. Of course I've raised the question with the DDG of what may be going on at Valadares, that's all quite legitimate. But that there's been corruption inside the IAEA? How can I suggest this without any proof?'

'Of course, of course, a very difficult situation. So let's go over this. Who could have been involved? The two inspectors, Müller and Cruz. What about any previous inspections?'

'This is the first inspection since the plant was opened to safeguards. Bob Haynes was responsible for planning these, and also visited Brazil earlier last year.'

'But I don't understand. If all these people were involved in a cover-up, why should files have been altered?'

'Perhaps Müller had decided he couldn't go along with it. He put the correct data in, and that was why he had to be stopped. Maybe he was threatened; although of course this is all absolutely without any proof, I am just trying to explain to you what I have been thinking.'

'But the Brazilian Nuclear Energy Commission, their Government, they must be aware of what's going on. It doesn't make sense. Why accept safeguards, and then . . .'

'Perhaps they don't know. Perhaps this is being done by the disaffected military.'

Vedyensky frowned and pursed his lips. 'Possible.'

'But this is only half of it. There is another link. Have you heard of Wolfgang Richter?'

'Richter? Remind me – oh, I remember, the rocket engineer. Yes, I have heard of him. Why?'

'Richter has met with Haynes on two or three occasions. On the surface at least, purely socially. Richter has a Brazilian wife, whose father is very rich, very well-connected and also, I believe, has links with some high-up members of the Brazilian Army.'

'How do you know all this?'

'I know a journalist.'

'Ah, yes, Nihal Senanayake – please go on.'

'There's no evidence to connect any of this, of course. It's just that I feel . . .'

'It all fits. Yes, it all fits very neatly.' Vedyensky frowned; he remained where he was, staring into space. Then suddenly he got up. 'Leave it to me,' he said.

'I thought I would talk to the DDG tomorrow.'

'No,' said Vedyensky, emphatically, 'No. Don't do that. Don't talk to anyone. I want to discuss this with one or two people first, we don't want to move too quickly and I must be sure.' He saw the expression of dissatisfaction on Dmitry's face and carried on: 'In fact you must proceed very carefully. Speak to no-one about your suspicions; be careful in everything you do. I take it you have told no-one?'

'Absolutely not.'

'I'll talk to you again tomorrow – we may need you to help us with some more information.' Vedyensky sat down at his desk. 'Good. You have done absolutely the right thing to tell me now, before taking it to anyone at the Agency.'

'There is one other thing. This is what has absolutely convinced me that there is something wrong.'

Vedyensky raised his eyebrows. Dmitry went on, trying to

underplay it: 'There was a break-in at my place last night. Nothing was taken but . . . I think that I'm being followed.'

Vedyensky's whole expression changed. 'When did you first notice this? How long has it been going on?'

Dmitry told him.

'Why have you not come to me before?'

'I went to the UN security people. They didn't seem so concerned. Then I thought perhaps I was being paranoid.'

'Tell me anything you can about this.'

'I have written down the numbers of some of the cars they are using. Let me see . . .' he searched in his wallet and produced a crumpled piece of paper which he handed to Vedyensky. 'The men seem to be Austrian, I guess they are from a private intelligence agency.'

'Hired by the Brazilian military, you think?'

'Perhaps. Or by Richter. But I wondered what else is going on . . . I thought perhaps my phone is tapped, the office could be bugged.'

'Almost certainly, tapping the phone is easy. That is the first thing they would do. We'll have someone from the Embassy round to do an electronic sweep, see what they come up with. We'd better do your apartment as well. This may be a little complicated if they are watching your apartment. How many flats are there in the building?'

'Three.'

'Only three. That is not so easy. Do people come and go a lot?'

'No.'

'Well, we could be the gas men . . . television repairs . . . no, this is a little too obvious. You had better have a little party this evening. You have invited a friend to stay. You will have to be there. They will carry out a silent search. Do you understand me? It is very important that we don't alert the listeners to what is going on. This is for your own safety, you understand? If we find any listening devices we will leave them in place so as not to alert them . . .'

Dmitry's heart sank. Vedyensky was beginning to take all this with an alarming degree of seriousness.

'They will come this evening. Invite them in, you are expecting them, old friends, huh? Talk about anything you like. Make it sound natural, all right?' Vedyensky had moved on now; he was deep in thought. 'What I want to know is, how have they got on to you?'

'I telephoned Eduardo Cruz. I realised at once it was a mistake. If he's been in on this, he could have tipped someone off that I was uneasy about it.'

'Of course, you must be very worried. I'll see to this at once. We'll arrange for you to be, er, looked after. You live alone in your flat, don't you?'

'Yes.'

'Got a spare room?'

'Yes.'

'All right, I'll organise something at once.'

'What will you do? Give me a bodyguard? Shadow my shadowers?'

Vedyensky grinned. 'Something like that. Don't worry, they'll be very discreet.'

Dmitry hesitated, and then he said, 'In that case, there is something else you should know. I've been seeing Haynes's wife.'

Vedyensky looked at him as if in deep astonishment. He said nothing, waiting for Dmitry to go on; but Dmitry volunteered nothing further, staring intently at a map of Vienna on the wall.

Suddenly Vedyensky roared with laughter. He said, 'My God, you have an unexpected talent for this. Someone has missed out on an opportunity here. This was your own idea?'

'No . . . yes . . . it was not like that . . .'

'Well? Has she told you anything of interest?'

Dmitry wished that he had never mentioned it. He tried to sound casual, but without success. 'No, not really. I don't think she knows anything.'

'When you said it might have been Cruz that alerted them to you, how do you know it wasn't through her?'

Dmitry had known this was coming. He supposed these people's minds must still run on in the old patterns – honeytraps, blackmail . . . 'That has occurred to me of course, in my most paranoid moments. But I can't believe it. No, it's ridiculous. In any case, I've told her nothing.'

'Haven't you asked her questions? Questions that might alert her to areas of interest to yourself?'

'I don't know. God, I don't know, I don't think so. I have tried to be careful. Anyway, that has nothing to do with this, it is just a coincidence.'

'In this business,' said Vedyensky softly, 'As you may learn, there are no coincidences. You have made quite a mistake, Dmitry Nikolayevich, in trying to do this on your own. We could have put someone with some training onto this, we could have helped you along a little. Now tell me about this relationship with Haynes's wife. It's still going on, is it?'

'Yes.'

'I take it you've gone to bed with her?'

'For God's sake! Is this really necessary? Does it matter –'

'Come, come, you can be frank with me, Dmitry Nikolayevich. Is this a casual matter, of convenience to you, or to her, or is it more serious?'

Dmitry shifted from one foot to another; he thought, Vedyensky has no need to ask these questions, he does it only because he enjoys it, or maybe it is some KGB trick, some way of making people feel humiliated, less able to stand up to them. 'It's serious,' he said.

'If we asked you to stop seeing her, would you stop seeing her?'

For the first time since entering the room, Dmitry looked Vedyensky in the eyes. 'No.'

Vedyensky said, 'You will have to handle this very carefully. Please don't see her for the next couple of days. Don't argue with me; this is too important. Just make some excuse. I'm only asking you to wait a day or two. Will you go along with this for me, Dmitry Nikolayevich?'

'Yes, yes.' Dmitry took a deep breath, trying to calm himself. Vedyensky walked over to him, laying his hand heavily on Dmitry's shoulder. He felt himself stiffen with resentment.

'You're not regretting that you came to talk to me, are you? You would have been very foolish not to. You see, I think you may be in very serious danger. You should stay away from Mrs Haynes for her own sake as well as yours.'

Dmitry was silent.

'You have the list from the security service of the precautions you should take? Good. Stick to them. You had better not contact me by telephone, unless you use a payphone. Don't use the one nearest your flat; sometimes they put a tap on that too. You can get a message to me on this number,' and he scribbled a number on a piece of paper and handed it to him. 'Don't come to see me again here. They are watching you, but they will just think you came to this function. I will meet you tomorrow afternoon at the IAEA at four-thirty at the bar on the seventh level. Can you manage four-thirty?'

'I would have to check with my secretary.'

'Well then, the cafeteria downstairs at six if you fail to make it. You must pardon me, but I have to go upstairs. Go straight home tonight, watch what you are doing; we'll have someone keeping an eye on you from later this evening.'

Dmitry mumbled some thanks.

'Some other little tips, Dmitry Nikolayevich. When you're under surveillance, you should never let them know that you know. No looking over your shoulder, jumping off trains just as the doors close, driving your car round two or three corners and stopping suddenly so they nearly run into you. Those kinds of capers are strictly for spy movies.' Vedyensky patted him on the back. 'Don't look so downhearted, Dmitry Nikolayevich, you may have turned up something very important. Really, you are to be congratulated.' He opened the door and ushered Dmitry into the corridor.

Dmitry left the building and went to his car. He was now in a far worse state than he had been when he had arrived there. He was so angry that for a while he did not dare to start the car, he was afraid of crashing it. So now Vedyensky was going to run him like a common spy. He had been told not to talk to the DDG; not to see Katie. Thinking it over, he did not really believe he was in danger; Vedyensky would exaggerate that, it was in his interest to do so.

He drove home deliberately slowly and, once inside the apartment, poured himself a drink. He had better phone Katie, she was meant to be coming over; he would have to put her off. He picked up the phone. As it rang he was tense; he was afraid Bob would answer it. He did. He hung up instantly and put his head in his hand. But he would have to ring; he couldn't have Katie turn up under these circumstances. He rang again. This time Katie picked up the phone.

'Yes?' Her voice sounded uncertain, vulnerable. He knew she had been expecting it to be him.

'Katie, I can't see you tonight.'

'Why not?'

'There's something come up at work.'

'Nihal, I'll ring you back later. I was just going out.' She hung up. Dmitry put the phone down in despair. After fifteen minutes or so Katie rang back. She sounded furious. She said, 'Why did you ring me like that? You put me in an impossible position. I hate all this. What excuse are you making now?'

'Katie, can't we meet tomorrow instead. Something has come up at work.'

'I don't believe it. There is nothing that goes on in that place that requires you to be there late in the evening.'

'No, I'll be at home – but there's a report I have to finish.'

She sounded close to tears. 'If you don't want to see me, why can't you just say you don't want to see me?'

'Because it isn't true.'

There was a long silence. Then Katie said, 'I'm sorry.' Then she said, 'I'm freezing – I'm in a call box.'

'Don't be sorry. It doesn't matter. I'll ring you tomorrow, and we'll arrange something then.'

'I can't stand this.'

'Yes, I know. I just can't help it. I don't want things to be this way.'

'Well what way do you want them to be?' asked Katie. 'It seems to me the way things are suits you very well.' Her voice was angry and harsh. For a long time Dmitry did not answer; he was on the verge of tears. Finally he said, 'Katie, don't give me a hard time. Things are bad enough for me.'

Katie's voice changed at once. 'Mitya, what's the matter? Can't you tell me what's the matter?'

Instantly he reassured her. 'It's all right, there's nothing the matter. I have to go, Katie, I promise I'll call you tomorrow.'

They came at nine, two young men and a girl in a black Mercedes. The girl was attractive, dark, late twenties. She had a large suitcase and a bulky shoulder bag. The men carried them upstairs. Dmitry poured out the drinks and they clinked glasses and toasted one another. The girl kept laughing in a high, forced way which irritated Dmitry. She turned on the radio rather loudly and tuned in to some popular music. The two men talked and joked as they opened the suitcase. It contained a large quantity of electronic equipment. The girl's shoulder bag was also packed with counter-surveillance devices.

First they checked the phone lines. They used a large wiring analyser the size of a small television set, covered with knobs and electronic displays. They were talking politics, laughing and swearing a lot. Then there were some small hand-held instruments with aerials with which the men prowled the flat. The girl, Vera, came and sat beside Dmitry on the sofa. 'Come, Mitya, don't look so solemn,' she said. 'Aren't you pleased to see me? You haven't got another girlfriend, have you? Do you mind if I stay?'

'Yes,' said Dmitry, 'Yes, I do mind, as a matter of fact. Can't you stay in a hotel?'

'Do you hear that, Kostya? He wants me to stay in a hotel. You're not very hospitable, are you? Haven't you got anything to eat? I'm starving.' And she went into the kitchen. The men had started a physical search. They seemed to be going through everything; they examined the furniture, curtains, curtain rails, under the carpets, behind the pictures, inside every piece of electrical equipment. Then they went into the bedroom.

They must have been in the apartment for about two hours. Then the man called Kostya came and gave Dmitry a large wink. They packed all the equipment back into the suitcase and drained their glasses. 'We thought we'd all go out to eat somewhere,' he said. 'Want to join us?'

'Are you really throwing me out?' asked Vera.

'Yes, there's only one bed. Besides, someone else is coming to stay, a friend of mine. And I am too tall for the sofa. Really, let me get your coat. Can't you stay with Kostya here?'

'I am a respectable married man. There's no telling what my wife would say if she saw *her.*'

They left the suitcase in the flat and all went downstairs. Dmitry went with them; he felt he had to get out of the apartment, and besides, he wanted to ask them what they had found. Kostya climbed into the driving seat and indicated to Dmitry to get into the front. He headed downtown. Dmitry saw him look several times into the rear-view mirror.

'Well,' Kostya said, 'I should say things are fairly heavy. There's a tap on your line and two concealed bugs – sophisticated devices too, the kind which hop frequencies. And we've got a tail. What have you got, then? Atomic secrets, heh?'

Dmitry was feeling rather sick. He wanted to get out, to be on his own and think, but he felt he had nowhere to go to be alone. He was trying to think what he had said over the phone in the last few days, whether he had given anything away. He thought not, he had been very careful. He asked, 'Where were they, then?'

'One in each room . . . I know what you're thinking. That's what bothers everyone, them hearing what goes on in your bedroom. Don't worry, they've heard it all. You don't have any problems, do you? Your girlfriend likes it? Makes a lot of noise, heh? Don't worry about it.' And he laughed loudly.

Dmitry made his four-thirty appointment with Vedyensky in the delegate's lounge. They fetched some tea from the bar and sat down in the large, soft chairs opposite the window; the delegates had just departed back to the meeting and the place was quiet. Vedyensky asked, 'Did you have a good night?'

'Not very.'

'I can see that you feel upset about this. I'm sorry, I may have given you the wrong impression yesterday. You can of course mention your concerns to the DDG. But it all sounds a little fantastic, doesn't it? In any case, this might be the work of Richter rather than the Brazilians. We will have to see.'

'But surely they will have to take this seriously.'

'Look, you know the score as well as I do. The IAEA are powerless in a situation like this. They have no intelligence gathering facilities, they cannot investigate. If you are seriously interested in this being cleared up, Dmitry Nikolayevich, you are much better leaving it to us. Suppose you make a fuss and they are forced to do investigations into all the staff, the Brazilians will at once know that the secret is out. It will be much harder to establish what is going on. We have not been unaware of all this, Dmitry Nikolayevich. We have an agent in Brazil.'

Vedyensky paused; he lowered his voice. 'About Richter. We have been aware of his activities for some time. A copy of an extraordinary document which will prove highly embarrassing has been stolen from the Paraguayan Embassy in Bonn and leaked to the press. I think you know of this already – one of our operations, you understand. They are not going to be able to keep quiet about this for long. No, there will be a big noise about this very soon. Please, just do as I ask and don't do anything about all this just now. I am only talking of a few days.'

Dmitry shifted impatiently in his seat and sipped his tea.

'Now this question of your . . . lady-friend. We're not very happy about it.'

'But it's absurd. I'm sure she knows nothing about it. If you're suggesting she was somehow planted on me, you're quite wrong. I met her before I had the first idea . . .'

'You met her at Müller's funeral, didn't you?'

Was there anything these people didn't know?

'Look, I don't want to talk about this any further. You are making too much of it. It's distracting you from the main point of this.'

'Well, perhaps. In any event, you are to be careful, hm? We don't want anything getting back through her to her husband.'

'No. Of course not.'

'As to the next step, please be patient just for a few days.'

'I'm not happy about this at all. I can't see any reason . . .'

'But there may be reasons you are not aware of, which we are, Dmitry Nikolayevich.'

Dmitry stared gloomily out of the window. Then he said, half under his breath, 'You can't actually stop me from talking to the DDG, or Kaisler either, for that matter.'

Vedyensky stubbed out his cigarette. 'No. Of course not. But it would probably not be very good for your career.'

'Perhaps this is more important to me than my "career."'

'It is because we consider it so important that we are asking you to be patient.'

'I am not a patient man.'

'No, Dmitry Nikolayevich, we know that is not one of your virtues. Indeed, you are not really a very virtuous man, are you? You would be surprised to know what we know about you.'

Dmitry put his tea-cup down suddenly onto the saucer with a loud clatter and got to his feet. 'What is all this shit?' he demanded. 'What more of this outdated rubbish have you got up your sleeve? Faked letters of denunciation? Compromising photographs?'

Vedyensky looked astonished. Dmitry tried to calm himself. 'Porfiry Ivanovich, you cannot make these kind of threats to me any more. You can't have me sent back home if I don't do as you ask. I do not have to co-operate with you in any way unless I wish it. You know perfectly well that you and your people are becoming a kind of dinosaur.'

Vedyensky now looked at Dmitry coldly. Dmitry felt it; it was equally returned. He nearly shook with rage, but he thought, I mustn't make an enemy of him, these types can still be dangerous. He said, 'Excuse me, I have work to do.' Vedyensky rose and followed him, joining him again as he waited for the lift. Dmitry stared deliberately in the opposite direction.

'I only mentioned this,' said Vedyensky quietly, 'To try to make you realise the importance of doing things our way.'

'I can't imagine what you are talking about.'

'Oh, I think you can.'

'Then tell me.' The lift had opened; there were three people in it. They stepped inside. Dmitry continued, his voice raised in anger, 'Tell me in front of all these people. I am not ashamed of anything.' Nonetheless he felt his cheeks burn red, betraying him. Vedyensky flinched; the others looked away in embarrassment. When they got out Vedyensky suddenly said, 'Come here with me.'

He led Dmitry into a room to the right of the bank of lifts; it was a room for quiet and meditation. In the centre stood a large stone sculpture, shaped like a ring doughnut. Vedyensky ran his hand thoughtfully along its edge.

'Have you ever been in here before?'

Dmitry looked pointedly at a small notice on the wall requesting silence. 'You are not supposed to talk in here.'

'No, I know that. That is why I don't suppose anyone would have it bugged.'

Dmitry sat down abruptly on a raised platform at the end of the room and sank his face in his hands.

'You should be more careful about your behaviour, Dmitry Nikolayevich. Things may be more open these days, but you still have to be aware of your position. People are beginning to say things about you.'

'You don't have to threaten me,' he said. 'It will have the opposite effect to what you intend. It's true that things are different now; I would have thought you would have changed your methods.'

'I was threatening you with nothing; you have quite misunderstood me,' said Vedyensky; he seemed suddenly to have changed his whole approach. 'You are very highly thought of here; you are a credit to our country, a fine example of what our educational system and scientific training can achieve. Everyone says you are outstanding.'

Dmitry waved his hand dismissively. 'Please spare me all this. What have you brought me here to tell me?'

'Let us set all this other business aside. The fact is, you need our help. As you know the electronic sweep of your apartment showed, as you suspected, that your phone was tapped, via a transmitter in the junction box in the street. We'll be watching now to see when someone comes to replace the batteries, and make sure nobody gets access again.'

'Thanks.'

'We don't know how they got in – but this isn't too difficult. There isn't anyone else who has a key to your apartment is there? Your girlfriend?'

'No.'

'We also checked your office. That is more difficult, with a PABX system, but your line was also tapped – quite a complex matter because they had to use a repeater to get the signal out of the International Centre. They used a device in the base of the instrument itself. This we have also left in place. Just assume that everything you say is being recorded, heh?'

Vedyensky paused for a moment, as if to let this sink in, then carried on. 'Then the surveillance team . . . they are using three men, in eight-hour shifts. There are three cars, one ahead, one behind, one floating, he stays completely out of sight till he's needed when they want to change positions. That's all quite standard. They are using a private intelligence agency. If they were working for a secret service for a Western government, they'd be using more people; perhaps six men or more, they can afford it. They would probably be more discreet. But whoever that is would need a lot of money, because this kind of thing doesn't come cheap.'

'Can't you find out who is doing this?'

'Well, of course – and who is actually following you – but you see that won't get us very far, Dmitry Nikolayevich. These private intelligence agencies, they never know who their clients are. It's all done through dead-letter boxes, that kind of thing. We have to work that out in other ways. Now you had better let the whole thing drop. This is why I tell you not to talk to anyone. This journalist friend of yours, in particular. You see, they know you are linked to him. He's probably actually in the same situation as you.'

Dmitry was silent, thinking it all through.

'Boris Alexeyevich Kulagin will accompany you to your apartment tonight. You don't know him, his cover is a translator at the UN. I think you'll find him easy enough to get on with. You should be able to sleep a little more easily. Please let me know if there are any more developments immediately, won't you?'

'Of course.'

'In the meantime, try to take things a little more calmly. If you don't mind my saying so, you look dreadful, Dmitry Nikolayevich. You don't want your colleagues thinking you're about to have a breakdown.'

Boris Alexeyevich Kulagin moved into Dmitry's apartment that night. He came with a small suitcase and moved into the spare room. He seemed to be a man of few interests; he spent most of his time in the living room watching television while Dmitry sought refuge in the bedroom. Katie rang on Sunday and asked if she could see him and he said he had a Russian friend staying and he would try to meet her next week.

The only place he had any sense of safety was in his office. On

Monday he told Kulagin he would be working late. He sat in his office in the semi-darkness. When he worked late it was his habit to turn off the main lights and work by his desk-lamp; the fluorescent lighting always gave him a headache. It was nine o'clock. Suddenly he desperately wanted to see Katie; to hell with it all, he thought. He reached his hand out for the phone and then, slowly, reluctantly, let it fall again. He stood up and went to the window. The lights of Vienna shone in the darkness; the moon was almost full, lighting the underside of the clouds above it. Its light was so bright that it drowned out the stars.

He looked at his watch. Boris would be coming shortly; he couldn't stand it. He felt a desperate need to be alone; he couldn't face the thought of Boris Alexeyevich's heavy, silent presence in the flat, or the effort of trying to make conversation with him, nor the constant presence of his unseen watchers. On impulse he got stood up, left the office and went down to his car. He drove in the wrong direction for his apartment and turned right across the bridge, taking the road heading north, from the roundabout where the signposts pointed to the destinations of Budapest and Prague. He drove faster and faster, aware all the time of the headlights behind him; that would be the car following him, a discreet distance back. At the turn-off to Klosterneuburg he did not indicate, but suddenly cut across the lanes and pulled onto the slip-road at the last minute; the car behind him went on past, but he knew they would radio to the one behind to take the turning. The road wound up the hillside; he slowed down now and drove more carefully.

He circled aimlessly around the village, finally parking the car in a small car-park. He got out and walked slowly to the nearest bar; he saw the white car pull up further down the street. Inside, he did not even bother to buy a drink, but walked through into the little yard at the back, in which barrels of beer and crates of empty bottles were stacked. He climbed up on some and levered himself over the wall, scuffing his shoes and scraping his fingers on the rough bricks. He dropped heavily down into the street and brushed down his coat. It was all ridiculous; he hated himself for letting it get to him, for ending up playing their own game. He thought again of Vedyensky's warning and thought, to hell with him; to hell with the whole bloody thing.

He walked quietly down the road, his hands in his pockets, slipping a little on the patches of ice and snow which still lay on the ground up there. As he walked, he was not sure if he imagined a dark figure appearing briefly at the top of the street.

He walked on down towards the high walls which surrounded the abbey church and the baroque monastic buildings; inside the gateway he paused, standing on the frosty grass. The wind stirred in his hair and chilled him; he turned his collar up and hunched his shoulders. Often the buildings were floodlit, but tonight all was in darkness; he could only just make out the shape of the magnificent crown on the roof, a reproduction of the crown of the Holy Roman Empire. He stood still in the gloom; it was very quiet. Then suddenly, quite distinctly, he heard one footstep crunch on the gravel of the path outside. Just one footstep; and then silence.

Dmitry turned and ran across the grass to the shelter of the wall. He stood there with his back against the wall for some time; there was no further sound, and he was shivering with cold and with a fear which suddenly engulfed him from head to foot. Oh God, he thought, why did I come here? If they wanted to kill me they couldn't find a better time or place.

After a while he turned and walked along the wall. He thought he remembered there was another entrance; he didn't want to go back the way he had come. He emerged through the other gate back into the street; there was still nobody around. He walked quickly back towards his car. He walked faster and faster; dark shadows hung in every doorway. His shoulders were tense, waiting for the shot he feared; every few strides he had to consciously force himself to relax them. He reached the car, pulled out his keys and fiddled with the lock; it wouldn't turn, his hand was shaking. The relief he felt on slamming the door behind him was so intense he felt like laughing out loud. He started the engine, reversed suddenly out of the car-park, and drove back down the hill to rejoin the motorway.

At his apartment Boris Alexeyevich was sitting on the sofa drinking beer and watching a dubbed American film. Dmitry did not even say hello; he switched off the set without asking, went to the record player, and put on a disc which was already on the deck; he turned the volume up high and waited for the music to begin. It was Bach's St John Passion; the first great chorus had a demonic quality that perfectly suited his mood. Then he went into the kitchen and opened the fridge. He stared at its contents blankly; he didn't know how he was going to eat anything.

Boris Alexeyevich came into the kitchen after him. He switched on the radio and whispered, 'What happened to you? You're very late. You did not say you would be so late. I have reported you missing. Probably they are looking all over Vienna for you.'

Dmitry also whispered against the background noise. 'Well you'd better go out to the phone and unreport me.'

Boris shrugged. 'May I turn this down a little?'

'If you must.'

Boris said in a more normal voice, 'Where the hell did you go?'

'I went for a walk in Klosterneuburg.'

'On your own?'

'Yes.' Dmitry sat down suddenly on the sofa. 'I think I am going mad,' he said.

Boris Alexeyevich looked at him with something approaching concern. 'You take things too seriously, you never relax,' he said. 'You need to watch something like that American film. Or you need to go out, have a nice meal, find a woman . . .'

'Yes,' said Dmitry, 'Yes, I could do with a woman.'

'Well, then,' said Boris Alexeyevich, looking a little less morose, 'I can ring up a couple of friends of mine, secretaries at the Embassy, and they could come –'

'No, no, for God's sake,' said Dmitry, 'I'll just have something to eat and go to bed.'

He lay awake, staring at the ceiling, unable to sleep. Perhaps it was because he was so acutely aware of the listening devices picking up his every move. He thought of all the things he and Katie had said to one another in this room. They liked to talk to one another when they made love, tell one another what to do. He felt somehow violated. And what was he going to say to Katie? He couldn't ask her to come back here now. They had nowhere to meet. He couldn't explain to her. He supposed even seeing her was putting her at risk. The whole situation was absurd and horrible.

In the morning he got up early. Boris Alexeyevich was shaving at the kitchen sink. Dmitry was hardly able to eat. He cut himself some bread and buttered it, but it seemed unbearably dry; it seemed that no saliva came into his mouth. He poured himself a glass of milk. He hated milk, but it was nourishment; he gulped it down and poured himself another glass, wondering how much milk an adult had to drink a day to sustain himself.

At work, Dmitry couldn't concentrate on anything. He would read several paragraphs and realise that he had absorbed nothing from them. He shuffled papers uselessly on his desk. Hilde asked him several times for a letter he was supposed to have written. Finally he sat her down and dictated it to her. In the middle he lost the thread. She asked him with a mixture of irritation and concern, 'Are you feeling all right?' She was not the only person to ask him this question. One of his colleagues, at the end of a discussion, asked him if it was trouble about a woman. Dmitry shrugged and then said, 'Yes.'

'Can you tell me about it?'

'She's married. It's all going badly.'

'I see. Well, for goodness' sake, try to sort it out. People are noticing. Your work is suffering.'

'What work?' said Dmitry, bitterly, 'Pushing these papers around?'

At the end of the week Dmitry rang Katie from one of the call boxes in the main foyer. Katie's voice, at the end of the phone, sounded numb with misery.

She said, 'I thought it was all over.'

'No, I want to see you.' But where? It was impossible. There was nowhere they could be alone together. On impulse, he said, 'Let's meet on Saturday afternoon. We could go somewhere – I'll think about it. Let's do something nice together.'

'I'll have to arrange to leave Anna with someone. And then there's Bob . . . I'm not sure I can manage it.'

'Try. Try, and I'll ring you back later.'

They had agreed to go to Schönbrunn Palace, just outside Vienna. Katie left Anna with Bob saying she wanted an afternoon to herself and met Dmitry at the corner of the Obkirchergasse where he was waiting in his car. He drove her there and they chattered desultorily, not mentioning anything of importance; Katie knew that there was something wrong and didn't dare ask him what it was, anxious to avoid any argument or confrontation.

They walked through the vast, glittering palace, holding hands. The contrast between the beauty of the surroundings and the fear she felt was like something in a dream. Dmitry was silent, preoccupied. Katie said at last, 'If you would only explain to me what the matter is. If you're in some kind of trouble, I would understand.'

Dmitry said, 'It's nothing. You mustn't worry about it. Let's not talk about it now.'

'Why not? What else is there to talk about? You're not thinking about anything else, are you?' They had wandered ahead of the guide, neither of them interested in hearing the details of each room, both too impatient and immersed in their own thoughts. Dmitry held her hand almost fiercely, as if he was afraid she would let go. Katie was beginning to feel frightened of him. He didn't answer her; he seemed so distant, tense. She was by now so miserable that she began to think it didn't matter what happened to them as long as something could be decided one way or the other.

They passed through the last gilded room and went outside. The air was cold, the sun was beginning to descend, and the sky was clear, a pale greeny colour blending into gold. They walked down the paths between the formal gardens; their feet crunched on the snow. Suddenly Dmitry grimaced, as if in pain, and sat down on a low wall, fists clenched, looking at the ground.

'I'm sorry, I should not have gone on seeing you, I had no right to get you involved in this.' He spat the words out as if someone else was forcing them from him.

Katie looked at him in horror.

'But I wanted to get involved as much as you did, more so,' said Katie.

'I wasn't meaning that.'

'But what do you mean? I don't understand anything. If there's something you have to say to me, why don't you just say it? Why must you go on tormenting me like this?'

But it was Dmitry who seemed tormented. He seemed to be struggling with himself, trying to decide what he should say. Then he said, finally, 'Because it's no good, it can never work out, that's why.'

Katie sat on the wall next to him. 'But why not?' she asked.

Dmitry seemed suddenly to have changed his mind. She had felt he was about to reveal something to her, but now he simply said, in a much calmer voice: 'Well, to begin with, I have to go back to Russia eventually.'

'Without me,' she said.

He looked round at her and suddenly his face softened. 'Would you want to come with me, then?' he asked her, almost in wonderment. 'With Anna? It looks as if terrible times are coming there. Everyone will want to get out.'

'But not you.'

'No, not me. For better or worse, it is my country, and if everyone like me left there really would be no hope for us.'

'And that's more important to you than . . . than I am?'

'I don't know.'

'But it isn't like it was before,' said Katie. 'You don't have to defect, or anything. You don't have to burn your boats, do you?'

Dmitry shrugged.

'But that isn't all that's the matter,' said Katie. 'There's something else, isn't there?'

'Yes.'

'Please tell me about it.'

'No, it's not possible.'

'But is it because you are in some kind of trouble? Are you . . . is there . . .' she couldn't find the right expression, not wanting to put her thoughts into words because this would make them real, and the reality was too frightening. 'Are you involved in something . . .'

Dmitry seemed determined not to help her. 'What sort of thing?'

'Oh, for God's sake, Mitya, you know what I mean.'

'No, I don't know what you mean. You mean you think I am implicated in something sinister, do you? You think I am involved in intrigue or spying? You think perhaps I am abusing my position at the UN?' He made all this sound ridiculous, absurd; something unpleasant had crept into his voice. 'You don't have any thoughts like that about anyone else around you, do you? I don't suppose, for example, you have any such suspicions about your husband?'

Katie looked at him completely blankly. She said, 'About Bob? I don't know what you mean, Mitya, I can't think what you're talking about.'

Now Dmitry seemed really angry. He got to his feet; he looked back at the palace; the sky was growing dark and lights had been switched on inside. Absolutely nobody was around; it was freezing; their breath condensed heavily in the air. Katie looked at the ground; she was shivering. She wanted to get away, but at the same time, she wanted to understand what was happening; she couldn't bear to leave things as they were.

They were silent for a few moments. The wind blew through the square-cut hedges, which stirred and shed some snow; some birds flew up into the air with a sudden beating of wings. Dmitry said, much more gently now, 'Your hands are shaking.'

'So are yours.'

He took her hands in his and they looked at one another. The more they looked, the more they desired, and then against all reason they lay down behind the hedge on Dmitry's coat in the snow and made love to one another. It was cold, damp, uncomfortable, and messy because she still had her period, and neither of them felt any better for it afterwards; in fact Katie, pulling up her pants and tights, for a moment felt she knew what it must feel like to have murdered someone; she felt as if she had killed something inside her, all the good, warm things she had felt for Dmitry, leaving only the bare physical desire which nothing seemed to satisfy.

Dmitry too seemed disgusted with himself. He brushed the snow off his coat and put it back on in silence. Then he said, almost to himself, 'This is terrible. We can't carry on like this.'

'No,' agreed Katie. 'If you just wanted an affair, to see out your time here, let's please end it now.'

'Perhaps that is what I wanted in the beginning,' he said. 'I didn't think about it, much. But you're like a drug, Katie. I can't get enough of you. I never felt like this before.'

She turned and started walking back to the palace. 'Anyway, it doesn't matter now. We've agreed it's over.'

He caught her elbow, walking beside her, and made her look round at him. His face was pale, full of emotion, and he asked her, 'But is it?'

She broke away, starting to run. He followed her to the car park, his pace quickening so that he reached the car at the same time. He opened the door for her; she was breathing hard and wouldn't look at him. Once inside, she wrapped her shawl tightly around her neck trying to stop herself shivering. He started up the car and turned on the heating. He tried to talk to her but she stared steadfastly out of the window.

By the time they reached Vienna it was dark. As always, after an outburst of emotion, Katie felt better, and they had a cake and some coffee in a little restaurant near the station. It was warm and bright inside and Dmitry seemed a little more relaxed. Katie said, 'I don't understand you. You say one thing and do another. I get the feeling you have done something, something of which you are ashamed. And you don't talk to me about anything personal. You've never told me about what happened, for instance, with your marriage. Is it something to do with that, that you can't trust yourself with me?'

Dmitry ordered another coffee and took out a cigarette. Katie removed it from him without saying anything and he sighed, as if he had no alternative now but to talk to her. He said, 'It was a disaster from the beginning, with Masha. She was ambitious and deeply conventional. She wanted me to be something other than I was. I married her out of a kind of desperation, because it seemed to be a last chance – if you are not married at a certain age it begins to look odd. Did I love her? I don't know. If you had asked me when I married her I would have said that I loved her, but in the end I couldn't have done her any more harm if I had hated her and plotted for her destruction. God, how we made one another suffer.'

He drank his coffee and looked up at her. Katie said, cynically, 'Maybe you enjoyed suffering.'

'Yes, maybe; probably my whole people enjoy suffering. I am one of those people who think on the whole we get the kind of society we deserve. But maybe it's something in myself. I have not been very successful in my relationships with women. It seems I do not have the gift of causing happiness.'

Katie felt that she couldn't bear it; she thought she might be in for a long session of Slavic gloom, and she was now acutely aware that Bob and Anna would be expecting her back. The thought of seeing them, in the warmth of their own home, seemed suddenly attractive. She said, 'Well, I am not particularly fond of suffering. At least I don't actually suffer much with Bob.' She got to her feet. 'I'd better get back. You can always telephone me, if you want to see me. You will do, won't you?'

'Yes, all right.' Then he said, 'Take care, won't you? Watch out –'

'Watch out for what?'

'For . . . never mind.'

He made no move to follow her as she walked away. She left him lighting up a cigarette. She turned back to look at him as she closed the door and thought that never in her life had she seen anyone who looked so miserable.

And Dmitry sat at the table, smoking cigarette after cigarette, dimly aware of the KGB man in a raincoat sitting in the far corner. He was afraid to leave and walk out into the darkness; it was as if he expected that at any moment the sky might fall onto his head.

IX

But then: nothing happened.

Dmitry went to work, came home, tried to sleep. There was nothing he could do. Nihal had gone to Stockholm after all; there was silence from Katie. He felt completely deserted. He thought that if he sat tight and did nothing, perhaps the whole situation would somehow go away, resolve itself. It was impossible to go on living in this state of crisis for long.

On Wednesday morning Panini rang Dmitry. He said, 'You know, it occurred to me: we had a batch of tapes we had to pull off the machine when we were doing the back-ups. They've been sitting here for several weeks, since the beginning of January. It happens every so often, we get a faulty batch that don't record well. I was about to send them back when I remembered these were about the time you were interested in – some changes you had lost or something. Do you want me to see if I can get that file for you?'

Dmitry said, 'Hang on, I'll come down.' He didn't want to talk on the phone. He hurried down to Panini's office.

Panini, his shirtsleeves rolled up, gulping down a cup of coffee at once as if he had no time to savour it, made it clear from his attitude that he was being unusually helpful and expected gratitude. He said, 'It's not a big deal. There may be nothing, of course, it was only a thought. I can check it out if you want me to.'

'No, why not?' said Dmitry. 'Have a look for me.'

'Okay, I'll try and get it done for you in the next day or two.'

Dmitry returned upstairs. He didn't expect anything to come of it; he dismissed it from his mind. He went into his office and gathered up some papers; he had a meeting at eleven. Hilde was on the phone. He could hear her saying, 'He's just going to a meeting. No, he'll be here this afternoon. I'll be gone by then, but you could try. Can I take your name so he can call you back?'

Dmitry mouthed at her, 'Who is it?'

Hilde put the phone down. 'He didn't say . . . just said he'll call you back.'

'Look,' said Dmitry, shortly, 'You are not to go giving unknown people details of my movements. Next time make sure you get their name. Was it an internal or an external call?'

'Internal.' Hilde looked pained; she sat down at her desk. She was clearly beginning to find Dmitry impossible. She was still sulky later on that afternoon when she put some letters on his desk for him to sign. 'I'm going now,' she said, 'Is that all right?' It wasn't quite five o'clock.

'Yes, that's fine.' Dmitry was expecting Boris at half past five. Half an hour to kill. The phone rang; somebody wanted some information. He answered the question and put the phone down; almost instantly it rang again. He picked it up; it was Katie. Her voice sounded timid, hesitant.

'I'm in the building. I thought I could come up and talk to you. Are you busy? Can I come and see you now?'

Dmitry hesitated. He didn't know what to say; he didn't see how he could give a flat 'No.' He said, 'I can see you, but I am rather busy. There's someone coming to see me shortly.'

Katie said, angry, distressed, 'I don't want to see you if you can only squeeze me in for five minutes. I want to talk to you properly.'

He softened at once; after all, none of this was her fault. 'Then come. It's all right; I'll make time.' He could always ask Boris to wait. He hung up; he tapped his fingers on the pile of papers on his desk; he was nervous about seeing Katie. He could tell from the tone of her voice that there were going to be tears and remonstrations, and he didn't know how he could cope with them just now. And then – he was not sure whether it was his imagination – he thought he heard a very faint movement in Hilde's room, a slight metallic sound. He wondered whether he should get up and investigate it, but realised he was afraid to. He shifted his weight slightly forward in his chair and reached his hand out towards the phone.

The door opened, a man stepped into the room and shut it behind him in one quick movement. For an instant the man hesitated, perhaps because the main lights in the office were turned off and Dmitry was in shadow, illuminated only by the faint blue glow from the computer screen and the light of the desk-lamp. Then he lifted a gun with casual grace, bringing it up to aim at Dmitry's head. He wasted no time, he clearly did not intend to hang about. But Dmitry did a most unexpected thing. The moment the assassin entered the room, in the split second before he saw the gun, Dmitry knew he had come to kill him; it was something about the way that the assassin looked right through him, as if he had already ceased to exist. Most men would have frozen, ducked, or drawn backwards, and the assassin would have been prepared for any of these responses; but Dmitry suddenly stood up.

The first bullet caught him full in the chest as he rose, and not the head; he staggered back against the window, his right arm flung up in front of his face to shield his eyes from the horror of what was happening. The assassin gave him not an instant's grace before he fired again, two shots close together into the broad target of his chest. Dmitry collapsed behind the desk, falling hard on his back, one arm flung out. The assassin crossed the room and knelt down by his head, putting out his hand to loosen the tie and feel for the pulse in his neck.

The delicate touch of the fingers brought Dmitry out of shock; he thought for an instant someone had come to help him. He opened his eyes and took a deep, gasping breath. He and the assassin looked straight into one another's eyes for a second. Probably the assassin had no doubt in his mind that his target was dying, that most likely he only had a few minutes to live, but he would have wanted to be sure; he turned Dmitry's head away and transferred the gun back to his right hand to execute him with a shot to the base of the skull.

There was a sharp knock on the door and the handle turned. The assassin spun round and aimed the gun, backing away; as a figure stepped forward into the doorway he fired, twice. Dmitry was only dimly aware of what was happening but he saw the assassin toss his gun on top of the body by the door, take off his gloves and throw them down and then, without another glance at his victims, go out, closing the door behind him.

Dmitry lay on his back on the floor as he had fallen. One thought filled his head with unbearable clarity: 'I have been killed.' This thought did not seem to upset him; it just seemed strange; it surprised him that he could still think at all. He had been expecting one shot, then oblivion; when he heard the muffled shots he could not understand what was going on. But now something else was happening to him. He had begun to feel pain. It hurt him dreadfully to breathe; no matter how hard he tried, there did not seem to be enough air. He would have liked to have stopped, but he had no choice, he had to go on struggling.

A shudder went through him. He was cold; it was as if the angel of death had come and perched on his shoulder. He coughed involuntarily and swallowed a throatful of warm blood. He felt sick, but still detached, almost curious; he thought, so this is what it feels like to die. Then the telephone on his desk rang. It rang four times and was silent. The familiar sound seemed to bring him back to reality for a moment; he thought, if I could reach it, I could call for help. He raised his arm and started to try to roll onto his side but a pain so violent and terrible seized him that he nearly fainted.

Then he thought, Katie, Katie will come. Or Boris. Unless he has killed one of them; oh God, perhaps he has killed Katie. He turned his head and saw between the legs of the desk, lying in the half darkness by the door, the figure of a man and a dark stain of blood spreading over the carpet. Then he thought, it was Katie on the phone. She is not coming. If only I could breathe properly; if I could just get some air, if I could get to the phone . . .

Katie took the lift up to the twentieth floor. She was agitated; she didn't know what she was going to say to Dmitry, she thought perhaps it was a mistake to go and see him at all. As she stepped out of the lift she passed a man in a grey suit. She was vaguely aware that someone had stepped in as she got out, but she noticed nothing about him; she hurried along the corridor and paused outside Dmitry's room; she knocked, there was no reply, she knocked again. Then she opened the door.

The first thing she saw was the dead man lying face-down on the floor, his head covered with blood, and the gun lying next to him. She was stunned, but she neither screamed nor ran away; she knew as soon as she saw him that this was not Dmitry. Then where was he? She looked up and saw a hand emerging from behind the desk. Very slowly, as if dreaming, she walked across the room, round the desk, and saw him spread out on the floor, his skin very pale and blood soaking into his shirt. She stood for an instant frozen with terror; she thought at first that he must also be dead; then she saw and heard that he was breathing.

'Oh, no,' she said, 'No, no,' and he turned his head towards her. His lips moved, she heard him whisper, 'Help me,' and then, 'Can't breathe;' she saw fear and pain in his eyes, but she did not know what to do; she was afraid to touch him, afraid to see the damage that was done, afraid he would die or somehow fall apart in her hands. Seized with panic, she started to shout and scream for help, then, coming to her senses, scrambled to the telephone on the desk and dialled the emergency number for the UN medical service which was in the building.

A woman with an American accent answered immediately. Katie said, amazed that she could speak clearly, 'Room 2075, please come quickly, somebody has been shot.' The voice on the phone said, astonished, 'Shot?' and she half shouted, 'Please, hurry, just come, I'm going to call an ambulance.'

'Where has he been hit?' asked the voice, calm, insistent. 'I don't know,' she said, 'In the chest, in the lung, just please come quickly.' She slammed down the phone and then lifted the receiver again, dialled for an outside line, and then the emergency number. This time it took longer to get through; she asked for an ambulance and was clear-headed enough to tell them they could drive right up to the main concourse and stop at the revolving doors near the 'A' tower on the left. While she was talking she heard a man come to the door, exclaim with horror and then run off down the corridor. For the second time she hung up and then, her hands shaking, she turned back to Dmitry.

She thought, I must do something to try to stop the bleeding. She knelt beside him, clumsily pulled out her shawl from under her coat, rolled it into a ball and unbuttoned Dmitry's shirt to see where he had been wounded. There were three small holes close together in the chest from which blood and air were bubbling and gurgling with each agonised breath. The lung must be punctured, she thought, all the bleeding is inside, oh God, he is going to die. Not knowing what else to do, she pressed the shawl over the wounds. As she did so he cried out and shuddered, making feeble movements to push her away with his right hand.

'It's all right Mitya, I'm trying to help you,' said Katie in anguish and turned to look into his face. He was deathly pale and damp with sweat; his eyes were half open but did not seem to see her. He kept turning his head restlessly from side to side, as if by doing so he could escape the pain for an instant. Someone else had come to the door now; she could hear two or three voices outside. A man came and leant over her. 'I've called the doctor; they say they know, they're on their way down,' he said. 'Can I do anything?'

'Yes, please do something, I don't know what to do, I think he is dying,' said Katie; her voice broke and she laid her head on Dmitry's chest in a gesture of despair, not caring that the blood stained her cheek and soaked into her hair. The man did not do anything; he watched her helplessly. 'Why don't they come, oh why don't they hurry up and come,' said Katie, lifting herself up and rocking herself back and forth; Dmitry was worsening by the moment, she could feel him slipping away from her. She did not dare let go of him or take her eyes from his face; she wanted to be with him, holding him, at the moment of death. She stayed as she was, pressing the blood-soaked shawl against Dmitry's chest, watching his face grow still paler, almost blue in colour, his eyes drift shut, and hearing the terrible sound of his distressed breathing.

The man beside her left abruptly; she heard footsteps running and the nurse appeared. She bent over the dead man and Katie cried, 'Please, come here.' She did not care about the other man; but the nurse had already left him, saying in a shocked voice, 'He's already dead. There's someone else . . . ?'

The nurse knelt down beside her. She assessed Dmitry quickly, looking for any other injuries. She asked, 'Does he speak English okay?' and when Katie nodded, started to talk to Dmitry in a low voice, dispassionately, explaining what she was doing. First she put dressings over the wounds in the chest, taping them in place to make an airtight seal. Then she took Dmitry's left arm and folded it across his chest, holding it in place with a bandage. 'I'm going to lift him up a little and turn him onto the injured side,' she said to Katie, 'He's going to choke like that. Can you help me?' Katie nodded; as they rolled him onto his side Dmitry started to yell, a terrible, deep, anguished sound; a sort of convulsion went through him and he struggled to breathe; blood was gurgling in his throat. 'Cough that up and spit it out,' ordered the nurse; Dmitry must have heard her and did so, and Katie watched aghast as a quantity of bright red, frothy blood issued from his mouth. She thought for a moment that this was the end, there was a moment of complete stillness; but after a brief pause Dmitry went on breathing, even more rapidly than before.

When they turned him over both Katie and the nurse saw that he was also bleeding, more copiously, from his back. Katie could not bear it; she must have exclaimed at this outrage, but the nurse said, as if reading her thoughts, 'It's an exit wound.' She tore the shirt away, covered this wound too and then asked Katie to support his head and shoulders to raise them from the floor. Katie did this, kneeling in the blood and resting his head in her lap; she would have done anything to help him live. The nurse smiled at her reassuringly as she reached for the oxygen cylinder.

But Dmitry coughed again and retched violently; he flung back his head, his lips pulled back in a dreadful grimace, the teeth gleaming grotesquely through the blood. The nurse put the oxygen mask over his face and said, 'This will help you breathe. Take deep breaths, more slowly. That's right, you're doing well.' Her voice was soothing, calm. 'Try to keep still now, we're doing what we can, the ambulance is on its way. We'll get you to a surgeon very quickly now.' She looked up at Katie; there was no expression on her face; she did not try to reassure either of them that he would be all right, and Katie did not dare to ask. Then the doctor came in, with another man. He paused by the body for an instant; the nurse said, 'This one is still alive. He's been shot several times in the chest; I've sealed the wounds, he's breathing a little better now. I'll take his blood pressure; can you set up the drip?'

The doctor came over, putting some equipment down on the floor. He turned to Katie and said, 'Let us deal with this, please move aside,' but she relinquished her hold on Dmitry only reluctantly, moving back against the wall. She felt dizzy; she thought she was going to faint; she leaned against the wall and shut her eyes for a moment, but she had to open them again and keep on looking, as if only by her watching and willing him to be all right could he be kept alive.

Dmitry's breathing seemed to have steadied now. The doctor held his right hand; Katie was struck by the care, almost tenderness, with which he stroked the inside of his arm, looking for a vein in which to insert a line and set up a drip. He had trouble getting the needle in; gentleness gave way to brute force, he was swearing to himself; finally he had to take a scalpel and cut down to a deep vein. The nurse talked to Dmitry while it was being done in her low, gentle voice. The doctor bandaged the arm and stood up, holding the bag of serum in one hand, and with the other picked up the telephone and dialled a number. After a moment or two Katie realised he was phoning the hospital; he was asking whether they had a surgeon available. He would have to be there immediately, she heard him say; there wasn't much time. Then she heard him saying, good, good. He hung up and turned to the nurse. 'He'll go to the Laurenz Böhler, they have a cardio-thoracic surgeon there right now,' he said. 'The ambulance will be here in a few minutes. How is his blood pressure?'

The nurse muttered some figure, then added, 'It's still falling.' She pumped the bulb up again; Dmitry suddenly coughed again, moaned and shuddered. She took his hand. She asked quietly, 'Morphine?' but the doctor shook his head. He said, 'It won't be long. He's coping all right, better not to give him anything. He'll be at the hospital in ten or fifteen minutes.'

A silence fell over the room. There was nothing more to be done; Dmitry seemed to be drifting into unconsciousness now, his eyes were shut, he was quite still. Though this frightened Katie, she thought at least there would be no more pain. The nurse asked gently, 'Can you hear me?' and his eyelids fluttered. Katie heard a familiar voice outside in the corridor; it was the DG, Seppo Kaisler. He came into the room. He said, 'The police have been called. No-one is to touch anything here. Who is it that's been killed? How is Mitya Gavrilov?' And then the question Katie had been afraid to ask, 'Will he live?'

The doctor made a gesture with his hand as if to say that it was touch and go. Kaisler said, 'Do everything you can,' and went to the door where a group of people had gathered. 'Go home or get back to your desks,' he said. 'You can't do anything. Please move away now. Anil, come with me; I want to agree a statement for the press.' He turned back to the doctor. 'Tell the hospital I want to be kept informed; they can ring me any time, even at three in the morning. Where are they taking him?'

They continued to talk in low voices, but Katie didn't hear any more; she was suddenly overcome with fear. It occurred to her that Dmitry might never regain consciousness; she felt as if she had lost him already. It seemed an eternity, but could only have been a few minutes, before she heard more footsteps and the ambulance crew appeared. After a brief exchange with the doctor, they lifted Dmitry carefully onto the stretcher, lying on his left side, and carried him towards the lifts.

Despite Kaisler's efforts, a small crowd of people were still standing in the corridor, watching with astonishment and disbelief. Katie stayed beside the stretcher as they negotiated it into the lift. She clung to one of the ambulancemen, terrified that they might leave her behind and take Dmitry away from her. They emerged from the building into the rain; the ambulance stood on the bleak circular concourse, its headlamps shining into their eyes and the blue light flashing on the wet ground. Katie pleaded, 'I have to stay with him, please let me come,' and while no-one replied to her then, once the stretcher was safely stowed they helped her wordlessly into the ambulance. The doctor came in with her; the doors slammed shut and in seconds they were moving rapidly through the night, the vehicle swaying around the corners, the siren sounding.

She felt the vehicle accelerate as they swung onto the motorway; she knew the hospital was little more than a five-minute journey away. Katie clung to the seat, watching the two men check Dmitry's pulse, blood pressure, breathing rate. Her eyes were fixed on Dmitry's bloody chest, watching it rise and fall almost imperceptibly. Suddenly the phrase, 'Dead on arrival,' came into her head; she could not shake it out again, it repeated itself over and over in her head. The doctor and the ambulancemen were watchful, tense; she watched them putting another bag of clear fluid on the drip-stand.

The ambulance slowed down, went round two or three sharp corners and lurched to a halt; the doors were flung open, the stretcher lowered onto a trolley. Katie scrambled out after it through the doors into the brightly lit basement of the hospital. She noticed the pattern of large red dots on the vinyl floor which led from the entrance to the lift, like a trail of blood. They wheeled Dmitry into the lift and the door slid shut behind them; Katie had to follow, running, up the stairs. As she came up onto the landing a doctor in white with thin, fair hair and pale blue eyes was standing by the trolley; two more doctors and a nurse seemed to swoop on Dmitry; they turned him over and his arm fell outward, heavy, lifeless. There was something about the movement of it which struck terror into Katie. Under the bright lights his face was the colour of candle wax; his nose and cheekbones seemed sharp and thin as if the flesh had shrunk away from them; for a moment Katie thought that he was dead. Someone else must have thought the same, because she heard someone ask, 'Is he alive?' and the doctor replied, 'Just about.' Someone asked, 'What's the blood pressure?' and another replied. 'Not recordable.' The nurse was busy cutting off his clothes.

'All right,' said the surgeon, 'Let's get going with this. Get him in the emergency room.' Somebody asked him a question and he said, firmly, 'There's no time.' She heard him giving instructions, snatches of them reached her ears; each one of them filled her with horror, as if they were nailing her slowly into the floor. 'Right, emergency thoracotomy . . . I'm going to open him up straight away. I'll want him ventilated . . . Prepare for intubation . . . venous lines . . . Put him in the left lateral position . . . We need uncrossmatched blood and saline . . .'

Katie could see them through the open door pulling open a metal cabinet; a doctor yanked at the seal to open it and started to pull out the emergency equipment; there was an atmosphere of intense concentration and controlled haste. A woman dressed in a white housecoat came to her side and said firmly, 'Please come this way, you don't want to watch this.' Katie pushed her away violently and continued to stare at what she could see happening through the open door. The woman firmly took hold of Katie's arm; 'Please, you must come with me,' she said.

Katie did not want to move; she wanted to stay with Dmitry, to see everything that happened to him. Then they shut the door. Some kind of cry, as if it was herself who had been wounded, came from her mouth, and she thrust her fist into it to try to silence it. She was led downstairs into a room with two tables and chairs and a glass screen behind which the admissions staff sat, and asked to sit down at the table. Katie sat, her hands neatly folded in her lap, and stared at the table-top. She seemed to sit there like this for a long time. Then she looked at her hands. They were covered with blood, but the blood had all dried now, it was no longer that bright rich colour which had so astonished her. If he dies, she thought, I will never wash my hands – this is all I will have left of him.

'Would you like to drink something?' asked the woman. The voice made Katie jump; she had forgotten she wasn't alone. 'No,' Katie said, 'No, please, nothing.' Then she looked the woman straight in the eye and said, 'Is he going to die?'

'If he gets through the operation, he'll have a good chance. A chest injury like this is very serious, but many people survive worse. You must keep calm, you may have a long wait.'

Katie hardly listened; she knew the woman could give her only vague words of hope, committing herself to no opinion; and anyway, what did she know about it, she was not God. The woman went out and Katie was left alone. She sat in the silent room for what seemed hours. Katie felt a sudden hatred for God, if he existed; if Dmitry dies, she thought, I will hate you forever. It had the intensity for her of some irrevocable curse; she felt blinded for a moment by despair, hatred, and fear. How foolish she was to have hope; he had been shot several times; she had seen the surgeon's look of doubt; probably he was dead already. While some people clung to hope, refusing to admit that death was certain even in the face of irrefutable evidence, Katie had to prepare herself for the worst, pushing all hope into the furthest corner of her mind. In an instant she stood up, opened the door and started to run up the stairs. The nurse saw and tried to stop her, but Katie was too quick; she opened the door to the emergency room but there was no-one in there. The floor was littered with discarded sterile wrappers and there was a lot of blood.

The woman from the admissions department had caught her up now. 'You are not allowed in here,' she said. 'He's in the operating theatre. Please, wait quietly downstairs, and they'll let you know as soon as it's all over. If you behave like this, you'll have to leave.' Once again Katie was led down the stairs. The woman took a piece of paper from the rack on the wall above them and sat down opposite Katie at the table.

'Is he your husband?' she asked. Katie nodded; she did not know what else to say, if she told them he was a friend or lover they might send her away. 'Perhaps you could help us with some details,' the woman said, 'We have to fill out an admissions form.'

'Do you have to fill out the form even if he's dead?' asked Katie spitefully, and the woman said stiffly, 'But he's not dead. There's a good chance he'll be all right. Dr Tobenhaus is a wonderful surgeon.'

Katie was silent. She put up her trembling hand to stroke her tangled hair; it was stiff and matted with blood.

'Perhaps you could give me his name to begin with,' said the nurse.

'Dmitry Nikolayevich Gavrilov.'

'You'll have to say that more slowly. Which is the surname?'

Katie told her. She repeated everything slowly, spelling it out.

'His date of birth?'

This was terrible. She didn't know it. Hadn't he said his birthday was in December? 'December the twelfth,' she said, after thinking for a moment.

'The year?'

'I can't remember, I'm sorry.'

'Well, how old is he?'

'Oh, I don't . . . he's forty-five . . . no, forty-six. I can't think,' she said.

The nurse looked at her slightly oddly, wrote something down, and then asked, 'Address?'

Katie gave it.

'And you are next of kin?'

Katie nodded.

The nurse smiled, said, 'I'll be back with you in a moment,' and left the room. After a few minutes another nurse came back. She carried on going through the form; perhaps it was meant as a kindness to her, thought Katie, to give her something to do while she waited for news. She didn't know the answers to most of the questions. 'I can't bear it,' she said, suddenly getting to her feet, 'I can't bear not knowing. Would they come and tell me if he was dead?'

'Yes, of course,' said the nurse. 'It's been quite a long time. That's a good sign.'

Katie could feel hope awakening in her; this was more painful than her previous certainty that he would die. The door to the room opened; two men came in. They were both imposing, and, from their clothes, their manner and their voices, obviously Russian. The shorter of the two was complaining bitterly.

'This is the Russian Ambassador to the United Nations. He insists on seeing a doctor. There must be somebody here who has some information. What kind of a hospital is this?'

The nurse went out. A few minutes later she brought in a junior doctor. Before he had a chance to say anything, the Ambassador cut in. 'I have been kept waiting downstairs; no-one seems to be able to inform me of anything. What exactly is Gavrilov's condition? I must have some definite information now.'

'He's in the operating theatre,' said the doctor. 'I'm afraid I can't tell you much. He was in a very critical condition when he got here. He could be as much as five, six hours in surgery.'

The two Russians talked together for a few moments. The Ambassador turned back to the doctor. 'I want to be informed at once of any news. Please contact me at this number. We will make arrangements for him to be transferred to another hospital as soon as this is possible. I also want to know about security arrangements here.'

The doctor said, 'The police are downstairs. This is already being seen to. Perhaps if you come with me?'

They left the room. Katie cried, 'But I can't wait five or six hours.' She was desperate; she got up and began to walk aimlessly around the room. Her hands, her legs, were trembling; this didn't seem real, this couldn't be happening to her.

'Do you want to ring anyone and let them know?' the nurse was asking. 'Could anyone come and keep you company? Do you want to let anyone know where you are?'

'No, no,' said Katie. She looked at her watch. The babysitter would have left; Bob would be home by now and looking after Anna. She couldn't face calling him and trying to explain, or even begin to think about how she was going to deal with all this. She started to shake violently, finally giving way; the nurse put her arm around her and Katie began to cry. After a while she stopped; she sat still, feeling hollow, numb, exhausted. She had no idea how long she sat there. The nurse went to fetch her a drink and she was left alone, watching the admissions staff behind the screen chatting and tapping information into their computers and one or two people coming in to casualty. There was a woman with a crying child, a man with a battered face.

Eventually the young doctor came in. He said to Katie, 'I'm sorry, Frau Gavrilov, but the police are here. They are anxious to talk to you, if possible. They tell me you were the first person at the scene of the crime. If you could talk to them it might help locate the killer. '

Katie shot upright; she felt the blood drain from her face; when the doctor said 'Killer' she thought for an instant he must mean that Dmitry was dead; then she remembered the other man. She nodded. They took her to a room down the corridor. It must have been a doctor's office; there were files in a tray on the desk, posters on the walls, a filing cabinet. The policeman she took to be senior was a solid-looking man in a plain suit and a rather drab coat. She didn't take in their names or ranks. He said, 'I'm sorry, I realise you are very distressed. There seems to be some confusion. I was told you were his wife, but the Russian

Ambassador has just informed me he is not married.'

'No,' said Katie, 'I was afraid they would send me away. My name is Katherine Haynes. He was . . . he is my lover.' Her voice became suddenly stronger and she looked up at him; she loved the sound of the words in German, *mein Geliebter.*

'Please tell us what happened.'

Katie told them.

'We understand that you can only have missed the assassin by a few moments. You didn't see anyone, pass anyone in the corridor?'

'No . . . I don't remember. No, there wasn't anybody . . . I don't think I passed anyone at all . . . only someone when I got out of the lift.'

'There was someone by the lifts?'

'Someone got in when I got out . . . I don't remember.'

'What was he wearing?'

'I don't know . . . a suit, a grey suit.'

'Tall?'

'Not particularly.'

'Was he white? European?'

'Yes, European or maybe American . . . I wasn't paying any attention.'

'Was he carrying anything?'

'I don't know.' Katie tried to recall any details. The policemen kept going over it; was there anything she remembered; his shoes; his hands; his face; his hair; any distinguishing marks; was he carrying a briefcase. Katie said no, she couldn't remember, he didn't look like an assassin. But she thought he might have been quite young. That was unusual, at the IAEA. There weren't many men under thirty on the staff.

The policeman tried another avenue of questioning.

'Why were you going to see Dr Gavrilov?'

'To talk things over. I was upset, we were . . .' It was difficult to think of the right word in German. '*Wir hatten gestritten,* we'd had a disagreement . . . I can't talk about all this now.'

'Are you married?' Katie saw the policeman looking at her ring; she nodded.

'Was your husband aware of this relationship?'

'No . . . I don't know . . . please, I can't go through this, not now.'

'You must understand,' said the policeman, 'That although it's unlikely in a crime of this sort, we have to rule out sexual jealousy as a motive.'

Katie looked blankly at him. She couldn't make sense of anything; she didn't know what to say. She said, 'I think I'm going to be sick.' But she wasn't sick; she sat there, trembling. The policeman asked for her address and details of her husband's work, wrote it down in his notebook. 'Is there anything else you would like to tell us? You can't think of any reason, yourself, why somebody might want to kill him?'

'No; why should I?

'There wasn't anything about his behaviour – anything unusual – he didn't speak to you about anything that was bothering him?'

Katie said, her voice breaking, 'He never told me anything. If there had been something going on, he wouldn't have said, would he? Isn't that the way things are? Why are you asking me these questions? Go and ask the CIA, the KGB. What do I know about these things?'

The two policemen exchanged glances. The second one now spoke to her. He had a quiet, soothing voice. 'Don't get upset,' he said, 'Take your time. Perhaps you could explain to us why you said what you did just now?'

But Katie couldn't answer. She was racked with sobs. The policeman found a box of medical wipes on the desk and handed them to her. He got up and left her with the second man. There were voices outside. Katie too stood up and opened the door. A man whom she took to be the surgeon was standing talking to the policeman. He glanced up and saw Katie and instantly looked away again. Katie knew at once this meant bad news. She walked up to him, slowly, her body feeling as heavy as lead. The surgeon turned to face her.

'Sit down,' he said. 'My name is Tobenhaus; I have just been carrying out the surgery on your husband . . . please.' Katie sat, and the surgeon sat down opposite her. He looked exhausted.

'Well,' he said, taking a deep breath, 'He is alive. The operation was successful. We stopped the bleeding, we have removed two of the bullets and resected part of the lung. Fortunately the bullets did not hit any other vital structure, but we have had some problems. We will have to see. The next few hours will probably tell us.'

Katie said, sharply, 'What are you trying to tell me? What is wrong?'

'It may be nothing. The body has had a severe shock. He was almost dead when he arrived here, no blood pressure, then a brief respiratory arrest. Normally we would expect him to resume normal respiration after the operation and regain consciousness after half an hour or so but this has not happened. There is of course a possibility that there has been some damage . . .'

Katie said, 'You mean, brain damage.'

'Well, this is only a possibility, I would not want to lower your hopes at this stage.'

Katie wouldn't let this go; she pressed him further. 'But if he's not breathing . . . are you telling me . . . you might have been operating all this time on someone who was brain dead?'

The doctor looked increasingly uncomfortable. 'Look, personally I do not think things are so bleak. It's far too early to say. You should be quite hopeful. We'll let the sedation wear off, see how things go. As I said, the operation has been a complete success,' and he started to list all the things that had gone well, things which, if Dmitry had suffered brain damage, were of no significance.

The police were leaving. There was nothing for them to stay for. Katie stared at the floor and wondered if she would go mad. A nurse came round the corner. She was hurrying. She said to the surgeon, 'Please come here,' and he excused himself and left her. Katie lay down on the floor and felt the cold vinyl against her cheek. She tried to count to drive all other thoughts out of her head. There was a clock on the wall. It was after midnight. She wondered if they would let her see Dmitry. She wondered if she wanted to. If he was going to die, she would rather see him later, without all the tubes and monitors. But suppose he didn't die, and instead . . . she couldn't let herself think about it. Until now she had not thought there could be anything worse than death. Her whole body was convulsed with violent fits of shivering.

A nurse walked briskly down the corridor. She sat Katie up, put her arms round her shoulder. She said, 'It's all right, you know. He's come round. He started fighting the respirator, he's responded to some simple commands. They think he'll be all right.' Shortly afterwards the surgeon returned. He was smiling. He said, 'We've had a false alarm. They'll clean him up and transfer him to intensive care. In a little while you can go and see him.'

Katie sat and waited for perhaps an hour. Time had now lost all meaning, but it didn't matter. She would have waited forever if in the end she knew he would be all right. Another doctor came. He said, 'Just five minutes, please. He is very weak. We are giving him further transfusions. Pain is normally quite severe after a thoracotomy; we have given him morphine, he's pretty dopey. You can see him, reassure him if you like, but please don't ask him any questions.'

Katie was asked to put on a white coat over her clothes and, when she had done so, the doctor led her into the intensive care unit. There was an overwhelmingly oppressive atmosphere in the ward; it was dark, the walls were painted a deep green, and it was lit only by small lights at each bedhead. There were eight beds in the ward; Dmitry was lying in the nearest one to her in the centre of the room. She was afraid as she approached him. She remembered looking first at his feet, which stuck out from under the green sheet; she thought they must be cold. Then she looked at his face. It was very still; there was some faint colour in it; he was not dead. He was breathing on his own; to her surprise there was nothing obscuring his face except the fine plastic tubes which delivered oxygen to his nostrils. She hesitated, then put out her hand to touch his arm; it was warm, but he did not respond. He had intravenous lines in both arms, into which dark red blood and fluid flowed, tubes coming out of the chest to drain the blood and air and a monitor over his heart. They had cut him open from the middle of his chest all the way round almost to the spinal column; she could see the incision under part of the dressing, neatly stitched and beaded with fresh blood.

'There were three shots,' explained the doctor without emotion. 'One of the bullets went through, two lodged in the chest, one just millimetres from the heart, one shattering the fifth rib. Still, he's fit and healthy, there should be no problem. The loss of half the lung shouldn't affect him. He looks really terrible, it must be a shock to you, but in these cases people usually make a quick recovery.'

Katie stared at Dmitry's face; then he opened his eyes. He looked at her; she knew he recognised her. Relief and desire flooded through her; she wanted to embrace him; she wanted to possess him utterly, completely. She felt an instant's irrational envy for the surgeon who had saved his life, had put his hands inside his body. She saw his fingers tremble and realised with overwhelming pity that he was too weak even to lift his hand; she put her hand on his, slipping her fingers through his fingers, being very careful because of the intravenous tube.

'Mitya, it's all right. You're going to be all right.'

He murmured something she couldn't understand and then, more clearly, 'How bad?' He seemed confused. She saw him looking up, at the lines of blood going into his arms, at the tubes emerging from his chest, trying to work out what had happened to him. Then he looked at Katie; she realised she must be an alarming sight, her white face looking at him with a terrifying mixture of pity and love, her hair tangled and thick with blood. He shut his eyes again and murmured, 'Oh my God.'

'It's all right,' said Katie again, not knowing what else to say. 'The doctor has operated, he says you'll be fine.'

She was not sure if he had taken it in. After a while Dmitry opened his eyes again. His voice was blurred and indistinct; she had trouble making out what he was saying. He whispered, 'They will try again.'

This frightened Katie. She looked at the doctor, but he clearly hadn't understood him, perhaps not speaking English well. She said, 'No, Mitya, no; you are safe here.' His eyes, under the bright light of the lamp, were very blue, much bluer than she remembered. Now he seemed to stare at her as if he had never seen her before; something did not quite connect.

He said, making a great effort, 'Kaisler.'

She turned Dmitry's hand over, holding it gently with both her own. 'Please, don't distress yourself.'

The doctor tapped her arm. 'Enough, now.'

Dmitry said, 'Must tell Kaisler.'

'Yes, of course,' said Katie, nodding, 'He knows, he knows.'

'No, not this,' said Dmitry, struggling to make his meaning clear, 'Valadares.'

The doctor touched her arm again; he said, 'I'm sorry.' Katie leaned over and kissed Dmitry's brow. 'I'll come back in the morning.' Dmitry's eyes were shut; she didn't know if he had heard her. She went out into the corridor. 'You must go home,' the doctor said, 'He'll be all right now. You need some sleep.'

Katie went downstairs to the call-box. Bob answered the phone on the first ring as if he had been sitting by it, waiting; he didn't sound angry, on the contrary, his voice was very calm and controlled. 'Are you still at the hospital? They told me you were there. I came over but they wouldn't let me come up or speak to you. Why, for God's sake, didn't you phone me?'

'I couldn't, not till I knew . . . he's going to live.'

'Is he?' Bob sounded distant; she imagined this news would not please him. She supposed that he knew everything, now; at least she wouldn't have to break it to him. He said, 'I'll come and pick you up.'

'What about Anna?'

'No, Marianne's here. I asked her to babysit while I came looking for you. Wait there; it won't take me long.'

'It's all right, I can get a taxi.'

'No, it's better if I come.'

She sat by the entrance, near the coffee machines. A few haggard-looking people were standing in a group. Bob was there in ten minutes; he came through the doors and looked at Katie with horror. She knew she looked terrible, her eyes watery and red-rimmed, with blood on her hair, skin and clothes. He must have found this shocking, as if her lover's blood proclaimed her intimacy. Shocked out of his calmness, he started on her at once.

'What the hell were you doing with him?' Bob demanded. 'You don't know what's going on. You could have been killed yourself, you stupid little fool.'

'Please don't talk to me about it, I can't bear it. I thought he was dead, I thought . . .' and she began to cry.

'You told the hospital you were his wife. What's it all about? Marianne has been telling me about your lies. I suppose this means that you've been screwing him.'

'Yes, I have,' said Katie simply.

He stopped in his tracks. 'Since when?'

'Since . . . oh, since the end of January, I think.'

Bob struck her on the face. He hit her hard, so hard that she fell to the floor. She cried out and turned, scrambling to her feet, and began to run back down the corridor; Bob ran after her. He grabbed hold of her arms and she began to struggle to get free, kicking and trying to bite. She started screaming, 'Let go of me, let go of me, I'm staying here.'

'You're coming home,' said Bob. 'Stop, you're making a scene.' The receptionist came towards them; he said angrily, 'Stop this, you're disturbing people. They have problems of their own, you know.' Bob let go of Katie and she stood facing him, breathing heavily.

'Come on, you must come home,' said Bob, suddenly, firmly, switching moods in an instant. 'Think about Anna.'

Katie was too exhausted to protest further. He led her to the car and they drove home in silence. She was unable to stop shaking; her face was smarting from the blow, but she supposed she had deserved it. Half-way home, as if repentant, Bob took her hand in his, and she didn't take it away. They drove in silence; Katie was grateful not to have to explain any more.

When they got home Marianne stared at Katie with disbelief. Bob shook his head at her to tell her not to say anything and showed her to the door. He held out a black plastic bag for Katie to put her clothes in and sat her on a chair while he ran her a bath. With difficulty she controlled her shaking arms and washed her hair; the bath turned the colour of pale onion skins. When she was clean he held out a towel for her and helped her out of the bath. He dried her very gently, patting her as if she were a child. Finally he helped her into her towelling robe and put his arms round her.

This kindness was more upsetting than his anger. She said, 'I don't understand. Why are you being kind to me? I don't deserve it.'

He said, 'We can talk about that later.'

She said, over and over, 'I'm so sorry, I'm so sorry.' She went into Anna's room to check that she was all right, and kissed her forehead as she slept; then she went into the living room and stood there helplessly. Bob was sitting on the sofa, his head in his hands. When she came in he let them fall away in a gesture of despair. 'Oh, God, this is a mess,' he said. Katie knew she had hurt him terribly; she was overwhelmed by guilt. She sat down next to him.

'I thought there was something,' Bob said. 'You seemed different to me, but I trusted you. I just can't believe it. All this time, and with *him.* Why?' Katie couldn't answer. Then Bob said, very quietly, 'What condition is he in? The hospital weren't very forthcoming. Is he in intensive care? Is he out of danger now, do they think?'

'Yes.'

'Do you want to leave me for him? Is that what you've been planning?'

Katie said, 'No . . . oh, no Bob, it's not like that. I was going there this afternoon to try to sort it out with him. I couldn't carry on as we were. I think it was all over . . . I don't know. How can I know anything, after this?'

Bob stood up, asked, 'Do you want something to drink?'

'Some cocoa.'

Bob went into the kitchen. She heard him taking out the saucepan, opening the fridge; then she heard him suddenly groan and bang his fist on the table. He swore violently. He came back into the room, and stared at her. Katie looked at him, dismayed. He said, 'I can't bear this. What is it all about? He didn't tell you anything, did he? Anything at all?'

'No,' said Katie, 'No, nothing.'

Bob looked at her; she saw disbelief in his eyes. She said, 'He was trying to say something in the hospital . . . I didn't understand . . . someone's name, Valadares; I think that was it, Valadares. That doesn't mean anything to you, does it?'

'And that was all? He didn't say anything else?'

'No, he was very drugged.'

Bob went back into the kitchen and brought her the cocoa. He walked to the window, turned round, walked across the room, came back to her. He put his arm on her shoulder but somehow the gesture was without warmth. He said, 'I'll mention it to Kaisler in the morning. I'll be seeing him anyway. Listen, we'd better sleep. I expect the police will want to ask questions tomorrow. I suppose I will be considered a suspect, the jealous husband, won't I?'

Katie asked, 'Where were you, at half past five?'

'In a meeting. It doesn't matter about an alibi, if that's what you're thinking, Katie. Anyone can hire a hit man.'

Katie said, 'I just don't understand why.'

Bob sat and looked at her. 'Well, if he lives, as you say he will, we no doubt will know.'

X

Nihal had arrived back in Vienna on the Wednesday morning. He had returned to his apartment at midday and had lunch with Bradman Abeywickrema, the Sri Lankan friend who had been staying in his flat while he was in Stockholm. Bradman had made himself well and truly at home, moving in his books, a small television and even, now, his own chair; Nihal could see he was going to have trouble persuading him to move out again. Bradman had nowhere to go, and wanted to hang on in Vienna in the hope of getting himself some more work.

In the late afternoon Nihal had gone downstairs to chat to the people in the first floor flat. He must have stayed there in the end for a couple of hours. Then he had gone over to check the mail at his office in the Bankgasse. When he left at about nine o'clock it had started raining; he had on his wrong shoes; by the time he turned into the Tulpengasse his socks were hopelessly wet. He dug in his pockets for the keys, but noticed that the gate was open. A policeman was standing in the shadow.

Nihal hurried to the gates. Under the arch, in the shadow, lay a body under a black sheet. Nihal knew it was a body; there was a dribble of blood coming from it, looking black as oil in the light of the streetlamp. Nihal, horrified, asked, 'Who is it?'

'Someone from one of the flats.'

Nihal opened the door, checked his mailbox, and took the lift up to his flat. He opened the door and went inside. Bradman was not there.

The door to the balcony was open; the flat was freezing cold. A half-drunk cup of coffee was on the table. Nihal realised suddenly what had happened; it was Bradman, and he had fallen – or been pushed – from the balcony. He ran downstairs and said to the policeman in his terrible German, 'But this is my friend.'

The policeman nodded. 'Please, my colleagues are coming shortly. They will want to talk to you.'

Nihal waited for the police to come. There were several of them; the inspector spoke good English. He asked Nihal to identify the body; he pulled back the black sheet. Nihal looked with apprehension, but there was nothing horrible about Bradman's appearance; the injured side of the head lay against the ground, hidden from view; his eyes were open and the expression on his face was as innocent as a child's. So, this was death.

Nihal took a step backwards, said, 'Yes, it's him. You had better come upstairs.'

Nihal took the inspector up to the flat. He said, 'I haven't touched anything, not even the cup of coffee. I suppose you will have to fingerprint everything.'

'Tell me who your friend is.'

Nihal told him.

'Could this be a suicide? You say he was depressed and without a job.'

'Yes. He was depressed, he was penniless, he had no work, he was in a bad way. But he was not that depressed.'

'Had he been staying with you long?'

'Oh, he came about a week ago – he was in the flat while I was in Stockholm. I came back this morning.' Nihal could see exactly what had happened. 'They probably thought I was in the flat . . . I was downstairs with the neighbours. It must have happened at about eight-thirty, while I was at my office.'

The inspector took notes. He went over Nihal's movements down to the last detail. Nihal felt shaky; it was beginning to sink in. Then he thought of the incident when Dmitry stayed the night. He said, 'Another friend stayed the night about two weeks ago. He thought he heard someone on the balcony. I went to look; but there was no-one there. It's probably not connected.'

'Who was this friend?'

'He works for the IAEA.'

'His name?'

'Dmitry Gavrilov.'

The inspector did not write this down in the notebook; his pen had frozen just above the surface of the paper. He looked up. He said, 'Dr Gavrilov stayed with you two weeks ago?'

'Yes, it must have been Wednesday of the week before last.' Nihal knew that the policeman knew something; he stopped talking. They looked at one another.

'How well do you know Dr Gavrilov?' the inspector asked.

'Quite well – we meet for a drink from time to time. I see him at the Agency.'

'You don't know what happened this afternoon?'

'No, I haven't spoken to anyone. Why? What happened?' Nihal had begun to feel uneasy.

The inspector looked as if he didn't know what to say for a moment; he knew Nihal was a journalist; perhaps he didn't want to say too much. Then he said, watching Nihal very carefully for his reaction, 'Gavrilov was shot in his office late this afternoon. He was hit three times in the chest. Another Russian from the UN was with him; he was shot in the head.'

At first Nihal didn't understand; it was too horrible to take in. The words made sense, but he couldn't relate them to reality at all. Then all the strength seemed to drain out of his legs; he sat down on the edge of the sofa bed. He realised that he had not taken the warning signs seriously enough; now he couldn't pretend to himself any longer that this was some kind of game. He asked, still unable to believe it, wanting to be sure there was no mistake, 'You mean Dmitry Gavrilov is dead?'

The inspector was cool and impersonal. 'No; my information is that he arrived at the hospital in a moribund state and is undergoing emergency surgery.'

There was a long silence. Nihal could imagine Dmitry, at this very moment, laid out on the operating table; he wondered if there was any chance . . . and, oh God, somebody would have to tell Katie. He asked if he could smoke; it was ridiculous, of course, to ask for permission in his own apartment, but that was the effect these policemen had. He said, 'I suppose they could have been after Gavrilov when they came here tonight. But that doesn't make sense. But it wouldn't have been Bradman they would have been after. They killed him instead of me; I suppose that's an obvious mistake.'

'You mean that someone had reason to kill you?'

'It's possible they wanted to stop me writing a particular story.'

'Would you tell us about it?'

Nihal said, 'I suppose I have to. Do I have to do it tonight? This is rather a shock.'

The inspector said, 'Well, I imagine you may be wanting police protection. I think you should tell us all about it now, don't you?'

The inspector questioned him for over two hours, listening intently to everything Nihal said, and writing rapidly in his notebook. At one point he broke off and asked if he could use the phone; he seemed to be asking someone else to come. Then the inspector said that if what Nihal said was true, it was clearly a matter for the intelligence services, and someone would be joining them shortly.

An Austrian intelligence agent turned up a little later. He told Nihal he would be frank with him, and that it was very unlikely that they would ever clear up the crime. 'In these cases, you must realise that it is most unusual to ever get the killer. We are dealing with a professional. There is nothing to link them personally with the crime. The people who hire them never know their true identity and they do not know who they are working for. Usually they have two, three identities at their disposal, passports, and so on; they know all the tricks. It is not unknown for these people to have plastic surgery to change their appearance. We hope of course to get a description of this assassin from Dr Gavrilov if he lives, but by then he will probably have left the country.'

The inspector shrugged. 'Still, we must do what we can. Is there anything else you can tell us which you think may be of help?'

'No,' said Nihal. 'I suppose I will have to contact Bradman's family. Oh God, what will they think? I suppose in a way I am responsible. I should have warned him.'

'Well, you've got a story out if it, if you've the heart to write it,' said the inspector on the way out. 'If you're quick you can get something in the morning papers.'

Dmitry woke sometime in the night. The ward was in darkness, except for the light thrown by the individual lamps above the beds. The darkness and silence were tangible, oppressive. There was a sound of something ticking near him; it was too slow to be a clock; the sound irritated him. Eventually he realised it was the drip.

His mouth was unbearably dry; the drugs they had given him must have worn off a little, because now he was aware of pain, a deep aching which seemed to involve his whole left side. Breathing was painful and difficult, despite the oxygen. Nobody came to him; he supposed they had no need, they had the monitors. He could not sleep properly; he kept seeing, over and over, the assassin entering the room, the glint of the light on the metal of the gun, the horror of looking down into the black barrel. He still did not understand why he wasn't dead.

The door to the ward opened and closed; he saw the light from the corridor shine in. He heard muffled footsteps and thought someone might be coming, but no-one did. He must have dozed on and off; the night seemed interminable. It would have been all right if he had been able to stop thinking, but incoherent chains of thought kept breaking through the muzziness in his head. What frightened him most was the fact that they might still think it was not too late to silence him. Everything seemed ruined; his term in Vienna, his relationship with Katie, his health, perhaps his career. He felt utterly alone.

Towards morning something woke him again. A doctor, a man he hadn't seen before, was fiddling with his drip. For some reason this made him feel uneasy; in the dim light he tried to make out the man's features more clearly. He asked, 'Who are you? Where is the other doctor?'

'He's not on duty. There'll be someone coming to see you in the morning. That's done now; try to sleep.' The man went away. Dmitry thought; what could be easier than to send someone into the hospital, dressed as a doctor, to put poison in the drip. In panic, he called out, despite the pain this caused him. He called several times; they must have heard the desperation in his voice. In a few minutes, the doctor came, and a nurse; without even saying anything to Dmitry, the doctor took his left arm, put a band round the upper arm and turned the arm over to expose the elbow. 'Make your hand into a fist,' he said; when Dmitry did not respond, the doctor took the hand and roughly pressed the fingers together. 'Like this,' he said. 'We are giving you something now to help you sleep.' The nurse passed him the syringe.

Dmitry said, trying to express himself clearly, 'What are you giving me? I don't want it.' He felt the prick of the needle in his arm and the pain of the fluid being injected. For a moment he thought he would be sick. A feeling of light-headedness came over him; the bed suddenly felt very soft; he was sinking into it. Little fragments of thoughts broke off and whirled round in all directions. The green walls spun around very slowly, and in the distance, so far off as to be hardly visible, a small squat figure which was death crouched behind a hedge.

Nihal had spent a wretched night. In the early morning he had finally rung the hospital and established that Dmitry was still alive. Later he had tried to ring Katie but no-one answered; he assumed that she might be at the hospital. Nihal didn't know what to do.

At about midday he went up to the International Centre and took the lift to the twentieth floor. The area round Dmitry's office had been taped off and the police were at work. Nihal found Hilde having coffee with one of the other secretaries in the office. She was very upset and had obviously been crying.

Hilde had spoken to the police earlier. She had told them about the call she had taken yesterday morning; the man had had a faint accent, but she couldn't say what, North American, Australian; she was not very good at placing accents and her conversation had been brief. She said, 'I shouldn't have told him anything. Dmitry told me off for it; I was angry, I was getting sick of his paranoia.' Her face crumpled. 'Obviously it wasn't paranoia at all.'

Nihal went and spoke to the IAEA press officer, Anil Kumar, who was very helpful. The reports from the hospital that morning had been good; Gavrilov's condition was described as stable and it was anticipated that he would make a good recovery. Anil knew quite a lot about what had happened; he had been up there shortly after the shooting and had seen Gavrilov carried out on the stretcher. He had spoken to the man who had tried to help Katie and had gone to fetch Kaisler. He told Nihal that the assassin had left behind his gun and gloves; this might help the police. The gun had a silencer; nobody had heard the shots. There was no clue as to how he had got into the building undetected.

Anil said that there was also some confusion about Kulagin, the man who had been in Gavrilov's office. He was employed as a translator but Nihal might as well know, because the rumour was circulating everywhere, that it was said that Kulagin was KGB.

The Russians had made an enormous fuss. It was a diplomatic incident. The Ambassador had complained in the strongest terms about lack of decent security arrangements, both to the UN and to the Austrian Government. The security people were downstairs with Kaisler now being hauled over the coals. It had emerged that Gavrilov had been to the UN security staff two or three weeks ago and had been given no more help than the standard photocopied sheets of paper on personal security precautions. This was unforgivable.

Since the UN building had extraterritorial status the police had had to be formally asked in to investigate. Anil didn't know if they had any leads. He showed Nihal the Viennese papers, spread out over his desk; they reported only the bald facts under headlines such as 'Russian atom scientist shot.' Nihal sat and read through them. One of the papers mentioned that Gavrilov had a mistress who was married to another UN employee but did not name her. Anil gave him the official statement; it simply condemned the incident and said it had nothing at all to do with the work this respected scientist had been carrying out for the IAEA.

Anil's phone kept ringing; he answered then passed callers over to his assistant to read out the statement. He told Nihal that all the journalists were asking about espionage. 'They are obsessed with spying,' he said. 'Just because it's Vienna, he is a Russian and because of the nuclear angle. I tell you I am going crazy here.'

Nihal went back upstairs towards Dmitry's office. He thought how perfectly the building had been designed for an assassination. The curved shape of the building meant you could not see along the corridors for more than ten or fifteen yards and made it easy for the assassin to have entered the office without being noticed. Opposite the door to Dmitry's office was a link between the two corridors which ran along either side of the building, providing four escape routes. Nihal thought about it carefully. The assassin would have had to check that Hilde was not there. That had been easy; he had telephoned earlier, from an internal phone, to check their movements. He must have known he had to choose exactly the right time; he would have known he had to be quick. Still, it didn't take more than a minute to open a door, fire the shots, get out again. The assassin could have gone into her office and shut the door, entered Dmitry's office by the connecting door. Probably he had been interrupted, shot Kulagin, dropped the gun, and got out quickly. It was well timed, too; there were as many as 3,000 people leaving the building at the end of the day, and even if the alarm had been raised it would have been impossible to stop and question everyone.

Nihal looked at his watch. He walked down the corridor. It took only a few seconds to reach the lifts. This is where he would have been sweating, thought Nihal, waiting for the lift to arrive; it could take a few minutes at that time of day when the lifts were busy. Nihal timed the whole operation, from leaving the lift to getting out of the main entrance. The assassin could have been out of the building within a few minutes of the shooting. He must have taken the chance that the alarm would have been raised; that's why he had to leave the gun, in case they were searching people leaving the building.

It was a brazen operation. The man would have had to have the most immense self-confidence. He must have entered the building earlier in the day, and spent some hours in the building. He would have had to have got hold of a pass that gave him permission to enter. He couldn't get in as a visitor, because visitors had to check through the airport-style security at the front entrance. Nihal as an accredited journalist had a permanent pass and could get in unchecked; in fact, it had always occurred to him that this was a weakness in the security system. He took the lift to the press bureau on the ground floor.

Lopez Varga, who dealt with press accreditation, looked irritated when he saw Nihal coming. He said, 'Can I help you? I'm afraid I haven't got much time. We're incredibly busy. The police have asked us to check all the journalists accredited to us because of this business last night.'

'Will that include me?'

'Well, since you've been here so long, not really. We're looking mainly at people who've been accredited in recent weeks, especially for this refugee conference. We've got to contact every single newspaper and broadcasting station to check that they're known to them. What do you want anyway?'

Nihal smiled sheepishly. 'You've just told me what I want.'

'Cough,' said the nurse, leaning over Dmitry, putting her hand reassuringly on his chest. 'I know it hurts, but you must cough all that stuff out of your lung or you'll get an infection . . . There, that's much better. You'll be much more comfortable in a day or two when we take the chest drains out. I want to lift you up a little.' She and a second nurse rearranged the pillows. 'We might even get you sitting up a bit tomorrow. There. Are you comfortable? The police are here to see you.'

Dmitry could hear the doctor's voice: 'Don't stay long. Just ask what is absolutely necessary.' He turned his head. The doctor, impersonal in his white coat, asked Dmitry how he was feeling. He didn't bother to reply. Two policemen, in plain clothes, stood by the bed. Finally one of them cleared his throat.

'Herr Dr Gavrilov, I'm Fritz Altmayer, Inspector for the Austrian police, and this is my colleague Peter Doleszal. Are you happy to talk in English? We can arrange for an interpreter if you prefer.'

'English is fine.'

'Please tell us when you feel unable to talk any longer. We just have a few questions to ask you now.'

Dmitry nodded. They asked him to describe the assassin and to go through exactly what had happened. The inspector took it all down; the second man, Doleszal, kept his eyes on Dmitry's face and watched him intently. When Dmitry had finished Doleszal spoke for the first time.

'How did he hold the gun? That could be important.'

'With both hands – I don't think he used the sights – he aimed at my head but I stood up. He fired once, then two shots close together'

'And two shots at Kulagin?'

'Yes.' Dmitry asked, 'Is he dead?'

'Yes. He was shot in the head. He must have died instantly.'

Dmitry turned his head away and tried not to show the emotions that followed quickly after one another; horror, anger, guilt.

The police waited a few moments. Then Altmayer leaned forward. 'I'm going to show you four photographs. I want you to look at each of them carefully and tell me whether one of these is the man who shot you.'

Altmayer held them up. Dmitry looked; he was given plenty of time. He said, 'I don't know. The third one, it could be him.'

The two men exchanged glances. Altmayer said, 'You couldn't swear to it? Look again.' He held the photograph up again. Dmitry looked; he couldn't say for sure. The man looked similar, but he didn't have any certainty about it. This was strange, because when he closed his eyes he could see the man's face quite clearly in his imagination. He said, 'I don't know.'

'But you picked him out of these four.'

'The others are definitely not him.'

'Well, the man you picked is a likely candidate. He entered the building posing as a journalist for the *Chicago Tribune*. He had received his accreditation from Lopez Varga who saw him three weeks ago. He presented a letter from the editor saying he was attending the refugee conference, but the *Chicago Tribune* have never heard of him. Of course, it's easy enough to fake a letter.

'As for this photograph, it's possible it's not him. This is a problem we often have with such security passes. You send in the photos and they check the photo on the form is the same as that on the pass, but as long as there's a passing resemblance, nobody checks if it's really the person applying. Still, this is a help. But even if it is him, which you're not certain of, I have to tell you that the chances of tracking him down are quite small.'

'I see.'

Altmayer paused, then asked, 'Do you have any idea who might have wanted you dead?'

Dmitry looked at them both. Altmayer had a solid, not unkindly-looking face. The other man was polite but distant, courteous; he looked like a civil servant; Dmitry thought he was from the Austrian secret service. He did not know what to say. How could he begin to explain things? What would the Austrians do with such information? Or perhaps they already knew some of it; they would surely have their eye on Richter, he had operated on their territory, his propellant at least was being manufactured in Linz. He wanted to say nothing about the Brazilians till he had spoken to Kaisler at the IAEA. An unbearable weariness overcame him; perhaps it was best to say nothing. They wouldn't press him, not at the moment. He shut his eyes. He heard Doleszal say, 'Dr Gavrilov –' and the other man, 'Later. Leave it till later.'

But Doleszal persisted. He said, 'Herr Dr Gavrilov, this is very important. Two people other than yourself have been killed. Do you know of any motive? This shooting was in your office – we believe you were the prime target. This was a cold-blooded, professional assassin. These things do not happen for no reason. Do you know why? You only have to answer yes or no.'

Dmitry was confused. 'Two?' He saw the two men look at one another.

Altmayer said, 'A friend of this journalist you know, Nihal Senanayake. It appears to be a case of mistaken identity. Do you think this might be connected?'

'I don't know. Nihal . . . Nihal is all right? Who was killed?'

'His name was Bradman . . .' Altmayer couldn't pronounce the surname. 'He was staying in Senanayake's apartment.'

'My God.' Dmitry was distressed; he couldn't think straight. He could hear the doctor talking to them in German in a low voice.

Altmayer said, 'One last question, please; let me repeat; do you have any idea who might have wanted you dead?'

Dmitry made a great effort. 'Look. I understand the situation perfectly, I know you have to go through the motions.' He turned to Doleszal. 'Are you from the Austrian secret service?'

Doleszal made a gesture which could have been either denial or acceptance.

'I am sure you will already know some of what is involved – please don't come here asking me to exhaust myself answering your questions. This may involve a foreign government. Ask the Director General of the IAEA. I have not been able to speak to him.'

'The IAEA have issued a statement saying that this is nothing to do with your work there. I have just seen the Director General and he has confirmed this to me himself.'

'Please, is this an interrogation?'

But the doctor had already stepped in. He ushered the police out and Dmitry was left alone. After a few minutes a nurse came in and touched his arm. She said, 'A Mrs Haynes is here to see you. I have asked her to wait. Would you like to see her for a few minutes, or shall I ask her to come back later?'

Dmitry hesitated. He felt exhausted, he wanted to sleep; he hated Katie to see him in this state; yet he could imagine her distress if they told her she couldn't see him. He said, 'Yes, I'll see her.'

Katie had been kept waiting for something like two hours. She had asked repeatedly for information but they had told her nothing. Sitting there brought home to her the truth about her position; the doctors did not feel they had to consult her about Dmitry's health, or inform her of what they might be doing; she didn't have even the right to see him; her feelings, their relationship, might as well not exist. The dinginess and smell of the hospital brought back to her the agony of last night and filled her with depression. Finally, just as she was beginning to be anxious that there might be something wrong, the nurse came and took her up to the intensive care unit.

Dmitry lay awkwardly in the bed, his limbs seeming too long for it, half propped up on pillows, still attached to various tubes. He was unshaven and his face looked colourless, almost grey. He lay with his eyes closed; his breathing seemed shallow, with a slight catch in it as if it pained him. Katie sat down on the chair by the bed, and said quietly, so as not to disturb him if he was sleeping, 'Mitya?'

He opened his eyes at once. He looked at her for a few seconds and then, as if even this was too much effort, he closed them again.

'I had trouble getting in to see you,' said Katie, trying not to cry and to keep up some semblance of normality. 'Usually they only allow close relatives.'

Dmitry didn't reply. He opened his eyes and looked at her without expression, cold, detached. She felt as if he had crossed over some thin line that separated the living from the dead and was having trouble stepping back again. She had never felt more distant from him than she did at that moment.

She said, alarmed by this feeling, wanting to provoke some response, 'Bob knows about us.'

'Does he?' It seemed of no importance to him.

'Well, perhaps it's a relief. It doesn't seem to matter much just now.' She wanted to take his hand but something prevented her from doing so; she was afraid he wouldn't want her to. After a few moments Dmitry turned his head slightly towards her and asked, 'Can you do something for me, Katie? Can you make two phone calls for me?'

She said, 'Yes, of course. Who to?'

'Can you ring Kaisler? I want to talk to him. It's important. Do it from the payphone here.'

'Yes, I will.'

'And can you ring my sister for me? I'll give you her number in Moscow. She will go crazy when she sees the papers.'

'Yes, of course.' Katie took the number down. She asked, 'Is there anything else?'

'No.' He shut his eyes.

Katie reached out to him suddenly and touched him, unable to hold back. 'Mitya, I love you; I thought you would die.'

He said, in an almost agonised voice, 'I know.'

'What is it all about? You must tell me; I am frightened.'

He looked at her again with that blank look. 'I'm sorry, Katie. Look at me, I can't help you.' He closed his eyes. It was like a dismissal; Katie thought perhaps she should go, but she could not bear to, so she stayed there for a little longer, till she realised he was sleeping. She got up, handed her white coat to the nurse, and went downstairs. As she walked down the stairs she heard footsteps behind her; it was one of the Russians who had been at the hospital last night. She walked down faster; the man followed her.

'Mrs Haynes,' he said, 'Just a moment, I want to ask you . . .'

'No,' said Katie.

He touched her arm. She stopped and turned around; although he had spoken politely, there was something threatening about him. He said, 'They are not being very informative. How is he? Is he conscious? Has he said anything to you yet?'

'No.' Katie started to walk downstairs again; the man fell in behind her. She went straight to the payphone near the main entrance and picked up the handset; her hand fumbled with the purse. She dropped the change on the floor; he picked it up and handed it to her. She glared at him. He smiled and moved away a few paces, turned his back to her. She turned back and dialled the IAEA's number and asked for the DG's office.

The Russian came back. He reached across and put his hand on the phone, cutting off the line. He said, 'May I say something to you?'

Katie turned on him with violence. She didn't understand; she was frightened, but also angry. She said, 'How dare you? Leave me alone.'

'Did he ask you to make this phone call?'

'No.'

'Because if he did, he has put your life in danger as well. Do you realise this?'

The soft voice was menacing. Katie said, 'I shall call the police.'

'There is a policeman round the corner, if you want one. But you won't get much joy out of them. I assure you that I have your interests at heart. I will take you up to the UN if you like. The car is outside . . .'

Katie was shaking with fear. She wondered whether to run for the door; surely he couldn't do anything to her in a public place. All her worst fears and suspicions seemed to be true; wild thoughts raced through her head. She said, 'Get away from me.'

'Come and talk to me over here,' said the Russian, pointing to the area by the coffee machines. Katie shook her head. 'I am calling my husband. I don't know what you want. It's all over between me and Dmitry, if that's what you want to talk to me about. I am never going to see him again.' She picked up the receiver and dialled again; the Russian stood and watched her. She dialled Bob's direct line. His secretary answered. She said, 'Sue, is Bob there? It's Katie.'

He was in a meeting. She put the phone down. 'I am going home.' she told the Russian. 'If you try to stop me I shall scream.' He stepped towards her and she hit him very suddenly in the face with her bag. He put up his hand to protect himself but the bag still gave him a glancing blow and the buckle grazed his cheek. He looked at her in astonishment as Katie turned and rushed outside.

It was pouring with rain as she ran down the steps; the rain felt hard on her skin and it was bitterly cold. Her hand shook as she fished for her keys in her bag; she was soaked by the time she got into her car. She pulled out of the parking space; as she reached the traffic lights she saw another, blue car do the same.

Katie's hands were shaking on the steering wheel. She thought, this isn't happening. They are going to try to kill me too. She thought of turning back to the hospital; but she was afraid of the Russian. She tried to think where the nearest police station was; she didn't know. She thought she would go to the UN, it was just a five-minute drive, and she would be safe there.

She drove quickly. The heavy rain made her even more nervous and when she reached the motorway she steered into the outer lane and stayed there. At the turn-off to Wagramerstrasse she saw the blue car not too far behind. She would have to stop at the traffic lights. They seemed red for a long time; the blue car was just behind; through the rain-spattered back window she saw a door open.

She pushed down the button that locked the doors and heard the locks turn. They couldn't open the doors; but they could shoot through the window. She couldn't believe she was thinking such things. She had to drive away. There was a gap in the oncoming traffic; Katie thought she could make it and drove forward. Several cars hooted at her; an oncoming car had to brake and swerve; she had to halt in the centre of the crossing. Cars were hooting at her from all sides. She saw the lights change and shot forwards. She drove the short distance to the international centre at breakneck speed, piloted the car onto the side of the road, got out and ran. She didn't even bother to shut the door behind her; she was too frightened to look back. She ran up the steps to the entrance lobby and flung herself through the doors, dishevelled and panting for breath.

The security men stared at her as she paused, breathless, and sank to the floor. One of them came up to her, but she pushed him away, getting to her feet and heading for the receptionist. She said, 'I have to see my husband urgently. He's in the IAEA – Bob Haynes. Will you ring up to him please?'

He was still in a meeting. They wouldn't let her in without checking first; she was not on the list of expected visitors. Katie asked to speak to his secretary. Eventually they said she would come down. Katie was still shaking. Sue didn't understand what it was all about but said Katie was definitely Haynes's wife. Katie was issued with a visitor's pass; Sue took her through across the courtyard.

Sue said, 'Whatever is it? You look dreadful.'

'I have to go and see Kaisler. I'll explain another time; I'm sorry. I just had to get into the building.'

She left Sue and hurried to the DG's office. His secretary looked up from the typewriter and stared at her; she must have looked wild, still breathless and her hair all wet from the rain; she said, 'I have to see Dr Kaisler at once.'

'What is it about?'

'It's about Dmitry Gavrilov.'

The secretary knew who she was; she went through to Kaisler's room. She came back and said, 'He will see you in a few minutes. Can I get you a cup of coffee?'

Katie nodded. She sat down on a chair and tried to compose herself. Kaisler came out of his office and asked her to come in. He invited her to sit down.

He looked at her anxiously, as if he feared a hysterical scene. 'You are Bob's wife, aren't you? I think we've met. I have an important meeting shortly; perhaps you could be brief.'

'I've just come from the hospital. Dmitry Gavrilov wants to talk to you urgently.'

'We sent someone down there this morning, but apparently he wasn't allowed in to see him. You spoke to him, did you? How is he?'

'He said it was urgent that he spoke to you.'

Kaisler frowned. 'It's almost impossible today, but I will try – or I could ask Lascalles. Do you know why he has asked to see me?'

'No; of course not.' There was an awkward silence. Neither of them knew what to say; she supposed by now her affair with Dmitry would be an open secret, and she knew that Kaisler would disapprove; he hated anything irregular.

Kaisler stood up. 'This is all very regrettable . . . Don't worry, I will arrange something. And now, if you'll excuse me . . .'

Katie ran along the corridor to Bob's office. He looked surprised as she stepped in, but only for a moment. He came over to her, and sat her down on a chair. She felt absolutely drained, exhausted; she felt as if she couldn't do another thing.

It was a relief to find Bob looking his usual calm self. Often in the past this had infuriated her, but now she found it reassuring. He put his hand on her shoulder, 'Honey, tell me what's happened. You look terrible.'

Katie started to cry. 'I don't know what's going on. I am so frightened. Please, please take me home and let's talk about this.'

Bob put his arms awkwardly around her. He said, 'Okay, okay, honey – I'll cancel my appointments. Don't cry, I'll take you home. Don't worry, everything is going to be just fine.'

XI

Dmitry was transferred to a private hospital in the afternoon at the request of the Russian Ambassador. Immediately he felt better. From the window of the large, white room he could see the top of a tree; the pale afternoon sunlight shone down on it, gilding the branches. He lay very still, watching the light change. By late afternoon a thin ray of sunshine entered the room; he watched it shift slowly along the bed and eventually touch his arm. He was surprised by how warm its touch was on his skin.

It was very quiet. From time to time a nurse came to check he was all right or to do something to him. Dmitry's fear had given way now to a mild euphoria. They hadn't managed to kill him. He was going to be all right.

Now it was getting dark. Dmitry felt each minute pass as if it were twenty; he wondered if anyone would come. He had asked the nurse to ring Katie's number; the nurse had come back and said she had spoken to Katie's husband, who said she was resting and didn't want to speak to anyone. Dmitry, for the first time, felt acute jealousy; he had always tried not to picture her with Bob before, but now he could imagine her all too clearly with her husband, seeking refuge in his arms, asking him to protect her. And why hadn't Kaisler come?

When they came and told him that Lascalles was there to see him instead, he was bitterly disappointed. He had never liked Lascalles; he was one of the old school, wedded to the theology of safeguards. As he anticipated, Lascalles did not like what Dmitry had to say. He sat, embarrassed, awkward, by the bed, and listened to him with obvious distaste. When Dmitry had finished he sat in silence for a while, tapping his fingers on his knees nervously.

'This is a very delicate matter, as you know. We can't do anything unless we are officially informed by a government – you know the score. I am not doubting what you say, it is possible, of course, but unless we have proof . . .'

The full implications of what Dmitry was saying seemed to slowly sink in. He got to his feet and walked to the window, moved a vase of flowers a little to the left to centre it, and then came back again. 'But what you are suggesting is terrible. This could have appalling repercussions. You are suggesting a maze of corruption, in Brazil, over here . . . There will be a loss of confidence in the entire safeguards programme. It could adversely affect the whole nuclear industry.'

'Fuck the nuclear industry.'

Lascalles almost jumped, startled. He looked at Dmitry as if he were not sure that he had heard him correctly. Dmitry went on, very quietly, 'The report recommends inspection only in another six months. We can't let it go on. The reports have not yet gone back to the Brazilians. We can query it. We can say there were problems – samples were lost, the report was inadequate. Surely we can invent some rubbish that will justify a repeat inspection.'

'I think that would be difficult. The Brazilian Government would say that was our fault, they would not have to co-operate.'

'Not if they had something to hide. But I don't believe that is the case. I am sure they will want to get at the truth as much as we do.'

Lascalles was thinking aloud. 'It is a different matter if we had proof. There is this facility for special inspections . . . I will relay what you say to the DG, of course . . .'

But in the end this was not necessary. Kaisler came in person that evening. He said that Panini had looked at the faulty tapes and pulled off a file which Müller had altered two days before his death, in which he claimed to write the truth about Valadares. It seemed that they had been operating a second gas centrifuge cascade, undeclared to the IAEA. The cascade which had been inspected was producing highly enriched uranium; Müller claimed to give the correct readings. Müller himself, or someone else with access to his password, must have deleted this information a day or so later.

Kaisler said that he was acting at once. He had summoned the Brazilian Ambassador to the UN and was going to request a special inspection.

He sat and looked at Dmitry. 'I am so deeply sorry you have had to go through all this. Lascalles had mentioned to me before that you had had your concerns. He said he had given you a thorough hearing. I hope you don't feel let down by us; under the circumstances there was nothing we could do.'

'No,' said Dmitry, 'No, there was no proof. But I want to ask you – who will organise the special inspection?'

'Well, I don't know. I imagine Bob Haynes will, he handles the Brazilian inspections.'

'Because I am not sure . . . but I think he too may be suspect.'

Kaisler seemed stunned. 'Why?'

'I can't explain. It's just an instinct. He chose the inspectors – you remember there was some trouble about that? Then you remember he was opposed to my going, said it would create problems, which of course it did. And isn't it unlikely that Müller would have changed the file back himself? Someone must have done it, someone inside the IAEA.'

'Yes, you're right – that must be considered.' Kaisler hesitated. 'Of course it is an open secret now that you have been involved with his wife.'

'What has that to do with this?'

'I'm sorry, I shouldn't have mentioned it.' Kaisler frowned. 'Of course we will have to carry out an internal investigation . . . Don't worry, we shall get to the bottom of this. And you, try to forget it for the present. You must concentrate on getting well.'

Katie was woken by the phone. She picked it up, disorientated, and glanced at the clock; it was nine o'clock. She could hear Bob's electric razor buzzing in the bathroom.

'Hello?'

'This is Georges Lascalles from the IAEA. Is Bob there?'

'Yes, hold on . . .' She cupped her hand over the phone and called out to Bob.

He came in, took the phone from her, and sat down on the bed. 'Haynes here.'

There was a long pause before Bob spoke. 'I see. I was going to take this morning off, my wife is not well . . . Yes, I understand, but can't you tell me what it's about? Yes, of course I'll come . . . Ten o'clock is fine . . . See you then.'

He hung up. He sat very still on the edge of the bed. Then he said, 'Shit.'

'What is it?'

'The DDG and the Head of Administration want to see me. I'm sorry, I'll have to go.'

'That's all right. What's it about?'

'I haven't the slightest idea. I'll get you a coffee.' He came back in a few minutes with the coffee; Anna was following him. He put on his jacket and adjusted his clothes in the mirror. She thought he looked preoccupied, distracted. He kissed her cheek almost casually and went out.

Katie lifted Anna onto her knee and cuddled her for a few moments, rocking her to and fro. When Anna became fidgety Katie told her to go and fetch the snakes and ladders board. She was afraid to go out and she didn't want to take Anna to kindergarten. She thought, there is no reason to be afraid any more, it's all over now, but it was hard to be rational about such things. She wanted Bob to come back quickly; she didn't like to be alone. She remembered with a start that she hadn't rung Dmitry's sister in Moscow; she supposed it was too late now. She felt guilty, desolate, as if she had somehow managed to fail him in everything. She thought she had at least gone to tell Kaisler.

Bob returned at midday, looking pale and upset; his tie was crooked and even his suit looked strangely crumpled. She had never seen Bob like this before; she was shocked; she thought he looked ill. Anna came running out of her bedroom and tugged at his sleeve, but for once, he had no time for her. He brushed her away, saying, 'Anna, go and play. I have to talk to your mother.'

When Anna had been persuaded to go and watch television Katie asked, 'What is it?' A series of wild thoughts went through her mind; that the police might have accused him of trying to kill Dmitry, that he had been threatened, that somebody else had been killed. Anything seemed possible.

'I've resigned from the Agency. They haven't formally accepted it.'

'But Bob – why?'

'You're not to talk to anyone, least of all your friend Nihal, is that clear? Some of it will come out soon, he can wait till it's official, but you're not to say anything about me. It seems there has been a cover-up of a diversion of nuclear material in Brazil. Hans Müller was one of the inspectors who was involved; the other is in Argentina but can't be contacted yet. Of course this whole thing is indirectly my responsibility, I organised that inspection. But that isn't the problem. The problem is your dear Dmitry. Is the man off his head? You know him so well, tell me, is he unbalanced, or what?'

'What's happened?'

'Only that he's made an accusation against me, that I've been involved in the cover-up, that's all. They won't find a shred of evidence. They told me they were suspending me while they look into it. They were very polite, quite charming in fact. "Of course, it's only a formality . . . ," "We just have to be quite sure . . ." "You understand that this is a very delicate situation with Brazil." After six years with the Agency, this is what I get.'

'What did you tell them?'

'What did I tell them? I told them I thought Gavrilov was crazy, always have done. How the fuck do you know that he wasn't involved himself, I asked them. I told them he had some kind of grudge against me, that he was having an affair with my wife. Of course they knew that already, it seems that everybody has known all about it, everyone except me of course.' He shot her an accusing look. 'God, the humiliation. Can you imagine what it feels like? But I'm not staying on under the circumstances. In fact, I've had it with the whole goddamned place.'

Katie had never heard Bob talk like this. She was trying, very slowly, because she couldn't think straight, to put things together. Then she said, 'Is that why Mitya was shot? Because of this business in Brazil?'

'I imagine so.'

'But why? Because he knew something?'

'God knows why. These Russians are unfathomable, I can tell you.'

'But then, Hans Müller . . .'

'Yes, it looks like Lieselotte was right. I imagine they killed him also. Maybe he was going to spill the beans – either that or he thought better of what he'd done and killed himself.'

Katie wondered why, if Dmitry knew about this, he hadn't told her, confided in her. She would have understood. He wouldn't have had to go into details. Now she felt hurt and confused; she didn't understand why he hadn't trusted her if he had nothing to be ashamed of. And Bob, why had Bob never told her anything either? Or hadn't he known? She stared at him, unable to understand anything. Sympathy for him swept over her and she leaned forward and put her hand on his shoulder. 'But Bob, if you resign . . . What will you do?'

'Oh, I don't know. I don't think it will be too hard to get a job. Besides, like you, I've had enough of Vienna. I've had enough of all this shit here, I'd like to start over. How do you feel?'

She said simply, taking her hand away and stepping away from him, 'I don't know.'

He put his head in his hands for a moment; then he sat up, running them through his hair to smooth it, and looked directly at her. He said, 'Katie, in spite of everything, you believe I still love you, don't you? And Anna . . . I don't want a divorce. I'm prepared to forgive you . . . What do you think? Are you willing to try again?'

Katie knew this was the right thing to do; but it was still hard, even after all this, to give Dmitry up. With an effort she said, 'Yes, I think that's best.' And then, having said it, she realised that she did think it best, in fact, she felt she wanted nothing more at that moment than to get away from Vienna, to leave all this behind. Perhaps she and Bob could be happy again; perhaps they might even have another child.

Bob, seeing the expression in her face change, came and put his arms around her. 'So it's all over, now, is it, with Gavrilov? Are you sure? I can't stand the man, but I suppose he must have meant something to you, and I appreciate this must have been a great shock . . . I don't want you to regret this.'

Katie turned her face up to him, 'I'm sure.' She let him kiss her on the mouth; it was a gentle kiss, cold somehow, without desire. He slipped his tongue into her mouth and put his hand on her breast but as he did so Anna came and stood in the doorway, and, seeing her, he broke off, sat on the chair and held his arms out to her. Katie stepped back with relief. Then, without any warning, she felt despair strike her and she started to sob loudly, uncontrollably. Bob sat and stared at her, horrified, and Anna, unable to bear the noise that she was making, went and hid her face in his lap.

Katie did not feel able to go and see Dmitry and confront him with her decision. She knew that seeing him would be painful and difficult for them both, and she was not sure how he would react; it seemed unfair to hurt him further while he was already suffering. She knew that she should see him, but she kept postponing it, and the longer she postponed it, the more difficult it seemed to go. She had told Nihal she would write to him, and she tried, but her letters seemed painfully inadequate; she tore them up and burned the pieces so that Bob wouldn't find her half-formed expressions of love and regret. At a certain point she realised that she was not going to see him and she wasn't going to write to him either. She wondered if he would telephone her but he didn't; she thought that he must know by now that it was all over.

Nihal telephoned her to ask how she was feeling. She said, 'All right. Have you seen Mitya? How is he?' He asked her straight out, in accusing tones, 'Aren't you going to see him?' and she said, 'No, I promised Bob. We agreed we would give our marriage another go. I was going to write to him . . . I don't know. I can't go and see him now, Nihal, and risk starting the whole thing up again.'

She thought probably Nihal would tell him. Once or twice in the next few days she found herself by the phone, tempted to call the hospital and ask to speak to him, but every time she knew she couldn't do it. It was better left this way; she was sure from his silence that he felt the same.

Nihal finally went to the hospital at the end of the week. Dmitry was sitting in a chair by the window, wearing a dressing-gown over his pyjamas. A book was open on his knee but he wasn't reading it. The hospital had said that Dmitry was much better and would welcome a visit, but Nihal, who hadn't seen him since before the shooting, thought that he looked awful.

'How are you feeling?' Nihal asked, awkwardly, with that vague embarrassment the healthy feel in the presence of an invalid. He crossed the room and had a look at the view outside the window.

Dmitry said, 'Better. It's good of you to come and see me. Get a chair. Come and tell me what's been happening. You usually know all the news.'

'Well, the story's out, to some extent, as you'll see from the papers There'll be an emergency meeting of the board. That will be a waste of time of course – Collor's already announced an internal inquiry at CNEN. The head of the Valadares plant, Oliveira, that guy you told me about, has committed suicide; he shot himself in the head. Eduardo Cruz has disappeared – left his house in the morning as usual and never turned up at work. Recently he was spending large sums of money his wife couldn't account for. The other thing you might like to know is that Bob Haynes resigned. Nobody can quite understand why.'

'Resigned? Or was dismissed?'

'Resigned, I think. It's all being hushed up a bit, I only heard through Katie . . . Has she been to see you?'

'No, not since I was transferred here.'

Nihal hesitated, feeling awkward again. 'Has she written?'

Dmitry didn't reply. His hand was shaking; he saw Nihal had noticed this and said abruptly, 'It's because I can't smoke. I shall have to give up for good; I don't know how I'm going to manage it. So what have they said about Haynes?'

'That he resigned for personal reasons. He's leaving Vienna; quite soon, I think.'

'And I suppose you are going to tell me she is going with him.'

'Yes.' Nihal was angry with Katie; he didn't like the fact that it was he who had to break this news. He said, 'I'm sorry, I thought you knew. She told me she was going to write you a letter.'

There was bitterness in Dmitry's voice. 'Well if she does I certainly won't waste my time reading it.'

'Oh, it's not as bad as that. She's very upset, she's very concerned about you.'

'Oh, well, of course. But then, I hear so many expressions of concern from all sides. It's rather touching, really.' He shifted slightly in his chair and as he moved a sudden spasm of pain crossed his face; Nihal wanted to say something or offer to help, but found that he couldn't. Dmitry, recovering, went on: 'So, what I want to know is: will the IAEA come clean about the bribed inspectors? After all it won't create much confidence.'

'I imagine they will, if they can. It depends. If Kaisler thinks this will come out, he'll make something of it, try to turn it to his advantage, I suppose. You know, inspectors being vulnerable, the need to strengthen support, that kind of thing. Kaisler in any case is very keen on being open about these things. Of course, I could spill the beans . . . but I won't. Well, what would be the point? I was going to do that book for them . . .'

Nihal paused and went over to the window, gazing out at the tree. 'I made some inquiries about Liliana Richter for you, Mitya, by the way. There isn't anything very definite. It's true her father has connections with the military. He had connections with everybody . . . he is known to be right-wing. Probably he knew this guy, Oliveira. This Brazilian journalist I know was going to see if he could find anything more.' Nihal noticed that Dmitry seemed to have lost interest; he stopped talking at once. He asked, 'Are you tired? Do you want me to go?'

'Well, maybe . . . But come again soon, won't you? I rely on you to tell me what is going on.'

Nihal's feature was published in *North-South* without causing much stir at first. Then other people started picking up on it. Articles began to appear in the German press and there were other pieces in a London Sunday paper and the *International Herald Tribune*. One accused Richter of meeting with a representative of Pakistan secretly in Paris. Another paper claimed to have been leaked information that showed that RASAG was secretly pursuing missile deals with a number of Middle Eastern countries. Another accusation was that Richter had links with a Chilean company which was developing anti-tank missiles.

The German Government was clearly embarrassed. It tried to distance itself from the project, in particular the terms of the contract with Paraguay. In a TV interview the German Foreign Minister said, 'We did not know the full details, we were not asked about the details. This is a purely private affair between a German company and the development of the area.' When the interviewer pointed out that a copy of the contract had been sitting in the Ministry's files for over two years he refused to comment. When pressed further, he said that as far as he knew the RASAG project was for purely peaceful purposes. In any case, since no sensitive parts were made on German soil, it was not a German problem.

Shortly afterwards the Bolivian Ambassador stood up in the United Nations General Assembly and accused Paraguay of pursuing military ambitions and potentially threatening to invade the Bolivian Chaco, which unlike the Paraguayan Chaco, was known to contain oil. He hinted that there was American backing for the project. 'The RASAG project . . . is the barrel of a gun pointing at the heart of Latin America,' he said. The terms of the contract were attacked as 'Blatantly neo-colonialist . . . this is a violation pure and simple of the sovereignty of an independent state.'

Nihal had not been able to pursue the RASAG story further. He hadn't succeeded in getting money to go to Paraguay; and anyway, recent experiences had given him a healthy fear of poking his nose in where it wasn't wanted. He had also been busy with the IAEA end of the continuing Brazilian story. Eduardo Cruz was still missing; it turned out that he had been booked on a flight to Venezuela the day he disappeared but had never turned up. It was now feared that he was dead. Heads had rolled in the Brazilian navy. New accounts had been submitted by CNEN to the IAEA, but not all the highly enriched uranium produced at Valadares could be accounted for. A significant quantity was still missing; Brazil had been given thirty days to account for it by the UN Security Council.

After a week in hospital and ten days at a convalescent clinic, Dmitry had discharged himself and was now at home under a police guard. He appeared to be acutely depressed and hardly saw anyone, although Hilde came in every day to bring his mail and to deliver his shopping. Nihal was worried about him and made a point of dropping in regularly on some pretext or other, for example to show him a copy of a recent article by

Nihal's friend Jaime dos Santos which had appeared in the Brazilian press claiming that a hunt was on for the highly enriched uranium in secret military sites in Amazonia. One of the military from Valadares who had been arrested had been quoted as saying that he would not reveal what had happened to the missing material even under torture.

Dmitry had been told by Kaisler that there had been no definite evidence to implicate Bob Haynes, and that since he had strenuously denied knowing anything, no action could be taken against him; besides, he'd resigned. Articles had appeared all over the world criticising the IAEA's safeguards programme and it was clear that Kaisler didn't want to give them any further ammunition.

The day before they were due to leave Vienna Katie went to have lunch with Nihal at the International Centre. She had hardly seen him in recent weeks; she'd had the distinct impression that he'd been avoiding her, but when she met him he seemed as pleased to see her as ever. She deliberately didn't ask about Dmitry till the end; he told her he was fine, he had started back at work that week, but she thought she detected a faint disapproval of her which she found very saddening. She left Nihal with a warm embrace, making him promise he would write to her; and, after leaving him, on a sudden impulse went up to Dmitry's office on the twentieth floor.

When she emerged from the lift she began to feel shaky. As she walked along the corridor she thought, this is not a good idea. She reached his door before thinking better of it and turned and walked away back to the lifts; she pressed the button, thought again and turned back, retracing her footsteps. The door to Hilde's office was open; Hilde was sitting at her desk, typing, and frowned at her as she stepped in. She asked, 'Have you got an appointment?'

'No.'

'You're not meant to see him without an appointment . . . I'll go and tell him you're here.' She returned in a minute and said, 'He says he's very busy. You can go in if you like.' Hilde was hostile, protective. It occurred to Katie that she might be in love with him herself.

Dmitry was not sitting at his desk; he was standing facing the window, reading a document in a blue folder. He didn't look round when she came in. She shut the door behind her and said, hesitantly, 'I didn't know you were back at work.'

'I started yesterday.'

'You seem well.'

'Do I? So everybody tells me.' His voice sounded tired, as if he did not have the energy to talk to her. Katie felt a dry sensation in her mouth, and suddenly weak as if all feeling had drained out of her. She thought, I was right to end it, it would never have come right between us. She wished she hadn't come. He was still reading the file, intent, concentrated; Katie took a couple of steps towards him, putting out her hand to touch his arm without being aware that she was doing so, and as she did he suddenly turned round, evading her, and said abruptly, 'Please don't touch me.'

She snatched her hand back as swiftly as if she had received an electric shock. He folded the file, put it down on his desk, sat down, picked up the phone and pressed one of the numbers, asked Hilde to get someone on the phone for him. Then he hung up. Still without looking at Katie, almost as if he dared not, he said, 'Why did you come here?'

'I just came to say goodbye. I'm leaving Vienna with Bob. I expect Nihal told you.'

'Yes, he did tell me. I wish you well, then.'

She almost hated him at that moment; she knew she had to leave, but she could not stop herself from looking at him for a moment longer. The fact that he did not look at her enabled her to do so; she would not have been able to look him in the eyes. She felt at least relieved that there were no obvious signs of his injury, but she also thought that there was something changed about him. He looked thinner, paler, but it was not just that; some of that inner energy which had charged him was gone, and because he did not look at her or smile she had a strange sensation for a moment that he was not real, that this could not be happening, as if she was looking at a reflection in a mirror, or as if he had indeed risen from the dead.

She said, slowly and painfully, 'I did hope that I might keep in touch with you . . . that we might . . .' She could not bring herself to say, be friends.

'I see. Well, write and let me have your address.'

Katie could not speak another word; she felt as if everything was crumbling around her. She watched him for a moment as he started to go through some document at great speed, crossing out words and phrases, jotting things in the margin, writing something on a sheet of paper which he pinned to the front; he tossed it into his out tray and picked up another sheaf of papers. She looked on as he wrote out a memo, his handwriting large and childlike as he wrote in English. It was impossible to believe now that the same hand with which he held the pen had once caressed her, touched her most intimate places, had aroused in her the most immense desire and pleasure.

Katie turned to go. Hilde came in; she said, 'Excuse me. The Director General just rang to say he will see you now. There are some letters for you to sign; I'll leave them on your desk. They've confirmed you're going to the Buenos Aires conference. And Personnel rang, they want your medical report.'

'Yes, of course, it's in here, perhaps you could drop it in on them.' Then he turned to Katie and said, as if she were a casual acquaintance, 'I'm sorry, I have to go. If you'll excuse me . . .' He opened the door for her to leave.

Katie walked slowly down the corridor. The carpet and the grey walls absorbed all sound; she felt that if she screamed the place down nobody would hear her. She went to the lift. As she stood waiting, listening to the distant whirring of the cables in the long shaft, she wondered for an instant whether to go back and try to explain herself, give the reasons why she hadn't been in touch with him, to say everything that was in her heart, but she pushed aside this desire at once; she would only make a fool of herself. Better to put it all behind her as he had done and accept that it was finished.

The lift doors opened and she stepped in. She pressed the button for the ground floor and cast her mind back over everything that had happened, trying to find an image of him less painful than the recent ones to hold in her mind. As she did so she saw quite clearly Dmitry's face in the garden at Schönbrunn, looking at her as she said, 'It's over,' and his soft voice asking her: 'But is it?'

PART TWO

SOUTH AMERICA

I

Katie stood on a street corner in Asunción, watching the wind from the Rio Paraguay stir the pale green branches of a tree. Below her stretched the city, the low, white colonial buildings, the dusty squares, and then the muddle of wooden shacks along the river. The warm, clean air caressed her face and for a moment she felt happy.

She had come to Asunción two days ago to join Bob for three weeks; he had come out here to take a temporary job, as he had told Katie, with a German engineering company. Since leaving Vienna Katie had been staying outside London at her parents' house with Anna, while Bob jetted from one place to another for interviews, looking up contacts and trying to get some work. When Bob had rung to tell her that he would be away in South America for three months she had broken down on the phone and asked if she could come and join him; Anna would be fine with her parents for a short while. Bob had, somewhat reluctantly, agreed.

But since arriving in Paraguay she had been shocked to discover that Bob was working for Wolf Richter. He had told her almost as soon as she had arrived. They were sitting in a restaurant, half shaded on the balcony, a cool breeze stirring the branches of an overhanging tree and rustling in the palm leaves. The bright light, the warmth, the throaty roar of traffic and the cries of unfamiliar birds reminded her with a jolt of her lost tropical childhood, the paradise from which she had been banished at the age of eleven back to grey old England and the purgatory of boarding school. She closed her eyes in pleasure, feeling the sun on her skin, when Bob's words penetrated her dream.

'We're staying with the Richters, they've rented a house here, it's very pleasant. I'm working for his company.'

Katie's eyes flew open. 'But I read about it in the papers, Nihal wrote something. He's making missiles, isn't he? He's a crook.'

'Most of what Nihal wrote was quite wrong. They're not missiles, they're rockets – launching systems for satellites.'

'That's potentially the same thing.'

'That's not his intention. Look, it's work. I had to get a job – it's only temporary.'

'You shouldn't have taken it. What good is it going to do your career?'

'What he's doing is quite legal. In fact, it's an exciting concept, Katie. Of course he has enemies, because he's threatening the status quo, but there's enormous potential.'

Katie felt slightly sick. She didn't want immediately to start rowing with him, as soon as she had stepped off the plane. She studied the menu. 'I'm not interested in this kind of argument. I just wish you had told me what you were doing, that's all.'

After lunch Bob took her back to the large house on the Avenida Mariscal Lopez, a huge, colonial style mansion set among trees, with green shutters and a lantern on the porch. He took her upstairs, to a spacious room overlooking the garden, and she flung herself on the large, antique bed. The journey had taken her twenty-two hours, changing planes at Rio de Janeiro and São Paulo, and she was exhausted. She fell asleep almost instantly, sleeping right through to wake up at dawn to a thin blue light filtering through the shutters and a cock crowing hoarsely from the garden.

Bob was lying asleep beside her, naked under the sheet, his skin tanned and smooth. Katie felt light-headed and very sick. She got up, went to the bathroom and stood over the sink, retching. Was it the meal she had eaten yesterday? Surely she couldn't have picked up some stomach bug already? But she knew this feeling; she'd had it before. She realised with sudden horror that it was a very long time since she'd had a period.

She sat down heavily on a cane chair in the bathroom and tried to remember when it had been. She hadn't given it a thought, with the move from Vienna, trying to find a school for Anna in England, worrying about Bob's work. She knew that stress and travel often upset things, but she was not sure. She had been so tired, for three or four weeks now she had been feeling exhausted; she had put it down to disorientation and depression after moving from Vienna and all the trauma she had been through. But the moment she thought about it, she knew; she must have been suppressing it, not wanting to think about it. All the signs were there. In the mornings she had sometimes felt that characteristic twinge of nausea as she had poured the coffee at breakfast. How could she have been so stupid? It was well over two months. How could she not have thought of it before?

And if it were over two months, then it was Dmitry's child. She remembered now when she had last had her period. It had been ending that day she and Mitya had made love at Schönbrunn. She had thought that had been safe; obviously it had not been. She stood up and crept into the bedroom, searching in her bag for her diary. She knew her periods came, on average, every three-and-a-half weeks; but there had been shorter intervals. Her cycle had always been irregular, one of the reasons, she supposed, why she had not got pregnant easily after Anna. She tried to remember when she and Bob had first made love again; it hadn't been for at least a month after he found out about her and Dmitry, when he was with her in England. But it was possible. She supposed that she would know for sure if she asked a doctor; these days a scan could estimate the baby's age quite accurately.

But what could she do? She got back into bed, lying beside Bob, trying to work it all out. If she was pregnant by Dmitry, it might be best not to tell Bob and to go and quietly have an abortion. But she'd been brought up a Catholic; she didn't know that she could do this, and it was not as if she had found it easy to have a child. Then, should she write and tell Dmitry; perhaps he had a right to know. Or was that fair? And what would he do about it? Bob would, of course, assume it was his unless she told him otherwise. But surely he would recognise at once when the child was born that it was not his; or would he? Would she be capable of living such a lie?

If Bob knew the child was Dmitry's, he would want her to have an abortion, and this she would never do; so if she told him, she would have to leave him; and then there was Anna.

Then she thought, perhaps it won't come to anything, anyway. Her last pregnancy had ended in a miscarriage. It might be best to say nothing to anyone until she was sure; there might be no point.

She rolled over in bed, unable to sleep, and dreading Bob's awakening. A wind stirred the trees in the garden and through the closed shutters came the melancholy calling of some bird.

Katie crossed the street, coming from the doctor's, and felt a wave of irrational joy sweep through her. The result of the pregnancy test had been positive. She had asked at one of the big hotels for them to recommend her a doctor, and, having found one, been examined and told that she was between eight and ten weeks pregnant, though it was impossible to be sure.

Her first impulse was to tell Bob she felt ill and simply go home, to buy herself more time to think, both about the pregnancy and what Bob was doing, and to try to make a decision. But there were several reasons why she rejected this. Going home would mean a major confrontation with Bob, in which things were likely to come out; it would be expensive, as she had a cheap ticket which she couldn't change. Also, she couldn't face the thought of the journey so soon. And what would she do in England, with her mother watching her like a hawk? Her mother would be bound to notice something wrong. Perhaps she was better off leaving things as they were.

She went to have a drink in the Gran Hotel del Paraguay, and found a seat outside on the terrace. On impulse, she picked up some hotel paper and began to write a letter. She was writing to Dmitry. They had never been really honest with one another; neither of them had ever said what they had really thought. Perhaps it was a chance to say everything that they had left unsaid; perhaps he really had the right to know. She tried several times, agonising over every phrase, finally settling on the simplest version:

Dear Mitya, I'm writing to you because I have just discovered that I am pregnant. The child must have been conceived about the end of March. I am almost certain that it is yours. I have not told Bob; if I do I imagine he will assume that it's his. I don't know what I should do about it. At first I thought there was no point in telling you; I don't want you to feel guilty or that you have to do anything. But perhaps it's too important not to let you know and we have done too much harm to one another already by concealing things.

I find this letter hard to write. Sometimes I find it hard even to remember what you look like. I suppose this child, if it is ever born, would remind me. I have to confess that when it was confirmed that I was pregnant I was filled with joy at the thought that something positive might have come from our relationship. But perhaps it is not positive, perhaps it is another muddle. I was and still am comforted by the thought that had you died I might still have had something left of you.

I don't know what else to say. I'm here in Paraguay with Bob for three weeks. I hope that you are well and getting on all right at work and that you will at least write to me sometime to say what you are doing.

With love, Katie.

She took the letter to the receptionist, leaving the money for it to be sent express mail to Vienna. She asked the hotel if they could receive a letter or fax for her and they said yes. She scribbled a note that he could write to her or fax her at the hotel, sealed the letter in the envelope and handed it over.

At the end of the week, a week of unseasonal heat in which Katie had done what little sightseeing she could, Bob told her that he was going out to the Chaco to prepare for the rocket launch which was scheduled for next week. He said he thought Katie looked unwell and that perhaps she had better stay behind in Asunción.

'How long will you be away?'

'About a week.'

'But Bob, I came here to see you.' Katie couldn't help herself; she was tearful and emotional. She went upstairs to their room and Bob followed her, his face anxious and concerned. He sat down next to her on the bed and put his arm around her shoulders.

'Honey, what is it?'

'Bob, I'm pregnant.' She blurted it out; she couldn't conceal it any longer. Bob looked at her, astonished.

'Oh, but Katie, that's wonderful. Isn't it wonderful? Aren't you pleased?' Then he looked into her face, and she saw doubt and suspicion suddenly cross his features. He said, 'Katie? Is it . . . is it mine, or . . .'

The thought was obviously terrible for him to contemplate; he couldn't bring himself to mention Dmitry's name, and his face for a moment expressed the most horrible jealousy. Katie turned her face away from him. 'I don't know, Bob – I think so.'

'You think? What exactly do you think?'

This was terrible; what was she to say to him? She had been to the hotel earlier that day; there had been nothing from Dmitry. 'I just realised last week my period was late. I did the test . . .'

'So you mean it was when I was in England, last month?'

'I suppose it must have been.'

'Then why aren't you sure? What are you saying? You surely to God didn't see him in England?'

'No, Bob, no – of course not.' She turned her tear-streaked face up to him, looking him full in the eyes. For some perverse reason she found that, although she was lying, she was angry with Bob for not believing her. But he believed her now. He took her hand in his. He said, 'Then I don't understand. Why aren't you happy?'

'I am pleased about the baby, of course I am. But it's you, you're never here, you're just concerned with Wolf Richter and these stupid rockets.'

'Look, come with us – you can see it too. It might be fun.' He stood up and went to the window. 'Katie, I know you don't approve, but it's not for long. A couple of months and I'll be through. It's not as bad as you think.' He paused, and then his voice changed. 'Please don't mention this to either Wolf or Liliana.'

Katie sensed at once that he really meant this. 'No. No, of course not.'

'They might not appreciate it, and I am being well paid.' Bob came back and lay beside her on the bed. 'You'll be coming with us, then?'

Katie didn't want to go at first; she thought it might be dangerous, and she didn't want to become personally involved in this business; but on the other hand, she didn't want to be left here in Asunción on her own. At dinner Richter too invited her to come and was at his most charming, so she accepted. Only later, when she sat and watched him talking to Bob, she had thought: he has a cruel mouth; I wonder why I never noticed it before. That is what his face is, cruel.

The night before they were due to leave, Katie packed her things together and wandered downstairs, out onto the veranda. It was filled with exotic plants; their scent was overpowering in the still air. To her left a parrot sat on a metal hoop. Katie caught a glimpse of Liliana through the palm fronds; she was lounging on a chair by the swimming pool. Katie was amused to note that the brightly-coloured fine silk dress and scarf she wore perfectly complemented the colours of the parrot.

The phone rang somewhere in the depths of the house. A maid came out and hurried over to speak to Liliana, then returned inside. Liliana spotted Katie and called her over. She patted the chair next to her and Katie sat down.

'It's the Americans,' Liliana said. 'They are ringing Wolfie every day now, they are putting pressure on him. I think it is very serious – they have too much influence here. But the President is very keen on the rocket project; he doesn't want to stop it now, just when we are having such success; besides, the contract that we have with Paraguay cannot be cancelled.'

Katie stood up and said, 'Any contract can be cancelled.' She went and dipped her feet into the pool; little ripples spread out and the water splashed gently against the tiled edge. In the distance she could hear the faint roar of the traffic, and all around her the screeching of tropical birds.

Liliana shrugged. Then she said casually, examining her painted fingernails, 'Who does Bob know at the American Embassy?'

'I don't know that he knows anybody. I suppose he might do. Why?'

'I wondered . . . I saw him in a bar with this character from the US Embassy. You have to remember that everybody knows everyone else here, this is a very small place. It's hard to meet anywhere without it being noticed.' She continued to examine her fingernails.

Despite her languid attitude, Katie realised that Liliana was sharp and alert; she felt suddenly that she had under-estimated her. She thought, she is trying to hint at something; I have to pay attention to this. Something I can't understand is going on. Everything is significant; everything that has happened to me since we met Wolf Richter in Paris has been significant. There is a hidden thread.

'Did you remember?' asked Liliana, looking up suddenly, her voice becoming brighter, 'That people are coming this evening? It will be quite a party. You will join in with us, won't you?'

At ten o'clock they were sitting around the massive table in the dining room. The room was lit by candles, suspended in the huge glass chandelier; the light was reflected in the large gilt mirror above the marble mantelpiece. There were two generals, who had arrived wearing their absurd white uniforms with gold braided epaulettes. There were a handful of Germans, introduced to her as the range controller, the computer systems manager, another engineer; there was even Weiland himself, looking frail but with glittering eyes. There was also a blonde woman sitting next to him of such stunning appearance that she hardly seemed real.

Richter was enjoying himself. The meal was superb; dish after dish kept arriving on the table, fresh fish from the Rio Paraguay, meat, game from the Chaco, everything beautifully garnished and arranged; there were three different kinds of wine; everyone was getting drunk. Katie did not know what to think. She was sitting next to a round, soft-voiced, middle-aged Paraguayan who spoke to her in English. He did not know the way things were going in Paraguay, he said. This talk of democracy was all very well but people did not always know what was good for them. His own career was at an end; he was retired now. He talked about his daughters and his grandchildren, about a visit to Europe many years ago. Katie, for lack of anything else to do, chatted to him amicably. She felt she was lucky to be next to him; he was by far the most civilised person there, she thought.

She glanced across the table. Richter was drawing parabolas in the air with his finger. The generals were laughing. He mimicked something crude. She looked at Bob; he, too, was laughing. But now Richter had got onto his hobby horse. He would sell launches to whoever could afford it, he said. Brazil, Argentina, Chile; once one had launched one satellite they would all have to have one. Katie looked round the table, at the men's eager faces, at the women, silent, admiring. She thought, whatever am I doing here? How did I get into this? The Chinese had even shown interest, said Richter, the Indonesians, and of course there were so many opportunities in the Middle East.

There was a hush; everyone was listening to him now. '*Der Himmel ist für alle da,*' he said, 'The skies are there for everyone.' He lifted his eyes and made an eloquent gesture in the air with his hands; for an instant his face, which in daylight had always struck her as being crude and heavy, seemed almost fine. They drank a toast; Katie picked up her glass. The poetry of the phrase was not lost on her, but then, nor was the philosophy. It was the same old argument, she thought; she was tired of it. What use in pointing out to Richter that the money would be better spent on roads, on hospitals, on immunisations? What was that to him? He was not interested in these things, she wouldn't even waste her breath.

But Richter seemed to have read her mind. He was describing now the work they were doing on the land in the Chaco. First they had been flying in food for the workers on the project, but now they were drilling wells, irrigating the land, planting crops. They were achieving more in this small area than any of the UN development projects, he said. They were providing health care to the workers. The Indians liked them; they called them the 'friends who put fire in the heavens.' They had a sophisticated religion and mythology, the Guaraní, said Richter. Now he addressed Katie directly. Had she read anything about them? There were some works by a German anthropologist. Of course there had been talk about exploiting the Indians, but he exploited them a lot less than the Mennonites or the missionaries.

Katie looked at Bob. He didn't catch her eye; he was looking at Liliana; he seemed almost mesmerised. It was the way Liliana ate her food, so slowly, sensuously, the way she raised the glass to her lips. Katie watched her select a peach from the fruit-bowl, peel it, cut it, put out her tongue to lick the fruit before she put it in her mouth. Then Liliana caught Bob's eye, as if she knew that he was watching her, smiled, and looked at Katie. A tiny shock went through her; for an instant she wondered, why had I never thought of it before? Of course, that's why he wanted to come to work with Wolf; that is why he has dragged us half way across the world; he is still in love with Liliana.

After supper the man who had been sitting next to Katie took his leave. He smiled at her and kissed her hand. They all went to have coffee on the veranda. It was now quite cool outside. The wind stirred in the palm trees and wrinkled the water of the pool. Liliana poured coffee from a silver pot, passed Katie the tiny cup, and sat down next to her. She said, 'You have made quite a conquest. Did you like him?'

'He was charming,' said Katie. 'Who was he?'

'I met his daughter at a party the other day. She denies the stories that are told. That man was chief of police in one of the most repressive eras of the Stroessner regime. Apparently his excesses were so great that even Stroessner couldn't put up with him and to get him out of the way he was sent abroad as ambassador. Apparently he made a very good one.'

Katie could not disguise the shock which went through her at this. But then, she supposed that was right; even torturers were pleasant men, good fathers, husbands. Liliana sighed; she said, in a low voice, conspiratorial, confiding, 'I hate this town, there is nothing to do here. I asked to stay in Paris this trip but Wolf makes me go everywhere with him. He doesn't trust me. He is so jealous. You know, when Bob came to stay and Wolf was in Stuttgart he made the chauffeur sleep in my bed so that Bob wouldn't do so. The chauffeur was gay, you see.' She laughed with amusement.

Katie said, not amused at all, 'When did Bob visit you?'

'Oh, it was maybe three months ago. Didn't he tell you?'

'He told me he was in Paris, for an interview.'

Liliana laughed. 'Well I can assure you nothing happened – don't look like that. What's the matter? Are you feeling ill?'

'It's the heat,' said Katie, 'It's given me a headache. I'm very tired. I think I'll go up to bed.'

Katie lay in bed in the dark. She could hear the voices still coming up from below. The phrase echoed in her head; '*Der Himmel ist für alle da.*' The beauty of the phrase could not survive translation. Surely someone who could say this could not be without some imagination? She could not understand what Richter was about. He was not the kind of man who, obsessed only with the details of his project, could not look beyond that to its uses; no, he was only too aware of its potential, and of the fact that he could make a lot of money out of it. But human beings were strange and complicated. Her moral values, which had seemed so simple when she was young, were now all mixed up. Perhaps Richter genuinely thought his rockets would be used only for peaceful purposes, just as Bob – and Mitya, perhaps, too – had believed that nuclear energy could be separated from nuclear bombs. Or perhaps he didn't care about their use, was interested only in the technical achievement. She rolled over in bed; her head ached. She wished Bob would hurry up and join her, not because she wanted him there so much as because she could imagine him sitting down below, talking to Liliana, only too clearly. She felt suddenly angry; with herself as much as with him. After all, what right did she have to be jealous? She had lied enough to him; it was not as if she had been faithful.

It was two in the morning when Bob finally came up. When he saw she was awake he leaned over and kissed her. Katie did not respond. He crossed the room and took off his shoes; Katie sat up on one elbow. 'What are we doing here?' she asked. 'I can't stand these people. Sitting down to dinner with Nazis and torturers. Doesn't it make you feel ashamed?'

'Oh, come on,' said Bob, 'It's not as bad as that, you've got to face realities. What do you mean about torturers, anyway?'

Katie told him what Liliana had said. Bob frowned. He said, 'Are you sure that's true? There are so many stories.'

'Yes, but most of them are true,' said Katie. 'And hardly any of these people have been prosecuted. The same people who tortured and had people killed are now sitting behind their desks and getting on with their jobs. Why shouldn't it be true? I don't understand you. What are we doing here? I don't want to have anything to do with these kind of people.'

'Weiland is the only ex-Nazi –'

'I said Nazis. There's no such thing as an ex-Nazi, you should know that.'

'Weiland is not a war criminal. He's perfectly respectable, he has lived in the States for years, he worked with NASA –'

'Please, don't let's argue.' Katie changed the subject abruptly. 'Liliana told me the Americans are putting pressure on him to stop.'

'Yes, that's true. Articles are appearing in the newspapers, questions have been raised at the UN. Most of what is said is completely false. Nobody minded at first but now it's obvious he's having success with the rockets everyone is getting upset about it. Wolf has actually written to the UN requesting a team of inspectors to come to the site and verify that this is simply for peaceful purposes – actually that was my idea.'

'But what about the US? If they want it stopped, they can have it stopped, can't they?'

'It's not as simple as that. We have this legitimate contract. Rodriguez is very keen on the rocket project. They're crazy to attract foreign investment here. They want to develop the Chaco. Paraguay has always been about the most insignificant country in the whole of Latin America; this is something that gives them some prestige.'

'But it's not giving them any money, is it? There was an article in the paper here today arguing that the terms of the contract are quite unfair – that Paraguay won't get anything out of it except a free satellite launch until the company is making a big profit.'

'That's true. But it will make big profits, and then we'll see who's laughing.' Bob was getting undressed; he went to the bathroom to clean his teeth. He came back to the doorway in his pyjamas and stood looking at her.

'It's hot; do you want the air-conditioning on?'

'I can't stand the air conditioning. I wake up freezing cold. Why can't they have a thermostat on these things?'

'God, how you complain about everything.' He came to bed and, with a sudden affectionate gesture, started to stroke her but she pushed him away.

'I don't want to, Bob, the baby –' It was the perfect excuse. She didn't want him to touch her. 'Bob, are you sure it's safe in the Chaco? Supposing the rocket blows up on the launch pad or something. Anna –'

'It'll be fine. President Rodriguez is coming to see it personally. There might even be a representative from the US.'

'Is that what the man from the Embassy told you?'

'What man from the Embassy?' Bob's voice had changed subtly; there was a note of tension in it. 'What do you mean?'

'Liliana said you'd had a drink with someone from the US Embassy.'

'She must have been imagining things.' Bob lay quietly for a moment. She glanced surreptitiously at him; he was lying flat on his back, his eyes open; he was frowning. 'When did she mention it?'

'Earlier this evening. What's the matter? Is it very important?'

'No, of course not.' A silence fell; they were both lying still, both slightly tense, neither wanting to let the other know that they weren't sleeping. It must have been three or four in the morning, Katie thought; at that time, briefly, the traffic ceased almost entirely. Katie got up, went into the bathroom and started retching over the sink. Bob did not stir. She returned to the bed and lay there, crying soundlessly. She thought she might as well leave him, she might as well be on her own, she felt so lonely. She neither trusted him nor knew what he was thinking; she felt absolutely lost. Then she thought of Anna, waiting for them in England, and tears came into her eyes.

'Are you coming, then?' asked Liliana.

'I've packed. Will I need much?'

'It's quite comfortable there, don't worry.' Liliana tied a scarf around her head. 'We'll leave in half an hour. I'll drive us to the airport; Bob will be there already.'

Katie fetched her suitcase and waited for Liliana in the hallway. She came down the stairs like a model in her long dress, radiating perfume. They were going in the white Porsche. Liliana climbed into the driving seat, reversing the car out onto the road rather too recklessly for Katie's comfort. As they drove past the house Katie saw two men watching in a car just up the street. They were there all the time; they were not very discreet. Liliana had pointed them out to her before and said they were the CIA.

Katie asked, as casually as she could, 'Could we call in at the Gran Hotel del Paraguay on the way? I think I left a scarf there the other day.'

Liliana made the small detour and Katie ran into the lobby. The man at the desk said he would check if there was anything for her and came back with a folded sheet of fax paper. Katie unfolded it with shaking fingers. When she saw that it was Dmitry's writing she hardly dared to read it; perhaps it would be another cold rejection. But she had no other time; Liliana was waiting, and she had no wish for Bob to discover it. She moved across to the other side of the lounge and read it.

The letter said:

> Dearest Katie,
>
> I have wanted to write to you so many times but believed that you had put all this behind you and that it would be best not to be starting things up again by contacting you. I am better now, but I have not been well; it took longer to recover than I had first thought. You will be pleased to hear that I have now had to give up smoking.
>
> I know I have no right at all to say anything to you about what you should do but it seems to me that all my life I have suffered and caused suffering by not saying openly what I think or feel. Even worse is when I have rushed in impulsively and done things without thinking where they are going to take me. I may be guilty of that even now but I have to tell you that I want you to have the baby. This of course is

no use to you if I am not there to help you so I must say that I will support you, help you, live with you, marry you, if you want any of these things. If you are truly wanting to stay with your husband then that is different but you do not say anything about this in your letter.

You write in a very dignified way but it seems full of pain between the lines. I know how much I must have hurt you to make you deny your own wishes so much. Please do not do anything which you may regret later. If you want I will come and see you and we can talk about everything. I am leaving for Buenos Aires for ten days at the end of the week and perhaps I can route home via Asunción. Please ring me or fax soon so that I can arrange this.

As we say in Russia, I wait for your reply as a swallow waits for the summer,

Your loving Mitya.

When she had finished the letter Katie read it again, trying to make sure she had understood it. She went hot all over and then cold. She wanted to keep the letter, but she dared not. She tore it up, threw it in a bin and ran back to the car.

'Did you find it?'

'No.' Katie was sure Liliana would see that something had happened to her; perhaps she would think she was just upset about the scarf. But Liliana seemed unaware of anything but the car and the road. She was driving too fast. She had the roof down and her hair whipped back from her face where it strayed from under the brightly-coloured scarf. A lorry in front shed some of its load of earth, smearing the windscreen and narrowly missing them; Liliana swerved to overtake it on the inside. She turned the wipers on and squirted water to clear the windscreen.

'You know, Wolfie is a genius,' she said. 'He was explaining to me the other night. Do you know what he did? He needed something to open the valves to let the fuel up from the tanks to the engines so what did he use? A car windscreen wiper motor. Isn't that unbelievable? It worked perfectly.' And she roared with laughter.

Katie forced herself to smile. She was hardly conscious of the drive to the airport. She was in utter confusion. For an instant it crossed her mind that she could simply take the next flight back to Europe; she could simply turn up in Vienna on his doorstep and say, 'Here I am.' But no; he would be going to Buenos Aires; she could wait and go to meet him there. She tried to imagine his face when he saw her, his reaction to her, but she couldn't do it; she had to push the thoughts away instantly.

Bob was waiting for them at the airport. Richter's plane, a small jet, was standing on the tarmac with its engine roaring. Bob fussed around Katie, enjoying himself. She had never flown in a small plane before; the sensation of taking off was exhilarating; and as the plane banked steeply, she saw below the wide sluggish curve of the Rio Paraguay. She looked out of the window, peering into the flat wilderness which lay spread out before her. Below and ahead of them lay a sea of trees; they were still climbing. In spite of herself, she was excited.

'There's nothing much to see,' said Liliana, as they flew over the Chaco; 'It's all like this; there's absolutely nothing here.' Its emptiness was impressive. They flew north of the Trans-Chaco highway; a few ranches were dotted here and there and an occasional earth road cut through the forest. Finally the plane banked again; Liliana pointed out of the window. In the distance Katie saw a clearing with an airstrip; a group of buildings; and the rocket gantry gleaming in the bright sunlight. On the horizon she could see the mysterious grey hump of Cerro León.

'RASAG occupies this whole area,' said Liliana. 'There are hundreds of native workers; we've built housing for them over there. We've pumped up water and started irrigating; look – you can see the channels.'

They touched down. Clouds of dust from the strip of bare earth rose up and enveloped the plane. Richter was standing at the side of the runway to greet them. Katie looked around; when the engine cut out, the silence hit her. There was a hot, dry wind. The rocket gantry towered above the trees, thin metal tubes criss-crossed like a modern architectural sculpture. In the midst of it stood the rocket. It was still under construction; the bottom part was made up of a bundle of tubes; the top was almost square. Three men in yellow suits were working on the platform at the top of the gantry.

Katie looked at the rocket with astonishment; it was angular, ungainly with its cylinders of jointed tubes. She said, 'It doesn't look very aerodynamic.'

Richter laughed. He slapped her shoulder. 'What does it matter?' He said, 'That's only a detail. It doesn't have to look like a Porsche. If you have enough power, you can get anything into orbit.'

He left his hand resting on her shoulder; Katie instantly moved away, following Bob towards the buildings. He took her on a quick tour of the out-buildings; the computer room, the workshop. It was very hot; outside, barefoot soldiers sat sipping *yerba maté* out of gourds under a tree.

Bob took her back to the ranch, a big, solid house, with a wooden veranda. Inside it was air-conditioned and comfortable; there were leather chairs, rugs on the floor, hammocks hanging from the ceiling.

Bob showed her round, almost proudly. 'There's everything you need here. I've got to help Wolf – why don't you rest here? Our room's upstairs.'

'Is there a phone?'

'Of course. Why? Who do you want to call?'

'I thought I might ring Anna but it doesn't matter; I just wanted to be sure that someone could reach us here in case she was ill or anything.'

A woman came in, bringing them glasses of orange juice on a tray. The ice jingled in the glasses as she walked across the room. Bob took a glass, drained the contents down, kissed Katie on the cheek and strolled out. She watched him walk across the dusty compound to the control room. It was very quiet. She wondered if she could call Vienna. Perhaps they kept a record of all calls; perhaps they recorded them or listened in. She didn't dare to. Anyway, they would only be here a few days, she could call Dmitry when she got back to Asunción.

Liliana came in and sat beside her. 'Wolf will be working all night,' she said. 'It's always like this. There are always last-minute problems. He's anxious to keep to the schedule because of Rodriguez coming.' She stretched out her legs, yawned and sighed. 'I hope you bought a good book to read.'

Katie thought that she would be bored, but she wasn't. There was constant activity. While the men worked, Liliana stayed in the house and took endless phone calls. Katie began to realise that many of the calls were from people who seemed to be anxious to prevent or postpone the launch, and that Liliana, far from being an empty-headed beauty, was in fact a very shrewd negotiator.

Once when Liliana put the phone down with a gesture of triumph, Katie asked her: 'Who is this that keeps calling?'

'It's the Americans. They are getting tough. I thought all along it was a mistake to come to Paraguay; he would have been better off in Brazil. They are much more able to stand up to the Americans.'

'Why didn't he try Brazil?'

'Well, he did, there were negotiations with several governments, but you see, Brazil had already had their fingers burned with this Sonda space programme which France was helping them with. The two main aerospace companies are going bankrupt, their missile programme is in chaos. I think they were happier for Wolf to try it out somewhere else; after all, if it works, they can always buy the technology.'

There were also other calls in Portuguese which seemed to go on for hours and which Katie was completely unable to understand.

The day before the launch Richter was plunged into depression by the news that the President was unable to come and would be sending one of his generals, head of the air force, instead. He took this badly, as a sign that the President's position was weak or that he was trying to distance himself from the project. But there was nothing to be done; the launch had to go ahead as planned.

At ten o'clock in the morning they heard the drone of the general's plane in the distance. The atmosphere was tense. Everyone was standing outside in the bright sunlight waiting for him. They watched the plane circle, come down, the clouds of dust stream across the airstrip. The general jumped down out of the plane. Richter, his face all smiles, went up to him; he shook his hand; he put his hand almost delicately on the general's shoulder. They turned and looked at the rocket standing on the gantry; Richter was pointing out various features to him in his primitive Spanish, then pointed to the chairs which had been arranged on the veranda of the house.

Loudspeakers, crackling ominously, announced that everyone should prepare for the launch, and the young soldiers, carrying their rifles proudly, lined up along the fence to watch.

Suddenly everything went very still; the men spoke in nervous whispers. The wind sighed around the house; it set up ripples in the reservoir of water lying to the left of the building.

The countdown started. 'Three . . . two . . . one . . .' The bottom of the rocket lit with bright flame. A great balloon of red dust billowed up; the rocket began to lift from its launch-pad. Then the sound, the roar, hit them. Katie waited, tense and anxious despite herself, to see if the rocket would clear the top of the gantry; she wondered if it was her imagination that the rocket was tilting slightly. She glanced at Richter; he was frowning, biting his lip. The rocket was rapidly gathering speed, rising now in an arc; it was flying into the sun, Katie couldn't keep her eyes on it. There was something beautiful, impressive in its pure, arching flight, like an arrow from a bow, like an image of the soul's ascent to heaven; its power was awesome. Katie looked at Bob and smiled; instinctively she put out her hand and he slipped his arm around her waist.

The general smiled and turned to congratulate Richter; but Richter was clearly unhappy. He was explaining that one of the valves must have failed to open properly; the rocket should have gone straight upwards. Katie could sense his disappointment. But it must have gone a great distance; they could not feel the shock of its return to earth. Only later, in the distance, they saw a thin plume of smoke rising from the forests.

They drank the champagne that had been cooled for them; the general joining in, smiling politely. It was impossible to know what he was really thinking. Richter was already talking about the next launch. He was going to bring it forward. Everything else had gone perfectly; the next time they were using a cluster of sixteen pipes. The next day they would go out and retrieve the parts of the rocket, to try to see what had gone wrong with the operation on the valves. But they were all subdued; it was as if Richter sensed he was on dodgy ground, that he needed the President's enthusiasm above all else to ensure the continuation of the project, and that when he received the report of this partial failure it would perhaps sow the final seed of doubt in Rodriguez' mind. The general, smiling, shook Richter's hand and took leave of them.

They watched his plane take off and sat down on the terrace. Katie went back into the ranch and looked at the half-drunk glasses of champagne standing abandoned on the table.

Richter sat and banged his fist on the table, knocking over a glass so that the golden liquid spilt onto the floor. Liliana, alarmed, reached out and put her hand on his shoulder.

'Don't worry,' she said, 'It will not fail. You will not fail. Look at me!'

Katie was shocked because, although Liliana's voice was soft, her lovely face was both hard and cold.

For the first time, Katie felt some sympathy for Richter. She could see that he was genuinely depressed. He had worked desperately hard on the project and he was devastated by such a tiny thing as a sticking valve letting him down. Richter said that he would have to go back to Stuttgart to sort out a few things there and would be away a few days. Bob could stay here and supervise the recovery of the rocket wreckage. He also asked Bob about the possibility of getting UN observers to attend the next launch. He said that it was important that they did something to counteract all the propaganda against them; perhaps they should invite some journalists along, show it wasn't something sinister and secret. He had suggested this before but the military didn't like the idea; journalists were cover for spies as far as they were concerned.

Richter collected together the print-outs from the computer, sat down with one of the other scientists and started to go through them. With his customary arrogance stripped away, he seemed almost vulnerable, human. Katie continued to wonder whether she hadn't actually been wrong about him.

Bob came and sat beside her. He said, 'Are you okay? Do you mind staying here a few days? It's quite comfortable, isn't it?'

'No, I don't mind.'

Katie wandered off to bed, restless and unhappy. In the morning when the house was empty she phoned the IAEA in Vienna to ask if they had the name of the hotel Dmitry Gavrilov was booked into in Buenos Aires, but they said they could not reveal to her where he was staying for security reasons. If it was urgent she could leave a message and they would try to get it to him. Katie asked for the number of the conference centre in case she could get a message to him there.

As she spoke, Bob's shadow fell across the doorway. She looked up and him and smiled brightly. Suddenly it all seemed hopeless; she would have to wait. She went outside with Bob and watched Richter's Lear jet flying off into the sun.

II

Dmitry woke up in the middle of the night in his hotel room in Buenos Aires. After a while in which he waited intently for any foreign sound, he reached out for his watch. He felt an irrational sensation of fear as he put his hand out from the safety of the bedclothes.

It was three-twenty a.m. He sighed and let the watch fall back onto the table by the bed, closed his eyes, and tried to sleep again. This happened often, not every night, but often enough to be disturbing. Sometimes he woke from a nightmare; sometimes with an acute memory of the salty taste of blood in his mouth, the struggle to draw breath.

After a meeting yesterday when he had lost his train of thought and come to himself with a jerk, his head in his hand, uttering an audible curse, one of his colleagues had asked him, gently, concerned, if he was in pain. He had told him truthfully that he was not; his physical recovery had been remarkable. But he found it difficult to concentrate. He seemed to have lost his short-term memory. He couldn't hold a phone number in his head long enough to dial it without looking at it again. Someone would hand him something and he would immediately forget that he had been given it. He drifted around the conference centre, in and out of the main session, half-listening through the head-phones to the endless lifeless drone of the simultaneous translation. Sometimes he would tune in to Chinese or Arabic to listen to the unintelligible sounds. He wondered once or twice if he should see a doctor. The truth was that he was still afraid. He was not afraid of anything tangible; he knew that he was out of danger and that the nightmare was over. He was afraid of himself. A deep depression, which had hit him on discharge from the hospital in Vienna, kept taking hold of him. There were moments, increasingly frequently it seemed, when he simply felt he did not want to live.

When Dmitry had received Katie's letter before leaving Vienna it had thrown him into confusion. He had read it over several times on the tram on the way in to work and looked at the postmark; it had only been posted five days earlier. His first thought was to wonder what she was doing in Paraguay; then it seemed only too clear. Haynes, after all, had been deeply involved with Richter, and Dmitry's suspicions had been, presumably, well-founded. He had puzzled over what Katie was trying to say. At first he had taken 'I don't know what to do about it,' 'If it is ever born' and 'might' to mean that she was considering an abortion, something all too common in Russia; but then he had remembered that she had had a miscarriage and might be afraid of counting on this pregnancy continuing. What had struck him about the letter was her restraint, her uncertainty; it had given him an overwhelming feeling of sadness.

When he had arrived in his office he had told Hilde not to interrupt him for ten minutes, shut his door, taken a sheet of headed paper and started to write in his large, rounded handwriting. He had written the letter straight off, without any corrections, gone down to the fax machine, and sent it straight to the hotel in Paraguay.

He had heard nothing. Later, before leaving Vienna, he had phoned the hotel. They told him that no-one of that name was resident there or was booked in in the near future, but that they could take a message in case they arrived.

He rolled over in bed. He thought about Katie and was instantly filled with despair. What if she had gone to the States or even to England to have an abortion. Could she know what Bob was doing, what the implications were? He had no idea. He tried to put it from his mind, but somehow the failure of this relationship, more than all his other failures, tormented him. He believed that he and Katie had had the possibility of a genuine intimacy. The child was a symbol of that hope;

he suddenly wanted it, and wanted her, very much indeed.

He sat up in bed. He reached out, picked up the phone, and asked for an international line. He dialled again the hotel in Asunción. Once again they said that the señora was not staying at the hotel but that they could take a message for her. In despair, he hung up.

In the south of Buenos Aires is an old working class quarter by the Riachuelo canal where the old port used to be, called La Boca, the mouth. The *barrio* is famous for its brightly painted sheet-iron houses, made from materials taken from abandoned ships; artists have come to the area and added their pictures and sculptures to the vivid scene.

Dmitry was there with an old friend, Anatoly Makushkin, who was Scientific First Secretary at the Russian Embassy in Buenos Aires. He had phoned him in the morning; they had not seen one another for several years, but the moment Anatoly's deep voice had answered the phone, Dmitry had found himself on the same wavelength, echoing his expressions of delight.

'Why didn't you contact me sooner? I have been half expecting it. You are at this nuclear energy conference of course.'

'Of course.'

'What time are you free? I can come over and meet you.'

'Oh, I think from four o'clock. Shall I see you at the conference centre?'

They had met at four-thirty. The two men had embraced warmly, kissing both cheeks, then stood back from one another. They were the same age, but Anatoly could easily have been a decade older; he was slightly overweight, and his hair was greying. He had examined Dmitry's face shrewdly. 'Well, you look all right,' he said, 'You look very well. I'm glad. We were very shocked to read what happened, you must have had a terrible time. Did you get my letter?'

'Yes. Eventually. Thanks.'

'Have you seen anything of the city? If you haven't been there, I thought we could go to La Boca. It's very picturesque. We can walk there, and then find somewhere for a drink or a coffee.'

So now they were wandering in the late afternoon down the

narrow streets, heading for the waterfront. 'There's a place here that might amuse you,' said Anatoly. The bar, in a street near the water's edge, had a red blind on which was painted its name: '*El Samovar de Rasputín.'* A mural of the mad monk and cherubs flanked the door. They ordered beer and sat at a table under a chandelier; the walls were covered with pictures and artefacts; an old sign showed the place had once been an antique shop. The man at the next table watched them; he listened as if he could understand what they were saying, making Dmitry nervous. He and Anatoly chatted rather desultorily about the conference, about life in Buenos Aires, Vienna, and events back home. They finished their beers; Anatoly offered to buy another but Dmitry declined. He said, 'It's a bit oppressive here. Let's go and have a walk.'

Once they had left the bar and were strolling down towards the water, Dmitry felt able to open up a little more, 'Tolya, have you been following this Paraguayan rocket project? You don't know what's going on there, do you? Presumably you know what Wolfgang Richter is up to now.'

'Ah, yes,' said Anatoly. 'None of it is really secret now. It has been in all the papers. He launched his third rocket this week; apparently it was not entirely successful. Now he is building an even bigger one.' He paused to offer Dmitry a cigarette, which Dmitry declined, then lit one himself. 'Well, so far it has looked rather promising for Richter. The problem is that we have no links with Paraguay at all, there is no way we can put any pressure on them to stop. But there seems to be growing concern about him. Probably the terms of this contract, of which he was so proud, will be his downfall. It has made many enemies in Paraguay, as well as outside. But we are leaving any active steps to the Americans. I believe there have been some contacts between the KGB and the CIA over this. You know, we are even working together a little bit these days.'

'But can't the Americans put pressure on Rodriguez?'

'No, I'm not sure. It seems obvious that they could stop it at any time. But there are rumours about other activities which the company is involved in – maybe they want to string it along, see what happens, just until the time it actually becomes dangerous. In the old days, of course, we would have accused them of being in co-operation and so on, indeed I believe that has been the official line, but I think they are really just as anxious to be rid of Richter as we are.'

'What I don't understand,' said Dmitry, 'Is why the Americans let him start up in Paraguay. It's practically in their back pocket.'

'Well, the deal was signed by Stroessner, in his last days in power,' said Anatoly. 'The Americans had cut off aid then because of human rights abuses. So far Rodriguez has refused to be swayed. There has been diplomatic pressure, but the problem is he isn't actually doing anything illegal, not yet, anyway, not that we can prove. Did you see,' Anatoly gave a chuckle, 'That Richter had offered to solve the world's nuclear waste problem by shooting spent reactor rods into space? At the cost of several million dollars each, I gather.'

Dmitry laughed with him. 'Yes, he told me that idea himself, at a café in Vienna. I wasn't sure that he was serious.'

'You met Richter in Vienna?' Anatoly looked at Dmitry with amazement.

'He was a friend of one of my colleagues, Bob Haynes, an American, who I believe is now working for Richter in Paraguay.'

Anatoly looked at him sharply for an instant, then continued to walk, his eyes cast downwards. They reached the river's edge and stood there, looking out over the water. The shipyard itself was in decay; more of the boats lay on their sides, exposing their battered hulls, than were afloat; there was little sign of life. The late afternoon sunlight made the colours of the boats more intense; a light wind clipped the rigging of the boats against the masts with a rapid ping-ping-ping. The wind brought with it the rank smell of the polluted water; after a few minutes they turned away.

It was starting to get dark; they walked back toward where Anatoly had left his car. He said, 'You must come and see Nina and the girls. What about tomorrow? You said you had an official dinner tonight.'

'Yes, tomorrow would be fine. It's my last night.'

'Well, then. Come at eight. You have the address? Let me give it to you.' He scribbled it down on a page from his diary, tore it out and handed it to Dmitry.

The following morning Dmitry was standing by the entrance to the main conference hall when someone came up behind him and tapped his shoulder. 'I am Jaime dos Santos, you know, Nihal's friend, on the *Jorno do Brasil.* He told me to look out for you. Shall we go and have a drink?'

Jaime dos Santos looked about thirty; he was tall and lean, with a sensitive, intelligent face. They found their way to the bar. Dmitry bought the drinks and carried them to a table. Dos Santos sat close to him, nursing his drink. 'I have something to tell you. Nihal explained to me what had happened to you, told me you were someone I could trust. I have to say, for months I have been trying to find out further details about Project Solimões. There have been several of us onto it, but we have not got very far. We are trying to find out just how far the bomb project had got, how far Collor had got in dismantling it. What has happened to the bomb-making facilities for example? What has happened to the scientists working on it? They all appear to be in their posts. We have no idea at all what is happening.

'Then Nihal rang me about this lead with Carneiro de Amaral and his daughter, Liliana Richter. I turned up at the house pretending to be delivering something and chatted up the maid. I borrowed a friend's red sports car to impress her and took her to some night-clubs. I really turned her head. She was a bright girl; I think she saw through it; but anyway she went along with it. She didn't care too much as long as she was having a good time.

'We went through the kind of people Carneiro entertained, who he mixed with, where he met them. Eventually I got her to tell me about this meeting that had taken place in Carneiro's house back in December last year, just after the Foz do Iguaçu agreement had been signed.

'There were a number of the Brazilian Military there. Rear Admiral Oliveira, from the Valadares Centre, a man from the Brazilian air force, Air Marshall Gonçalo Cardoso Soares, a representative of a German company which I suspect was RASAG, and a Paraguayan General, Luís Hería Prieto. I told you she was a smart girl; she remembered their names. I have checked up on him; he is one of the anti-democratic elements who are not happy with the changes in Paraguay. You have to understand that a lot of the military there are very unhappy at seeing their power eroded, just as they have been in my country. In Brazil in particular they blame all its economic and social problems on weak government. They cannot see that a return to the military regime would be the very worst thing that could happen to us.'

Dos Santos had finished his beer. He was so gripped by what he was saying that he went on without needing any encouragement at all from Dmitry.

'Of course I can only imagine what they were discussing at this meeting. But here is the next thing. This colleague of mine had established that there have been flights between the Paraguayan Chaco and a military site in the south of Brazil. From there are regular military flights to Cachimbo, in Amazonia; you know, the place where they built the test bores for atomic bombs. One of the planes, a small one, was stopped in the north of Paraguay, near San Pedro Caballero. They said they were looking for drugs. A Paraguayan journalist who was investigating this was later dragged out of his car in broad daylight and shot by people who they claimed were drug-runners. The story was in the papers; nobody has done much in the way of investigating it. The journalist was found with seventeen bullets in his body. As you may imagine, other journalists are not very anxious to look into what he found.'

'Have you published anything about this?'

'Not yet, we don't have enough evidence. There have been so many crazy stories circulating about the rocket project. What are we to suppose? A number of the military have been arrested already. Nobody can understand why they haven't found out what is going on. The Brazilian government cannot be behind this thing, but why haven't they exposed it?'

'I don't understand. Oliveira is dead. The scandal at Valadares has been looked into. I thought this was all over.'

'Look. They still haven't accounted for all the highly enriched uranium that was produced at Valadares. Who knows where it is. It's even possible it's be sold for vast sums to Libya or Iraq. Nobody knows how many people might be involved, how high up this thing is going to go. Maybe they don't want the extent of it to be known. It's always like this in such situations. You have to flush these guys out, one by one. It takes a long time.'

'But this possible connection with Richter. This I don't understand. You're surely not suggesting he has tried to lay his hands on an atomic warhead? Why should he do such a thing? Hold the world to ransom?' Dmitry's voice expressed his contempt for the very idea.

'No. No, I agree, that would be too incredible. No, I'm not suggesting that. But maybe it's the other way round. Maybe the Brazilian military want a rocket to launch their bomb.'

Dmitry shrugged. 'The intelligence services must know what's going on. They must know if this Richter really is a threat.'

Dos Santos snorted. 'Yes, but it's only once things become public that there is ever any action. Anyway, you can tell all this to Nihal. You're going back tomorrow? Greet him for me, won't you? Tell him to watch the Brazilian press.'

'I will. And you, be careful won't you?'

'Sure.' Dos Santos shook Dmitry's hand and turned to go.

Dmitry stood outside the entrance to the conference centre for a few moments, to breathe in the fresh air. He watched dos Santos walk down the road, heading for the car park. The United Nations flags were fluttering in the breeze. Dmitry turned to go back in through the doors when he heard it happen.

There was a squeal of brakes and a muffled cry. Dmitry spun round to see a car reverse back over a body on the ground and lurch across the grass. He saw the car drive down to the main road, screech across the pavement and smash into an oncoming truck. Then the door swung open and a young man leapt out and ran into the side streets so fast that he caught only a glimpse of a white tee-shirt, jeans and white trainers.

A knot of people who had been standing by a nearby car crowded round the body. The uniformed men at the door started running towards them. Dmitry walked over slowly behind them. Someone ran for an ambulance but the security guard who was there said it was already too late as he waved at the gathering crowd to move away.

Dmitry pushed his way through them. He looked down at the body. Dos Santos was lying face down; there was blood; fortunately he couldn't see the young man's broken face. He thought, this can't have happened. If only this could not have happened. He felt as if an enormous weight had suddenly descended on him. He felt as if he had been handed the poisoned chalice; this thing would not go away from him.

He told the security guard where the police could get hold of him if they wanted a description of the incident and pointed out the direction in which he had seen the man running. He went back into the conference centre, into the main hall, sat down, and put on his headphones. He could not listen to one word. So it was still going on. Had they known who dos Santos was talking to? Did they know he was here? Who was he going to talk to about it? There was no point in hoping the police would get anywhere. He was not going to go to the KGB again; not after what happened last time. There was no point in going to a newspaper; he had not enough to go on, and no way to convince them. He didn't want to ring Nihal and then put him at risk. He hadn't the slightest idea what he could do.

Why had they killed dos Santos here, in Argentina? Wouldn't it have been easier to kill him in Brazil? They hadn't – and this was too terrible to think about, this must surely be a product of his paranoia – known that dos Santos had made contact with him? But what did that matter – what did he know? Besides, it had happened too quickly – there hadn't been time to set up a killing.

And what if Richter really was involved in this nuclear diversion business? What had a RASAG representative been doing at a meeting of these military types? What was Richter hoping to do? If he had dreams of commercial success it was the worst thing he could get involved with. Nobody was going to let him get mixed up in something like this. None of it made the slightest sense.

The easiest thing, the best thing that he could do, would be to walk away from it. In any case, there was nothing it was in his power to do. He would ring dos Santos's paper now and tell them the manner of his death and what he thought was behind it. That was the end of his responsibility. He would go and see Tolya this evening and return to Vienna tomorrow. He was not going to think about it any more. He tried to listen to the final speeches, forcing himself to concentrate.

He was called out of the final session to give a brief statement to the police. They said it seemed to be a clear case of hit and run. Dmitry asked if the car had been traced; he was told that it had been reported stolen earlier that afternoon. Probably it was a young joy-rider. The police couldn't account for his presence near the conference centre; but they didn't think there was anything more to it. Dmitry did not try to persuade them otherwise; he didn't want to spend hours with them explaining about Project Solimões and the Paraguayan rocket project. He would leave it to dos Santos's paper to raise that with them later.

After the police had gone Dmitry left the conference centre in a taxi. He didn't want to go back to his hotel; he was too restless; he wanted to keep busy. On impulse he decided to go and wander round the fashionable Barrio Norte, where Anatoly lived. He got out of his taxi at one of the coffee houses, walked in one entrance, out the other, just in case anyone was following him, and took a bus, a Buenos Aires *colectivo*. He consulted the map he had in his pocket. After turning off the Avenida 9 de Julio the streets became like those in Paris; grand nineteenth century apartment buildings, shops selling fashion clothes, interior decoration, art, antiques. He stepped off the *colectivo* and wandered aimlessly along the streets. He looked in the shop windows, but he did not want to buy anything; what would be the point? Even the bookshops did not entice him. Suddenly he laughed aloud. In his youth he would have given anything to travel out of the Soviet Union; Buenos Aires would have sounded like a magic incantation on his tongue. Now that he was here he felt no joy at all; he would have felt the same despair had he been anywhere.

He was on the Avenida Santa Fe, walking northwards slowly, irresolutely, trying to spin out the time till eight o'clock, when the sun sank behind the buildings. A blazing stream of copper light shone across the street and caught on the metal of the shop signs, the bonnets of the cars and *colectivos,* filling the air with a strange luminosity. The light shone on his hands, turning them deep gold, on the fabric of his dark coat, on the pavement which seemed to melt beneath his feet. His heart seemed to stop for an instant and then to pound again, stricken with an unbearable mixture of beauty and pain. If God were ever to enter the world, he would come in such a blaze of light as this, he thought, stopping to look into the light for an instant before the intensity of it hurt his eyes. In another moment the sun passed behind another building, and he was cut off, left behind in an inky darkness for a moment till his eyes adjusted to the coming twilight.

He felt dizzy. Something had happened to him; he could not say what it was. He turned into a side-street shaded by plane trees and began to walk faster and still faster. He came to a little square and sat down on a bench; there were children in the park, their mothers and nannies gathering up coats and jackets and calling that it was time to go home. He thought, I am not going to run away from this. He felt that it had somehow been given to him; there must be some point in it. He was not going to sit and do nothing about that young man's death. It must be possible for him to do something; he had to get to the bottom of it somehow. He could not just sit there and let these people carry on their killing.

He looked at his map; he was only a street or two away from Anatoly's apartment. He had an hour and a half to wait until he was due there; after a while when the square had emptied he got up, bought a paper, *La Nación,* at a news-stand, found a café, and sat down to read it over a cup of coffee.

On page three was a short item:

> Rocket launch in Paraguay
>
> A third rocket launch from the RASAG site in north-west Paraguay took place yesterday watched by Air Force Chief General Martinez. The launch was not an unqualified success as the rocket failed to follow its planned trajectory after a fuel inlet valve malfunctioned. The launch of a larger, sixteen-engine rocket is planned for next month.
>
> RASAG's rocket activities have been strongly criticised by the governments of Brazil and Argentina, although both governments have behind the scenes expressed interest in the cut-price rocket since the scrapping of Argentina's Condor programme and the bankruptcy of both Brazil's major aerospace companies. The Bolivian government has accused RASAG of using a secret US military airstrip situated in the uninhabited Chaco region.

> Recent reports that a plane stopped in the north of Paraguay was carrying sensitive military equipment have been strenuously denied by representatives of RASAG and the Paraguayan government.

Dmitry ordered another coffee. He looked at his hand; it was shaking slightly. He would have given anything just then for a cigarette. He tore the item out of the paper, folded it into his wallet, and read the rest of the paper. At quarter to eight he got up and walked out into the night.

Anatoly and Nina welcomed him warmly into their apartment. Nina explained that it was the maid's night off; she had just prepared something simple, there were no other guests. The two girls, aged seven and nine, were already in their pyjamas, their faces freshly scrubbed, their hair still slightly damp from the bath. They hovered nervously in the doorway and giggled whenever Dmitry looked at them.

'Come and say hello properly,' ordered Anatoly, 'And then go to bed.'

They sat at the end of the grand table and ate a homely meal, some Ukrainian-style dumplings stuffed with meat and onions, followed by fresh fruit. Anatoly was generous with the wine; inevitably they talked about the worsening situation back home, till Nina changed the subject and they began talking about old times. The children wandered in from time to time to ask for a drink or to peer at the visitor and Nina shooed them out again. They were not allowed to do this at official dinners, she explained, but tonight was different. Eventually she went off to read them a story. Dmitry's feeling of isolation was intensified; he could not bear the atmosphere of peaceful domesticity, contrasting with his own isolation. Anatoly must have caught his fleeting look of sadness, for he suddenly asked:

'So you never found the right woman to marry, Mitya?'

'No.'

'What went wrong with you and Masha? I thought she seemed just right for you; very clever, very sensible.'

'Perhaps she was too sensible.'

'Nina saw her last time we were in Moscow, you know. She has married again, a professor at the Lebedev Academy.'

'Has she? I never hear from her these days.'

Anatoly offered Dmitry a cigarette which he declined. Then he said, 'You know, I always thought that the trouble with you was that you were too fond of your sister.'

Dmitry smiled. 'Well, you have to admit that other women did rather pale in comparison.'

'Why did she marry that creep Oleg? I never could work it out. She must have had a hundred proposals. All the men were crazy about her. I was myself. My God, she was beautiful. I would have done anything for her, I swear I would have died for her if she had asked me to.'

Dmitry said, with a touch of irony, 'Fortunately that wasn't necessary.'

'Nina still can't bear it if I mention her. She wasn't even too keen on your coming. She is very jealous, not that she has ever had much reason to be – well, now and then, you know . . .'

'No, I don't know.' Dmitry was surprised.

'You disapprove of me, Mitya.'

'Not at all. I don't disapprove of anyone. It's just I would hope that if I were lucky enough to have a loving wife like Nina, I wouldn't see the point in being unfaithful.'

Anatoly switched the subject. He said, 'I shouldn't really tell you this, but I heard today some news which might interest you, in view of what we were talking about yesterday.'

'I saw what was in today's papers.'

'Yes? Oh, well, that's already out of date. I gather the US Ambassador is going to see Rodriguez again to issue an ultimatum that the US wants the rocket project cancelled. But that's not all. Richter's investors too are getting a little anxious. He has apparently been seeking other alternatives to Paraguay, and the Americans are not happy about this. I believe they are going to try to stop the project altogether. There appear to be links, you see, with this business in Brazil, and he has also been dabbling in the Middle East. They've decided he must be stopped at all costs.'

'How?'

'Oh, we have intelligence that they are planning a para-military operation. A few days and it will all be over.'

For an instant Dmitry felt relief; then a terrible thought occurred to him; he couldn't shake it out of his head. He was thinking of Katie's safety. He struggled to think clearly. 'Where exactly are they based? The Chaco is a big area, isn't it? Are they actually out there now?'

'I imagine so. They would have been out there for the launch.' Anatoly seemed suddenly nervous. 'Why, what's on your mind?'

'Tolya, you're very careless. When I was in Vienna I had an affair, I was in love with Haynes's wife. She is there, in Paraguay, with Haynes. This Richter has armed security men, he has the support of half the Paraguayan military. If the CIA goes in, there may be shooting. They could blow them all up. Anything might happen. If they're going to destroy Richter, are they going to care if a few innocent people get in the way?'

Anatoly said, taken aback, 'Yes, in that case, I can see your concern, but she must know the score. She knows he's not out there growing soya beans.'

Dmitry winced. He held the wine glass in his hand, swirling the dark red liquid round and round in it. Anatoly said, his voice changed, worried, 'You're not thinking of trying to warn her, are you? You couldn't take that risk.'

Dmitry said, 'You shouldn't have told me, Tolya.'

Anatoly had a tense, alarmed look in his eyes, though he kept his voice low and even. 'Well, perhaps you should warn her to get out. But what if she tells them? What if she tried to leave and they find out why? Perhaps she's actually in less danger if you leave well alone.'

Dmitry got to his feet and walked to the mantelpiece, unable to keep still. He said, 'It's my fault she's there. From the beginning I decided to tell her nothing, to protect her. It's because of that she's there now. If I had told her the truth about her husband she would never have gone with him.'

'This affair, is it all over?'

'Yes – that is, I thought so. I don't know .'

Dmitry had drained his glass; Anatoly replenished it. He said, 'I'm sorry, I made a grave mistake in telling you. How was I to know that you would be so upset by it?'

Dmitry took another gulp of wine. It was good wine, but he didn't notice the taste of it. He walked across the room. 'You know, you remember when we used to have those abstract arguments at university, about whether the greater good is worth the sacrifice of a few innocent people? Those situations we used to invent, sometimes you argued one way, sometimes the other. The trouble is, the equation was always too neat. In real life, the edges are all blurred, we can't tell who is innocent and who is not, we don't know what is going to happen, what would have happened if we had chosen differently. Besides, when we love some of those people who are to be sacrificed, it all looks rather different .'

Anatoly laughed. 'Yes, I remember. You were always obsessed in these arguments with what you called the truth.'

'Well, when you have been fed nothing but lies and stupidities from the cradle – things you knew made no sense, which you knew not even the person who told you them had the slightest belief in –'

'Yes, it's coming back to me now. Scientific truth, religious truth – of course that was always a little dangerous – artistic truth, well, that was dangerous too – scientific truth was the best. That's why you became a scientist, wasn't it? You could go on looking for the truth without it being political, without being disapproved of.'

'Well, maybe that was the original intention. I should have stayed with pure science. Now I could hardly be working with anything more political.' He turned and continued to walk up and down on the Persian carpet. 'But the fact is, nobody really wants to know the truth about anything. To be honest with you, this whole business with Brazil has really upset me, Tolya. I was ignored; I was used. I told them there was a problem in the first place.'

'But maybe they were right to be cautious. There was rather a lot at stake, Mitya.'

'Yes. My life, for instance.'

Anatoly could not meet his eyes. He stood up, went to the cupboard, took out a bottle of vodka and two glasses, and poured some out. Dmitry sat down and put it on the table without drinking it.

'She wrote to me, about two weeks ago,' he said. 'She told me she was pregnant with my child. I wrote back and told her that I wanted her to have it, that if she left her husband I would marry her. She hasn't written back.'

Nina had come to the door, but when she heard what he was saying, she turned and walked out again.

Anatoly was shocked. He said, 'My God, I see. I had no idea.'

'No, of course you had no idea. How could you have?'

Dmitry sat and stared at the table, tracing the pattern on the cloth with his finger. He was thinking, perhaps it is already too late, perhaps she has already had a termination. He found the thought unbearable. The idea of this child affected him immensely; he recalled the sensation of holding Olga's first-born son in his arms, so tiny, so perfect, so unspoiled. It had been like the birth of hope itself. He and Olga had looked at one another; they had smiled; they had kissed; they had promised then to put the past behind them. Even Oleg, the happy, proud father, had seemed different; Dmitry had felt quite fond of him on that day.

Anatoly said, nervously, 'What are you going to do?'

'Well, I could go and see her. It's only an hour's flight to Asunción.'

'You're crazy. They would never give you a visa with a Soviet passport.'

'I can travel on my UN *laissez-passer*.'

'Only on official business, surely.'

'They won't know if it's official. I expect I would get told off when I get back.'

'How would you find her?'

'Oh, I'd find her. You can find out anything in South America if you pay enough.'

'You're mad. It's too risky.'

'You wouldn't try to stop me?'

'How could I? I can only tell you that it would be dangerous, for her as well as you.' He struck his forehead with the palm of his hand. 'My God, I am an idiot to have said anything.' He stood up, clearly anxious to end this conversation. 'I had better take you back to the hotel.'

Nina came back in with the coffee and put the tray down on the table. She looked at them both uncertainly, not understanding the cause of the heavy atmosphere which now permeated the room. Her husband, who had been so looking forward to seeing his old friend, now sat with a completely closed expression, what she called his bureaucratic face, staring at the floor. Dmitry got up suddenly. He said, 'I am sorry, I'm not feeling so well. I think I had better go back. Thank you for a delightful evening, both of you.'

Anatoly said, 'I will take you in the car.'

'No, no, I can get a taxi.'

'It is no trouble to get the car out.'

'No, really, I would rather go on my own.'

Nina said suddenly, 'Tolya, let him go.' She had no idea what had happened, but she wanted Dmitry out of the apartment at once; she had a sudden conviction that he was dangerous, that he brought havoc wherever he went. Dmitry kissed both her cheeks and then stood back; he held out his hand to Anatoly, who took it and shook it, formally and without warmth.

'Have a good trip back to Vienna.'

Nina saw him to the door.

In the middle of the night Dmitry woke up. He was wide awake and terribly thirsty. He got up, poured a glass of mineral water from the bottle in the fridge, and drained it. Then he sat on the edge of the bed and started to think.

It had not occurred to him until he spoke to Tolya to go to Paraguay. But was it so impossible? There were always ways of finding out what you needed to know. Why not find Katie, and get to the bottom of this Richter business? Haynes must know what was going on.

No. How could he even think of doing anything so stupid? It was quite possible that Katie wasn't there. She might never have received his fax; someone might have intercepted it. And what if Tolya were right, what if it were more dangerous to warn her than to let things be? He got up and walked over to the window. What would Tolya do, now that he had realised his mistake? Perhaps he would try to make sure that he did get on the plane tomorrow. There were ways; people were taken ill, drugged, escorted to the airport. He had seen this happen himself once, in Geneva. But surely these things didn't happen any more?

Or Tolya might tell the KGB *rezident* at the Embassy. No, he wouldn't do that, he'd be in trouble, the KGB were always complaining how the straight diplomats gossiped. But then, he needn't say that he had given away the information. He, Dmitry, might have found it out for himself. But there was no point in going if he hadn't contacted Katie; she might, after all, be safely in Asunción. On the other hand, he didn't know what the CIA might do. It was not beyond them to put a bomb in Richter's car, and Katie might be in it. They didn't care who else they killed.

He couldn't sleep; at three a.m. he took a sleeping pill and set the alarm for half-past seven. His flight to Vienna left Ezeiza airport at twelve-thirty-five, he would have to check in by eleven-forty-five, that gave him four hours. He woke up feeling drugged and exhausted. He showered and shaved and left the hotel before breakfast. He asked the receptionist to confirm his flight and told her that he would return to collect his baggage, which was packed and ready in his room.

He walked a few blocks to the nearest café and ordered a roll and coffee. Then he went to the telephone and looked up a private detective in the Buenos Aires phone directory.

There were quite a few. He picked one that looked promising and rang the number. He thought it was too early, nobody would be there, but a man answered. Dmitry asked to speak to the *jefe*; the man replied lazily that he was the *jefe*. His name was Luís Portillo.

Dmitry said, 'I want to know if you can get me an address and telephone number in Paraguay.'

'There's the phone book,' said Portillo lazily.

'This number won't be listed in the phone book. It's in the Chaco. I just want to know if you can get it or not.'

'Of course I can get it, for a price. I have a contact on the international exchange.'

'I need it this morning.'

'Well, that shouldn't be a problem, I have some Paraguayan contacts who can help me. Whose number is it you want?'

Dmitry told him. There was a silence; then Portillo said, 'I see. This might be a little more expensive. It will cost you five hundred dollars.'

'That's okay. I'll pay in dollars, cash, in a couple of hours.'

He went out to a call-box and phoned the hotel. Oh yes, said the receptionist, somebody had been in to ask after him. A Russian gentleman; two gentlemen, in fact. Did he want to leave a message where he could be contacted?

Dmitry said he would be back at eleven and wanted her to have a taxi ready to take him to the airport.

He bought a South American travel guide at a news-stand and turned to the pages on Paraguay. He read it drinking a coffee at a bar and then went to Portillo's office. It was half-past ten. He climbed up a narrow flight of stairs to the offices on the first floor. In the reception area a surly-faced girl typed up a report from a tape. She took Dmitry through to Portillo's office.

He was a small, plump man, in a baggy suit. Piles of files, papers, directories covered his desk; there were two phones, wired up to a tape recorder; a map of Argentina on the wall; two battered filing cabinets. Dmitry stood there, awkwardly, taken over by a sudden sense of unreality; Portillo waved him into a chair.

'It wasn't difficult; rather too easy in fact, everyone knows everything in Paraguay, it's such a small place. But since you're paying good money, I'll fill you in on what I know. You have the money?'

Dmitry counted it out and handed it over. Portillo left it lying on the desk between them.

'Before I give you this information, I think I should first ask who you are and why you want it.'

'I'm an old colleague of his, I'm visiting Paraguay, I want to look him up.'

Portillo looked utterly unconvinced.

Dmitry said, after a pause, 'If I wanted to kill him I would hardly say so.'

'No. But I've been in this business a long time, one gets the feel of things. You are also German?'

'I'm from Vienna.'

Portillo sighed, then shrugged and leaned forward on his desk. 'In the Chaco, they are using this big *estancia* in the region north of Mariscal Estigarribia. There is a road running north towards Cerro León;

it is in the wilderness. They have had electricity taken out there, water, everything. This is a rough map of the region. I don't suppose you'd get near it, the whole area is a military zone. There is a phone number for the house, here it is.' Portillo handed him a piece of paper, and then, with a swift movement, swept up the dollar bills and stuffed them in his pocket.

Anatoly and another Russian were waiting for him with his luggage at the hotel. Tolya appeared genial; only his eyes betrayed something more calculated. 'Mitya, I came to see you off. I wanted to say I was sorry about last night. You are on the Lufthansa flight?'

'I'm sure you checked.'

'You have a car coming for you? We are going out to the airport ourselves. You don't want a lift?'

'I've ordered a taxi.'

'Good. Good. Well, look after yourself, won't you?'

They shook hands.

On arrival at Ezeiza International Airport Dmitry checked in his suitcase. He looked around for Anatoly but couldn't see him; he did, however, spot the other man browsing through the papers in the kiosk. The flight was called, and Dmitry passed the security checkpoint, out of sight of the departure hall. Dmitry walked a few steps with him, glancing back. There was no sign of Anatoly's companion; perhaps they thought this evidence enough of his departure. He went back to one of the phone booths and slowly dialled the number in the Chaco; he did not even know why he was doing it, it seemed pointless. There was a long silence; the line did not connect. He hung up, picked up the receiver again, and dialled one last time.

The phone rang and rang, but no-one answered. He dialled again, one last time in desperation. A woman's voice answered; it was Katie.

Katie was standing in a pool of sunlight by the window. She was on her own in the house, and when the phone rang she hadn't bothered to answer at first, thinking it wouldn't be for her. When it rang the second time Katie answered cautiously, 'Hello?'

'It's me, Mitya.'

She was so stunned to hear his voice that she didn't know what to say. Then she said, 'Where are you?'

'In Buenos Aires. At the airport. I –'

The line went dead. Katie looked at the handset, bewildered; then she quickly hung up. She would not have believed that the sound of his voice could cause so much pain. She looked at the silent phone as if it were hostile; then, as she knew it would, it began to ring again. She snatched it up but again the line was dead. She hung up, unclenched her hands and stood listening to the silence. She waited, but nothing happened. She went slowly into the kitchen to get some coffee. She looked out of the window while she waited for the kettle to boil, looking at the shadows shifting almost imperceptibly on the wooden floor. Then suddenly the phone started to ring again.

She darted towards it, hesitated for a second, then picked it up. 'Yes?'

'There was something wrong with that phone, I couldn't get the tokens in. Listen to me, this is important. Did you get my fax?'

'Yes, just two days ago, on my way here. How did you find me here?'

'With difficulty. But you must leave at once. Can you get away?'

'Why? I'm coming back at the end of the week.'

'You have to leave there now, at once. There is going to be trouble.'

'What sort of trouble? I don't know if I can leave. You don't understand, we are miles away from anywhere. There aren't even any proper roads.'

'But there is a road. I've looked at the map. Aren't you near Mariscal Estigarribia?'

'Yes, but the road is just a dirt track. It's the main smuggling route from Bolivia. I couldn't go by myself. I don't understand.'

There was silence; Katie thought the line had been broken; then Dmitry's voice came back, clear and decisive. He said, 'Katie, you are in danger. You must leave and not tell anyone, no-one, do you understand? I can get a flight to Asunción today or tomorrow and try to meet you.'

'Mitya, I can't get to Asunción.'

'Then I'll meet you in Mariscal Estigarribia. Do you know the town?'

'No, I've never been there. I'll try to, but it's a military town, there's nothing there'

'The guide book says there's a hotel – the Hotel Alemán. I can be there tomorrow night. Will you do this for me? Will you promise me – oh shit, the money's running out.'

Katie said, 'Give me your number,' but there was only the long, high, disconnected tone. She waited by the phone, hoping he might ring back, but the phone stubbornly remained silent.

At the Lufthansa desk the girl looked as if Dmitry had gone mad when he asked if they could retrieve his baggage because he wasn't going on the flight.

She said, 'You're checked in. There is no refund.'

'I don't care. I just want my suitcase.'

'Well, I hope you realise we will probably have to delay the flight. Give me your ticket and boarding pass.'

He handed them over. She came back in a few minutes, handed it to him, and said, 'I have informed them. You will get your suitcase. Please wait here. Do you wish to re-book?'

'Not until I know my plans. Can I pick up the suitcase later? I have an urgent appointment to make.'

The girl looked at him oddly and he went hot all over; he realised they might think the suitcase had a bomb in it, no doubt they would check it thoroughly. He turned and walked away but no-one stopped him. He took a taxi back into the centre to the UN offices and asked to see the resident representative on an urgent matter. He had to wait some thirty minutes, then the secretary showed him in.

The res. rep. was a dour-faced Dutchman. He got up from his desk to shake Dmitry's hand and gestured to the chair, but Dmitry didn't sit down.

Dmitry explained that he had been at the nuclear energy conference. He said, 'I've had to change my travel plans. I need to get a visa for Paraguay. I know all travel is supposed to be approved in advance, but this is exceptional.'

The res. rep. looked tired and bored. 'Paraguay. But you're from the IAEA, aren't you? They're not going for nuclear power in Paraguay, surely? They've got all this hydroelectric power from Itaipú.' He raised his eyebrows slightly, clearly waiting for enlightenment.

'I was supposed to see somebody here, but I discovered he's in Paraguay. Someone from the Paraguayan Atomic Energy Commission. I thought I could go and see him on my way back.'

'Is this official business or unofficial?'

'It's . . . it should have been official. I mean, if I had seen him here it would have been official.'

'Can I see your *laissez-passer?*'

Dmitry handed it over. The res. rep. studied it carefully. Then he looked up at Dmitry. There was obviously something about this that he didn't like. He said, 'You must know how the system works. Any private detour has to be included in your travel authorisation. Can I see it, please?'

Dmitry felt in his inside pocket, 'It's here somewhere. Whatever do you want it for, anyway? I explained to you that this is a last-minute change of plan.'

'Well, I'm afraid our system isn't designed to cope with last minute changes of plan.'

Dmitry said, desperately, 'Well, supposing I had to take a flight back routing through Asunción – can you not even get me a transit visa?'

The res. rep. sighed. 'Are you new to the UN, or what? Anyone travelling on official duty must take the most direct route. I'm afraid this all sounds quite fantastic to me. I don't understand why you don't just travel on your national passport.'

'I am a Russian.'

An amused smile crossed the res. rep.'s features. 'Yes, of course. I suppose in the case of Paraguay that would present some difficulties. But I can't help you. Mind you, I think things are getting better since Stroessner went. You could try the Embassy. I must point out that this would still be irregular, but, no doubt you're aware of that.' He handed Dmitry back his *laissez-passer.*

Dmitry left the UN offices, chilled by the cool breeze blowing outside. He walked over to a nearby phone box and rang the airport about his suitcase. The woman from Lufthansa told him that someone from the Russian Embassy had already collected it. Dmitry hung up. He stood there, irresolute. He was in trouble. Everything was against his going. People like him did not behave like this. God knew how he would ever explain himself. He found another phone box and rang the Paraguayan Embassy; a woman answered. He asked if it was possible for a citizen of the Soviet Union to obtain a visa for Paraguay.

The woman laughed; she had a pleasant, musical voice. 'Well, never in the whole time I have worked here has this happened,' she said. 'When did you want to travel? Of course you can apply for one, and we will send off to Asunción, but really I think it is quite likely it would be refused. Well, I don't know, things are changing, but in any case, it would take some time.'

Dmitry hung up; that was it then. At that moment he would gladly have renounced his nationality and everything that went with it. Well, it was too bad about his suitcase, he would have to do without it. There was no way he was going to contact the Russian Embassy. He at least had his toothbrush and shaving things in his briefcase. He found a tailor's shop and bought himself a spare shirt and two pairs of underpants and went to find a cheap hotel for the night.

He strode along the street. The more he thought about his suitcase, the more it bothered him. Had Tolya collected the suitcase himself or had he informed someone else? Perhaps the KGB would now be onto him. They knew he had not gone; they knew he was still in Buenos Aires. They might try to look for him; it was conceivable they might check every hotel. Or they might inform the police that he was missing, that he was ill, that he was off his head. But what would be the point, when they knew he couldn't get a visa? Then there was his fear that the Brazilian plotters might be on to him again. They might now know that he had seen dos Santos – if that were so he wasn't safe anywhere. He would do better just to go home.

Then he thought of Katie, waiting for him at the hotel in Mariscal Estigarribia, sitting on the bed in the darkness in some awful room, waiting and waiting, and him not coming. It wasn't possible to do that to her; she would have gone there at some risk.

He went into a bookshop and looked in an atlas. There must be ways of crossing the Paraná. Wasn't there a ferry between Posadas and Encarnación? They might not check on passports – his UN *laissez-passer* looked impressive. He was on a diplomatic grade. Would some local border guard even know it had to be visaed? Then he thought of Iguazú. He remembered reading somewhere that there was a lot of smuggling over the border, the immigration controls were very lax. Traffic crossed the river daily, between Brazil, Argentina, Paraguay, to work, to market; he could fly to Puerto Iguazú on the Argentine side. He could cross into Brazil. From Foz do Iguaçu there was another bridge into Paraguay. The distance from there to Asunción was about 400 kilometres, and about 600 kilometres to Mariscal Estigarribia. It might take as long as twelve hours, depending on the roads.

He went to a café, found a phone and rang Aerolineas Argentinas. Yes, a woman told him, there were flights to Puerto Iguazú in the morning, from the domestic airport. The earliest was at six-fifty. She could book it now, but it wasn't full, there would be no problem. But Dmitry didn't want to make a reservation. He imagined they might check all outward flights.

He went back into the street. He felt light-headed and dizzy from lack of sleep, he hadn't eaten all day and the sun was very hot. He walked to the Palermo park, picking up a sandwich and a cold drink on the way. He sat down under a tree and had some lunch, then he rested his head on his briefcase and shut his eyes. He woke up suddenly, completely disoriented; he looked at his watch to find it was five o'clock. His suit was crumpled, his head was pounding, he felt like a tramp. He thought he had better go and find himself a hotel.

Dmitry took a *colectivo* to one of the seedier areas of the city. Old low houses with dark courtyards lined the streets. He found himself a small hotel and took a room under a false name. The woman at the desk, who was about sixty, plump, but not completely unattractive, said lazily, 'Passport?'

'I don't have one.' He didn't want to leave it in case they did check the hotels.

'Any other identification?'

'No.'

She looked at him shrewdly and then shrugged. She handed him a key. 'Is it just one night?'

'One night.'

'You pay in advance.'

He paid and went upstairs. The room was horrible. It was cramped, badly papered, had a cracked washstand, and looked out over a dank courtyard. He lay down on the bed. A couple were having sex in the next room; the bed banged rhythmically against the wall and he could hear the woman groaning. It occurred to him that it might be a hotel used by prostitutes. He tried to blot the sound out but despite himself it aroused him. He decided to go and get a meal; he took his briefcase with him. On the way out the woman said, 'Are you coming back?'

'I'm coming back.' But he thought he might find somewhere better.

It was getting dark. He was overcome with a fierce desire to see Katie; no, not to see her, to fuck her. The violence of it frightened him. He suddenly thought, what am I doing? It had seemed to him that they had loved one another; that was why he was going to Paraguay. But he remembered all too clearly that by the end love had had very little to do with it. Why was he going? He couldn't think that he could enter a country illegally and not face the consequences. What would the IAEA do? Already they were expecting him back tomorrow. His colleagues had been expecting him on the plane. He had not even thought to ring them or send a fax – he must do that in the morning. He could say he had been taken ill. Or that he had decided to take a couple of days holiday; they would be sympathetic, in view of what had happened.

He could ring Katie. He could ask her to come alone, he could meet her here in Buenos Aires. He went to find a call box. It didn't work. He found another one. The phone rang and a man's voice answered so he hung up. He started walking again. Abruptly he came to a halt. He had been walking, blindly, not aware of where he was going, and now he had no idea where he was. He was in a dark street; there were few street-lights. This was not a good part of town. He could be robbed and murdered. He could see, ahead of him, a shadow in a doorway. He turned and walked quickly back up the street. He walked faster and faster, then ran several blocks till he saw a street with bright lights and traffic; he jumped on the nearest *colectivo*, went to the back and stared out of the window.

The vehicle pulled out onto another main road. Now he recognised where he was; he was on the Avenida 9 de Julio. He got off at the next stop, found a café and ordered a drink. He saw a policeman walking past; almost instinctively, to hide his face, he turned his head away and put up his arm to run it through his hair. Then, suddenly, he put his head in his hands. He could not imagine how this had happened to him, walking like a madman across Buenos Aires, unable to go back to his sordid hotel, concealing his identity, afraid that out of every dark side street somebody would come to apprehend or kill him.

Taking hold of himself, he went and found another hotel; he had to bribe them to accept a reservation without a passport. He lay there on the uncomfortable mattress, listening to the sound of traffic roaring past and watching the pattern of the lights from the headlamps on the ceiling. Eventually he must have fallen asleep. Waking with a start, he realised his alarm was bleeping; he got shakily out of bed. He could hardly remember where he was and what he was doing; then he realised he had to catch the early morning flight to Puerto Iguazú.

He took a taxi to the airport. He had cut the journey a bit fine, and was afraid that he would be late and miss the flight. At the airport Dmitry saw from the departure board that there was a half-hour delay. He went to the desk and bought his ticket. Now he began to fret about the delay. The whole journey might take much longer than he thought. Supposing he were late, that Katie didn't wait for him . . .

He sat on a plastic airport chair and looked out of the window at the huge expanse of the Rio de la Plata. Dawn was breaking; there was a red, hazy bar of light over the water, fading to gold above; in this light the water seemed black and solid, lumpy like molten rock. He sat and looked at it for a long time; then realised with a start that they were calling his flight. He thought, I shouldn't go. This will lead to disaster. But he went and boarded all the same.

III

As soon as she had put the phone down, Katie began to regret her decision. It was not that she didn't want to be with Dmitry; the moment she had received his faxed letter she knew that she wanted to be with him, that she only wanted the child so much because it was his child, and that he offered her an escape from what was clearly to her now a dead marriage. But to meet him here? To begin with, she had no idea how she was going to get to Mariscal Estigarribia. What kind of excuse could she make? Who could she get to take her? She supposed she could say she just wanted to go back to Asunción, but then Bob would urge her just to wait another day or so. Besides, there was no reason to go by road rather than by air. She wondered if she could just say that she was bored and wanted someone to drive her there so she could have a look around. Did that sound odd? Was it suspicious? Supposing Bob offered to go there with her?

The second thing that worried her was how Dmitry was going to get there. He might not be able to get a visa; he was a Russian and, despite the changes, Paraguay was still firmly anti-communist. Besides, the whole area was crawling with the military, they were extra vigilant because of the rocket project. But what if he did come and she wasn't there?

She went upstairs and packed a few things into her shoulder bag. If she took any more they would be suspicious. Bob would be occupied with supervising the arrival of the rocket parts due in that day; he was in charge while Richter was in Europe. She decided not to tell him anything; she decided just to go.

Bob hung around the house all morning, waiting for the expected flight. Katie was tense and irritable, trying hard to keep up a semblance of normality; finally she told Bob she felt sick and went to lie down on the bed. The rocket parts arrived on the plane at two o'clock. She saw them unloading the numbered steel tubes and start to assemble them. Bob would be fully occupied for several hours; the problem was that he had a view of the house and all he had to do was look up to see her leave.

She went and found one of the drivers, a small, middle-aged man known as Mito, sitting sipping a can of *gaseosa* under a tree.

'Mito, I have to go and get something from Mariscal Estigarribia. How long will it take to get there?'

Mito looked blank. 'Maybe one, one-and-a-half hours.'

'So there's time to get there and back before dark?'

'Of course.'

'Could you bring the car round to the back of the house?'

'Now?'

'Yes, now.'

He did as he was asked. Katie left a note for Bob saying she was feeling ill and going to Asunción and to call her there tomorrow. She said she was sorry but she couldn't stand it in the Chaco any longer and she didn't want to disturb his work; she told him not to worry. Bob must have noticed the jeep leaving, but there was no reason for him to suspect she was in it and no-one took any notice of them.

It was hot, very hot. The jeep bumped around on the unmetalled roads, and Katie began to feel anxious about the pregnancy. It took just under an hour and a half to reach Mariscal Estigarribia. They drove round in the heat and dust looking for the hotel. When they found the Hotel Alemán Katie's heart sank. It was a low wooden building at the side of the road with a plastic Coca-Cola sign outside, a porch with some wagon wheels, and no sign of life. Katie walked round into the courtyard. Some tired-looking banana trees with tattered leaves leaned against the wall, and a few chickens were scratching in the dust. Three grubby, half-naked little girls ran out and stared at Katie. Then they started laughing and ran back in through an open door.

Katie asked the driver to wait outside. They were used to that; they would sit there waiting in the car all day unless told otherwise. She wondered what she should say to him. She didn't want him to go back; he would tell Bob where she was. In the end she went out and told him he could go off and get himself a drink or something and come back at seven. Then she went back to the hotel and called out to see if anyone was there.

She walked through the open door and into what appeared to be the dining room; there were chairs and plastic-covered tables. A man came out of the kitchen. He was wearing only a pair of baggy shorts over which a beer gut protruded.

'Can I help you? We have single or double rooms, breakfast included, all air-conditioned.' He spoke Spanish with a heavy German accent.

Katie said, in German, 'Just one room, for me. Someone may be joining me later.'

'Then you need a double; let me show you.' The rooms were in another building across the courtyard. He led her into one; it was reasonably clean, but small and absolutely basic; just two small, hard beds and a massive air-conditioner on the wall. The man turned it on; the noise was terrible. He switched it off again. 'There is a bathroom,' he said, indicating a door at the side. 'The other rooms are smaller and cheaper.'

'No; this will do,' said Katie.

'My name is Feldman; welcome. You are not German, but you speak it very well. Where are you from?'

'I am English,' said Katie, 'But I lived in Vienna.'

'Would you like anything to eat?'

She had a supper of grilled meat, rice and manioc. At seven, the driver came back. Katie said, 'I'm not feeling very well. I don't want to drive back. We'll stay the night here – I can get you a room.' She was embarrassed by him. She didn't want him to see Dmitry if he arrived. She wondered if there was anywhere else she could send him.

'Don't worry, I will sleep in the car,' said Mito.

Katie went back to the hotel room and sat on the hard bed in the darkness. At this point she wanted only to cry; she didn't think that Mitya would come and she was afraid of Bob coming after her. She worried about what would go through his mind; he would be anxious rather than suspicious; he would ring Asunción, find she had not arrived, and then what would he do? He would be crazy with worry. Perhaps she should call him and say where she was, that she'd felt ill and decided to stay here; but he might come to find her. Then if Mitya arrived, there would be a dreadful scene.

But Mitya might not come; she would go back to Asunción in the morning and wait for him there. After a while she began to think this was the best thing. She didn't know what to say to him; she was nervous of how she would respond to him; she didn't want to make love to him here, she felt it would somehow be wrong, as if real love could not exist in such sordid surroundings. Why ever hadn't she said she would meet him in Asunción? But even now he was probably on the road.

She lay down. She couldn't sleep. She kept listening out for any sound, any car pulling up outside, that might be Bob, or might be Dmitry. She kept looking at her watch. Hours went past, so slowly that the night was endless. It was dreadfully hot, oppressive, as if there might be a storm, but she couldn't bear the noise of the air-conditioner. For the twentieth time she looked at her watch; it was nearly midnight.

Then she heard the sound of a car and voices outside.

The flight from Buenos Aires to Puerto Iguazú took just under two hours. Coming down, once they had got below the cloud, the plane banked over the Iguazú Falls; Dmitry could see them spread out before him in the jungle, clouds of white spray rising up out of the foaming water.

Most of the people on the plane were tourists; from the airport there were buses going to the cataracts and across the border to Foz do Iguaçu in Brazil. The sky was overcast and the air was damp as Dmitry climbed into the Brazil-bound bus. He glanced impatiently at his watch. It was eight-thirty. The bus carried him along a straight road through the sub-tropical jungle. Before the bridge the customs officials and police showed no interest in checking passports but waved them through; this bode well, thought Dmitry, for crossing into Paraguay.

It began to rain. Foz do Iguaçu, especially without sunlight, was a depressing place. The traffic was jammed, the skyscrapers loomed behind the huge hoardings, everywhere people were scurrying to work, their thin shirts soaked by the rain. At the bus station Dmitry did not know what to do next. He stood with his briefcase in his hand, wondering whether it was best to get another bus or try to get a lift in a private car. He hovered there, unable to decide. This was absurd; he should turn back; this really was the point of no return.

He walked in the rain down towards the bridge. He was wet through, but it didn't matter, it was so warm. The rain eased; a moist wind blew in his face. Across the river the new town of Ciudad del Este sprawled in front of him, hideous with its tower blocks, building sites and shanty towns. The road sloped down to the bridge; underneath it ran the Paraná, unexpectedly narrow in its deep channel through the red earth.

There was a steady stream of traffic crossing the bridge; most of it seemed to be waved through without a hitch, at least on the Brazilian side. Dmitry turned around and held out his arm to hitch a lift. The first few cars sped past; then a large lorry; then a battered car with Paraguayan number-plates pulled up. Dmitry asked, in Spanish, 'Can you take me across the bridge?' The man shrugged and Dmitry opened the door and got in. The driver started the car. The steering seemed wobbly and the engine made an unhealthy noise.

'Where are you going?'

'Only to Ciudad del Este.'

'American? German? Tourist?'

'Tourist, yes.'

'You have been to see the cataracts?'

'*Sí.*' They were a major tourist attraction; people must cross the border all the time to see them. He thought, if they ask to see my passport I could tell them I'd been over to the Iguazú Falls and left my passport behind in the hotel.

They crossed to the Paraguayan side and the frontier police did not take the slightest notice of them. The driver pulled up and said, 'You want to get out here?' Dmitry nodded. He felt like laughing; it was absurd that he had expended so much energy over the question of how he was going to cross the border. The car drove off leaving a trail of noxious fumes and Dmitry set out in search of a bank and a garage from which to hire a car.

It was late afternoon by the time he reached the outskirts of Asunción. He drove into the centre, and was surprised to see a yellow tram trundling down the middle of the road; it reminded him instantly of Vienna. Another tram came up behind him; he had to drive onto the pavement to avoid it. He felt confused, so tired he could no longer drive safely. He thought that if he didn't get anything to eat or drink he would collapse. He parked the car behind a stand of yellow taxis and wandered down the street.

Near the corner was a bar with a wooden sign which said: 'Bavaria Bar.' It occurred to Dmitry that he could ask for information there; perhaps they might know the Hotel Alemán. He wandered inside, sat down at the bar and beckoned to a plump, attractive Paraguayan woman who was serving. He looked around. The bar had a low wooden ceiling and paintings of chalets and cows in green meadows on the panelled walls. The woman came over and took his order, beer and some sausages.

'Is the owner German?' he asked.

'Yes – Ludwig Grüber. He'll be here shortly. You want to speak to him?'

'If it's possible.'

'Sit down over there. It won't be long.'

Dmitry moved away from the bar and sat down at the table she had pointed out. He looked at his watch. It would take at least five or six hours to reach Mariscal Estigarribia, depending on the state of the roads. He thought again of Katie waiting in the hotel. The girl brought a plate of spicy sausages and salad and a cold beer. She asked, 'You are German too?'

'No, but I speak German. I wanted to ask for some advice about going to the Chaco.'

'To Filadelfia? To the Mennonite colonies?'

'To Mariscal Estigarribia.'

'Why? There's nothing there, it's a military town. Do you have some special reason? I'll ask Señor Grüber . . .'

Dmitry ate and drank. The air was now dusky in the street; the bar began to fill up. There was an overpowering smell of spicy sausages; the heat from the grill fought with the heat from the street outside. After a while, a sour-faced German of about fifty came over to him. 'Yes?'

'I'm going to Mariscal Estigarribia, I wondered how long it would take me, how good the roads are.'

'It will take about six or seven hours. The road's good to the turn-off to Filadelfia, they've started to asphalt it but I don't know how far they've got. There aren't many gas stations, fill up when you see one. Take plenty of water. Why are you going to the Chaco? Hunting?'

'Perhaps.'

'The problem is that this is a military zone. If you're going beyond Mariscal Estigarribia it helps to have some kind of written permit. There have been lots of stories of people being stopped and turned back north of there. In any case, there are military checkpoints along the trans-Chaco highway. You have to carry your passport and maybe some kind of *permiso* .'

Dmitry listened in silence. Suddenly the whole thing seemed impossible; he was overcome with a sense of futility. Why hadn't he thought this through? A bead of sweat dripped down his nose and he didn't have the energy to wipe it away. He stared at the naïve paintings of cows in green fields with desperation.

Grüber tapped his shoulder. 'Here, why don't you talk to the colonel? He knows all about the Chaco.' He called over to a man sitting nearby, 'César, this man wants to know about the Chaco,' and introduced him – 'Colonel César Madregón. He is retired, he fell out with the previous regime.' The phone rang, Grüber excused himself and went out of the door at the back.

The colonel came over and sat down beside Dmitry. Even in ordinary clothes he had a definite military bearing. He was in his fifties; he had probably put on weight recently and his belt was pulled tightly over his belly. His face was creased and there was a warm and friendly look in his eyes. He had brought his beer with him and poured out another glass. It was so cold that the sides of the glass frosted instantly.

'The Chaco,' he said. 'You are going to the Chaco? Have you some special purpose?'

Dmitry said, finding it an effort to get the words out, 'Señor Grüber mentioned hunting.'

'Ah! You want to hunt the *tigre*, eh? Well, this I can arrange if you would like it. You will have to come with me. It is illegal, of course, but that is of no consequence. You want to hire me as your guide?'

Dmitry sat upright; he grinned; in an instant this man had become his salvation. He asked, 'How much?'

'A hundred dollars a day. When are you wanting to go?'

'Tonight.'

'Tonight.' César Madregón raised his eyebrows. He repeated, as if he had not quite understood him, 'You want to go tonight.'

'Now, in fact.'

'Now.' Madregón looked at him; then he suddenly slapped his thigh and roared with laughter. 'Well,' he said, 'Why not now? Of course, why not?'

Dmitry looked him in the eye and decided that he liked this man. César Madregón stood up. 'Well, then,' he said, 'Finish your beer. Do you have a vehicle? Anyway, it's better if we go in mine. You can buy the petrol. We'll go past my house and pick up some things. It's on the way. You have any equipment?'

'Equipment?'

'For shooting *tigre*.' He held up his hands to mimic the action of firing a rifle.

Dmitry laughed. 'They don't let you bring them on the aeroplane, you know.'

'Of course, of course. You have everything with you?'

Dmitry pointed at his briefcase. 'Everything.'

'You travel light, eh?'

'The airline lost my luggage.'

'Hah!' Madregón roared with laughter. 'Well. Come.' Madregón's jeep was parked outside. They bought petrol, Madregón tossed four large bottles of mineral water and a supply of cigarettes in the back. Dmitry pulled three hundred-dollar bills out of his wallet and handed them to Madregón. 'And the petrol – here's something to cover that.' Madregón grinned and put the money in his wallet. He reversed the jeep into the road and they drove for ten or fifteen minutes to a suburban street where Madregón pulled up outside a wooden bungalow. In a matter of minutes he had collected some bags, a crate of beer and a case of what Dmitry assumed were rifles and flung them into the back of the vehicle. Within minutes they were speeding through the city. César Madregón pointed out various landmarks, which mostly seemed to represent some site of plot or intrigue. 'This is the Club des Officiales where the coup that ousted Stroessner was planned. This is Stroessner's old house – two journalists were arrested recently for taking photographs of it. Do you want to see Rodriguez' house? No? Well, it's not on our way. It's an enormous mansion, a chateau, there's not another house like it in all Paraguay. And where do you think he got the money for it, eh?'

Dmitry shrugged. They were in a queue of traffic leaving the centre; he glanced at his watch. It was just after six. The light was strange. There were great holes in the clouds through which the sky glowed with a dirty yellow colour. By a curious illusion the grey clouds seemed transparent while the sky itself seemed dense, opaque. They drove past a tangle of cheap houses in which lights were being lit, past carts drawn by horses and slow-moving bicycles, then out onto the huge curving bridge over the vast width of the Rio Paraguay. From the top of the bridge Dmitry could see the endless, flat, grey-green expanse of the Chaco spreading out before him, doubly mysterious in the half-light. The sky seemed low and threatening.

Madregón said, 'We may have trouble. It may rain tonight.'

'Is that a problem?'

'Once we're off the asphalt highway, yes. But maybe it will hold off. I think so.'

'Does it rain much in the Chaco?'

'No, but when it does rain, the water sits on top of the ground. The roads are hard when they are dry, but a little rain and you cannot drive, you slip about all over the place. You understand me?'

Dmitry was having trouble with the Paraguayan Spanish, but he got the gist of it.

'You didn't tell me your name.'

'Mitya Gavrilov.'

'But this is a Russian name?'

Dmitry said vaguely, 'Yes, the country of my origins.'

'Well, we have some Russian connections here, you know. Some of the Mennonites came from Russia, did you know this? Also there was a famous cartographer, Juan Belayev – you have heard of Juan Belayev? There have been a number of Russian immigrants in the old days. Now of course it is impossible to imagine a Russian in anti-communist Paraguay. You are from Germany?'

'From Vienna.'

'Ah, Vienna. They have trams there too, I think? I have seen them in pictures.'

Over the river they came to the first military checkpoint. Madregón wound down the window. The soldier, barely sixteen, eyed them nervously.

'Where are you going?'

'Visiting friends in Mariscal Estigarribia.' Madregón chatted for a minute or so, then the soldier waved them on. As they drove downhill through Villa Hayes the road began to straighten out. There was no traffic, and soon it was quite dark. The road ran straight ahead of them into the darkness, the headlamps illuminating it a short distance ahead, lighting up the stems of the palm trees on either side. From time to time Dmitry caught a glimpse of water gleaming under the palms. César Madregón kept talking. At times Dmitry listened, then his thoughts overtook him; Madregón's voice came in waves as if he was listening to him on a badly tuned radio.

'We are very excited here, you know,' said Madregón. 'At first we were all a little sceptical. Rodriguez after all was a military man through and through, and his daughter married to one of the General's sons. But it does seem that he is serious about democratising, there was too much pressure on him from all around. Even in Paraguay we cannot escape the tide of the times. Everywhere in the world the time of the dictator is coming to an end – this is the benefit we are all reaping from the end of the cold war, no? The US no longer has to support all these dictatorships in the fight against communism, because the fight against communism doesn't signify anything any more.'

As the kilometres rolled by and the landscape remained the same, monotonous, uninhabited and eerie, Dmitry began to have an odd sensation, as if they were driving off the edge of the world – not just of the physical world, but from the whole past structure of a world which was transforming itself. Madregón was right. The old order was breaking apart, yet people continued to think along the old lines, unable to reorganise their mental habits. The outlines of the old system remained, though everything had crumbled within. Dmitry felt a pain in his head, as if his own mind was disintegrating and reforming itself while he sat there, weary, in this car, holding himself upright and still clutching his UN *laissez-passer* in his hand as if this alone could guarantee his existence. He had the strangest sensation that he was letting go of everything, a consciousness of leaving the world he knew behind, and was heading into the vast, uninhabited heart of the continent, the *tierra incognita*.

'*Impresionante*, eh?' said Madregón.

Dmitry jerked awake. He must have fallen asleep for a moment. He sat up and peered out into the dark.

Madregón was still talking, one hand on the wheel, the other making eloquent gestures in the air. 'They are planning one day to develop the Chaco. Imagine, in this whole area, half of Paraguay, live only two per cent of the people. Some of these are the *indígenas*. The problem is there is no water, there are no power lines. See that big radio tower for telecommunications over there?'

'Do the US have a military base here?'

'Do they? Well that is a good question. There is an airfield near Mariscal Estigarribia. It was built with American engineers – it is huge, asphalted, seven kilometres long. No-one really knows what it is for. One rumour was that it was to land the space shuttle; others that it is just a strategic point, in case they ever need to land large numbers of troops in south America. The Americans use Paraguay as a listening post, you know. They can take in five countries.'

'But isn't there something else going on in the Chaco? I read something in the paper in Buenos Aires – something about testing rockets?'

'Ah, the rocket project. Yes, indeed, it's true. This is an extraordinary business. That is why we have to be a bit careful, these days. It's a German behind it – they say he made a secret deal with Stroessner in his last days in power; but nobody really knows what is going on there. A journalist went to report on it, and never came back. His body was found a few days later. They said it was drug smugglers.'

Madregón leaned towards Dmitry. 'Listen, I can tell you a very strange story about this. Don't ask me any questions about it, because this is all I know. It happened a few weeks ago, though of course it was not reported in the papers. Two Indians in the forest near Cerro León came across a silver object – something made of shiny metal, cylindrical. They tried to open it, messed around with it, trying to see what it was. When they got home they became very sick and in a few days they died. I didn't believe this, there are so many odd stories told in the Chaco, but a pilot friend and I decided to go and have a look. We overflew the area in a light aeroplane and we did indeed see this metal thing in the forest, but there was no airstrip, we couldn't land. And then a military aeroplane came and chased us away from the site.'

'What did it look like, this object?'

'Round, metallic – hard to say exactly how big it was.'

'And the sickness which overtook the Indians?'

'Oh, there were several versions – they got old overnight, they shrivelled up, they vomited blood. I don't know if a doctor ever saw them, I don't even know if it's true. There was talk of digging up the bodies to see what had happened; but you have to understand that there have been stories like this before, of people seeing spaceships and other strange things in the forest. The Chaco is the kind of place where anything could happen and no-one would ever know about it.'

'On the contrary,' said Dmitry, 'These days everyone knows everything about what is going on. This rocket project, for instance, is hardly a secret.'

'No; this is something very curious,' said Madregón. 'It does not seem to be anything to do with the Americans, and in fact, there have been rumours that the Americans have recently tried to persuade Rodriguez to drop it. There's no doubt that if the Americans wanted the rocket project cancelled Rodriguez would have to comply.'

'But then,' said Dmitry, 'If they stop him here, in Paraguay, what's to stop him going somewhere else, maybe somewhere which isn't so amenable to US influence?'

'Hah!' said Madregón. 'You are right of course – yes, that must be why.' He glanced sideways at Dmitry. 'Very good. I like the way you think.'

They stopped to fill up with petrol at Pozo Colorado. Dmitry peered at the map. What looked there like a fair-sized town seemed to consist of a military post, a filling station and cheap café, and a few wooden houses. The proximity of the soldiers standing guard across the road made Dmitry nervous.

'Don't they ever ask for our papers?'

'Sometimes. Most of them know me. Want a cigarette? Some *maté?*'

Madregón took a thermos flask and a wooden cup out of the glove-box; he poured water into the cup and handed it to Dmitry. The liquid was green and tasted dreadfully bitter.

Madregón took the cup from Dmitry and drank. 'So where were you thinking of staying the night? There is a good hotel in Filadelfia.'

'There's a hotel in Mariscal Estigarribia – the Alemán.'

'The Alemán.' Madregón shrugged. 'I've never heard of it'

He started up the jeep and drove on. The landscape was changing subtly. The palm trees had given way to thicker forests which had been cleared here and there for grazing cattle. Exhausted though he was, Dmitry couldn't sleep; the eerie sensation which he had felt earlier grew even stronger. The two men were silent now; there was nothing but the noise and vibration of the car, the headlamps on the road, the outline of the trees, the dark sky.

Some kilometres north of the turn-off to Filadelfia, past the next checkpoint, they came to the end of the tarmac. Huge earth-moving vehicles stood silent and abandoned on the road. The jeep bounced down to the old earth road running alongside the earthworks. At once they slowed down; a fine dust blew in through the windows. Madregón wound his up.

The road shone white in the light of the headlamps, which turned every hollow into a pit of darkness. They jolted along the unmade road for some time; conversation was now impossible as Madregón concentrated on manoeuvring the jeep. Finally, round the corner, the headlights lit up a wooden sign proclaiming 'Welcome to the city of Mariscal Estigarribia.'

Ahead of them, up the road, a brick gateway blocked the entrance to the town. Soldiers stood on either side. Madregón stopped and wound down the window. He handed over his card and said to Dmitry, 'Your passport?'

Dmitry handed Madregón his UN *laissez-passer*. The soldier wrote down the number and the registration number of the car. Madregón took Dmitry's pass and studied it.

'United Nations?' he said. 'And you want to go shooting *tigre?* You are not, I hope, a member of the UN environment programme?' He handed the passport to the soldier who wrote the details down. Through the gateway was a wide, dusty street, lined with bottle-shaped trees whose swollen trunks were painted white. They drove slowly, past the brick church, a tiny post office, the brick-built houses of the military. There was no sign of any hotel. Eventually Madregón found a soldier on the street and asked him. Dmitry understood nothing; they were speaking Guaraní. Madregón turned the jeep round and headed back towards the gate.

'It's just outside the town here – I can't imagine what it is like. I have a friend here I'll stay with. You want me to collect you in the morning?'

Dmitry nodded. Then he said, 'I have to tell you, I have been guilty of a small deception. I did not come here to shoot the *tigre* – I came to meet a woman.'

Madregón stopped the jeep. He looked at Dmitry in astonishment and then roared with laughter. 'But you should have warned me,' he said. 'That is much more dangerous!'

The Hotel Alemán lay hidden behind some trees. Dmitry climbed out of the jeep; Madregón stopped the engine. The silence struck him at once; an eerie silence, which after a few moments was filled with the sound of insects and the rustle of the wind in the dry trees. As he walked towards the entrance the fine dust of the Chaco clung to his shoes.

Madregón called after him, 'I'll come back in the morning. I hope she is there for you.'

Dmitry walked into the hotel. A man was there, asleep in a chair; he lay with his mouth open, and didn't stir. Dmitry tiptoed past him. There was no sign of anyone around. He walked into the courtyard; everything was in darkness. Then a light came on and a door opened. It was Katie. She was standing in the doorway. She whispered, 'Come in.'

IV

Katie stood still, her heart fluttering with apprehension, as Dmitry walked into the room. They stood facing one another in the stark light from the dusty fluorescent tube. Dmitry looked exhausted, his pale skin almost blue in this ugly light; there was an uneven stubble on his chin and his shirt was sticky with sweat. He looked too large, out of place, in this miserable room. He looked as she had expected him, and yet, different. She felt nervous, almost shy; hesitantly, she held out her arms towards him.

He stepped forward and embraced her for a moment, then held her away from him, staring at her face intently, and then her body. Neither of them spoke. He sat down on the bed next to her in sudden weariness, still holding onto her hand, and Katie sat down beside him. She said, 'I didn't understand what you were saying, on the phone. Why am I in danger? You frightened me. Shall we leave at once?'

'No, I'm exhausted. I couldn't drive anywhere tonight.' Then he asked, 'Do you have a car?'

'Yes, it's outside.'

Dmitry lay down on the bed and shut his eyes for a second. Katie was afraid to touch him; the room was so sordid, with the furniture so cheap, the sheets rough and grey, and their reflection distorted in the cracked mirror above the basin. Abruptly, Katie switched off the light.

He asked, 'Is there somewhere to have a shower?' She pointed to the bathroom. In the darkness she heard him taking off his clothes. He put on the light in the bathroom and she heard the water running. She, too, was sweaty; it was unbearably hot and humid in the stuffy room. She slipped off her night-dress and followed him.

The water was lukewarm, but refreshing. She stood under the shower with him, running her hands over his body; then he put his arms around her. She had forgotten the feel of his skin, its softness over the hard and angular bones, and the infinite gentleness of his large, sensitive hands. To touch him gave her a feeling at once of rightness, belonging.

She turned her face up to him, shutting her eyes as the water ran over her face. 'I was afraid I wouldn't feel the same about you.'

'And do you?'

'Yes.'

He began to kiss her, gentle kisses on her eyes, her cheeks, her mouth; he was aroused, but she was half afraid of him; pregnant, and having had one miscarriage, she was uncertain about making love. She left him abruptly and went into the bedroom, half-heartedly drying herself. He followed her, leaving the light on in the bathroom, casting a softer light into the room.

'Katie; what is it?' He came to sit beside her, and she turned to him, gazing at the long red scar bisecting his chest. She ran her finger along it, thinking how she had last seen him, so distant and untouchable. His skin was very pale, with that translucent quality she remembered; against it the scar showed up harshly. He had lost some weight.

She asked, very softly, 'What is going on, Mitya? Tell me, why did you come? If you say I am in danger I must believe you, after what happened. Is it because of Richter?'

He hesitated for a long time. 'I heard that they are going to destroy the rocket range – Richter, everyone there, might be killed.'

'They?'

He didn't answer her. Katie looked at him, not saying anything either. Her first thought was that she should warn Bob; but she knew Dmitry wouldn't let her. If she warned Bob, he would warn Richter, and so on. She must be very careful about what she said or did. And how did Dmitry know this? Once again she felt the prickly touch of fear.

He ran his hands over her body, kissing her, turning her towards him. She resisted. She said, 'No, Mitya, I can't, not now, I'm afraid – the baby.' He said, 'I can be very gentle,' and she said, 'No, you don't understand. I lost the last baby, at three months. And I do so much want this one.' He took her in his arms then, lying down, pulling her against him, stroked her arms and neck and hair. She felt him against her, his penis hard against her thigh, and she also felt the stirrings of desire; but she didn't give into it. She felt him gradually relax, softening; after a while she realised he was asleep.

Katie could not sleep. The bed was far from comfortable; the mattress was lumpy and sagged on one side. The air was unbearably hot and humid, but if she got up and put the air conditioner on, it very rapidly became too cold. She had to pull the sheet up to protect her from the mosquito which whined overhead. She was alarmed, afraid; she wanted to get away, to get back to safety. Eventually she must have slept because she woke early, quite soon after dawn, feeling sick and headachy; Dmitry was already awake and dressed, sitting on the end of the bed, waiting for her.

He said, 'We should go. It's already light.' They looked out of the window; the sky was overcast and heavy and it felt as if there might be a storm.

Katie went into the dining room. There was no sign of anyone. She fetched some orange juice and bread from the kitchen and left some money on the table so as not to disturb Feldman. Mito was still outside in the car. She told him they were taking the car and he should wait here for someone to collect him. She said she wasn't well and was going to Asunción.

The clouds were dark, oppressive, and cast a grim shadow over the endless expanse of grey-green trees. Dmitry drove fast, raising a cloud of dust; Katie said, 'Don't drive so quickly. It doesn't matter. We're not in that much of a hurry.'

'It would be best to get to the metalled road before there's any rain.'

The landscape looked gloomy without the sun and Katie felt her spirits sinking. Dmitry, sensing this, started to sing to cheer her up, some Russian song about a crocodile. Katie put her hand on his thigh and he glanced at her; he laughed; she was not sure she had seen him so happy before. She said: 'Are you enjoying this?'

'Yes? Aren't you?'

'Do you love me?'

She said it unthinkingly; she had never asked him this before. He replied as lightly, automatically, 'Of course I do.' He had never admitted it either; she did not know why it made a difference to her to hear it said, but it made all the difference in the world. She felt high with happiness. The possibility of danger, the fear that Bob might follow her, her tiredness and nausea, all evaporated. The car, bouncing over the unmade road in the centre of the continent, became the container of all that was precious to her; her unborn child, her lover; only Anna was missing, and they would be with her soon. She said, 'Then everything's all right.' And then the first raindrops fell.

Dmitry switched on the windscreen wipers, but the rain was falling so fast that they could hardly see. The car slipped on the wet surface of the road; it spun clockwise; Dmitry straightened it out, then it spun in the opposite direction. They had been travelling quite fast; he could not get control of it; they bounced over the rough ground at the side of the road and the vehicle seemed to make a massive leap, ending with a crunch in the thorn scrub. They sat still, stunned. The noise of the rain on the roof was deafening.

Fortunately they had both been strapped in. Katie said, 'You were going too fast.' Dmitry turned to look at her. He said, 'I don't think there's much damage. We'll just have to wait until the rain stops.'

But it went on and on raining. It rained for over an hour. Thunder and lightning roared overheard. The rain was so heavy that it seemed to form a solid wall around them.

When the rain finally stopped it did so quite suddenly. Dmitry climbed out and examined the front of the vehicle. The lights were smashed and the bonnet was slightly buckled. Then he looked at the road. Water was lying everywhere; it lay on the grass all around them; it would take time to sink into the parched earth. He said, 'We'll have to wait for a while before trying to drive any further.'

They sat and waited. Eventually the sun came out; the road was steaming. But the car would not start. The engine growled but did not come to life. After several attempts, afraid of running down the battery, Dmitry got out and opened the bonnet.

'Is it the battery?'

'I don't know. Perhaps water has got into the electrics somehow. I'm afraid I'm not very good at this. I might be more use if it was nuclear-powered. Look in the front there, maybe there's a manual of some kind.'

There wasn't. Katie stood in the boiling sun and watched him checking over the engine. 'What will we do if we can't start it?'

Dmitry didn't reply. There was no shade; the sun was directly overhead. She looked up the road, lying like a red gash across the landscape, and then, in the distance, towards Mariscal Estigarribia, she saw the sun glinting on something. Whatever it was, it was on the road and moving. She said, 'Mitya, I think there's a car coming. Perhaps they'll be able to help.'

Dmitry stepped away from the engine. His hands were black with grease; he stood behind her and rested his forearms on her shoulders, peering into the distance. The vehicle was coming slowly, negotiating the slippery road with care; it grew imperceptibly bigger, and in the fierce sunlight and the mist of steam rising off the road it was impossible to make out anything clearly. Finally it became clear that it was a jeep; there were two men sitting on the back. They held in their hands objects which might have been sticks but which were more likely to be rifles.

The jeep drew to a halt a few yards from where they were standing. They couldn't see the driver's face at first; then as he climbed down out of the jeep and turned his face to them, Katie started violently. It was Bob.

They remained as they were; Dmitry standing behind Katie, unable to think of anything to say. In the back, the two men casually lowered the rifles to point in their direction.

Katie was aware that by standing as she was in front of Dmitry she was protecting him. She leaned closer against him; Bob looked at Dmitry as if he could not believe what he was seeing. His face was tight with anger. He said, 'What the hell are you doing here?'

Katie began, 'Bob –'

'Let him answer me. And get away from him.'

'No.'

The two men got out of the back of the jeep and stood not far away. They moved carefully, so that one of them always had a rifle covering them. They looked insolent, amused. Katie did not like the way they handled their weapons, as if eager for a chance to show their skill. She said, 'Bob, tell them to put those things away. One of them might go off and hit us by mistake.'

'That would be less likely to happen if you got away from him.'

'Bob, please be reasonable. I'm in love with him. I'm leaving you. I want a divorce.'

'You expect me to believe that? That he turns up here only to run away with you?' Bob stepped forward, took Katie's wrist and dragged her away from Dmitry. Perhaps it was because Dmitry's hands were black with engine grease that he didn't try to hold on to her; or perhaps he thought it was better not to start a fight. Once Katie was out of the line of fire, one of the men deliberately slipped the safety catch off the rifle and aimed it more accurately at Dmitry.

Katie started to shout in desperation; Bob was so angry that she thought he might do anything. She said, 'You're not going to let them kill him –' and she grabbed her husband's shirt with one hand, raising the other to strike out at him. Then she stopped, realising its uselessness.

Bob's voice was very quiet and controlled. 'No, that won't be necessary.' He turned to the men. 'Tie his hands and get him in the back of the jeep.'

The taller of the two men stepped forward. 'Put your hands behind your back.' Dmitry did so without a protest; he kept his head held up and smiled at Katie reassuringly. Katie said in a low voice, 'Bob, you can't do this. What are you doing this for? You must have gone mad.' She had never felt so frightened. Then something happened; perhaps Dmitry had made some sudden movement, perhaps he had spoken some insult, but the guard who had been tying his hands struck him suddenly in the stomach with his rifle butt. Dmitry doubled up; the guard hit him again, and then a third time, on the back; they were heavy blows. Katie screamed; Bob restrained her; Dmitry fell to his knees, still doubled over, swaying to keep his balance with his hands behind his back.

The guard gave Dmitry a final kick in the side and he fell forward onto the road.

Bob said, 'That's enough.' He kept an iron grip on Katie's wrist. He said, 'Have you got your things in the car? Get them out and put them in the jeep.'

Katie did as he told her. She would have gone to Dmitry at once but she was too frightened; the two men were lifting him to his feet. He was covered in red mud and his face was white with shock and pain. He made no resistance as they took him to the jeep and half threw him into the back. Katie climbed into the front with Bob.

She asked, 'Where are we going?'

'Back to the rocket range. I have a feeling they will be interested to meet your friend there.'

Katie said, 'I can't believe this. Something's happened to you. How can you behave like this?' She turned round to Dmitry; he was sitting upright and didn't look too bad. She tried to keep calm, to think of the best way to handle this. They drove back to Mariscal Estigarribia; they had to go very slowly because of the condition of the road. When they reached the town Bob said, 'We can't drive on, the road will be impassable. What the hell do we do now?'

Katie suggested the hotel. One of the soldiers stayed in the jeep and the other came with them. He had untied Dmitry's hands. Feldman didn't seem in the least surprised at seeing them. He showed them two rooms. Bob left the soldier watching Dmitry in one while he took Katie into the other.

Katie struggled to keep her voice calm and reasonable. 'Bob, whatever has happened, please let me go home with Mitya. I can't live with you any longer. There's something about you; you frighten me. I don't want to have anything to do with Richter and all this, I want some kind of normal life for myself, and Anna, and this other baby.'

'What do you mean, a normal life? What kind of a life do you think you'll have with Gavrilov? Don't you realise what he's up to? He's just making use of you.'

'That isn't true.'

'Are you so sure of that?' Bob looked at her, white-faced, deeply shaken as well as angry.

Katie's voice was very quiet. 'Bob, it's all over between us and there's no point in seeking revenge.'

'Why shouldn't I seek revenge? That Russian bastard has fucked everything up all along the line. You don't have the least idea – you are letting yourself get involved in things you don't understand. Are you really expecting me to believe that he's come here just to find you? You think I'll just sit back and let you go off with him, and this child you're carrying, and go God knows where? Is that really what you think I'd do?'

Katie said, 'I think this other baby is his.'

Bob stared at her with such coldness that her mouth went dry and she could feel sweat breaking out all over her. He moved towards her. He said, 'That's not possible. You told me that was not possible.'

'I lied about the dates. It's already three months.'

'You lied about the dates.' His voice rose in disbelief. 'My God. I would never have believed you could do this. And you say you want another baby – you're not fit to be a mother!'

A look of disgust came over him, as if he could not bear to think of what she had done. 'I don't understand how you can even touch that man. He is repulsive. And what the hell do you think he's doing here? Well, we'll find out, won't we?'

The threat behind this brought Katie to her feet. 'What are you going to do? You can't hold Dmitry like this. He is nothing to do with this rocket business. Why don't you just let him go back to Asunción?'

'So that you can join him there.'

'Whatever you do I'm going to leave you.'

'We'll see.' Bob left the room abruptly, banging the door behind him. Katie sat on the bed in torment. The walls were very thin; she could hear Bob talking to the soldier in the next room. Then he came back and said they would all go and have something to eat. Katie followed him into the dining room. Dmitry was already there, with the two guards, at the table. The atmosphere in there was unbearably oppressive. The windows were open, but there was hardly a breath of air; Bob walked up and down uneasily. Dmitry looked up at Katie when she came in but his face showed no expression. He shook his head slightly as if to tell her to say nothing to him.

Feldman came in and tried to make conversation. He put the food on the table with some Paraguayan beer.

Bob said, 'Sit down,' and Katie sat at the table. It was like that; he had absolute control over all of them.

Bob turned to Dmitry. 'But there's more to it than this, isn't there? Why did you come here?'

Katie put her hand on his arm. 'Bob, I've told you the truth –'

Bob ignored her, pushing her hand aside. 'I could get rid of you altogether. I could tell these two men to take you out to the rocket range and shoot you. You realise that, don't you? It would be perfectly legal. The territory is RASAG's. Nobody could do anything about it.'

Dmitry looked Bob straight in the face. He said, 'You have the power to do that, of course, if you want to, if that is the kind of man you are.'

Katie watched Bob's face. It was twisted with anger. Katie could see how Dmitry threatened him in every way, physically, intellectually, morally; no wander Bob hated him. She said, 'Please don't talk like this, Bob. Don't say such things, you don't mean them.'

Feldman came in and cleared away the plates. Bob said, 'You don't have any playing cards, do you? We could play cards to pass the time.'

Dmitry said, 'Isn't it chess that one plays with death?'

Feldman came back with a bottle of whisky and a pack of tattered playing cards which he put on the table. He clearly didn't like the atmosphere in the room, and hastily went out again. Bob knocked back a large glass of whisky and began to shuffle the cards. 'Can you play poker?'

Dmitry looked straight at him. 'Of course, it's only too easy to deceive when you hide the cards; but you should know that chess, even though you can see the whole board, is also a game of deceit.'

Bob looked up, sharply. 'What are you trying to say?'

'How much did they pay you, the Brazilians, to organise that inspection? You tipped them off, didn't you, about Müller, you covered up for him. Did you know they were going to kill him?'

Katie went hot and cold all over. Bob got to his feet; he was outraged. 'Is that what you think? Is that what you've told her? Is that why –'

Katie grabbed his arm. 'No, Bob, he's never said anything –'

'You're a fool.' He spat the word out at her. 'You're both fools. You don't know anything, you don't understand anything, you're meddling in things you can't begin to comprehend –' he broke off and turned to Dmitry. 'Or do you understand things only too well?'

Katie looked from one to the other of them in utter confusion. Could this be true? If so, Bob would have known all along the reasons for Müller's death, even had a part in it – no, that wasn't possible. What could be his motive? But if it were, he would be capable of anything.

Dmitry went on, quietly, 'Who was behind it? Who was your contact in Brazil?'

'I thought you told me you were here for Katie? What are all these questions? Do you think I am going to answer them?' Bob turned to one of the men. 'For God's sake watch him. Take it in turns to sleep. If you hear anything in the corridor, check it out.'

He took Katie's hand and led her into the next room. As soon as they were alone, Katie knew what he was going to ask her. The whisky seemed to have had an instant effect on him. He said to her, 'Get into bed. I want you to make love to me.'

Katie said, 'No. Anyway, it would not be love.'

'You're still my wife.'

'Do you think I could bear to touch you after what you let those men do to Dmitry this morning, after what you've said? Besides, you're involved with crooks. There was something about them, wasn't there? All that money, that power. It fascinated you, didn't it? You wanted to be like them, you wanted to lead that kind of life. Well, I find it empty. Liliana, Wolf, they have nothing in their heads. Wolf just likes to play with things, cars, rockets, missiles; Liliana can think of nothing but clothes or money. You've lied about her, too – I hope you didn't go to bed with her that time in Paris because it would be like going to bed with a mannequin. I can't imagine it would be very satisfying.'

'Get on the bed.'

'No, I won't. I won't just do what you say like this. Anyway, I thought that I disgusted you.'

'Yes, you do,' Bob was keeping his voice low. 'But the walls in here are thin. I want that son-of-a-bitch to hear you, I want him to hear you fucking me, and I want you to sound as if you're enjoying it. What did he do to you, that bastard, what did he do to you in bed that you liked so much? Show me, go on, show me. After all, you want him to live.'

Katie woke early in the morning. She had cried for half the night; she felt desperate, disgusted and shamed, and terrified of what would happen to them. The room was mercifully empty; Bob wasn't there. She looked out of the window to see if the jeep was still parked outside; it crossed her mind that they might already have taken Dmitry off somewhere to shoot him; wasn't dawn the traditional time for executions? She pulled on her clothes and went to the door; as she opened it Bob came in. He had taken a shower; his hair was wet. He looked clean and composed.

'Where were you going?'

'To see where you were.'

'Come here.' They went next door. The room was still in semi-darkness; the curtains were drawn. The guard, Virgilio, was sitting on the chair with a gun in his lap. Dmitry was sitting upright on the bed; he looked as if he hadn't slept much. He shot Katie an agonised glance as she came in; she looked at the floor. If she had looked at his face she would have been unable to hold back the tears.

Bob turned to Dmitry. 'My problem is what to do with you now. The easiest thing would be to have these guys shoot you; but I wouldn't like to have that on my conscience. I think it might be better if I just hand you over to the military. Maybe you'd like to explain what you're doing here to them. You got your passport there?'

'Why do you want it?'

Bob picked up Dmitry's jacket and took the two passports out of his pocket. He flipped through them. 'One Soviet passport. That will interest them, I'm sure. You didn't get a visa.'

'No.'

He held up the UN *laissez-passer* and flipped through that too. 'This isn't visaed either. So you're an illegal immigrant. And it's outside UN regulations, surely? This isn't much use to you here, is it? I think we may as well get rid of it.' He tossed it into the round glass ashtray, tipped a generous quantity of whisky onto it, and struck a match. Dmitry made a move to get up off the bed but the guard pushed him back. They watched the flames shoot up; Dmitry watched mesmerised as darkness spread across the shiny red cover like a stain.

'All right,' said Bob, 'Let's go.'

But the burning of the passport had had an extraordinary effect on Katie; it seemed gratuitously cruel, as if Bob had stripped Dmitry naked. She knew he meant him to suffer; she flung herself at Bob, digging her fingers into the flesh of his neck and tore at it with her fingernails. The two guards stepped forward; seeing his opportunity, Dmitry leapt up and grabbed Virgilio around the neck; there was a brief struggle and Dmitry pushed him away, holding in his right hand the man's revolver. He backed away to be out of reach, holding the gun as he had been taught, long ago during his national service, for target practice; standing sideways on with his legs apart, almost as if he were fighting a duel, sighting along the whole length of his outstretched right arm, his left eye closed. He aimed at Haynes because he was in the middle. Something in him had turned; it gave him a wonderful sense of power to threaten those who had just been threatening him. At the same time he was tense, nervous, unsure of the weapon in his hand. It occurred to him that he did not know how many rounds were in it or even if there was one in the presenting chamber.

'For God's sake don't make me use this,' she said, 'I am not a very good shot. If I aim for the heart I am quite likely to hit you in the face or in the belly, but at this range I am unlikely to miss you altogether.'

Nobody moved.

'Katie, get out into the courtyard.'

Katie turned and fled.

Nobody moved in the dim room. Through the tattered curtains came a thin pencil of light in which the dust danced.

Bob said, 'Put it down, Gavrilov, and let's talk about this.'

'Talk? You've held me at gunpoint for twenty-four hours and told me several times you want me dead. Put up your hands. And you, Virgilio, put that pistol down on the table. Do it with your left hand, very slowly.'

Virgilio put his left hand in his pocket and slowly pulled the gun out. They were all three frozen; Dmitry could see the fear on their faces. As Virgilio put his hand out towards the table he made a sudden move. Dmitry fired. He seemed to do it in slow motion; he remembered struggling to hold the sights steady while his finger seemed to take an extraordinarily long time to take up pressure on the trigger. Then the gun suddenly went off. It made a deafening roar in the small room. The bullet struck Virgilio at the base of his neck; it hit the artery and bright orange-red blood shot out with such violence that it sprayed across the floor like a fountain and hit Dmitry's shirt. Virgilio fell to the floor, crumpling as if he was a marionette and someone had cut the strings. He lay there with blood still pouring out of him. Dmitry stood transfixed; he had never seen so much blood before; it lay thickly on the floor like bright red paint. Dmitry had to step back to stop it wetting his shoes.

Virgilio was dead almost instantly; his open eyes looked up towards the ceiling, his mouth hung open in shock. Dmitry stared at him in disbelief; he almost expected something else to happen, to see the soul depart visibly; surely it took more than this to make a man die? He was acutely aware of everything in the room; the silence, the smell of cordite, the sunlight lying in a thin beam across the floor. He thought what an irony it was that he, who had survived three shots from a trained assassin, should have killed with his first bullet.

He had let the recoil lift the gun upwards; now he brought it back down into line again. Haynes had gone completely white; he obviously thought Dmitry might feel he had already gone too far and might as well kill him too. And indeed, Dmitry for a moment felt such an intense rage that he almost thought he might pull the trigger. The anger was at himself; he was not sure that he had really had to shoot. He knew at once that this act would have its consequences; that one way or another he would have to pay for it. If he could have unravelled the thread of his life which had led him to this point and started out anew, he would have done so.

For a few moments after the gunshot sounded, there had been an extraordinary stillness in the room. Now, suddenly, sounds started to filter in from the street outside and from the other rooms; shrill, alarmed voices, shouts, confusion. Dmitry's hand had started to shake with reaction; he suddenly wanted only to get away. Katie had appeared in the doorway; she cried out, 'Oh my God, what have you done?' He pushed her back, trying to stop her from looking at the dead man. There seemed to be blood all over the room; it looked like a slaughterhouse.

Dmitry saw her staring at him and looked down at the blood which had splashed onto his shirt and said, 'It's okay, it isn't mine. Katie, take the bags, put them in the jeep.'

She hesitated. Bob said, 'For God's sake, Katie, you can't go with him now, you've seen what he can do.' Katie looked at him, then left the room.

Dmitry said to Haynes, 'Now you are going to tell me what is going on. If you don't I am going to shoot you just like him. After all, why not? I could hardly be in a worse position than I am already.'

Haynes obviously believed him. He said, 'For God's sake. What do you want to know?'

'What is Richter up to in Brazil?'

'In Brazil?'

'I mean the connection with this nuclear diversion. You know all about that; come on, tell me. How is Richter involved in this?'

'He's not involved.' Haynes saw Dmitry's hand tighten on the gun and panicked. 'It was Liliana. Her father had the idea – and Heinrichs, Richter's right-hand man. They had a meeting. It was a group of right-wing in the Brazilian military. They had the idea of making a bomb – they wanted to show the government how much power they had. RASAG was supposed to supply them with the launching system, but nobody in the Brazilian aerospace programme would have gone along with it. It was a very small group of people.'

'Their names?'

'Oliveira was involved, an Air Marshall – I don't know his name – a Paraguayan general, too, Luís Hería Prieto. It was a crazy idea. They were prepared to pay a lot of money. Heinrichs knew what bad shape the company was in and he wanted the money. I guess he has more power than Richter – he controls the financial side, he does the ordering.'

'And had they supplied the Brazilians?'

'That's correct, with the sixteen-engine model: Richter hasn't even tested it yet – that's happening next month. As far as I know they've done nothing with it, it's just sitting in sheds waiting for the propitious moment. It was transported to Cachimbo by plane via various locations.'

'How did they manage to conceal this?'

'Well, no-one knew what it was for – it doesn't look much like a rocket, you know. Just pieces of tubing and various metal boxes – could be anything. The transportation was quite easy. Some came direct from Germany, some routed via Paraguay. There's been a lot of drug trafficking between Bolivia, Paraguay, Brazil – a lot of the military are involved in it, they turn a blind eye.'

'Have they built a bomb?'

'I don't know.'

Dmitry said, 'If you don't tell me the truth I shall shoot you in the leg.' He was getting nervous; he could hear people shouting outside.

Haynes said, 'I don't know – that's the truth, I don't know. I know they had the intention. I don't know who else might have been involved on the Brazilian side'

'And you? What about you? Did you know all this? What was your role? In Vienna, did you tell them I knew?'

Bob's face was grey with fear. 'I swear to you – I wasn't involved.'

Dmitry wanted to ask him dozens of questions, but he knew there would be no time; perhaps there never would be time. They looked at one another. It would have been hard to say who was the more frightened. Somebody outside was shouting for the soldiers to come. Dmitry said, urgent, alarmed, 'Give me the keys to your jeep.' Haynes dug in his pockets and pulled them out.

'Throw them on the bed.'

He did so. Dmitry picked them up. Then he said, 'I want you to pick up that pistol, those rifles, any other weapons, and put them in that suitcase over there, and then put it by the door. Hurry. If I were you, I wouldn't come out of this room till you hear we've driven away, because if you do, I will certainly kill you.'

He looked out of the window. Two young soldiers were coming; they had their rifles ready, they looked nervous. Feldman was standing in the courtyard arguing with Katie. The soldiers asked Feldman something; he turned and pointed towards their room. Dmitry turned to Haynes and said, 'Have you got any money? Give me what you have.'

Haynes pulled out his wallet. His hands were quite steady. He said, 'You've got to be out of your mind.' He held it out. Dmitry, remembering the golden rule that you should never get within reach of the man you are holding at gunpoint, asked him to toss it on the floor. He bent down to pick it up without taking his eyes off Haynes or Luís.

'I'm going outside,' he said. 'I don't want you to move from here. Do you understand me?' Haynes nodded. Dmitry put the revolver in his pocket and went out, shutting the door. The two soldiers stood in the courtyard. They looked at him blankly; he had no way of knowing what they were thinking.

Dmitry said, finding it hard to think of the right words in Spanish,

'This is a private fight.' Even as he said it, it sounded absurd; surely the word *lucha* – fight, could apply only to some great cause, not some sordid squabble in a hotel room. He said, '*Está una cuestión de amor.*' They stood and stared at him. He had no idea if he was getting through to them; he could see that they didn't know what to do; they were so young, they came from abject poverty, to them Dmitry appeared a powerful and important person; they did not want to get into trouble. Dmitry could see Katie watching him across the courtyard; he hated what he was doing. He pulled out his wallet and Haynes's and began counting out the greasy ten thousand Guaraní notes, then hundred dollar bills. 'How much?' he asked. 'How much do you want?'

The soldiers looked at one another.

'Go and tell them it was nothing,' said Dmitry.

One of the soldiers held out his hand. Dmitry thrust the notes into it. Some of the notes fell to the ground; the second soldier bent to pick them up. Then they both hesitated, still looking at Dmitry with this curious mixture of awe and curiosity. Then one said, 'You want a doctor?'

Dmitry didn't understand; he did not realise that they took the blood on his shirt to be his own. He said, 'It's too late for a doctor.' They fell back, wide-eyed, as if he was already a ghost; they turned and left the courtyard. Feldman came up; he said, 'What is going on?' He too looked at the blood on Dmitry's shirt in horror. 'Has somebody. . .?'

'We are going,' said Dmitry, 'He will pay the bill.' He handed Feldman Haynes's wallet. Katie had already got into the jeep. She was sitting there, white-faced, her hands pressed to her cheeks, and she was shaking. Dmitry flung the suitcase in the back and fiddled with the keys. He was amazed that his own hands seemed so steady. He started the jeep and drove down the road; they had to pass near the military checkpoint. A little road ran to the left; he turned down it. Maybe there was another way. If he could cut off the corner, they might not be seen. He drove over rough ground between the trees. Katie said, 'Dmitry, it's no use. There are military checkpoints all along the road.' Then she said, 'Oh my God, what will they do if they catch up with you? Did you have to kill him?'

'Do you think I wanted to?' They rejoined the main road; nobody seemed to have seen them. Dmitry could not quite believe what had happened; his hands had begun to shake on the wheel. He tried not to think about it; he tried to blot it from his mind. After a few miles Dmitry suddenly stopped the jeep. He opened the door and got out.

'What are you doing?' Katie asked.

'I'm going to get rid of these guns. Perhaps I should keep the pistol; there are still five rounds in it. Shit! I don't know what to do. We can't risk being found with a van-load of guns, and this gun is a liability anyway. Perhaps I should keep the pistol.' He opened the suitcase and took out the rifles, carried them a distance off the road and threw them into the undergrowth. Then he tossed the pistol away and finally, with a violent gesture of despair, the revolver.

'Mitya, are you sure?'

'They're no use to us. I don't want to take the risk of killing anyone else, haven't I got enough on my conscience?'

Katie said nothing. Dmitry climbed back into the jeep. She said, 'You look as if you've killed someone. You've got blood on your shirt.'

Dmitry took off the shirt and went and hid that in the undergrowth too. He came back and took another one out of the bag. 'This is my last shirt.' He looked down at his shoes and then went off again to wipe them on the grass. Nausea and revulsion suddenly overcame him and he turned away to be sick by the roadside. He went to the back of the jeep and pulled out his Soviet passport. He was convinced it was a liability. If he was stopped, he was arguably better off without it. He could claim his UN *laissez-passer* had been lost. He asked, 'Shall I throw this away too?' Katie understood him. She remembered hearing that people had trouble if they even had a Soviet or Cuban visa in their passport when they entered Paraguay and she didn't know if that had changed yet. Dmitry went and buried the passport by the side of the road. He straightened up, looking back over the scene, trying to fix the shapes of the trees and the undulations in the road in his memory just in case he should have need to come back, but there were no particular landmarks; besides he did not expect he would be able to remember.

He came back to the jeep. Katie was staring at him; he could not bear the expression on her face. He suddenly hit out at the side of the jeep with his hand. 'Why did I have to kill him? He was only doing what he was told. I talked to him last night, you know. He seemed quite a decent man. Perhaps he has a wife, a lover, children. What made me think

I had more right to live than him?'

Katie said, 'Don't think about it now, Mitya. You said you had to do it.'

'I would have done much better to have killed your husband.'

'No, don't say that!'

'So you still care for him, after everything. If you knew . . .' He stopped himself; he wondered for a moment whether he should confide in Katie, tell her what Haynes had said, ask her to tell someone in Asunción, maybe the UN res. rep., maybe the American Ambassador. But he was afraid to do so. Anyone so far who had had any information had been killed, or nearly killed; it was like a curse. She was best protected by her innocence.

'No,' said Katie, 'Of course, I don't care for him, not now, not after this. But I can't wish him dead. You frighten me, Mitya, you have so much anger in you.'

He climbed into the jeep. He felt it too, as if some violence which had been inside him all his life had suddenly found a circumstance in which it could find outward expression, in his own blood and that of others. He had played with the idea of death, he had considered in his darkest moments taking his own life, and now he had found in himself the capacity to inflict it also. He was profoundly shaken. For a while the death of Virgilio in the hotel room had revolted him, he realised that he had crossed over some border; he knew that he could kill and would kill again if he needed to. For that reason he felt he could not afford to carry arms; it would be too much of a temptation. He kept thinking of that moment when he pulled the trigger; the instant of no return, the explosion and the powerful recoil, a split-second flash of triumph that the shot had gone home.

They sat in silence for a few moments, not looking at one another. Then Dmitry started the engine; they drove a little further; then, turning around a bend in the road, they suddenly saw the glint of cars ahead and a barrier across the road. Dmitry stopped the jeep, slammed it into reverse and drove backwards about fifty yards, till they were out of sight. He stopped and looked at Katie.

'There's nowhere else to go. If we go back they'll pick us up in Mariscal Estigarribia.'

'Isn't there another road?'

'No. Perhaps we should have gone the other way and headed for Bolivia. But there'll be roadblocks on that road too, I expect. There's nothing else for it, Katie, I shall have to give myself up.'

Katie didn't say anything for a while as the full hopelessness of the situation sank in. Then she said, 'What will they do to you?'

'Once I can establish who I am I'll be all right. You must carry on and get to Asunción. Go straight to the resident representative at the UN office and tell him what has happened. If I'm imprisoned he can negotiate for my release.'

Katie tried to reason with him. 'They might not bother to wait. They might just shoot you.'

'Yes, they might. But I don't think so. Not until they have established who I am. Things are different in Paraguay now that Stroessner's gone.'

'I can't go on alone.'

'Yes, you can. No, listen. Don't argue with me. There is one other chance. You go on with the jeep. You'd better hurry, they may have seen us. I'll walk right round the roadblock and join you on the road the other side. I'll have to walk for miles; it might take some time. If that fails I'll try to join you in Asunción.'

Despair was written all over Katie's face. 'I've never driven a jeep.'

'I'll show you. Look – it's just the gears.' He quickly ran through it with her. 'Don't worry about me. The important thing is that you get safely to Asunción, and get out of the country. I'll be all right in the end, I promise you. If anyone comes, if the police contact you or anything, if they question you about the shooting, say you didn't see what happened. You were not in the room; you didn't see it. That's all you have to say. Don't say that I admitted I did it. Tell the truth, what you saw, but no more, just that you didn't see.'

'Of course, of course, I promise.'

'Now drive carefully.' He kissed her swiftly on the mouth, and got out of the jeep.

Katie said, 'What about your things?' Dmitry picked up his briefcase, deciding it was better that she didn't have it. He took a bottle of mineral water and some bread.

'Wait for me the other side for as long as you reasonably can, but if there's a patrol or something, you go on, won't you?'

Katie's face bore a terrible, stricken look. She said, 'I shall never get over it if anything happens to you.'

'Nothing will happen to me. It's you I'm worried about. Go on now.'

Katie hesitated for a moment longer and then, without a backward glance, threw the jeep into gear and started to move. He watched her ascend jerkily through the gears, gathering speed. He turned and ran as fast as he could over the uneven ground till he was out of sight of the road, then started to walk away from the road in the blistering heat.

It was much more difficult than he had imagined. The roadblock was opposite a military fort. He had to try to keep to the scrub rather than the open ground to cut down on the chances of being seen. There was little shade against the intense sun, and once he was walking he found he soon became unbearably hot. His belly and ribs ached from the blows he had received yesterday and he was exhausted from lack of sleep. After an hour of walking he changed direction; he sat down under a *quebracho* tree and had a drink, leaning against its bulbous trunk. It was hard to resist the temptation to lie down on the parched earth and doze. When he left he abandoned the briefcase.

He walked for about two hours. He wished he hadn't asked Katie to wait. He seemed to have had one bad idea after another. He thought of her sitting in the car in the heat, vulnerable and afraid. In any case, if they got through this roadblock there were all the others. When he tried to head back to the road it seemed further away than he had thought. Eventually he reached it, a straight line running into a haze of heat, mirages shimmering on the surface. There was no sign of Katie. Then he saw a vehicle in the distance; it came closer; it was a jeep. He thought of diving into the undergrowth but it would be too late; they would have seen him; he couldn't bear to be pursued through the scrub like a hunted rabbit. It would be better to give himself up; if he did so, they were less likely to shoot him. Dmitry stood still. His heart was pounding; he was afraid that when they saw him they might shoot anyway. The jeep stopped. A soldier got out, carrying a rifle. He shouted, 'Put your hands up and come slowly towards us.'

Dmitry did so. He walked towards the soldiers, hands raised. His limbs felt heavy and drained of power, as in a dream. A few yards away he halted. They stared at him with blank, puzzled faces. Then Dmitry said, 'I'm lost. My car broke down; I was robbed.' He thought that they must have passed the abandoned car on the road.

One of the soldiers, who seemed to be in charge, said, 'Come here. Put your hands here.' Dmitry put his hands on the side of their jeep and they searched him. Then they said, 'You have no papers?'

Dmitry repeated, 'They were stolen.'

'Come with us.'

He climbed into the jeep and they drove back to the roadblock. There was some discussion; the soldiers came forward and asked him to get down. He said, 'You were not anything to do with the English señora?'

Dmitry hesitated, and then said, 'What English señora?'

The soldier shrugged. He turned to his companion and spoke in Guaraní; Dmitry couldn't understand them, he stood in silent despair. They took him through the gate into the fort and sat him on a bench in the compound. They said, 'Wait,' though he could hardly do otherwise. Two of the soldiers stood guard; the other went into one of the buildings. For a long time nothing moved.

V

What seemed hours passed. Dmitry shifted uneasily on the bench. The soldiers stood near him, waiting, expectant. Dmitry's head had begun to hurt. He had had hardly any sleep for two nights; he was thirsty; the heat was intense. It was obvious that they didn't know what to do with him. He had given too much money away to the other soldiers; if he had kept some for a bribe, probably they would have let him go.

An officer emerged from one of the buildings and came over to him. He asked a series of questions. Where was he from? What had he been doing in Mariscal Estigarribia? Dmitry mumbled his answers. He denied knowing anything. The officer was not impressed. Finally he shouted something at the soldiers who indicated to Dmitry to get to his feet. They took him to a truck and told him to get inside the back. Dmitry said, 'Where are we going?' but they didn't answer him.

The jeep headed northwards and east, back on the road on which they had come. The late afternoon sun made long shadows; the air had cooled a little, there was a faint breeze. It was the hour for the jaguars to hunt; Dmitry stared into the distance, hoping for a glimpse of one. They were heading back to Mariscal Estigarribia. The name, which had seemed to him so romantic when he had first read it, now revolted him. The sun was setting as they arrived at the checkpoint; the light was a rich yellow colour; the breeze on his damp shirt made him suddenly feel cold. Or perhaps it was not the wind; it might have been fear. He did not like the way the soldiers were looking at him. They escorted him into the red brick building.

Dmitry stood and blinked for a few moments as his eyes adjusted to the darkness. A powerfully-built uniformed man got up from behind a desk. His face was more European than Guaraní, but he had black, impenetrable eyes. He introduced himself as the Commandante, Vargas. He spoke a good Spanish, his voice smooth and well enunciated; Dmitry had no difficulty in following him.

Vargas said, 'I understand you were picked up at the roadblock. You have no papers?'

'My papers were stolen.'

'So. Tell us who you are and what you were doing here.'

'I am an employee of the United Nations. I have diplomatic status. This is all a misunderstanding. I –'

Vargas made a dismissive gesture. He sat down and took a sheet of paper from a drawer. He said, without emotion, 'Your name, please?'

'Dmitry Gavrilov.'

'Spell it.'

Dmitry did so. He stumbled over the letters; finally Vargas passed him the paper and he wrote it down himself.

'Your nationality?'

'I am an international civil servant. My country of origin is of no importance.'

'Why not? Why should you wish to conceal it? Are you an American? You do not look like an American and you do not speak like one either.'

Dmitry said, 'I'm from Austria. Part of the United Nations is based there.'

'And you claim to represent the United Nations. That should be easy enough to check. Perhaps you could give me the name of the resident representative here in Asunción?'

Dmitry was suddenly fearful. If only he had looked this up. 'I'm sorry, I don't know his name.'

'You don't know his name.'

'No, I haven't met him.'

Vargas looked at Dmitry coldly with his black eyes. Dmitry felt utterly confused; he didn't know how much Vargas knew; he felt he was being played with. Vargas said, 'You wouldn't be here to see Wolf Richter, would you, by any chance?'

Dmitry thought for a moment and then said, 'No.' His hesitation however had told Vargas something; he continued, 'Do you know who I mean?'

Dmitry wondered if he should deny knowing him. Perhaps it was a trap. On the other hand, it might be worse in the long run to lie about it. He said, 'I have read about his project in the papers.' A feeling of hopelessness descended on Dmitry; he did not know how to explain himself. He did not want to lie, and yet he did not think they would believe the truth.

'So you are here because of Richter. You admit this?'

'I am not admitting anything.'

Vargas's eyes narrowed. He looked back to his piece of paper. 'But if you are not here on official United Nations business, and you are not here to see Wolf Richter, then what kind of business are you here on?' His voice had a hard edge to it; he gave the impression he was struggling to remain patient, that he was giving his prisoner every chance to put his case.

Dmitry was in torment. He thought, they must know what has happened. He wondered if he wouldn't do better just to come out with it all. Even now he could probably have defused the situation. If he had been more relaxed with the soldiers, had he started out by telling them what had happened, had addressed them man to man; had he said, 'Look, this is all about a woman. You know how it is . . .' he might have ended up sitting playing cards and drinking with them. But he looked like a man who was hiding something; his whole appearance implied guilt.

Finally he said, without conviction, 'It is a kind of holiday.' His words sounded wooden, hollow. He wondered whether it would help him to mention Cesar Madregón; on the other hand, he didn't want to get him into trouble. He decided to risk it. He said, 'César Madregón brought me here. We were going to shoot the *tigre*.'

'But it is not the *tigre* you have shot, is it, Señor Gavrilov?' Vargas looked him directly in the eye. 'Wait a moment.' He called somebody in, handed him the sheet of paper, and told him to put a call through to the UN offices in Asunción. He looked at his watch. He said, 'It may have to be in the morning.'

The man went out. Vargas continued to look at Dmitry with a cold detachment which frightened him. 'So tell me your real reasons for visiting this part of the country. You cannot expect me to believe it's a holiday. You have admitted that you know about the rocket project. You have shot one of the guards from the rocket site. These are not the actions of someone who is here for some innocent purpose.'

Dmitry did not know what to say. He didn't know whether it was better to admit it and defend himself, or to keep silent. Whatever he said might incriminate him still further. He was so tired he couldn't think straight. The only people who had seen the shooting were Katie, who had promised she would not testify against him, Haynes, and Luís. They might have trouble proving what had happened. Besides, if a case ever came to court, he was sure that justice could still be bought in this country. The problem was, it was most unlikely ever to come to court.

Vargas got to his feet, scraping his chair across the floor with a loud noise which made Dmitry jump. 'Come with me,' he said, 'I want to show you something.' They went out through the door into a corridor and then into another room. Something lay on the ground under a blanket; flies were buzzing round it, there were dark stains on the floor. Dmitry at once felt dizzy and weak. The blanket formed the shape of a man. As yet, even in the small, airless room, there was no smell. Vargas kept his eyes on Dmitry's face as he drew back the blanket to expose the man's face. Dmitry did not want to look; he couldn't bear to be confronted with what he had done, but he knew he had to; then he thought that perhaps in some curious way it would even help him.

He took a deep breath and looked. They had not closed Virgilio's eyes; the lips were drawn back from the yellowed teeth; Dmitry could not take his eyes off the bloody hole the bullet had torn in the man's neck. Once he had started to look, once he had overcome his initial revulsion, he could not stop himself; he felt he had to study it, to understand it, to see what he had really done. But the more he looked, the more terrible it seemed. It was obscene, to think that an action of his had transformed the living, breathing, miracle of human life into this repulsive lump of dead flesh. He looked at Virgilio's rotten teeth, dissolved away by too much *gaseosa;* soon the lips around them would be rotting.

He turned and looked at Vargas and stared directly into his face. If Vargas expected some obvious reaction which would reveal his guilt, he didn't get it. Surely, anyone would be upset seeing such a sight unless they were hardened through their job to death. Dmitry felt he had to say something; he said simply, '*El es muerte.*' It sounded as if he was surprised; it sounded false.

With a flick of his boot Vargas kicked the blanket back over the man's head. 'You are not going to deny that you have done this?' he said.

'I will neither deny nor accept it. I do not believe that it is in my interests to say anything.'

Vargas said, 'Come,' and they went back to his office.

Dmitry said, quietly, 'I insist that you contact the UN resident representative in Asunción. He will be able to establish my credentials. If you believe that I have killed this man you should hand me over to the police to face the process of justice in Asunción.'

Vargas said, 'You are a fool. You think you have the right to see a lawyer, have a trial, to withhold information? This is a military matter. You are in a military zone; there is no civil authority here. We have a military project here which we have a duty to protect; you are quite likely to be a spy, a saboteur. We would be quite within our rights to simply take you outside and shoot you right away. Nobody would ask any questions; nobody would challenge us. Do you understand me?'

Dmitry had started to sweat. He understood perfectly. He said, 'But there would be an outcry. I am a foreigner, a UN employee of high rank; there would be questions asked.'

'Yes, there would be questions asked,' said Vargas, 'But there would not be any answers. Let me tell you a little story.' He leaned back in his chair as if he had all the time in the world. 'A year or so ago, a man from Norway disappeared in the Chaco. I cannot recall now what business he was on. Eventually when he did not turn up questions were asked by his relatives. The Norwegian Embassy in Buenos Aires made investigations, but he was never found. So what happened? Was he killed? Did he change his name and go into Bolivia, and then who knows where? Is he working somewhere here in the Mennonite colonies under another identity? Nobody has the slightest idea. No-one has ever discovered what has happened to him.' Vargas shrugged expressively. 'That is the kind of place the Chaco is,' he said.

Dmitry stood in silence. Outside, through the open door, it was now quite dark. The soldiers shifted restlessly behind him. Vargas smiled. He was probably enjoying himself; life must be pretty boring in Mariscal Estigarribia. 'I think I have been remarkably patient, don't you?' Vargas got up. 'Well, have you no explanation to give us? You are not going to tell us you are *periodista*, a journalist? That is the usual excuse. Why will you not admit that you shot this soldier? Let me tell you this; it is the guilty man who is protected by the right to silence. This is the fundamental flaw in all systems of justice. In my experience, the innocent man always protests his innocence. He would say that he had not done it, or he would describe in the greatest detail what had happened, he would want to confess, because it would be in his interest to do so. Or he would say he did not mean it, it was an accident, it was self-defence. Was it self-defence, Señor Gavrilov?'

Dmitry opened his mouth to say something, but the words would not come. He was paralysed with indecision. Vargas got to his feet. 'I don't think you can realise the seriousness of your position,' he said. 'Come on, talk to me. Do we have to force it out of you?'

So it had come at last; the threat of physical abuse. Dmitry had been expecting it; it did not make him feel any more frightened. He said, 'It was self-defence. I gave myself up willingly. I need not have done. I would not have done so unless I was innocent.'

'So,' said Vargas, 'Explain to us what happened; exactly what happened.'

Dmitry was having trouble with his Spanish. He was exhausted, confused, his head was throbbing, the right words would not come into his head. 'They were holding me at gunpoint. The American threatened to take me to the rocket range and have me shot. I thought that he was serious. There was a struggle, I got hold of a gun. I didn't mean to fire it; I never had any intention of killing him.'

'But you did kill him. With one shot. That was a very unfortunate accident. Why did the American – Haynes, I think is his name – want to have you shot?'

Dmitry hesitated. It was so easy to say, because I was running off with his wife. Why didn't he say so? They might just believe him. But he was afraid to mention Katie's name. He had visions of them arresting her on the road to Asunción and asking her questions, trying to force her to incriminate him, something he had stupidly made her promise not to do. He didn't think that she would willingly do what she thought would betray him; she would lie, to save his skin; they would know she was lying; it could get very unpleasant. He thought they would not treat her badly, not these days, not in Asunción, and especially not a British citizen, but she would be frightened enough – and she was pregnant. He decided he would keep her out of it.

He said, 'Perhaps he also thought I had come here to find out about the rocket project, or to interfere with it.'

'Exactly. That is what I also think. Come on, we want to know the whole truth; how you came here, who sent you, what you have found out. We want names, dates, places. This is what Richter's men have asked for.'

Dmitry felt an overpowering sensation of depression and helplessness wash over him. 'But I have no such information. I've told you, this is a mistake.'

The phone rang, loudly. Vargas snatched it up. He answered in monosyllables. Then he slammed the phone down. 'We have contacted the UN. It seems the resident representative has never heard of you. He has no knowledge of anyone of your name being in Paraguay.'

Dmitry closed his eyes.

'We have also checked with immigration. They have no record of you either.'

Dmitry said, 'I crossed the border at Ciudad del Este. They did not ask to see my passport.'

'And where is your passport?'

'I told you; it was stolen. The American, Haynes, took it from me in the hotel.'

'Ah, yes, the American; the American who is working for Señor Richter. But unfortunately for you, it appears that you are not working for Señor Richter; in fact, his people are very anxious to find out who you are and why you are here. They have asked us to find out from you. Come now, be reasonable. This is your last chance to tell us.'

Dmitry said, 'Please, I have had nothing to drink. If I could just have a glass of water –'

Vargas nodded to one of the soldiers. He turned and went out, returning in a few moments with a small glass. It seemed absurd in the circumstances, but Dmitry wondered how clean it was. You were not supposed to drink unboiled water outside Asunción. Probably he would get dysentery. He gulped it down; it was not enough, but he didn't feel able to ask for more.

Vargas said, 'All right, let's have the full story. You entered the country at Ciudad del Este. When was this?'

'Thursday morning.'

'How did you get to Asunción?'

'I hired a car.'

'At about five-thirty you met with Cesar Madregón at the Bavaria Bar. You told him you wanted to come to the Chaco on an illegal hunting expedition. He drove you here. We have the number of the vehicle and your passport number which the soldier recorded. The soldier could not recall any details of your passport.'

'It was a UN *laissez-passer*. The red diplomatic one.'

'I see. Madregón took you to the Hotel Alemán. He left you there but you didn't stay the night. Where did you go?'

He didn't want to mention Katie. 'I wandered around.'

'All night?'

'Well, I slept.'

'On the ground.'

'Yes.'

'Why not in the hotel?'

'I didn't like the look of it.'

Vargas sighed. 'The next evening you turn up again, with Haynes, his wife, and these two soldiers, Luís Castellanos and the unfortunate Virgilio Rojas. In the morning there is an argument. You shoot Rojas. You steal the guns. You bribe two soldiers. You escape, driving off, with the Englishwoman. Have I got all this correct?'

Dmitry supposed they had talked to Haynes, Luís, Feldman. It was hopeless to deny it. He said, 'They threatened to shoot me.'

'Yes, I am sure they did. You were a danger to them, weren't you? You were here to sabotage the rocket project?'

Dmitry said, 'Who has told you this? Haynes? He is a liar. He has . . .

how do I say . . . I don't have the word . . .'

'Can you speak English?' asked Vargas abruptly.

Dmitry switched language with great relief. 'My Spanish is not so good.'

'No, it's not bad.' Vargas spoke with an East Coast accent. 'Myself, I learned English at West Point. Perhaps you will now find it easier to explain yourself.'

Dmitry shifted uneasily on his feet. The whole atmosphere in the room was oppressive; the soldiers with their guns; Vargas, who probably had never had such an interesting case to deal with before; the unvoiced threat of violence. Vargas got to his feet. He said, 'Sit down.' Dmitry sat. Vargas came over to him; the purpose of him sitting seemed not for his own benefit, but so that Vargas could look down on him. He said, 'You are really in a very unfortunate situation. You expect me to believe this extraordinary story? Well? Where is your motive? Why do you behave in this bizarre manner? Have you any explanation?'

Dmitry said, 'It is all a terrible mistake. I keep asking myself, how did I get into this situation? I have no way to explain myself. I can only think I have gone mad.'

Vargas appeared perplexed by this admission. Dmitry hung his head; he half expected Vargas to hit him. There was a knock at the door. A man came in, a colonel. He addressed Vargas. They talked together, very quickly, in Spanish; their voices were flat in tone and the words, broken abruptly by pauses, came out like rapid machine-gun fire. Dmitry tried to follow what they were saying. He heard them mention Richter, Haynes, the rocket project. He heard the word, *espía*, spy. Then Vargas turned to him. 'My colleague is from military intelligence,' he said. 'He also would like to talk to you.'

The colonel sat down. Dmitry wondered what military intelligence were involved with in the Chaco; perhaps it was with non-existent troop movements on the Bolivian border, perhaps, more likely, with drugs. They went over the whole story again, half in English, half in Spanish. Dmitry's head was aching. He kept saying, 'Please, I haven't eaten, I haven't slept.' They asked him what he knew about Richter. He told them he knew only what he had read in the newspapers. Dmitry was several times on the point of telling them about Katie, but he didn't think that they would believe that either. It was also his last card; he would only play it when absolutely necessary.

He said, 'Please give me time. Please let me think.'

Vargas said, 'So that you can think up more of these lies? We want the truth. We have been extremely patient with you, much more patient than you might have had the right to expect.'

There was a long silence in the room. The soldiers at the door shifted on their feet; one of them stifled a yawn. Dmitry was beginning to feel a sense of hollow dread, as he imagined a man might feel who was about to be led out to his execution. He thought, for some reason, of being beheaded; he imagined the sensation of laying his cheek on the cold block. Perhaps it might even be a relief to know that it was all over; what disturbed him most at that moment was not knowing what was going to happen. Suddenly, unable to bear the silence any longer, he asked: 'What are you going to do with me?'

The question seemed to infuriate Vargas; he had obviously been considering this very point. 'Take him away,' he said to the soldiers. 'Let's see whether a night in a cell makes him more talkative. We'll check out what he says in the morning.'

They took him out and escorted him to another building. He was led down a corridor and into a small room with a heavy door and a tiny, high window. They took everything off him but his clothes, even his watch and belt. There was no bed, nothing in the room but a bucket in the corner. The door was slammed behind him and he was left alone. A little later a soldier brought in a glass of water and a mug of thin stew in which a few lumps of meat were suspended. Dmitry ate it hungrily. There was nothing to be done; he lay down on the hard floor and tried to sleep. His head ached so much that he could hardly bear to rest it on the concrete; but he was so exhausted that eventually he slept.

He was woken in the night by a distant rumbling sound which at first he took to be thunder. But the sound was different; hollow, booming, flat. It sounded like bombs exploding. Weird flashes momentarily lit up the walls of the room. He lifted himself up and went to peer out of the window; he could see a strange, pale light in the sky over the flat expanse to the north. He could hear raised voices and see a group of soldiers staring into the distance. There was another bang, louder and clearer now;

something bright lit up the sky a long way off, and now the glow in the sky was turning red. Dmitry knew what it was, now; he thought, my God, they are blowing up the rocket range. He could hear a telephone ringing; there were loud voices. A truck filled up with soldiers and roared off down the road. Then he heard a plane fly overhead.

After about ten minutes he heard voices in the corridor. The door opened and two soldiers came inside. Without saying a word they pushed him out into the corridor and propelled him along to the office.

Vargas was waiting for him. He said, 'Now we are going to get at the truth from you. We have had nothing but lies and evasions. It is no coincidence that you are here. Sit down.'

They forced him down onto a chair. Dmitry felt the difference in their mood at once. While before he had felt that perhaps Vargas did not really care, that he was puzzled by him and, although he wanted to know why he was there, was not in any desperate hurry to find out, he now saw that he was deadly serious. The door opened and the colonel came in. He had been drinking whisky. His clothes looked dishevelled, as if he had just pulled them on; perhaps he had just got out of bed or come from the whorehouse. There would be nothing much else to do here in your spare time but drinking and whoring. He looked unpleasant. 'We have been wasting our time,' he said to Vargas. 'In Stroessner's time we would have known what to do with him. Let's try him in the *pileta*.'

The phone rang. Vargas answered it. He went outside and started to shout orders. The colonel came and leaned over Dmitry, putting his hand on his thigh. He squeezed it, gently, almost caressingly; Dmitry instinctively shrank from his touch. 'You see,' said the colonel, breathing whisky fumes all over him, 'We can do absolutely anything we like with you. Anything. Do you understand me?'

'Yes, I understand.'

The colonel turned to the soldiers by the door. 'All right, you know what to do with him.' The soldiers nodded and took him out of the room.

They walked down the corridor. The two soldiers looked at him with blank, impassive faces. They opened a door and indicated for him to go in. Dmitry had intended to stay calm and dignified, whatever happened, but when they asked him to step into the room his will failed him. His legs trembled uncontrollably and they had to push him over the threshold.

He stood there, uncertain. The room was about fifteen feet square and was lit by a single bulb on the ceiling. Perhaps it had been designed as a storeroom. There were cobwebs and dust; it looked as if it had not been much used. There was nothing in it but a chair and a large tin tank, the kind that might be used as a water storage tank or as a cattle trough. One of the soldiers turned on the tap on the wall above it. The sound of the water running made saliva pour into Dmitry's mouth.

The soldier turned to Dmitry. 'Take off your clothes.'

Dmitry felt his knees continue to shake; he knew now what they were going to do to him. He had heard it was a common means of torture in Latin America; cheap, effective, and leaving no external marks on the body. He said in a low voice, trying to keep it controlled, 'You do not have to do this. I –'

'We don't want to do it,' said the soldier. 'We don't like doing it; it would be much easier if you just told us something. Why don't you just tell us what Vargas wants to hear? Then we will not have to do anything to you.'

The second soldier was more threatening. He said again, 'Take off your clothes.'

A third soldier came into the room. Dmitry hesitated; then the second soldier, unexpectedly, hit him hard across the cheek with the back of his hand. Dmitry felt a warm, salty taste in his mouth; he felt his teeth gingerly with his tongue, afraid that one was broken. He felt absolutely terrified; bravery had no meaning in this situation; worse even than the thought of pain was the thought of humiliating himself. For a moment he felt like bursting into tears.

He started to undo the buttons of his shirt with trembling fingers; he saw them watching intently, as if eager to see what lay underneath. He took his clothes off, one by one, prolonging the process as long as he reasonably could, and folded them neatly into a pile on the floor. He stood in front of them, naked. His body looked unnaturally white in the dark room and compared with those of the soldiers; dark veins stood out against his pale skin; he thought how unattractive white skin must look to other races; it made him feel doubly vulnerable. The soldiers hesitated; they seemed uncertain; he thought for a moment they were almost afraid of him, reluctant to make a direct approach, because he was so much bigger than they were; perhaps they thought he would resist them. Then he saw that they were staring at the huge scar on his chest. One of them pointed to it; 'What is this?' he asked.

Dmitry clutched at this pitiful straw which had been offered him. He said, 'It was a heart operation. I have a heart problem.' He thought perhaps if they believed he had a weak heart and might die they wouldn't torture him. The soldiers conferred; one of them went away. Dmitry was left standing in the room.

The second soldier said, 'Turn round. Put your hands behind your back.'

He did so. They tied his hands and ankles together tightly and pushed him forwards. He could not put his arms or feet out to balance himself, so he fell flat on the floor. He lay there, stunned, the air knocked out of him, listening to the sound of the water filling up the tank. It was agony to hear the water and not to be able to drink it. When the tank began to sound full they turned off the tap. There was a silence that lasted so long Dmitry wondered if it would ever be broken. He sat up with difficulty and looked at the soldiers.

The door opened suddenly and the colonel came in. He looked at Dmitry. 'What is this? This is not a heart operation. What are these? They are bullet wounds. You have had surgery to the chest, no? This is interesting. How did you get these? Who has tried to kill you? Why?'

Dmitry didn't know what to say; everything pointed against him. The colonel said, 'There is nothing wrong with his heart. You can carry on.' He went out. One soldier stood by the door; the other two grabbed Dmitry on each side and pulled him to his feet. He gulped in as much air as he could before they plunged his head down into the water. They were holding him by the hair, by his arms, pressing down on the back of his neck; he resisted, of course, but it was no use. As he went under he swallowed some water; he felt an instant of relief as his thirst was finally quenched; then began the unbearable pressure of wanting to breathe.

He wondered how long they would hold him under the water; he wondered if they ever misjudged and actually drowned somebody; he wondered too about the missing half of his lung, and whether that would mislead them about the length of time he could hold his breath. His head felt as if it would burst; he couldn't hold on any longer; he was going to have to breathe; air bubbled out of his mouth as he was forced to exhale. Now it was agony; he was dying; he was drowning. The water started to rush into his lungs and they pulled him out.

He gasped for air, coughing, choking, gulping; then, before he felt he had caught his breath, they pushed him back under again. He tried frantically to resist, to get more air into his lungs, but he was already hitting the water. This time it was only a short interval before he had to draw water into his lungs; again, just at the critical moment, they pulled him out.

Dmitry thought, I can't stand much of this, it's no use, I will have to tell them something. But what could he tell them? The truth would only make it worse, and they would probably not believe him. He started to say something, but again, before he could get the words out, they plunged him into the water. This time he had hardly any air in his lungs; he discovered it is much harder to hold air out than to hold it in. He made a desperate effort, tried to thrash his head under the water; he felt the strength of the soldier's hands gripping him and his own strength ebbing out of him. There was a roaring in his head and a moment of unconsciousness; then he was lying on the floor, coughing water up out of his lungs. He was making a dreadful retching noise; he was vomiting water. They let him lie there for a moment. Then they pulled him up onto his knees against the side of the tank and slammed his head down into the water.

There was nothing he could do. They hardly even gave him a chance to beg for mercy. When he was out of the water he was gasping for air, unable to speak. Once or twice they asked him, not unkindly, if he had anything to say, but he did not know how to answer them. He had no idea how long this went on for. At one point he passed out again. He came to his senses lying on the floor which was now wet and slippery with water. He needed to urinate, but couldn't bring himself to tell them; sooner or later he would have to do it on the floor and then he would have to lie in it.

He looked across the room, his cheek pressing on the cold floor. The soldiers were talking. One of them had lit a cigarette; the smell of the smoke gave Dmitry a strange sensation, like a flashback to a former world. They were talking mostly in Guaraní; the sound of their voices was almost soothing.

For some reason he got the impression they were talking about fishing. One of them was holding out his hands as if to show the size of his catch. He heard the names of various rivers: the Paraná, the Pilcomayo, the Paraguay. He looked across the room to them; two of them were drinking *yerba maté* while the other smoked. They glanced in his direction, saw that his eyes were open, laughed and continued to talk. Dmitry felt himself drifting in a kind of daze. He saw in his mind's eye the vast sweep of the wide South American rivers, the patches of water hyacinths rotating slowly on the surface as they drifted downstream, the huge fish that swam sensuously beneath the surface. It was like a dream that lasted for a moment in the brief interval between unconsciousness and full awakening; then he could not escape the reality of the bare, dirty floor, the pain in his tightly-bound hands and feet.

After a few moments the soldiers came over and pulled him to his feet. The thought of going back into the water was unbearable. Dmitry said, 'Please, no more. You don't have to do this to me. I will tell you what you want to know.'

'Go on then,' said the soldier, 'Tell us.'

Dmitry heard one of them open the door and shout something. He heard footsteps from along the corridor. Everything seemed to come out of Dmitry in an unruly jumble. He said, 'I am Russian. It is true I am employed by the United Nations. I was at a conference in Buenos Aires, on nuclear energy in the Third World.'

The colonel came into the room. The second soldier said, '*El es ruso.*'

The colonel looked impressed. '*Ruso?* he said. 'The Russians too are interested in rockets, isn't that so? So you admit you are a spy?'

'I am not a spy,' said Dmitry, 'I am a scientist.'

'What kind of scientist?'

'A physicist.' Dmitry did not know if he had used the right word; perhaps *físico* could also mean doctor, physician. He tried to make it clearer. He said, 'I am a specialist in atomic energy.'

'Atomic energy?' The colonel was clearly astonished; he turned to the others and muttered something. Dmitry only heard the one word, '*Bombas.*'

He jerked his head up. 'No,' he said, 'Not bombs. I am not an expert in bombs. On the contrary, I work for the International Atomic Energy Agency. We are an agency of the United Nations dedicated to promoting the peaceful uses of atomic energy.'

He had heard the phrase so often at the conference last week in English, in Spanish, in every language, that it rolled easily from his tongue.

The colonel stared at him. If the situation had not been so desperate, it might almost have been funny, for the colonel's stare combined the most perfect mixture of amusement and disbelief. He asked one of the soldiers something, who left and returned a few minutes later with the commandante.

'*Existe, esta organisación?*' the colonel asked him.

'*Sí, existe,*' Vargas replied.

'I see,' said the colonel. 'So you were sent here to stop Senõr Richter, is that it? To see if he is making any bombs?'

Dmitry said, 'No, that would be impossible. He could not make bombs here, it is a very sophisticated process. I have reason to believe that he may have supplied missiles to Brazil, and that the Brazilian military may be trying to make a bomb.'

Vargas, sitting on the chair, leaned over him. He said, 'How do you know this? Where did you hear it? Tell me; this is very interesting.'

Dmitry said, 'I heard it from a Brazilian journalist in Buenos Aires, Jaime dos Santos. He was investigating it. He was killed within ten minutes of telling me. I myself was shot two months ago because I knew about the plot to remove highly enriched uranium from the Valadares Centre in Brazil.'

The two men conferred for a moment. Vargas went on. 'What did this journalist tell you? Tell me everything he said.'

Dmitry told him. When he gave the names of the men at the secret meeting Vargas sat upright. He said to the colonel, 'Hería Prieto – I know him. He is very right-wing. I know he has contacts in the Brazilian army. His daughter lives in Brazil. But this is unbelievable. Have you any evidence to support this claim?'

'No, but there will be evidence – if I am allowed to communicate to anyone. Haynes admitted it to me. He knows . . .'

'Where is Haynes?'

'I don't know. I left him in the hotel.'

Vargas spoke again to the colonel. He said, 'But the United Nations didn't send you here. They do not operate this way, they would go through the government. I cannot believe you would come alone. Were you sent by your own government? Are you an agent of the KGB?'

'No, I swear it, I came alone.'

'But there must be others with you – the ones responsible for this attack on the rocket site.'

'No.'

The colonel moved nearer. He said, 'He is still lying. Let us try him again in the *pileta*.'

Dmitry said, desperate, 'This attack has nothing to do with me or my country. I can tell you who has blown up the rocket range; it is the CIA.'

The colonel laughed unpleasantly. He said, 'Of course, you would say this. It is a nonsense. The Americans have other ways of influencing things, they do not have to resort to such crude tricks. On the contrary, this is the sort of thing that would be done by communist agents. You, I take it, are a communist?'

'I am a scientist; I am not interested in politics.'

The colonel shrugged. 'Where you come from you are all communists.'

Dmitry shook his head. 'Why are we talking about communism? Communism is over, finished.'

'You think so?' The colonel leaned forward. 'You think communism is dead, do you? You, a Russian?'

'Oh, communism has been dead for some time,' said Dmitry, 'It's just there are some who don't realise it yet.'

Vargas laughed. He said something to the colonel and he laughed too, loudly and unpleasantly. Vargas leaned forward, cupping Dmitry's chin in his hand and forcing him to look up at him. 'Why did you say it was the CIA? Where did you get this information from?'

Dmitry, not knowing what to say, said feebly, 'I can't remember.'

The colonel hit him in the face. Blood poured into his mouth. He felt he had no dignity, sitting naked on the floor, still bound, blood dribbling from his mouth.

'I heard it from an official at the Russian Embassy in Buenos Aires.'

'Ah,' said the colonel. 'Finally. You will give me his name?'

'Anatoly Makushkin.'

'He is a high ranking officer?'

'He is First Scientific Secretary. He is a real diplomat. He is not in the KGB.'

'Then where did he get his information?'

Dmitry said, dully, 'Embassy gossip. I suppose, in the end, from the KGB.'

'So,' said the colonel, 'Now we have it. Do you think I am not aware that the United Nations has always been used as a cover for spying by your country? You are an agent sent by the KGB. You have been caught in the act of espionage. In the course of carrying out your duties you have murdered a Paraguayan soldier. Who are the others working with you?'

'There are no others.'

'Then who carried out the attack on the rocket range? I want their names. I want all the details. Come on, tell me. Tell me or I can assure you things will get even more unpleasant for you.'

Dmitry's voice shook with utter desperation. There was nothing more he could tell them. He said, 'No, this is the truth. I have told you the truth.'

The colonel moved forward; Vargas restrained him. He said, 'No, this is enough for now. I want to make some phone calls.' He turned to Dmitry. 'Let me tell you at once I am not convinced by what you have said. You should have come out with it in the first place; you should not have lied to us. I can assure you I do not like treating you in this way. But if I discover that you have still been lying, you will regret it, I promise you.'

They took him back to the cell. They untied his hands and feet and threw his clothes in after him. Dmitry at once got dressed; he lay down on the floor and fell asleep almost instantly in exhaustion. When he woke up it was day. He felt completely still and calm; it was as if he was incapable of feeling anything else. He looked out of the window. Clouds drifted slowly across the sky; he looked at them curiously; he thought how infinite were the number of shades of grey. After a while he began to feel sick with hunger. He got to his feet and started to stumble round the room. He wondered how long they would hold him here, whether he would ever get out.

He didn't know how he would cope with prison. He thought suddenly of his days at the Physico-Power Institute in Obninsk. He could see clearly in his mind the double walls, the multiple fences of electrified wires separated by strips of freshly ploughed ground and the military patrols with their guard dogs. It had seemed almost like a prison to him then, working long hours and leaving every evening to go back to the prison of his home. He put his head in his hands. He thought of the dark winter evenings, of Masha and her long silences; he remembered how he would put his arms around her, try to make her respond to him, and how all too often she would freeze and simply push him aside. He had sought comfort with other women; Masha too had not been faithful to him. Despite his own behaviour, this had infuriated him; it was the way she had taunted him with it. Once, very drunk, he had actually assaulted her; the worst thing was it had made him feel better until he had woken in the morning to see her bruised face and been stricken with remorse. It was like something out of a bad play. He could not imagine how he had done these things.

Now he put his head between his knees and groaned aloud. He was bewildered; he could not understand what he had done to make things turn out so badly. But wasn't that the way life was? Why had he thought that he was entitled to escape, to have a good life, when all around him, now and in the past, was the vast suffering mass of humanity? What had made him think that he should be immune? And he saw that in some curious way he had brought this on himself, as if he had chosen it, wanted to suffer. Maybe in some way he had thought it would help him to expunge the guilt.

He felt himself trembling. He would not have been able to describe to anyone how degrading, how disturbing, this violent assault upon him had been. He did not feel any animosity towards the torturers; rather, he felt it for himself. It was as if they had all been involved in some debasing and unpleasant ritual from which none of them had been able to extract themselves. Of course he should have spoken right away to Vargas. He should have given him the benefit of intelligence and judgement. Later, lying on the floor, trying hopelessly to sleep, Dmitry thought of what he himself would do if he had in his power someone he believed had planted a bomb on the rocket site which might, at any moment, blow up Katie. Under such circumstances he would do anything to get the information, including threats and actual violence; he would himself become a torturer.

VI

Katie reached Asunción by dark. She went straight to Richter's house because there was nowhere else to go. She asked the maid to bring her some toast and hot chocolate and she went up to her bedroom. What else could she do? She felt ill and exhausted and it was too late to contact anyone official that night.

Katie went into the bathroom and turned on the shower. When she took her clothes off she noticed there was a tiny smear of blood on her pants. She stared at them as if in hope that if she looked for long enough she would see that it was a trick of the light, that she had imagined it, that it wasn't there. This was just how her previous miscarriage had begun, an innocuous little smear of blood; there had been no pain till much later. She sat down on the bed; she felt numb with exhaustion and despair.

She thought, I can't bear it. If Dmitry was here with me and everything was all right I could just about cope with it; I cannot face it on my own. Everything is doomed. She felt a sudden wave of anger that this might have been caused by Bob, that it might indeed have been his intention. Desperate, she showered and crawled into her bed. She lay awake for hours, hardly daring to move, occasionally getting up to check if there was any more bleeding; there wasn't. Perhaps it was nothing, she thought, perhaps it will be all right.

In the morning she phoned the UN office. They said the res. rep. wouldn't be free till the afternoon, so she made an appointment to go in and see him, trying to explain briefly what it was about. Then she got the number of the Russian Embassy in Buenos Aires and rang that. She had to hang on for what seemed hours. Eventually she managed to get through to Anatoly Makushkin. He had a soft voice which she found it difficult to hear over the telephone. When she explained why she was calling there was a long silence. Then he said, 'I warned him not to go. I told him something like this would happen.'

She said, 'Isn't there anything you can do?'

'Of course, the Ambassador will make enquiries. I expect he will be released eventually, they won't be able to prove anything against him. What have they arrested him for? Suspected espionage or something like this?'

Katie said, 'The problem is, he shot a soldier. It was self-defence.'

Anatoly said, 'Oh, good God.'

'You must do something. He is not even with the police, he's with the military. If they know that people are concerned about him they are less likely to do anything awful. You must do something right away.'

Anatoly's voice sounded cold and far away. He said, 'I will go and talk to the Ambassador. Do you have any other information that could help us? You had better write it down and fax it to us. I am sorry but I cannot help you any more. Ring me if you hear anything yourself.'

Katie hung up. She walked upstairs, very slowly, and checked her pants; there was another tiny smear of blood. She lay down on the bed again. Then she thought, it's no use, I can't stay here. If it's going to happen, it's going to happen. She asked the maid to ring for a taxi and went downtown to the UN offices.

She felt a sense of relief in entering the building with its familiar atmosphere. There were posters on the walls stating the intention to solve by some miraculous means all the world's problems: Health for all by the year 2000; decade of clean water and sanitation; a new charter for children. Secretaries sat typing and important-looking men held earnest conversations. The res. rep. was a tall, thin, Scandinavian, aged about forty, with washed-out features and thinning, pale hair. He kept looking at her through the plate glass in the partitions which divided up the office and frowning as if he didn't want to see her. She had to wait some time to see him; at length the secretary took her in. He shook her hand and asked her to sit down. He said, 'I'm sorry, I don't quite understand what this is all about.'

Katie tried to explain. She said a friend of hers, a UN employee from Vienna, had been arrested in Mariscal Estigarribia. He was not here officially, she said. Would the UN be able to do anything to get him released?

Nilson said, in a voice which was as washed-out as his appearance, 'What was he arrested for?'

'He shot a soldier. In self-defence. They were threatening him.'

Nilson winced. 'Shot? You mean, killed?'

Katie nodded. Nilson stared at her and scratched his head. He looked out of the window at the rooftops and then up at the sky. 'You will have to tell me more than this,' he said. 'What was he doing there? Who is your friend?'

Katie told him.

'From the IAEA? An expert on uranium enrichment? Good God. There is an atomic energy commission here, as a matter of fact, God knows what it does – I met the director at some dinner or other, nice man – but you say he was not on official business? He came in on his national passport? What the hell was he doing in Mariscal Estigarribia?'

'He came to meet me.'

'You live there?'

'My husband is working for Wolf Richter.'

'Ah; Richter; the rocket man.' Nilson sighed. Katie looked at the wall, at a photograph of the Pope shaking hands with some UN dignitary. It was underneath a poster for family planning. Nilson frowned even more deeply. 'I don't see what you expect me to do. I suppose they will bring him to Asunción, there's nothing out there. Perhaps I can arrange to see him. He will want legal representation, I suppose.'

At that moment the phone rang. Nilson picked it up. After a few minutes he said, 'There is somebody here talking to me about it now. Okay, thanks.' He hung up, turned to Katie. 'My deputy had a call this morning from the commandante at Mariscal Estigarribia, asking if we knew this Dr Gavrilov. He's has sent a fax to New York to ask if any such person is employed by the UN.'

'He has a senior post at the IAEA. Please, can't you contact them and tell them who he is? They might be capable of anything. Surely if they know he is from the UN that will give him some protection.'

Nilson said, 'Maybe.' He looked more and more unhappy. 'We could get in touch with them and say he is a UN employee. Maybe we could try the Minister of the Interior, I'll ring him myself. I'm not sure what else we can do. You say he was here on holiday?'

'I . . .' Katie thought she might as well come out with everything. 'He came to meet me. He couldn't get a visa.'

'So he entered the country illegally?' Nilson got up. 'This is inconceivable. Has he gone off his head? Do Vienna know about this?'

'I imagine not.'

'The IAEA will have no choice but to revoke his diplomatic immunity immediately. We can't prevent him from facing justice here. But it is a very special situation right now in the Chaco with the rocket project. You say your husband works for Richter? They must have much more influence there than we do. Why don't you try to get them to sort it out? As I understand it they have complete immunity from Paraguayan law.'

Katie, realising that it was hopeless, suddenly started to cry. Nilson looked acutely embarrassed; he asked his secretary to get her a cup of coffee. 'I am really sorry, I have things to do. Is there anything else I can do? Do you want me to send a fax to the IAEA? They should surely be informed in any case?'

Katie said, bitterly, wiping away her tears, 'What would be the point?'

The secretary took Katie outside. She drank her coffee and tried to take hold of herself. She didn't want to go back to the house; she was afraid that Bob would come after her, and the thought of seeing him was unbearable. She didn't know what else she could do to help Dmitry. Perhaps she could achieve as much at home, phoning people, appealing to the Paraguayan Ambassador, to the Russian Embassy, to the UN. Most important of all, perhaps she could get hold of Richter and beg him to help, though she supposed this was unlikely. Besides, what would happen to her if she had a miscarriage and had to go into hospital? She thought of Anna, waiting for her back at home; she was due back in a few days time anyway. She felt she had lost everything else; she had a sudden irrational fear that something would happen to Anna and that she would lose her too. She turned to the secretary. She said, 'Can you ring the airlines? I want a flight out of here as soon as possible – connecting to London. And can I make a call to England? I'll pay for it.'

Dmitry sat on the floor of the cell, waiting for something to happen. He had sat there for hours, hardly moving. He had lost all sense of time; from the angle of the sun he gathered that it was sometime in the afternoon. At last he heard someone coming to the door. The two soldiers came in, tied his hands and feet again, and sat him on the chair. Somebody else came in and stood in front of him. Dmitry didn't look up for some time; at length a soft voice said, 'Are you not going to look at me?'

It was César Madregón. Dmitry looked up in astonishment; when he saw the kindly weather-beaten face he could have laughed out loud. Madregón said, 'Get me another chair,' and a soldier went and fetched one. Madregón sat down on it.

'I don't want to get your hopes up,' he said, 'They agreed that I could see you. There is talk of having you transferred to Asunción. Vargas has gone there to see Rodriguez. I imagine the civil authorities will want to handle things properly. They have this anti-corruption drive, you know, they are taking it all very seriously. Everyone is very anxious to clean up Paraguay's image abroad.'

Dmitry felt relief sweep through him. He said, 'I see.'

'However, I think things are still fairly bleak. The charges against you are very serious, you know. An additional complication is the rocket project. As you know, the Paraguayan authorities have no jurisdiction over the RASAG zone. None of the people working there can be prosecuted under Paraguayan law. So they could simply hand you over to them; indeed, under the terms of the contract, they may even be compelled to do so. I don't know what these people are like. I imagine they are not particularly pleasant.'

Dmitry shook his head.

'Well, how did you get yourself into this mess?' Then, to the soldier standing by the door, 'Does he have to be tied up? I want to offer him a cigarette.'

The soldier said, 'They don't want to take any risks. He might be violent.'

'That's all right,' said Dmitry. 'I don't smoke.'

César Madregón lit his cigarette. He said, 'Well, I really am sorry. It would have been a pleasure to hunt the *tigre* with you. I don't have much influence with anybody these days but, I'll do what I can. This is still the kind of place where it matters who you know, a word in the right place, that kind of thing. Good luck, eh?' He put his hand on Dmitry's shoulder in a friendly gesture. Dmitry couldn't help himself; he flinched, as if expecting a blow. Madregón noticed. A deep frown crossed his amiable face. He took his hand away and hesitated; then he turned abruptly and left the room. The soldier untied him, then he too went out.

Alone, Dmitry stared at the floor. In a way, things were worse now. A ray of light had come into the darkness and stirred up hope. Feverish thoughts whirled round in his head. Perhaps Madregón would fix it; perhaps they wouldn't dare do him any further harm. Katie would have rung the Russian Embassy in Buenos Aires; Tolya would surely move heaven and earth for him. Except, the Soviet Union had no links of any kind with Paraguay, no consul, no trade mission; perhaps they would be able to work through another embassy. Perhaps the UN might be able to exert some pressure; he didn't know.

He paced around the cell in a state of growing agitation. He tried to think of the line the UN would take. Would the resident representative come out to try to see him and establish what was going on? Presumably they would have informed the IAEA by then. The IAEA would be horrified. Illegally entering a foreign country and shooting one of its citizens wasn't the kind of thing they advocated among their representatives. They would strip him immediately of his diplomatic status. He would be dismissed. This hadn't occurred to him before; it struck him like a thunderbolt. Somehow he had been imagining that if he got out of this life could go back to normal; he hadn't been thinking beyond the next moment. Thinking about it, the UN probably wouldn't do much for him. He would be an embarrassment to them. They would write a few letters, make a few noises, but basically they wouldn't do anything to help him. And Katie should have arrived in Asunción the previous night. If they were going to do anything they had had plenty of time to do it.

Dmitry stopped, clutched his head, and turned round; he started walking round the cell in the opposite direction so that he would not get dizzy. What would have happened to her? She should have seen the resident representative, phoned the Russian Embassy, and then got out of the country. That was what he had told her to do. But she might not do it. She might still be there in Asunción, talking to the British Embassy, visiting lawyers, trying to find somebody who might be able to help him. He tried to imagine what she would be feeling. Then he started to think about the baby. He imagined Katie with the baby, a little human being who looked like him but might never see him. He couldn't bear it.

He forced himself to sit down. Earlier the hours had slipped by in a timeless daze; now every minute counted. It began to grow dark. It must be about time they brought him something to eat. Then he heard raised voices outside; he stood on the chair to look out of the window and saw the soldiers marching somebody across the road. To his astonishment, he recognised Bob Haynes.

They seemed to have him under arrest. There were two fair-skinned men with them too, whom he assumed were Germans from the rocket site. He sat down. Perhaps Haynes had been asked to come here and explain what had happened. This was terrible. God knew what he might say about him; he was vindictive enough. Dmitry sat, perfectly still, straining to distinguish and understand words; they were speaking German. Haynes sounded angry. Dmitry went again to the window but there was nothing to see.

He heard the telephone ring. Then he heard raised voices from outside and a crowd of soldiers gathered outside the entrance to the building. Then Dmitry's blood turned cold. Haynes's voice had changed; it had turned to fear and horror. Some soldiers dragged him out of the building and stood him in the road under a streetlamp. They were shouting at him. A fair-skinned man, presumably a German working for Richter, was standing with Vargas; he held a semi-automatic pistol in his hand. Two or three of the soldiers were also holding guns.

They started firing into the dust around Haynes's feet, laughing, goading him. And then Haynes did what they were waiting for; he turned and started to run. He only got a few yards. Dmitry thought it was the German who fired the shot that felled him. One of the soldiers walked over and fired two more shots into the body. Several more went up to have a look. One of them kicked the body over onto its back. Then one of the soldiers turned round, touched the German's arm, and pointed straight at Dmitry's window.

Dmitry could not move. He was paralysed with fear. He thought, they will be coming for me now. He looked down at the floor; every mark, every imperfection on its grey, dusty surface seemed immeasurably clear and important; he felt that even in this there was something beautiful. He wanted to understand what it was; he wanted to understand everything; and now there was no time left, just a few precious minutes; he wanted them to last forever. He heard the soldiers talking and a door slamming, and some boots scraping on the floor. Footsteps came towards him; he tensed himself, he felt violently sick, he thought his bowels would open. He started to pray violently for a miracle, oh God, please, don't let this happen, don't let this happen. And then, completely unexpectedly, the footsteps seemed to halt in their tracks, the voices died away, and, looking out of the window again, he saw the German get into his jeep and drive away.

Dmitry flung himself face downwards onto the floor and started to laugh and then to cry. After a while he sat up and rested the back of his head against the wall, hot tears pouring down his face. Eventually, the tears stopped coming. He felt completely calm and quiet. He found himself wishing, in some strange, primitive way, that he could make some payment for this unexpected reprieve. What nonsense was he thinking? But something was burning inside him, struggling to get out. He vowed that if he ever got out of here, if he had another chance, he would lead a different kind of life, a new, pure life of which his love for Katie and their child was the symbol, a life free of hatred and suspicion, of mistaken cowardly and violent acts. He desperately wanted to purge himself of these things, though he did not have the slightest idea how.

He shut his eyes; weariness overtook him; he must have fallen asleep. He woke to hear the door open. He sat up, startled, confused, blinking in the daylight. He had no idea for a moment what time it was, nor where he was. A soldier was standing in the doorway; he was telling him to come out. Dmitry stumbled into the corridor; he had the unpleasant sensation that something terrible had happened; it was like trying to recall a bad dream. The soldier took him into Vargas's office.

Vargas was not there. Instead, standing impatiently by the desk, glancing at his watch, was the bulky figure of Wolfgang Richter.

'Sit down,' he said, staring at Dmitry. Dmitry sat; Richter sat down opposite him. He looked haggard; he hadn't shaved; he seemed anxious and distracted, emptied of all his previous energy. His voice was flat and drained, he looked quite different from the prosperous, dynamic man Dmitry had last seen in Vienna. His shirt was grubby and there were sweat stains under his arms; perspiration gave his face a shiny, flaccid appearance.

Richter put his hands face down on the edge of the desk and leaned forward. 'I met you in Vienna,' he said; 'I remember. What the hell are you doing here?'

Dmitry was not in the mood to play games, 'I am tired of interrogations. What is the point of asking me? Nobody has told me anything.'

Richter asked, 'Are you KGB, or what? Are you behind this business?' Dmitry sat in silence. There was hardly a sound. A fly buzzed against the window. Dmitry's head ached; he passed his hand across his damp forehead. He felt ill; he wondered if he had a fever. It occurred to him that he hadn't been taking any malaria pills.

Something about Dmitry's silence seemed to rattle Richter; it was as if he wasn't sure quite where he stood. Suddenly he said, almost to himself: 'They called me in Stuttgart. They said the President wanted to see me; that there was a crisis. Rodriguez told me he was going to cancel the rocket project. He had got wind of a plan by some Brazilians and a Paraguayan general to hold their governments to ransom. He was furious; said the rocket project was being used by anti-democratic elements.

'I told him I didn't understand. Then he called in this commandante, the local guy, Vargas, I had met him before. He's the man who interrogated you. He told me what you had said. He said they could already substantiate part of this claim; Luís Hería Prieto, the Paraguayan general, had confessed to it. They had a statement. He read it out to me. I must confess I couldn't take in all the details.'

Richter got up. He walked to the window. Dmitry's head was

buzzing; a dreadful irony was dawning on him; that the information that had been dragged out of him so reluctantly under torture had been used as he would have wished it, to terminate the rocket project. He looked at Richter, bewildered; he couldn't understand why Richter was telling him all this.

'Then they brought in someone from the CIA. They said they also had evidence that this was true. Then Rodriguez said there had been an accident at the rocket range. There had been explosions and a great deal of damage. He said rumours had connected it with the CIA. The CIA denied it. You seemed to be the source of these rumours. Where did you hear this?'

'From someone in the Russian Embassy in Buenos Aires. The only reason I have to think it's true is that it happened.'

'You mean from the KGB, don't you? Is this their idea, then? Were they responsible?'

Dmitry said, 'I don't think so. It's not in their sphere of influence. Anyway, they are all running round in circles these days not knowing what the hell to do about anything. We have more than enough problems to deal with at home.'

Richter tapped his fingers on the desk. 'Well, I'm going out there now to have a look and assess the damage.' He paused to look over at Dmitry. He asked again, 'And you – who are you? What are you doing here?'

'I was involved with Bob Haynes's wife. I wanted to get her away. Haynes knew about the plot, you know; he told me that himself.'

Richter said, 'Yes, that's right, I remember, you were with her in Vienna at that café. So you were screwing her, were you? God, these women. Do you know who is at the root of this? Liliana. My God, why did I ever trust that woman? No, it's not true, I never trusted her. But who could have imagined she would get up to something as crazy as this?' Richter ran his hand through his dishevelled hair. 'She was fucking Heinrichs, did you know that? I have already instructed my lawyer to file divorce papers. This has nearly ruined me. I will have lost all credibility. Nobody is going to believe I was not behind this. The CIA gave me a very clear warning . . .' His voice tailed away and he stared woodenly out of the window.

Dmitry could not help at that moment feeling sorry for Richter. Maybe this was genuine; perhaps he really didn't know about the Brazilian plot. He thought then that perhaps Richter might have some sympathy for him; his own dreams had come to nothing, perhaps he could feel some pity for someone else's ruined life. The two of them sat, looking at the pitted surface of the desk, in the airless room. Richter went on talking, as if he were thinking aloud.

'On the other hand, it's possible nothing will ever be proved. Heinrichs gave the Brazilians instructions to destroy the rocket. The government have apparently now recovered all the weapons-grade uranium. I don't believe they had a bomb ready. I don't believe they ever could have pulled this off.'

He cleared his throat. 'The trouble is I have no taste for violence. That business with Haynes last night; that was uncalled for. All right, so he had betrayed me, he was passing information to the CIA.'

Dmitry stared at him, stunned. Was this what lay at the bottom of this business? So if Haynes had been working for them here, in Paraguay . . . this could change everything. Perhaps they had been making use of him all along, exploiting this fortuitous connection with Liliana. Perhaps he had been working for them all the time, in Vienna. This would explain a great deal; the CIA might have wanted to keep quiet about Valadares as much as the KGB, and for the same reasons.

Dmitry continued to stare at him. 'But you would have sold Brazil the rockets, anyway. You once said you would have sold them to anybody. You know it could be easily adapted. How do you know what they would have put on top of it?'

Richter looked at Dmitry directly; it was curious, but even if he looked him straight in the face, it was as if his eyes never connected. He said, 'No, you misunderstand me. I would have sold them to the government. The Brazilian government, especially now under Collor, is as responsible as anyone. What would it matter to me if Brazil had the bomb? Why does it matter so much to you? You have enough of them, don't you?'

'I understand that point of view absolutely. What concerned me was that this was a violation of an international agreement. Brazil have undertaken not to produce a bomb. But haven't you been a little naïve?

You must surely realise what kind of people an organisation like yours would attract.'

'I did not expect to be betrayed like this.'

Richter lit a cigarette; he remained seated, almost as if he were too tired to move. He looked at his watch again. 'How are you feeling?' he asked unexpectedly. 'I hear they gave you rather a rough time. That's the trouble with these people, they don't know any other way to get information out of someone. They didn't do you any serious damage, did they?'

'I don't think so.'

'Look,' said Richter, getting up suddenly, walking over to the window and swatting at the buzzing fly. 'You have caused a lot of trouble for me, one way and another. On the other hand, it seems you are a victim of this business as much as I am. I can't think what is going to be achieved by leaving you to rot here in a Paraguayan prison. Have you seen the state penitentiary in Asunción? My God, what a place. It's a disgrace – drugs, violence, corruption – I don't suppose you'd last out very long there. And the food, the smell . . .' His face wrinkled in an expression of absolute disgust.

Dmitry sat very still. Richter turned round to face him. 'Well, if I have a word with them they'll release you. If I claim you are attached to the RASAG project, I imagine you will have immunity, even if the contract has been cancelled. We are flying everybody out of here as soon as possible.'

He leaned over the desk. 'Well, come on,' he said. 'You can come with me. What's the matter with you? Do you want to get out or don't you?'

The Lear jet turned on its wingtip and lined up to land on the thin strip of parched earth. Out of the window Dmitry saw the shadowy outline of Cerro León on the horizon.

'When I've divorced Liliana,' Richter said, 'I'm going to marry my secretary. She's a nice girl – Sylvia. She's got less up here than Liliana. It's always best to have a woman with no brains. Don't you agree?'

They came in to land. Dust flew up as the wheels touched ground and obscured the view. When they opened the door Dmitry saw the rocket gantry rising above the trees; the top of the rocket could be seen glinting in the centre of the metal scaffold. He stood and stared at it. It looked bigger than it actually was; there was no sense of perspective in this vast wilderness. To Katie it had seemed impressive; to Dmitry, who had worked with the vast SS-9s, it seemed little more than a firecracker. He felt suddenly deflated. Was this what it was all about? He wondered whether Richter would seriously have had any success with these things.

A driver was waiting to drive them towards the site. There had been a massive fire; for perhaps a mile to the east there was blackened ground, still smouldering in places. A smell of charred wood and something acrid, metallic, hung in the air. Part of the house itself was in ruins. He thought, thank goodness Katie hadn't been there. Perhaps I did something right, after all.

'Was anybody killed?'

'Yes – eleven of them. A few more suffered burns; they were flown to hospital in Asunción, but they'll be all right. If it was the CIA, it shows what vandals they are. It's a useless waste. I gather that they had persuaded Rodriguez to cancel the project in any case.'

They climbed down from the jeep and walked towards the gantry. 'They have destroyed millions of dollars worth of computers,' said Richter. 'Of course we had back-ups but this will set us back about two years. Most of the technical staff have already gone; they didn't believe we could guarantee their safety.' A group of RASAG workers, their women and children, had come out of their huts when they heard Richter coming. 'You must excuse me for a while,' he said, 'I have some business to attend to.'

Dmitry held back as the workers approached Richter. They were appealing to him; they didn't want to go, they didn't want to lose their jobs. They were asking if the agricultural projects would continue. Richter gave them bland assurances; he said they would be compensated. Then he turned to one of his colleagues and began giving instructions for the dismantling of the rocket.

Dmitry sat down in the shade under a tree in a daze and watched Richter at work. One of the battered old Argosy transport planes was sitting on the runway; men were loading boxes onto it. The sun began to descend; its slanting rays shone in Dmitry's eyes and a dry wind blew in his face, bearing on it the faint, spicy scent of the *palo santo* tree.

A young German wandered over with a canned drink; he handed it to Dmitry and introduced himself as the range controller. He said that this destruction was terrible; he told Dmitry about his native wife. He said he had grown fond of her and couldn't bear to leave her behind, but there was no point in pretending he could take her back to Germany. 'It was a nice dream,' he said, 'But the trouble with dreams is one has to wake up again to real life, isn't that so?'

Later, in the Lear jet heading for Rio, Richter kept up a long monologue, shouting above the noise of the engines. He was explaining that he was considering launching his rockets from a stabilised ship at sea. Of course there were various technical problems, but these could be overcome. Dmitry turned to look at him. For someone who had been up all night, who had just supervised the closing down of his project, he seemed remarkably animated. Dmitry wondered if he would ever understand him. Perhaps he was just an idealist, who had been used by people more ruthless than himself. Perhaps he was really a man from another age, like one of the Spanish explorers searching for Eldorado; an anomaly here at the end of the twentieth century. He was indeed a man following a mad quest in which he could never succeed, because Dmitry saw that even if he could make it work technically, politically he would never be allowed to get away with it.

Perhaps he would turn himself to more realistic ends; he might go where the money was, and that was for missiles. Possibly he would be able to find someone else to subsidise his dreams, perhaps someone in the Middle East. Dmitry turned his head away, closed his eyes, and tried to sleep. Somehow he felt this was not going to be the last that would be heard of Wolfgang Richter.

EPILOGUE

It was pouring with rain. Nihal walked down the gloomy street in Kilburn, holding his umbrella. It was one of those bleak, bitter February days which Nihal always associated with the memory of his past years in London. He had been in London for a three-day conference and had just found time to call in and see Katie and Dmitry for tea before catching the seven-thirty flight back to Vienna.

He found their flat without too much difficulty; it was on the ground floor of a three storey Victorian house. He rang the bell; he could hear the baby crying indoors. The cries became louder, rising to a crescendo; Katie opened the door, the baby against her shoulder. She looked extremely pleased to see him.

'Nihal, how wonderful – come in.' Katie took his umbrella and propped it by the door in the gloomy entrance hall. She took him through into the living room; it was a double room with the original dividing doors and a kitchen area at one end, untidy and poorly decorated, but with a warm fire burning in the grate. The baby had stopped crying, and Katie turned towards Nihal to show him off. 'What do you think?' she asked. 'Don't you think he looks like Mitya?'

The baby did indeed look extraordinarily like his father. He was, thought Nihal, quite remarkably, yet endearingly ugly. Katie's face radiated adoration as she gazed down at the crumpled little face. Nihal made suitable noises of admiration but the baby was unimpressed and after a few moments it started crying again.

Katie went to the door and called upstairs. 'Mitya! Come down. Nihal's here.' She put on the kettle, filling it with difficulty by the spout because the sink was piled high with unwashed dishes. The baby carried on fretting on her shoulder.

Nihal asked, 'Why is he crying? Does he need feeding?'

'I don't know,' said Katie, 'Anna was never like this. I've only just fed him. Mitya won't be a minute, he's finishing a translation.' She went to the door and called up to him again.

Dmitry appeared in the doorway and greeted Nihal warmly. His hair had grown longer and he was wearing a shapeless woolly which Katie proudly said she had knitted for him. Dmitry told Nihal to sit down on the sofa, at the end which didn't have a hole in it, and then peered at the baby.

'What's the matter with him?'

'Mitya, if I feed him again, will you make the tea? There's a cake in the tin.' She sat down on the armchair, pulled up her jumper and latched the baby on to her round, pale breast. The baby whimpered and then started to feed; Katie sighed and leaned back on the cushions. Dmitry walked across the room to Katie, stood behind her and looked down at her and the little baby, quiet now and sucking rhythmically at the breast. Almost unconsciously, he pulled a stray lock of her hair back from her face and arranged it on her shoulder. Katie smiled at him; for a moment Nihal felt like an intruder, shut out of this sudden and complete intimacy between them.

The kettle was boiling. Dmitry abruptly broke away and went to make a pot of tea. 'So how's Vienna, Nihal? What are you working on?'

'Well, actually, I'm still following up the RASAG story. Richter has just signed a deal with Libya. He's transferred his test site to a remote area in the Saharan desert south of Zurbah. It's a perfect spot for testing rockets; even more deserted than the Chaco, and, of course, it's outside US influence.'

'Does he still claim it's for launching satellites?'

'Yes, that's what he says. But the trouble with these people is that an idea turns into an obsession and then they don't care who pays for it or what the end result is. I don't think there's much doubt about what he's doing now.'

Dmitry carried a tray from the kitchen and placed it on the table. He poured out the tea into the Russian glasses Nihal recognised from Vienna and cut generous slices of cake. Nihal went on, 'Gaddafi has been rather vague about its intentions – simply said that the project is peaceful. But there's some more evidence turned up about abortive missile deals RASAG was making with Pakistan, and with a secret project backed by a number of German companies to sell missiles to Saudi Arabia.'

Dmitry seemed not to be concentrating; he frowned as he passed Nihal his tea. Then he went to the door and called upstairs; Anna came down, looked shyly at Nihal, and helped herself to some cake. She had grown much taller since Nihal had last seen her and her face was thinner, having lost that infant chubbiness. She went up to Katie and began to stroke the baby's head; Nihal noticed that she did it rather roughly.

'Not while he's having his milk,' said Katie, gently. 'He doesn't like it.'

'Yes he does.' Anna reached out her hand again. Katie tolerated this for a moment, until the baby started whimpering, and then firmly took it away. 'Shhh, he's going to sleep. Go and have another bit of cake.'

Anna went over to Dmitry, took another slice of cake and climbed up onto his knee. She sat there, leaning back against his chest, swinging her legs, perfectly at ease.

Nihal sipped his tea and, when no-one else said anything, carried on. 'RASAG's new chairman has denied absolutely that there is any truth in this. But there's no doubt that after he'd been kicked out of Paraguay Richter was in deep trouble. After all, his credibility had been destroyed. The company was nearly shut down; Heinrichs was being prosecuted. How he managed to keep going I don't know. At one stage he offered to sell the whole thing to another armaments company just to be shot of it.'

Katie asked, 'Nihal, how can you go on with this? Aren't you afraid?'

'Well, a bit, but Richter himself has much more reason to be. I phoned his new wife, Sylvia – you know, the girl I met in Paris. I couldn't get him through his office so I rang his home number. She told me there had been two attempts on his life; in one his bodyguard was shot, and in the other there was a bomb in his car which killed the driver. She said he was very careful about who he met these days . . .'

'And Liliana?'

'She's in hiding, in Brazil, as fas as I know.'

'And how's the IAEA?'

'Oh, all right. There's been all this Iraqi business – that's had them running in circles. Probably the whole safeguards system will be reviewed. What about you? I was thinking of you a lot over those dramatic days in August . . .'

Katie looked up from the baby, who appeared to have fallen asleep. 'We never stopped listening to the radio. Mitya wants to go back, to see for himself, but I couldn't face taking the children.' She lifted the baby from her breast and laid him gently in the Moses basket on the floor. For a few moments there was peace; then he began to cry again. Dmitry gently lifted Anna off his knee, stood up and started to rock the basket but the baby carried on inconsolably. He picked it up and peered at the little crumpled face. 'Sasha,' he said, 'What is the matter with you?' Nihal found it strangely touching to see the little baby held so gently in his enormous hands. 'You can't be hungry; you can't have your mother's breasts all the time, you know, I shall get jealous.' He walked up and down, but the baby would not be pacified. After a few minutes Nihal had had enough of the noise.

'I'm afraid I must go, or I'll miss my plane.' He got to his feet. 'I'm sorry it's been so short. Perhaps next time . . .'

'No, it's lovely to see you. I'm sorry we're in such chaos.'

The baby was now working himself up into a fury and Dmitry handed him back to Katie.

'I'll walk you to the station,' she said to Nihal.

'I'd come too,' said Dmitry, 'But I've got a deadline for the morning.'

Katie put on Anna's coat and hat and gloves, wrapped the baby in a shawl and tucked him in the pram in the hallway. Nihal helped her carry it down the steps. Dmitry shook Nihal's hand and closed the door behind him. Walking down the road, the baby finally stopped crying; instead, Anna started to complain that she was cold.

'Come on,' said Katie, 'We're not going far.' She turned to Nihal. 'I'm sorry. It hasn't been a good day. This is the first big job Mitya's had for this company and he's anxious to get it done on time.'

'What's he working on?'

'Oh, it's just a technical translation for some company hoping to set up a joint venture in Russia. We didn't have enough money so he took on too much work. It was all such a mess, Nihal; after Bob died I discovered he only had a small life insurance, he was in the process of taking out another but he never signed the forms. And of course Richter wouldn't pay anything.' She sighed, turning to Anna to pull up her hood and wind the scarf more tightly round her neck. 'Then Mitya lost his job, and he was ill over Christmas; he was in hospital with a nasty chest infection, so he got behind with everything . . . And he keeps saying he wants to go back to Russia. I sat with him you know, those three days in August, seeing him weep first tears of shame and then of joy. He couldn't bear the fact that he wasn't there to be part of it. Now he gets these fits of Russian melancholy and then he drinks too much.'

'Well,' said Nihal, with a shrug of his shoulders, 'You made your choice, Katie; nobody's perfect.'

'You shouldn't have started going on about Richter,' said Katie. 'He'll be upset now; he hates to talk about it.'

'Does he? Why? I thought he'd be interested.'

'Well, he lost rather a lot, didn't he? It's affected him rather badly, he feels it's the end of his career. He can make some kind of living out of translating but it bores him.'

They came to the underground station. Katie put her arms round Nihal and held him tightly. 'For God's sake, Nihal, be careful. Haven't you learned how serious this can be?'

Nihal released her reluctantly. 'I don't think Richter is such a serious threat. He has much more reason to be afraid than I have. Don't worry about me; I'm fine.'

Katie watched his small, familiar figure walk up the steps to the platform and waved him goodbye. She felt like crying, as if part of her life was going with him. Abruptly she turned round and pushed the pram back down the road in the pouring rain, the baby howling, and Anna running ahead of them, skipping and chanting a song, the Russian one about the crocodile.